For the people who introduced me to dice:

Alix
Charity
Christine
Jess

Here's to more inglorious beginnings, wolf pets, and goblin buddies.

MUSEUM
of
MAGIC

BETH REVIS

SCRIPTURIENT
BOOKS

If we shadows have offended,

Think but this, and all is mended,

That you have but slumber'd here

While these visions did appear.

WILLIAM SHAKESPEARE

A MIDSUMMER NIGHT'S DREAM

FOREWORD

The book you are holding in your hands came about due to chaos and chance.

This book, from its very first inception, was designed to be written in a totally new way. Every week, I outlined a chapter with a variety of paths for the characters to take. I drew a tarot card to set the mood and then used elements of chance to determine how the story unfolded. I mostly used dice rolls, but spiced things up with coin flips, more tarot, or by drawing options from a cup. Each chapter ended with a chance for readers to vote on the direction for the next chapter.

The end result is this book, a story that was impossible to plan, guided by fate and readers.

You can see traces of this in the design. Every chapter opens with the name of the tarot card that was drawn as it was written, as well as a quick summary of what the card means. This story was originally published on both Kindle Vella and my Patreon, and the sequel is being written in the same style. You can read *House of Hex* and vote on the story's development now!

Please follow me on social media or via my newsletter to discover new, exciting stories as they unfold. Find more information at bethrevis.com.

PROLOGUE

THE UNOPENED, UNSHUFFLED DECK

The little iron bell tinkled as a tall, thin woman pushed the door open. She blinked as she transitioned from the bright, sunny outside to the darkened room, and Emmi knew she had only seconds before the woman spotted her behind the front desk. She allowed herself one deep breath with closed eyes before painting a smile on her face.

"Hi!" she called cheerily in the tone of voice borne from years working in the gift shop.

Emmi could tell immediately that the woman had never worked retail. It had nothing to do with the expensive leather bag on the woman's shoulder and everything to do with the way she had no idea that Emmi's bright smile was one hundred percent a customer service smile and not in any way real.

"Oh! I didn't see you there." The woman grinned, the edges of her red lipstick straining. "Did you just pop up here by *magic?*" She waggled her fingers.

"Ha. No," Emmi said. Three sentences in, and the woman was diving straight for the kitsch. "I just work here." And live here. The Museum of Magic was built from one of the oldest buildings in America, with the bottom floors devoted to the museum and the top floor—formerly the attic—reserved for

Emmi and her grandfather. But Emmi didn't tell the woman that. Whenever a guest found out that Emmi wasn't just a summer employee but an actual descendent of the resident historical witch, with the same last name as the one carved in stone over the doorway, the tour turned the spotlight from the various mystical artifacts into an interview about what Emmi knew (not much more than any other seventeen-year-old), whether she had magic (no), or whether she'd ever seen magic (obviously not, since magic wasn't real).

"Well," the woman said, her gaze sliding past Emmi and roving around the foyer. "This is just a charming little...museum."

She said that last word as if she was dubious it was accurate, despite the laminated sign in the window.

"Welcome to the Museum of Magic," Emmi said, repeating the same words she'd heard her grandfather tell guests for years, the same ones she herself had started parroting once she'd gotten old enough to take over the family business, at least during the summer and weekends. "This building is the former residence of Elspeth Castor, a witch who fled the persecutions of the English witch trials only to find herself accused of witchcraft in the American colonies. Elspeth Castor arrived in America on the *Speedwell*, the ship that accompanied the *Mayflower* across the Atlantic, and she was the only person on either ship to disembark at Provincetown instead of Plymouth."

Emmi eyed the woman. She looked a little bored, her eyes flitting around the foyer at the pictures hanging from the wallpapered hallway depicting the story Emmi was telling. Emmi skipped some of the details about her ancestor, and dove straight to the salacious points.

"The original pilgrims, as we all know, nearly died that first winter in America," she said.

"Thanksgiving, Native Americans, all that," the woman muttered. Emmi blinked several times, but otherwise didn't let her emotions show—not that the woman noticed. She expected that sort of vague abridgment of history when the local fifth graders came for their annual trip to the museum, but... Ah, well. Emmi still had to get the woman to pay for a ticket into the museum.

"Oh!" the woman said as Sabrina stepped daintily over the counter. The woman laughed. "You're the wrong color! Why are you orange?"

Oh my god, Karen, you can't just ask people why they're orange, Emmi thought, wanting to quote that movie, *Mean Girls,* but biting her tongue just in time—the joke was old, and she doubted it would land well. "Meet Sabrina," she said, gesturing to the ginger cat.

"Like the teenage witch?" the woman chuckled. Sabrina jumped off the counter toward the woman, who bent down to make little *tsking* noises at the cat. Sabrina, who had never met a stranger, butted her head right against the woman's outstretched hand. Emmi smiled at her cat. Sabrina *was* the wrong color— Grandfather had taken Emmi to the shelter in the hopes that she would pick a black cat, something very apropos for the museum. But Emmi had fallen in love with Sabrina and her orange whiskers.

The woman looked up, and Emmi knew she was going to ask for either the restroom or the gift shop and then leave. Before she could, though, Emmi rushed in with the rest of her pitch. "So what the history books often leave out—and what's never mentioned at Thanksgiving dinners—is that the pilgrims blamed Elspeth Castor for their harsh living conditions," Emmi said. She heard the theatrical pitch to her voice and leaned into it. "Elspeth had joined the *Speedwell* out of desperation, fleeing the witch trials of England, and although she had thought that she would be safe in America, the pilgrims had decided the strange woman was a witch. Dropping her off, alone, in Provincetown had been their solution. But Elspeth lived. And the pilgrims were convinced that she had cursed them."

There it was—Emmi had the woman's attention. "Throughout the first winter, the pilgrims sent hunting parties to track down and kill Elspeth, believing the only way to stop her curse was to kill her. They were, of course, unsuccessful."

"What happened?" the woman asked somewhat breathlessly. Sabrina wove between her legs, demanding more attention. It was a mark of how much the story had engaged the woman that she ignored the cat.

"Elspeth lived. She became known as a wanderer, and there are records of her as far south as Virginia and as far north as Salem." Emmi added emphasis to that last word—Salem. She knew what it meant for the tourists. Although the witch trials were most famous in Salem, they had extended throughout the region, the paranoia about witchcraft causing many a smaller village to hang an innocent woman. Just to be safe, of course.

The tourist, however, frowned. She seemed to be counting on her fingers. "But...that would mean Elspeth had to have been around a hundred years old. And the date carved in the stone doorway was 1666. The Salem witch trials were in—"

"1692," Emmi finished for her. And the pilgrims landed at Plymouth in 1620. Great. This woman had a kid's problematic idea of Thanksgiving with smiling Native Americans passing around turkey, but she skewered Emmi on bringing up Salem. On the one hand, she was right—Elspeth had died before the infamous witch trials. But Emmi hadn't lied—Elspeth had been recorded as a visitor of the town, just a few years before she died. Not too long before the fanatics started looking for witches...

"Elspeth's connection with witchcraft extends throughout the region in the earliest ages of America's colonial history," Emmi said, switching tactics. "If you'd like to learn more about her and the way this one remarkable woman witnessed history, tickets to the museum are only eight dollars, and..."

Emmi trailed off as the woman shook her head. "Nah, I was just stopping by off the interstate. Saw a sign for this place at the gas station. Do you have a gift shop? And a bathroom?"

Emmi's smile tightened at the corners. "Sure," she said. She led the woman to the side room—formerly Elspeth's sitting room, now converted to a shop with a bookcase full of tomes about history and witchcraft, a table of crystal globes, a carousel of postcards, and a glass case featuring more expensive items, such as handcrafted beaded necklaces and voodoo dolls, which, despite being highly anachronistic and not at all contemporaneous to Elspeth Castor's history or this region, were their best sellers.

The woman did a quick turn around the shop, then beelined to the restroom. A few moments later, the tinkling iron bell at the door alerted Emmi that the woman had slipped out without buying a single thing or even thanking Emmi for her time. Sabrina mewed at the door, offended at being ignored.

Sighing, Emmi crossed over to the front door. It was summer, so the air was warm and muggy, the sunlight lingering heavily in the sky. She checked her watch. Emmi had been at the museum all day, and the woman from the interstate had been the only person to come inside. It was still technically an hour before she was supposed to close, but Emmi went ahead and flipped over the sign in the window and locked the door before drawing the black curtains in the front of the house closed.

"Boring day, huh, Sabrina?" Emmi told her cat. Sabrina rolled on her back, paws up and belly exposed. For most cats, this would be a sure trap to a clawed hand, but Grandfather often joked that Sabrina was half-dog. Emmi gave the ginger cat a good scratch on her white belly, and the cat's rumbled in a purr of bliss.

Standing back up, Emmi put her hand on the stone doorway, one of the more unique features of the house. Like many of the colonial houses in New England, the Castor house was made of planked wood. It retained much of its original charm, from the gabled roof to the massive chimney in the center of the house. And those original features included the stone doorway. Carved from one massive, solid boulder, the square stone had been roughly chipped away to the proper shape and then jammed against the wooden planks. The small stone landing and steps were made of the same material, an ostentatious detail on an otherwise typical colonial house.

As with many of the buildings of the time, the house had grown in size as it grew with age. Perhaps if Nathanial Hawthorne had gone a bit more south he would have become enamored with the rambling, multi-leveled house with six gables rather than the seven gabled one he wrote about. Still, despite its age and quirks, Emmi loved her home.

Even the museum part of it.

With her grandfather away for the summer, Emmi had become accustomed to the shadows in the corners, the creak in the floorboards, and the drafts around the chimney that seemed to loom larger when she was alone. Growing up in Nick Bottom, Massachusetts, every kid in school had known Emmi to be the weird kid who lived in the witch's house, and no one—*no one*— ever had a sleepover at the Castor house. But none of the items on display ever bothered Emmi.

It helped that she knew they were all fake.

Not fake in terms of history—the pointed black hennin hat had been verified by a textile expert to have been made in the late medieval period. Several larger museums had offered to buy some of the books in the library, a few of them handwritten from the seventeenth century. The clippings of herbs carefully compiled in jars had labels written with Elspeth's own hand, dating from 1616 to 1670. They were all real.

But they were *not* magic.

Emmi made her way through the museum, cutting off the lights in each room. The house was labyrinthine, some rooms requiring a slight step up or down as they'd been added on by subsequent generations. Emmi's grandfather had remodeled the space for a final time, converting the old sprawling homestead into the museum and restoring as much of it as possible to its original state, an enormous project that had left them teetering on the edge of broke for as long as Emmi could remember. The sitting room was the gift shop. The dining room now charted the progression of religious fanaticism and the shifting perspectives of witchcraft. The conservatory displayed Elspeth's personal garden of herbs used in potions. One bedroom showed how witch practices shifted as they moved from England to America in the colonies. Another displayed torture devices used to draw out confessions from accused witches—that was always the most popular room with the elementary school visits.

It was all a matter of history, a history Emmi loved and respected. She knew Elspeth Castor's past about as well as she knew her own, and she valued that history deeply. But while the fifth graders who giggled at thumbscrews were charming in their own way, and the people like the woman from the interstate were always a bit of a bother, the guests who aggravated Emmi the most were the ones who *believed*.

As a descendent of Elspeth Castor—and as the heir to the Museum of Magic in the tiny town of Nick Bottom—Emmi was absolutely never supposed to tell anyone how little she believed in magic.

But she knew, without a single doubt in her mind, that it was all nothing. It was the one truth Emmi believed more than anything else:

Magic. Was. *Not*. Real.

THE SUN

ILLUMINATION AND AN IMPORTANT JOURNEY

Twilight fell fast. The windows were nearly all the original glass from the seventeenth century, little diamond shapes framed by black-stained wood, the uneven thickness casting weird shadows across the thin carpets covering the hardwood floors. There were no overhead lights in the lower floors of the house. While the attic had been remodeled to be a more modern living space, careful placement of lamps and candles served to set the mood in the museum area. The lingering scent of smoke from the candles drifted through the museum.

It was long past time for Emmi to go upstairs. There was no reason for her to dawdle in the museum area. She had dinner—leftover Thai food—in the fridge. She could stream a show, blast some music, eat, fall asleep with Sabrina on the couch. Again.

But Emmi couldn't seem to talk herself into turning in for the night. Instead, she checked the computer behind the desk in the foyer. Sabrina hopped up on the counter to watch Emmi's fingers dance across the keyboard. Grandfather always told her that she was supposed to only use the computer for keeping track of sales and updating the museum's webpage, but Emmi always ignored him, quickly closing tabs whenever her grandfather came by.

But he wasn't here to fuss at her now.

Despite telling herself that she was getting online only to check her socials and email, Emmi knew she was really looking for a message from him. Grandfather had left for a trip to Europe almost a month ago in an attempt to track down some artifacts that were potentially linked to Elspeth Castor from before she'd left England. His emails had been daily at first; he hadn't been abroad in more than two decades, and he'd combined business with pleasure, visiting museums and cathedrals, wandering the streets of London and more.

Grandfather had flown out on a one-way ticket, intending to take his time. Emmi had known that there was a definite possibility that he would not return until it was time for school to start back up for the fall semester. And he was often scattered, the epitome of the absent-minded professor, as his history students at the local community college attested.

Still...it bothered her, the silence.

"Where is he?" Emmi asked Sabrina.

Sabrina stood up, arched her back in a stretch, and hopped down off the counter, padding over the thin carpet down the hallway. "Don't get lost!" Emmi called after the cat. Sabrina was a dearheart, but also dumb. She was well known for wandering around the house, getting into one of the rooms she usually ignored, realizing she wasn't where she'd intended to go, and simply screaming until Emmi found her and carried her back to the main hall.

Emmi frowned at the computer as she deleted the spam and then had nothing left in her inbox. Just to be sure, she checked the trash folder. Then she looked up Grandfather's socials to see if he'd posted something—a status, a picture, anything.

Nothing.

Emmi turned the screen off and stretched; the stool in front of the desk computer wasn't that comfortable. The pad Thai upstairs was calling her name—

Crash!

Emmi jumped up, so startled that the stool clattered to the

floor behind her. *What had that been?!* It sounded like glass shattering, and more concerning, it had definitely come from inside the house. Had someone smashed a window? Sabrina wasn't the brightest, but she was actually pretty careful and hadn't broken anything before. Other cats may knock knickknacks off shelves, but Sabrina never did, navigating the house with more care than most tourists.

Emmi started down the hallway to investigate, her heart racing, when another sound burst from the other side of the house—someone was knocking on the front door so hard that it shook in its frame.

Emmi froze, unsure which direction to go first. The pounding on the door intensified, and a cold chill raced up her spine. It was irrational, but dread filled her stomach—she absolutely did not want to answer the door. She couldn't explain the instinct, just...

She turned and headed down the hall, toward the sound of the crash. "Sabrina?" she called, hoping this was just a case of her cat knocking into something.

It didn't take long to discover the source. It hadn't been a window that had broken. It had been a large clay stoppered bottle on display by the fireplace.

The chimney was the straight spine of the house, a wide hearth on the bottom floor with bricks that cut through the second floor and the attic, warmed by the wooden logs burned in winter. The hearth was cold now, pieces of a broken pottery scattered in the remnants of ashes. Sabrina stood nearby, licking her paws and sitting primly.

Also there was a boy.

"What the—" Emmi muttered, staring.

The boy looked up.

"Oh," he said. "Hello."

"You're naked," Emmi said.

"I am not!" the boy protested, and he straightened from his position on the floor at the hearth, ash streaking his bare knees.

Once he was up, Emmi could see that he was... somewhat...clothed.

"You're wearing leaves."

The boy looked down at himself. "How observant you are." His British accent dripped with sarcasm.

The leaves clothing him were old, dried, and looked as if they'd fall off him at any moment. But even as the boy stretched, the plant detritus somehow stayed around his waist. "Who are you, Peter Pan?" Emmi asked, still reeling from the impossibility of his presence.

"Pan?" The boy laughed, the sound deep. He wasn't a boy. He was a young man, maybe a year or two older than Emmi—but he was slender-built and lithe, giving him a youthful appearance. As he stepped closer, Emmi realized he was at least a head taller than her, although her estimation of his height was thrown off by his chaotically floofy chestnut hair.

The pounding on the door grew louder. Emmi turned her head toward the sound. When she turned back to the boy, he was frowning.

"You definitely do not want to answer that door."

Emmi gaped at him. Who was he to pop into her home, break her crockery, and make demands, all while wearing nothing more than leaves? "I'm answering the door," she said, although there was a question in her voice. She *shouldn't* trust this boy, and yet... there was something niggling in her mind, warning her to believe him.

"I'm telling you, don't."

Emmi felt her ire rising. "Who are you to tell me anything?!" she demanded. Remnant thoughts or not, she didn't like being ordered about.

The boy swept into a capricious bow. "How impolite of me. My name is Puck. Sorry for breaking your bottle. But also, don't answer the door."

Emmi blinked several times, accidentally timing her eyelids to the pounding on the door. "Right," she said finally. "Okay." She turned and marched down the hall, toward the door.

"Where are you going?" The boy—Puck—called, chasing after her.

"To answer the door."

"But I said—"

Emmi swung open the door.

The man who stood on the threshold towered over Emmi. He wore a dark brown cloak, his face hidden in the shadows of the raised hood, but Emmi could still see the rough strands of a steel-grey beard poking out. His fist was raised; Emmi had opened the door just as he was about to beat on it again.

"Yes?" she said impatiently.

The man ignored her. His eyes flashed—they literally seemed to reflect light—and he growled, the sound dark and rumbling in the back of his throat. "*You*," he snarled, glaring at Puck.

Puck waved his hand with a flourish. "Me."

The man—Emmi could still not clearly see his face, but she was starting to think of him as Greybeard—whirled toward her. "Give me the fae."

"The what?" Emmi asked.

"Let me inside, and I will take care of it."

"I'm not an 'it,'" Puck said, somewhat sullenly.

"Let me inside!" Greybeard said, his voice raising a notch.

"No!" Emmi shouted back. Who was this man to beat on her door and demand entry? Fear washed over her, cold and sour. He was big enough to easily knock her aside and do as he liked. Emmi cast a furtive look to the front table, where the computer was—and the landline phone Grandfather insisted they keep for the museum. Where was her cell phone? Not in her pocket. She must have left it somewhere. But she was pretty sure she could get to the bright red telephone on the desk and call for help if this man—

"Girl," Greybeard growled. "I'm asking for your safety, as well as mine. Let me come inside this house."

Doubt filled her mind. None of this made *sense.*

Puck laughed. "He can't come inside without an invitation."

"What, like a vampire?" Emmi asked, her head bouncing between the two.

"Yes," said Puck.

"No!" roared Greybeard.

"Okay, well, I'm not letting you in." Emmi crossed her arms and glared at the man. He clearly meant business, and he put her on edge.

Puck laughed.

"You can go, too!" Emmi said, rounding on him. "I don't even know how you got inside, but—"

Emmi's voice faded as the man at the door loomed even larger. "You may deny me entry," he snarled, "and I may not be able to enter. But my weapons are under no such laws."

Blades blossomed at the man's hands, the edges sharp, but the color dark black. Iron? In one swift motion, he threw his hand out, and three knives flew down the corridor. With a squeak of terror, Emmi ducked—just in time, the whistling knife slicing through her loose hair before landing in a thud against the wall.

Emmi hit the floor and rolled toward the front desk, which had both cover and the phone. She tripped on her fallen stool, throwing herself behind the relative safety of the front desk. A blade point pierced the thin, painted plywood, inches from her face, and Emmi scrambled back. Okay, so it wasn't great cover. But it was the best she had. Emmi pulled her knees to her chest, breathing hard. What the hell was going on?

Through the sound of her rattling, shaking breath and the thudding of her heart in her ears, Emmi became aware of a different sound. Like wind. Like...

She peered around the edge of the desk.

Puck stood in the center of the corridor, his wrists held together and his palms open, a blast of wind erupting from his hands. Greybeard gripped the stone doorframe, his feet skidding across the stoop. His hood had flown back, and Emmi saw a man who looked too young for such an ostentatious beard, late thirties perhaps, with clear green eyes and a face marred with scars that stretched from his cheeks down to his chin, disappearing in his beard. His eyes, squinting against the blast of wind, found Emmi.

"Girl!" he shouted over the blast, "do not fall for this devil's tricks!"

Emmi stared at Puck.

The boy had his attention focused on Greybeard, but Emmi had eyes only for his hands and the impossible wind that blasted from them with the force of a hurricane.

"What—?" Emmi whispered.

The wind faltered. Puck glanced back at her, something on his face that she couldn't read—

And then an iron knife sliced into his arm, glancing off his bicep before thudding into the red telephone on the desk with enough force to slam it to the floor. Plastic and metal shattered. There went one means to call for help.

Puck fell to one knee, clutching his arm, as blood spurted through his fingers.

Green blood.

Panic rose in Emmi's throat, choking her. Greybeard used the pause of Puck's blast to pull another weapon out from beneath his cloak.

A crossbow. The bolts were jet black, all metal. Iron. He leveled the weapon at Puck.

"Just go!" Emmi screamed. She picked up the broken phone, swinging it by the plug she'd yanked from the wall, and hurtled it at Greybeard. Bits of red plastic flew off it as it slammed into Greybeard's face with a bell-ringing thunk.

Dazed, the man blinked.

And that gave Puck just enough time to blast him one more time. The wind hit Greybeard right in the chest, and the man stumbled down the steps, tripping to the sidewalk. Emmi slammed the door shut, twisted the lock, and pulled down the heavy wooden crossbar just for good measure.

Knees wobbly, Emmi turned around.

The foyer was trashed. Black iron throwing knives peppered the wall. Papers—every brochure Nick Bottom, Massachusetts, had to offer—were scattered everywhere, falling like confetti in the aftermath of Puck's wind blast.

And there was Puck.

Clothed in leaves.

Bleeding.

And grinning up at her like a triumphant idiot.

"Well!" he said cheerily, standing up and wincing only a little as his arm was jostled by the movement. "That was exciting!"

TWO OF SWORDS, TRANSPOSED
INDECISION, CONFUSION, AND INFORMATION OVERLOAD

"Exciting?!" Emmi gaped at the boy, who seemed completely oblivious that any of this was out of the ordinary at all.

"A bit," Puck said. He tread over the brochures to peer at the front desk, an utter mess between the wind he'd magically made, the knife throwing, and Emmi's grab for the telephone. He looked at the computer curiously.

"Look," Emmi said, slamming her hands on the table and drawing his full attention. "I am absolutely going to need more information on this situation than 'exciting.' What is going on? Who even was that man?" She paused, a horrible thought flooding her mind. "Do you think he's going to try to come back in?"

She looked at Puck as if he had the answers. He shrugged. "Maybe. I mean, Hunters do have the reputation of being persistent." His British lilt belied the gravity of the situation.

"I need to call the police," Emmi said flatly. She stared blankly at the spot where the red telephone usually was. "Cell phone."

She could barely process her thoughts, but once she said those words aloud, she focused on them. She needed to find her cell phone and use it to call the police. There was a man who had tried to kill her, or at least hurt her—no. No. Don't think about that. Find the cell phone.

Numbly, Emmi retraced her steps. She had thought her phone was at the desk, but it wasn't. That left the other place where the entire world had gone sideways. The hearth where she'd found Puck.

She stopped so suddenly that Puck, who'd been following on her heels, bumped right into her.

"Why have I even let you stay here? I don't know you! And you're dressed in leaves!"

Puck grinned at her. "You do seem very caught up by that detail."

"Also you did magic! And bled—are currently bleeding! Green!"

Puck looked down at his arm. "You know, it sort of detracts from your observational skills if you go about announcing everything multiple times. Makes me doubt you've really noticed it the first time."

"Go!" Emmi pointed to the corridor, at the end of which was the locked and bolted door. Her finger trembled. She didn't entirely trust Puck, but she also didn't *not* trust him, not after all that.

"No, thank you," Puck said simply.

"I—but—"

Puck stared at her with an amused quirk in his lips and very firmly did not head to the door.

With a growl of frustration, Emmi turned on her heel and marched to the giant fireplace. There in the ash were the remains of the bottle that had been on the table by the hearth. And on that table was her phone.

Emmi snatched it up, unlocking it. Puck watched a picture of

Emmi and her grandfather light up on the home screen before Emmi switched over to the call feature. "Police," she muttered, suddenly realizing why there were so many drills for children to learn how to dial 911. When the time came in a real emergency, Emmi was so shocked she could barely register what to do next, much less how to do it.

"Yes, police," Puck said. "They're absolutely not going to help in any way, but by all means, feel free to 'call' them."

Emmi flicked her eyes to him.

"I mean, I'm sure they know how to deal with a Hunter. And they'll be very prepared to negotiate witch handling. You can definitely trust the authorities when it comes to witches."

The screen went blank again as Emmi forgot to punch in the numbers. "Witch—what?"

Sabrina padded over. She'd tracked ashy footprints all over the seventeenth century rug and looked rather pleased with herself. Puck ignored the cat as she wound her way through his bare legs.

"Are..." Emmi recalled the way Puck had made the wind blow, the way he bled green. "Are *you* a witch?"

"No, of course not," Puck said. "You are."

Sabrina mewed in indignation at being ignored. Emmi didn't spare a thought for the cat. "I'm a witch." She had meant it more as a question than a statement, but her voice was flat.

Puck bent down and scratched Sabrina. "Obviously." Sabrina went limp with bliss at the attention, plopping on the floor immediately.

"No," Emmi said. "I'm not."

"No point arguing about it, but feel free if you'd like." Puck didn't hesitate to rub Sabrina's belly, which meant he either didn't have much experience with cats or he just understood Sabrina's innate desire for attention more than most people.

"No, it's just—I'm *not* a witch. No one is. Witches aren't real."

Puck raised an eyebrow and looked around the room. A

portrait of Elspeth in the tradition of John Singer Sargent but painted a century before he had been born hung over the mantel. A broomstick leaned against the stone hearth; it not only looked old, but it *was* old. Emmi had seen that exact same crooked broomstick in photographs of her mother when she was a child, and it had looked ancient then. On the opposite wall, a display case showed the medieval hennin hat—the traditional pointy hat that was used by merchants to stand out in crowds and then got ascribed as being a "witch's hat." Beside it was the actual huge cast iron cauldron Elspeth had used in the 1600s—for cooking food, as many people did then. Hanging above it was Elspeth's scrying mirror, spotted with age but still reflective.

"Okay, look," Emmi said. She was about to break the one rule she and her grandfather had—never, ever cast doubt on what Elspeth was. They wouldn't be very good museum curators if they didn't believe in the thing they were showcasing. "Magic and witchcraft and all that? It's just not real."

"Sure it's not," Puck said. He straightened, much to Sabrina's chagrin, and twirled his fingers over his body. The leaves he'd been wearing melted and shifted, turning into a regular pair of blue jeans and a gray sweater layered over a black t-shirt. Emmi's shock was replaced by confusion; the outfit was the exact same design as one of the people on the brochures scattered around the foyer wore. A young man with a Starbucks cup in one hand and a Tanner Outlet bag in the other, enticing people to shop for Kate Spade purses and GAP jeans at the strip mall up the interstate. Emmi had stared at that rack of brochures long enough to both recognize the outfit immediately and sort of hate it, despite the fact that it was just a sweater and jeans. And that it looked pretty darn good on Puck.

"What?" Puck asked at her look, his tone purposefully innocent but his eyes wicked. "It's just leaves."

Emmi blinked, and the leaves were back. Blink again—sweater and jeans.

"Okay. Okay," Emmi said, tossing her hands up. "You're magic. Magic is real. Now get out."

Puck smirked. He decidedly did not get out.

"What is it going to take to make you leave?" Emmi said.

"You could banish me," Puck offered. "Since you're a witch. Although I'd rather you didn't, for the record. Would make things complicated…"

Emmi growled in frustration.

"Why is it so hard to believe?" Puck asked. "You're the descendant of Elspeth Castor."

"Who was also not a witch."

Puck went from somewhat bemused to sharing Emmi's disbelief. "You really do think that, don't you?"

"Obviously."

"What do you think that was?" Puck pointed to the shards of the broken bottle still littering the ash.

Emmi shrugged. "Some pottery."

"A witch bottle."

Emmi knew enough of her history to know what Puck meant by "witch bottle." In fact, she herself had affixed the label on the wall behind the table; Grandfather had insisted she take more of an interest in the museum.

Witch bottles were used in the sixteenth and seventeenth centuries as a form of "good" magic that was almost deemed acceptable by the church. Mostly superstition, these bottles were used to ward off hexes or protect a home from bad magic. Clay bottles were filled with specific items, like nails, a bit of wine, even urine from the person who needed protection, and then stoppered up and hidden somewhere. The witch would then be unable to harm the person or curse the home.

According to the legends.

"It's just an old bottle," Emmi said. "And whatever people believed about it didn't change the fact that it was nothing more than hocus pocus."

"Perhaps if a regular mortal had made it." Puck shook his head. "But it was made by Elspeth."

That much had been printed on the sign by the table. Elspeth had written in one of her many journals about the bottle—that it was for protection of her family and that it must remain in the house. Sealed. Not broken.

"Elspeth Castor was one of the last great protectors," Puck said. He was all serious now, speaking as if he were concerned that Emmi didn't know all this. "Her magic was unique in that it was to protect not just her kind, but *all* kinds."

"Kinds?" Emmi asked, shaking her head.

"The mundane and the mystic," Puck explained. "Witches are mundanes who can see through the mysts between realms."

"Mists?" She didn't bother trying to hide the doubt in her voice as she waggled her fingers in a poor imitation of fog.

"Mysts. With a 'y.' As in 'mystical.' Witches can see through the mysts. Strong ones can help shape them."

"Well, I've never seen through any 'myst.'"

"Until the bottle broke." Puck looked down at it purposefully.

"Until *you* broke it," Emmi accused.

Puck looked affronted. "I did not! Well, not directly. It's not like I just pushed it over."

Emmi crossed her arms over her chest. She was still holding her phone; she still had half an idea to use it to call the police. "I want answers. Now."

"I've been *trying* to give them to you. It's not my fault you don't believe me."

"You've given me no reason to!"

"Aside from saving you from the Hunter."

"Aside from—oh." Emmi paused. That was a good point. "So how did you get here anyway?"

Puck gestured to the chimney.

"You came down the chimney," she said flatly.

Puck nodded.

"Like Santa Claus."

"Like who?"

Emmi blinked. "No. Sorry, no. I absolutely do not believe you just popped out of my chimney, knocked over the bottle, and fought off a random creep..."

"Oh, I didn't descend down it!" Puck said, laughing. "Yeah, I can see how that's confusing. No, it's just the ash sigil."

Puck reached past Emmi and grabbed the ancient broomstick that was standing at attention. Flipping it with his wrist, he brought up the ragged straws and plucked one from the end. Carefully, he used it to etch a symbol in the ash.

For a moment, nothing happened.

Then, the symbol burned. The gray-white ash was long cold, but a red fire shone through it, growing hotter, turning yellow, then blue. Wispy images Emmi could almost make out reflected in the flames. She leaned in closer.

"Careful," Puck said, pulling her away. "Unless you'd fancy a quick teleportation to the Orkney Islands."

Now that he named it, Emmi could recognize the shapes of the islands, those cold northern shores in Scotland. It seemed almost real enough to step through, but then, like a flickering candle flame blown out, it evaporated in smoke.

"Is that where you came from?" Emmi asked, a little breathless. It was hard to keep denying magic when it was happening right in front of her.

"No. Just the first sigil I could think of."

Emmi had done loads of research on witchcraft—or, more aptly, the perception of witchcraft among the public in history. She knew that during Elspeth's time, it was a common assumption that witches travelled by broomstick and often flew out of the chimney of their house. In her essay for AP American History, Emmi had written about how this was a leftover from medieval sexism; brooms and cleaning hearths were associated with women, and women were the ones most often at the end of an accuser's finger.

But now she was starting to see a different picture. A broomstick by a fireplace was a common enough feature that even now, centuries later, it didn't look out of place. If it took drawing a symbol in ash for teleportation spells to work, maybe the association with hearths and chimneys and broomsticks wasn't just about superstition and sexism, but based on a crumb of truth.

"All right," Emmi mused aloud, her phone's screen blank in her hand. "So, you came through my chimney. With magic." She wanted to doubt it, but the evidence was pretty blatant. "Why?"

For the first time, Puck seemed a little unsure of how to respond.

"Why did you come here?" Emmi pressed. "What do you want?"

Puck sighed. "There's a reason I showed up at the same time as a Hunter. Witch bottles are protective magic. And the spell Elspeth Castor made to ensure her lineage's protection was failing. I could sense it; I knew it was weak and about to break. And I knew that meant Hunters would come for you."

Emmi raised her eyebrow. Puck *had* come, and he *had* helped her fight off Greybeard, but...

"Why would you help me?"

The question came out smaller than she would have liked, more vulnerable. It was one thing to start believing magic was real; it was an entirely different thing to believe that she was at the epicenter of it. That she was worthy of magical protection—from her ancestor or from Puck.

"You have Elspeth's blood, and it seems pretty clear that you've got some of her magic, too," Puck said. "And her magic is the magic of protection. That's how she survived for as long as she did, with pilgrims and witch hunters and dark fae all on her track. She cast a powerful enough spell to protect her descendants for centuries." He took a deep breath, ruffling his hair. "But she also cast spells to protect the mystical from the mundane and to protect the mundane from the mystical. *All* her spells are fading."

Emmi wasn't sure what that meant—neither that her ancestor

was that strong nor that her magic was failing now of all times, after so long.

"I came here for the same reason that Hunter came here," Puck said. "We both think you may have the same power Elspeth did. The only difference is, I want you to use it to help bring back her protection spells, and he wants to kill you before you can do that."

FIVE OF PENTACLES

PERSEVERANCE, CHANGE FOR THE BETTER, AND RENEWED HOPE

E mmi sat down on the floor in front of the hearth, the splattered gray ash and broken pottery shards as impossible a puzzle as her own life.

"I don't know what to do," she muttered to herself, although she realized belatedly that Puck could hear her. He didn't say anything, though, giving her time to process.

The helplessness washing over her made her think of Grandfather. Even when she was little and both her parents were still alive, Grandfather had been there for her. They had all shared Elspeth's big old house together. But first cancer, then a drunk driving accident had whittled her family down to just her and Grandfather. He was the rock, the one steady thing in Emmi's life.

He and this house.

And now the house wasn't what she had spent her life thinking it was. It had been easy to pretend the old Castor house was steeped in legend but actually harmless. To find out that the magic was real? The house may never fall, but that knowledge had cracked the foundation of Emmi's life.

The only stable thing left to her was Grandfather. And he was gone.

"Wait a minute." Emmi twisted around to look at Puck, who

crouched next to Sabrina on the other side of the room, under the scrying mirror and beside the big black cauldron. "Grandfather's in England now. He was tracking down some of Elspeth's artifacts. Is he...is he caught up in all of this?"

Puck straightened, shrugging. "Maybe," he said. "The Hunters would likely target here first. Elspeth's magic was centered around the bottle. But they are vicious. They may go after him, if for no other reason than they could use him to force your hand."

Emmi's heart thudded in her chest. She still wasn't sure about what was real and what wasn't, nor where her power lay. But while she doubted the magic in her blood, she wasn't about to question her willingness to do *anything* to save Grandfather.

"Okay," Emmi said, decision made. "I may not believe...any of this, but I want to make sure Grandfather is safe."

A strange look passed over Puck's face, a shadow gone before Emmi could guess his thoughts. "Spoken like a true Castor," he said, his voice carefully neutral.

Emmi raised an eyebrow. "What's that supposed to mean?"

"Your magic is all about protection. That's what the witch bottle originally was, a protection spell. A pretty powerful one."

"That you broke," Emmi muttered.

Puck shrugged. "So make another one. You *are* a Castor."

Emmi's gaze shifted to Sabrina, licking her paws. Probably getting rid of the ash. It was summer; they should have cleaned the hearth long ago. But the ash added to the aesthetic of the room, Grandfather always insisted. Emmi stared down at the broken pieces of pottery scattered over the stone, spilling into the gray dust.

"I have no idea how to make a witch bottle," she confessed. Emmi had affixed the label for the museum's collection on the wall behind the bottle, and she had, of course, studied it for when she gave tours. Witch bottles were used primarily in England— and English colonies—in the Tudor era, and each one was unique. There were some common themes on contents, but all

Emmi knew about *this* witch bottle was that the insides rattled when she shook it. Grandfather had contemplated getting the bottle x-rayed to examine the contents, but they'd decided it was too expensive for such an unpopular item in the museum, one most people ignored.

"Don't you have..." Puck said, waving his hand. "Books or something?"

Emmi snorted. "Yes. We have books." There was a whole library on the second floor, with books older than Elspeth, some in coded language, some bound in gilded leather, some nothing more than folios with etchings. Emmi had spent her childhood in that library. She knew there was nothing in there about how to make a witch bottle. Elspeth had gathered books about history more than witchcraft, another reason Emmi had grown up believing Elspeth had been maligned for her gender and her oddness, not because she was an actual witch.

"Maybe I can figure out how to make it retroactively?" Emmi mused, staring down at the mess on the floor. If she found all the contents, perhaps she could just put them in another bottle, mumble some hocus pocus, and Grandfather would be okay? Emmi shook her head. It couldn't be that simple, she was sure. But it was a start.

Emmi thrust her hand into the ash, feeling around in the soft, cold powder for...something.

"What are you doing?" Puck asked.

Emmi pulled her ash-stained hand out, gripping a pottery shard. "If I know what kinds of things were in Elspeth's bottle, that's at least a start, yeah?"

"I suppose." Puck peered closer. "Do you intend to glue it all back together?"

"No." Emmi tossed the shard down on the carpet, gently enough to ensure it wouldn't break. "Unless you think I should?"

Puck shrugged. "You're the witch, not me."

Emmi sighed, staring at the broken bit. With the curved side down, she could see the stain of something dark reddish-brown on the inside of the bottle and groaned.

"I read about how liquid was sometimes poured into the bottle, too," she said, picking it back up and looking at it closer. It was going to be far harder to know what things to add to the bottle if some had evaporated. "This could be wine?"

"Or blood," Puck said cheerily.

Emmi pushed it away and focused on the hearth. Digging her fingers into the deepest pile, she felt something that seemed to be a rock. When she pulled it up, though, she wasn't so sure. Roughly heart-shaped, the pale gray stone was porous and strange, perhaps broken from the bottle's base, perhaps a palm-sized rock made of some soft stone.

"That could be blood, too," Puck said.

Emmi dropped the heart-shaped rock. It also had a reddish-brown stain on it, but darker and more mottled than the stain on the pottery shard.

Sticking up out of the ash she'd just disturbed, Emmi saw a charred bit of a page. The paper was so old that it crumbled on the edges when Emmi touched it. Not smooth like modern processed printer paper; this felt thick and rough, the ink on it browned and scratched into the page.

"Handwriting," Emmi muttered. This hadn't been made by a publisher with a press but by someone's personal pen. Not Elspeth—Emmi knew her ancestor's curling scribbles. This was a heavy hand, as if the writer were angry.

"What does it say?" Puck leaned over her shoulder.

The words were definitely Roman letters, but the hand-writing was thick and calligraphic. It was written in an old style, but almost illegible. "I don't know," Emmi said, dropping the paper.

A strange tingling sensation on her neck made her feel almost as if she were being watched. Emmi paused, looking around the room. There was no one there but Puck and Sabrina.

Distracted, Emmi ran her fingers over the mounds of ash

again. "Ouch!" she yelped, jerking her hand back. A razor-thin cut sliced through her palm.

Sabrina mewed, jumping into her lap. "I'm okay," Emmi said, petting her cat with her good hand. She needed to be careful. The ash itself could still have splinters or debris, to say nothing of the sharp bits of the broken bottle. Pushing the ash mound carefully with the back of her hand, Emmi scattered the gray fluff, revealing a dirt clod and something shiny.

"A coin?" Puck reached down and plucked it up. Emmi let him examine it; she was distracted by the dirt. It was so dark it looked black, not like the soil near the house. Slightly bigger than a pebble, it crumbled a little when she pinched it—definitely a clod of earth, not a rock.

It's just some dirt, Emmi tried to tell herself. It may not have anything to do with the bottle at all. But she still put it next to the pieces she'd excavated from the hearth.

"This is old." Puck tossed the coin to Emmi.

Old—like the writing on the paper. She should have expected that. The bottle had been made by Elspeth sometime in the seventeenth century. Of course the contents would be old, too, and judging from the dirt and the coin, English instead of American.

Emmi stood carefully, a thin line of blood seeping through her hand. Her mind swam with possibilities, and it didn't help that both Puck and Sabrina looked at her with expectant eyes, as if she was supposed to know what to do next.

But she didn't. None of this was normal.

Grandfather is missing, she reminded herself. That, too, wasn't normal.

She looked down at the pile of items she'd pulled from the ash. There was more in the hearth, surely, but she didn't even know what to do with what she'd found. Stuffing a bottle with wine—or blood—some stones, dirt, coins, and paper didn't seem enough to save Grandfather.

Her hands hovered over the items, and she almost picked up

the heart-shaped stone. *It's definitely a rock*, she thought. *Not a bit of the bottle that broke funny. It's a strange rock.*

The stain on it, however, made her pull back. If that was blood...she didn't want to think about having to make something or someone bleed. She clenched her fist over the thin cut on her palm; it was barely bleeding, but enough for her to be worried that she would ruin the spell if she contaminated it with her own blood.

Instead, Emmi plucked up the charred paper with handwriting on it. That was something she could handle. Even if the language was archaic, it was definitely English. Like badly-spelled Shakespearean. Her eyes blurred as she tried to focus on the writing, smudged with soot and burned edges cutting off some of the words.

I can handle books and papers. A part of her wanted to flee to the library upstairs. Libraries were safe. Libraries were home. If this paper was the closest to normal in this impossible situation, she could focus on it.

It's not enough. The voice in her mind was both panicked and certain. She was supposed to remake a medieval witch bottle, imbue it with magic *somehow*, and save her Grandfather? And also save the world from Hunters who just broke into people's houses and started throwing knives?

Her heart rose up her throat, and Emmi felt panic kicking in. It didn't help that Puck was *right there* watching her. In his gray sweater that was supposed to be on an outlet mall brochure, not on a boy who made violent winds burst from his palms. He was the magic one, not her.

"So, what next?" Puck asked eagerly, his eyes alight with excitement.

"I don't know!" Emmi snapped. Puck jerked back at her violent tone, but it wasn't his movement that caught her eye.

It was the mirror.

On the wall opposite the hearth, the old scrying mirror, ancient and spotted. The dull surface only ever reflected the room. Schoolchildren on field trips would dare each other to say "Bloody Mary" in it.

But it was only ever just a mirror.

Except now?

It did not reflect the room.

Instead of the wall and the fireplace, the mirror now reflected an outdoor scene. Dark clouds in a twilit sky over a rugged cliff in front of crashing waves. An old stone building—a church, perhaps—barely visible in the mist.

As Emmi stepped closer, an image of a person came into focus, timed with Emmi's steps. The person did not have Emmi's face, did not even wear her shocked expression. It was a woman, older than her by more than two decades at least.

And she was *furious*.

THE DEVIL, TRANSPOSED

FINDING STRENGTH, BEING ON THE RIGHT PATH BUT FEELING TRAPPED

Emmi was barely conscious of her feet moving across the carpet, slowly drawing her closer to the mirror.

To the woman screaming inside the mirror.

It wasn't screaming, not exactly. There were words. The woman's mouth moved up and down too purposefully to be anything but words.

But the mirror was silent.

It didn't matter that the woman's entire face strained with the effort it took to shout; no sound came out. Her fists were curled near her face, shaking with effort. Emmi shook her head a little, lips parting. "I can't hear you," she whispered in a strangled voice.

"What?" Puck asked.

Emmi ignored him. The woman's eyes were on her and her alone, red-rimmed and tired-looking. When Emmi shifted a little, the woman's eyes followed her. But even when Puck moved behind Emmi, the woman's gaze did not flicker to him.

So much about the woman seemed—pained. Not just the corded muscles of her neck as she screamed silently or the white knuckles of her fists. She had been shaven, a short and uneven stubble of brownish hair across her scalp. Whoever had done this to her had not been gentle and had used a dull blade that scraped across her skin, leaving gashes more than nicks. A trickle of dried blood from a particularly brutal scrape tracked around a small mole over her left ear.

The woman wore vaguely medieval clothing. Not Renaissance Faire garb, but actual medieval clothing, a rough brown kirtle over a dingy white smock. Emmi knew enough about the clothing from that time to know that while the woman was fully covered, these were considered underthings. She lacked a proper gown—and from the looks of the dark gray skies and the goose-bumps along the woman's skin, she could do with a woolen cloak as well.

But it was hard to focus on any of these details as the woman did not cease screaming in the mirror. Whatever message she was trying to say was obviously urgent, and the longer Emmi went without understanding her, the more distressed she seemed.

"What do you think she's saying?" Emmi asked. Puck stood behind her now, close enough that if she leaned backwards, she'd fall against him.

"Who?" Puck asked.

Emmi whipped around, staring at him. Puck seemed completely oblivious about the woman in the mirror, not perturbed at all. He was watching *her* as if *she* were the oddest thing in the room. Not a medieval woman screaming in a mirror.

"What..." Horror washed over her. Somehow, Puck *not* seeing the woman was worse than how she did see her. "What do you see when you look into the mirror?"

"You. Me." Puck looked behind his shoulder. "This room. Why? What do you see?"

"Not that." Emmi turned hollowly back to the mirror. The woman was watching her. As she spoke to Puck, the woman had silenced, but as soon as Emmi turned her full attention back, she started screaming again.

"What do you—?" Puck started.

"Shh!" Emmi hissed. She concentrated wholly on the woman's mouth. She shouted the same thing over and over again, Emmi was sure of that. Just...three words. Perhaps she could...she could figure this out?

Emmi watched as the woman's teeth bared in the first word, lips snarling. Then her mouth slammed shut before bursting out the next word. She ended with a furious scream-like word that stretched her lips wide.

Emmi found herself copying the woman's lips, imitating the way her tongue and teeth moved. "Sss," she said, copying her. "Mmmm—my! Lah? No..." The woman cycled back to the first word. "Sssss...ay! Say! Say...my...nnnn. Nae." Emmi huffed a breath, realizing the woman's words. "Say my name."

She didn't take her eyes off the mirror as she repeated it. "*Say my name.* That's what she's saying."

"What who is saying?" Puck asked gently. He may not see whatever Emmi saw, but he believed her. That was oddly comforting.

"I don't know," Emmi said. "A woman. Medieval. She's in the mirror—wait!" Emmi rushed to the mirror, splaying her hand on the cold glass, streaking soot and ash over the surface. "She's fading! She's—"

And just like that, she was gone. The storm clouds in the distance of the woman's outdoor horizon were the last to evaporate to nothing.

Emmi's eyes shifted focus from the reflection to her own hands. To the paper she still clutched. She spun around to Puck. "There was a woman in the mirror," she said.

"Yes, I gathered."

"She wanted me to say her name."

"Will you?" Puck was, at best, idly curious, and his lack of urgency in the situation made Emmi want to punch him.

"No!" Emmi shouted. "I don't *know* her name!"

"Yes," Puck said. "I can see how that would be a problem."

Growling, Emmi ignored him, looking back at the mirror, but

it showed nothing now but her own grim face. *I can figure this out,* Emmi thought. The witchcraft part? That was confusing. But this? This was history. And Emmi *knew* history.

"That beach—rocky, curving—that is like the coastlines of Scotland, maybe northern England," she said, musing aloud. "Not really a cliff like Dover, more like...craggy. There was at least a little sand on the beach below her. And a rock! I remember a rock in the water, big, like an island."

"These very specific details will surely help you solve this mystery," Puck said. "A rock, you say?"

Emmi ignored him. "She was definitely dressed in medieval or early Renaissance clothing. Hard to pinpoint the exact time with nothing but a kirtle really; they were used for centuries. Brown dye could have been any era. There was a building," Emmi said, remembering suddenly. "A stone building—maybe a church? Behind her shoulder."

"Good thing there aren't that many medieval stone buildings in Scotland during the Middle Ages." Puck sounded sincere, but Emmi knew he was being sarcastic.

"Or Renaissance," Emmi growled.

"Yes, let's add a few more centuries to our possible time frame for the mysterious mirror woman," Puck said. "It's always best to broaden the scope rather than narrow it."

"Not helping," Emmi muttered. With the mirror now just a normal mirror, she had nothing to do but look at the paper still in her hand. She brought the writing closer to her face. She'd noticed before that the handwriting was old, not just in age but also style. "I think maybe the woman was Renaissance, at least if she was linked to this paper," Emmi said. "It's not Middle English. It's, technically, modern English. But like Shakespearean. Badly-spelled Shakespearean."

She glanced at Puck through her eyelashes. It hadn't gone past her notice that Puck was named after a Shakespearean character. She wondered if it was his real name, or if he'd mocked her by picking the name of a famous fae. If it was his real name, Emmi wondered if Puck was *the* Puck, servant to Oberon, king of the fae. Or maybe that was all myth.

Focus, Emmi, she told herself. Holding the old paper up, Emmi read the words carefully and slowly. "'The description of the fourth kind of Sprites—no, I mean, Spirits." The spelling really was bad. "'Called the...Pharoah?" She forced herself to interpret each individual letter. P. H. A. I. R. I. E. What on Earth? But then she sounded it out, the same way she'd sounded out the mirror woman's words. The "ph" became an "f" sound, and it clicked—fairy. "'What is possible therein, and what is but illusion,'" she finished, guessing at the last word as it was torn off from the ripped page.

"Well, that doesn't make much sense," Puck offered.

"It tells us some." Emmi headed to the door, Puck on her heels. "This is probably around the early 1600s, I think, judging from the way it's written. The library may have something."

"You have a library in your house?" For the first time, Puck sounded impressed. Emmi spared a glance at him as she headed up the stairs to the second floor. Okay, noted. Magic mirrors didn't faze the boy, but a room of books was awe-inspiring.

Elspeth Castor's library wasn't exactly the dream-like fantasy that Beast presented to Belle in the Disney cartoon, but Emmi certainly felt like nowhere in the house was as magical as the aisles of mahogany shelves and meticulously recorded books. She went straight to the row of records from seventeenth century England, an eclectic mix of fiction and nonfiction, folios and bound copies mingling with handmade journals and scrolls of maps.

"How do you know where anything is?" Puck asked, eyes wide.

Emmi looked back at the paper. "I..." How *was* she supposed to find the exact paper that matched this one, and why did she think it would help her find the name of the woman in the mirror? And how did any of that help her remake a broken witch bottle and bring her Grandfather home? The impossibility of the situation washed over Emmi, and she felt her heart racing, her pulse pounding in her ears.

"Hey," Puck said, noticing her rising panic. "Hey, hey, hey. What's wrong? You have books. Books make you happy, yeah?"

Emmi snorted through her heavy breathing. Puck had only known her for a few hours, and he'd already honed in on how much of a nerd she was. The ridiculousness of that idea calmed her enough to say, "I don't know how to find what we need."

"So use your magic." Puck said it so simply that Emmi jerked fully out of her shock.

"I don't have magic. You're the one who blasted wind out of his hands."

"You're the one who saw the woman in the mirror," Puck pointed out. "Not me. You have a different sort of magic."

"The kind that can see things," Emmi said sarcastically.

But Puck nodded. "Yes. Exactly. You can see through the mysts, into the mystical."

"Well, I'm not seeing anything here."

"Have you tried?"

"Yes!" Emmi shouted, but then she stopped. She was seeing, but was she *seeing*? How did one turn on such a power? She hadn't really done anything to see the woman in the mirror.

Emmi took a calming breath. She shut her eyes. Another breath. She let her body relax. She took a step forward, another.

And bumped her nose into a book.

Opening her eyes, she saw the spine and, with a trembling hand, she pulled it from the shelf.

"It didn't work," Emmi said, lifting the book up to shove it back into place.

"Why do you say that?" Puck grabbed the book and flipped through the pages.

"That's *MacBeth*." Emmi's voice was flat. "It's not whatever this came from." She waved the burnt scrap of paper at Puck's face.

"There's witches in this," Puck said, pausing. "Maybe you

need this book, not the book the paper came from. Your magic could have pulled you to this title."

Emmi shook her head. Yes, there were witches in *MacBeth*. They stole the show, what with their double, double, boil and trouble. But it was fiction, and it wasn't what she needed, witches or not.

Emmi snatched the book out of Puck's hands, intent on reshelving it, but the cover fell open, exposing the first page. And just as Emmi had caught movement in the mirror before she saw the woman, she thought—for a moment—she caught a swirling glimmer of gold over the page. She focused in on the words, reading the opening lines of the play. "'When shall we three meet again, in thunder, lightning, or in rain?'" She looked up at Puck. "You were right."

"I usually am. About what?"

"This was what I needed to see." She pointed to the words, no longer shining. "The storm. There was a storm behind the woman in the mirror. And a storm here, in the text." Her mind raced, trying to recall the details she'd learned. "The witch hunts in England started because of the witch hunts in Scotland. The king—James. James VI of Scotland. After he was married, his boat almost sank on the return journey from Denmark. He blamed witches. He started the witch hunts because of the storm."

"Uh-huh," Puck said, nodding but clearly not following along.

"When Queen Elizabeth died, she was the Virgin Queen. She had no heirs. James the Sixth of Scotland became James the First of England. And Shakespeare wrote *MacBeth* to, well, to suck up to the new king." Emmi looked down at the paper in her hand. "This has something to do with James, I'm sure of it. James and the first witch hunt. Or..." her gaze slid over to the book she still held. "Or it has something to do with Shakespeare, and James's connection to *MacBeth?*"

Puck shrugged. "No idea."

It didn't feel like enough. These clues were too distant from the witch bottle, and none of it seemed powerful or important enough to save the woman in the mirror who so clearly desperately needed help. Needed Emmi to say her name.

And how will this help me find Grandfather? Emmi thought.

"I don't know what to do," she said helplessly.

"What if we go there?" Puck said. "Maybe you'll see—I mean, really *see*—something if we go there."

"Go where?" Emmi held up the copy of *MacBeth*. "To the Globe?"

"The globe?"

"The Globe Theater, where Shakespeare did all his plays." How could a boy named Puck not know about the Globe?

"Sure." Puck shrugged. "Or we go to the random Scottish coast from the mirror, if you can figure out where that was. There was a big rock, if you recall, that'll help you locate it."

"Okay, let me grab my passport and just hop on a plane." Emmi rolled her eyes. They'd saved for months for Grandfather's trip; she knew the credit card he'd given her for emergencies wouldn't cover an international flight, much less any other expenses.

"A...plane?" Puck shook his head. "Why wouldn't you just use an ash sigil?"

She remembered then the magic design Puck had drawn in the hearth's ash, the way it had shown the Orkney Islands.

She could go. To see. Or...to *see*. They could go right now.

She just had to decide where. The Globe Theater? Or pinpoint the Scottish coast and find the woman in the mirror? No—the Shakespearean connection felt too tenuous.

"Scotland," Emmi said, looking at Puck with determination in her eyes. "We need to go to Scotland."

But first, they had to figure out *where* in Scotland to go.

THE KING OF CUPS
DEEP FEELINGS AND FINDING THE RIGHT PATH

E mmi stared down at the open book in her lap. It still felt...
not enough. Like she was missing an essential piece of the
puzzle. Idly, she turned the page, scanning the words of
the infamous Scottish play.

"'Fair is foul and foul is fair,'" she muttered.

"Reasonable words to live by," Puck said amiably.

She turned the page and gasped aloud.

"What?" Puck leaned over the book. Someone had circled the
lines in the play where the first witch said:

> *But in a sieve I'll thither sail,*
> *And, like a rat without a tail,*
> *I'll do, I'll do, and I'll do.*

And in her grandfather's handwriting, Emmi read the scribble
in the margins: "'Storms and News from Scotland.'" She traced
her finger under the last three words—her grandfather had underlined them emphatically.

"Scotland again." Puck sounded rather unimpressed.

"And storms."

"Still not exactly helpful."

Emmi looked back at the circled text. Sailing in a sieve? That was ridiculous. She tried to picture a person stepping into a boat-sized colander, the holes making it sink immediately. It was impossible—if someone were to do such a thing it would be... "Magic," she whispered.

She glanced down at the paper in her hand, the soot-streak, burnt-edged scrap that had been in the witch bottle. It, too, spoke of fairies and impossible, magic things.

"There's a reason why *MacBeth* featured witches, and why it's called the Scottish play," Emmi said, dropping the book to the floor and standing. She rushed to the book shelves, Puck watching her. "Shakespeare wrote it for King James. And he added the witches because...aha!" She crowed triumphantly, tapping a book. The King James Version of the Bible—commissioned by the same King James who watched *MacBeth* when it was originally performed for him. And beside it, *Daemonologie*.

She pulled the slender volume from the shelf. "James wrote this before he became King of England," she told Puck, who shrugged, seemingly not seeing the connection.

Emmi scanned the pages of *Daemonologie* quickly. Black-and-white etched illustrations near the back caught her eye, and she slowed down, flipping the pages to the chapter header.

"News from Scotland!" she said, thrusting the book at Puck. She snatched it back before he could focus on it, reading quickly. "The news is witch trials!" she exclaimed. "James heard the dittays —the testimonies—himself." Her eyes puzzled through the difficult Scottish spelling. "It all centers around a place called 'North Barrick Kirk.'"

Finally Puck looked interested. "Now we're narrowing it down, Castor. A town."

"And a building," Emmi said. "'Kirk' means church. The church in the town of North Barrick."

Puck grabbed the book from her hands and shoved it back beside the Bible. "Let's go!" he said, racing to the stairs, back to the hearth room.

Emmi was slower, looking at her phone. By the time she entered the room, Puck knelt in front of the cold hearth, pooling together a small pile of ash. "North Barrick, you said?" he asked.

Emmi held her phone out, showing a tiny spot highlighted on the map labelled "North Berwick."

"The spelling must have changed through the years."

"You sure that's the right place?" Puck asked, squinting at the screen.

Emmi zoomed in on the map, changing it to street view to show a tiny white church with a digital label above it that read: "Saint Andrew's Auld Kirk, location of the North Berwick witch trials."

Puck's eyes widened, but Emmi just pocketed her phone. "This has got to be it."

Nodding, Puck turned back to the ash pile, tracing a mark into it with his finger. The wide hearth illuminated with an image of a green field and a white building. He stood up, brushing off his knees, as Emmi bent down to look into the perfect picture of a Scottish town.

"We just go through it?" Emmi whispered, peering in close.

"Yup." Puck pushed her in the back, and Emmi stumbled forward. Her left foot struck the gray brick of the hearth, but her right foot hit the soft grass-covered earth of a small patch of land on a peninsula. Salty air blew up her nose, and Emmi spun around, gasping. Puck casually strolled forward, nothing but a strange glimmer of golden light at his back.

"We're...here?" Emmi said, eyes wide.

"Yup."

Emmi had longed to go to Scotland—anywhere in the United Kingdom, truthfully—her whole life. She was raised on stories of England, fed a steady stream of fairy tales from the moors, and constantly reminded of her own heritage by way of the literal landmarks in her town directly highlighting her prestigious ancestor.

But to be here? Now?

Her heart pounded in her ears, and Emmi moved in a slow circle, taking it all in. The ocean lapped at either side of the slender, short peninsula they were on, a paved walkway curving up the side. She and Puck stood near a building with a large sign proclaiming it was a bird center—and the big statues of birds along the wall emphasized that, to say nothing of the tourists, many of whom had binoculars to look at a rock out in the sea. A nearby sign called the rock home to a flock of gannets, whatever type of bird that was.

It was summer, and both this little grassy area on the raised peninsula and the beaches below were crowded with tourists, none of whom seemed to have noticed Puck and Emmi magically appearing out of nowhere.

"Do you *see* anything?" Puck asked.

Emmi shook her head. Her gaze roved over to the small white building in the center of the lawn. On her phone, it had seemed like a garden shed, but in real life, Emmi could see the stone outlines in the grass that marked the ruins of a much larger building. Although most of the tourists were more interested in the bird center, Emmi grabbed Puck's hand and drug him over the lawn to the remains of the old church.

Everywhere there were signs of the witch trials. Iron cauldrons spotted the grassy lawn in front of the white building. Signs detailed the history of the trials. But despite Puck's impatient noises, Emmi couldn't *see* anything other than what was right before her eyes.

Nothing mystical.

She tried to focus, but she didn't know how. All she was doing was giving herself a massive headache as she squinted at the outlines of where the old building had been.

"Come on, Castor, you should be able to do this."

"Not. Helping," Emmi hissed.

She stared at the stones of the church's foundation.

She saw nothing but stones.

"Hey." Puck's voice was gentle, and, for once, serious. "You *can* do this."

"How?"

"No idea." Puck shrugged. "But I know without a doubt that you can."

Well, that was something. Emmi forced her shoulders to relax, unfocused her eyes. Breathe in. Breathe out. She shut her eyes.

And when she opened them, she saw much more than stones.

"There you go," Puck said, a hint of pride in his voice.

She could—distantly—see the white of the remaining building, the old church's porch, and the grassy lawn spotted with the foundation of the rest of the old church. But more present was the golden lines of the actual church as it had really been, rising up from the ground with a pointed roof, multiple rooms, windows and doors. Emmi turned, and the bird center was gone; the tourists, too. Facing the town with her back to the ocean, all the buildings blurred together, shimmering and melting so she couldn't really see any of them at all.

The only clear image was the church.

"Do you see the woman from the mirror?" Puck asked, his voice clear as a bell, the only sound in her ear.

Emmi shook her head. She took a step forward, and even though she didn't see anyone, she crashed into a person.

"Sorry, sorry!" she said, flailing blindly.

Puck gripped her arm, steering her through the crowd of tourists she couldn't see. He tried to draw her forward, but she stopped. "There's a wall!" she exclaimed.

"Not any more," Puck muttered, and Emmi realized that the wall she saw, the one so vividly in front of her, was nothing but air in reality.

"What is this?" she asked, holding her hands in front of her.

"When something big happens—an important celebration or alliance sometimes, but usually something traumatic—when something big enough to cross between the mundane and the mystical happens, there's an imprint left on the world. No one can see it but the seers. Like you."

Emmi gazed up at Puck. Although the tourist had been invisible to her, Puck was real. When she looked up at his face, though, he flinched. She recalled that he had been able to tell that she was seeing with the magic before she said anything; she wondered what he saw when he looked at her.

"What about the woman from the mirror?" Puck asked again.

Emmi turned her attention to the ghostly imprint of the church.

"It is rare for people to be caught in the veil tapestry," Puck said. "But it happens. And it sounded like you were seeing someone trapped in a traumatic time in the mirror."

Emmi nodded, agreeing, but she was still pretty sure the woman wasn't here, only the church.

Puck's hand clenched on her arm.

"What is it?" Emmi asked, feeling the urgency in his grip. She blinked again, and the golden light was gone; the church was nothing but ruins. She was seeing with her own eyes, firmly back in the real world.

They were surrounded by ponies.

"What the—" Emmi started.

It was clear she wasn't the only one confused and shocked. All the tourists were pointing, many of them taking pictures. About a dozen or so blackish-brown ponies stomped, tossing their heads as they spanned out in a circled around the remains of the church. Not just the one white building, but the entire old church, the full one. The one Emmi had seen. It was as if they could see what she had seen, the original walls still in tact as they positioned themselves around the echo of the church that had witnessed the rise of the witch trials.

"Your magic is linked to the land; animals are linked to the land," Puck said quickly under his breath. "They felt your magic, and they came."

"I summoned the ponies?" Emmi stared at them. They stood

eerily still, even though their nostrils flared from exertion and foam speckled their dark coats. They must have run from...somewhere. Just to stand in a circle.

The ponies's eyes were strangely hooded, dark but rimmed with light fur, puffy at the top. They kept in a tight formation, carefully circling the ruins.

Except for one. One of the ponies broke from the others. With the building long gone, it could have easily crossed the grassy field, but it didn't. It trotted around the perimeter of where the old church would be, turning at the long gone corners.

The dark dun pony stomped, drawing to a halt right in front of Puck and Emmi. It dipped its head as if in greeting. Puck's grip on her arm tightened.

"What is happening?" Emmi asked through clenched teeth as the pony stared at them.

"Sorry, folks, sorry!" a loud voice called. Emmi looked around for the source and saw a man in a dark green shirt and khaki slacks rushing up. He looked winded. "The ponies usually stay on the Law, but today they must have fancied some treats!"

The crowd laughed, and it was like a spell was broken. The ponies broke their formation around the church, tossing their manes nervously. Other people in similar green shirts started coaxing the ponies back toward the road, herding them away.

A flash of dark caught Emmi's eye. She sucked in a breath as, on the other side of the crowd, far too far away for her to get a clear image, she saw the unmistakable outline of a cloak. Not only was this unseasonable in the warm summer weather, but that cloak was exactly like the one the Hunter had worn when he'd attacked Emmi and Puck at her home.

"Puck," she said urgently.

"What?" He was still focused on the lone pony that hadn't moved, the one that had stopped right in front of them.

Emmi looked at the crowd again, but the black-cloaked Hunter was gone.

"Oy, Oberon!" the man in the green shirt shouted, jogging

over to Puck and Emmi. He had a rope lead that he slipped over the pony's head. "Sorry, folks, you must smell nice for my lad to be so focused on ya."

With the rope around his neck, the pony seemed to relax. "They're wild Exmoor ponies," the man explained. "They stay up on the Law of a day, but something spooked 'em bad enough for them all to rush down here." He pointed to a big grassy hill on the outside of town, the area known as the Law where the ponies lived.

"I'm sorry," Emmi said. "Did you say Oberon?"

"Aye, that's his name." The man scrubbed the pony's neck with his knuckles. "They're wild, but they're still my lads," he said fondly. "They've all names." He turned to Emmi. "America, eh?"

She nodded.

"Come to see the gannets?" He nodded to the bird center.

"No, actually. The church."

"Ah, old Andrew! Well, so, are you coming from or going to Edinburgh?"

Emmi was having a hard time following the man's accent, particularly after everything that had happened. "Sorry?"

"Just, anyone's interested in the church means they're interested in the witches. So it'll be Holyrood for you, yeah?"

"Yeah," Emmi said, even though she still wasn't sure what he meant.

"Ah, well, get on with ye," the man said, this time speaking to the pony. The pony named Oberon.

Once the man and the pony were several paces away, Emmi reached into her pocket for her phone. She tapped in Edinburgh and then Holyrood, the name of the old palace of Scottish kings. Of King James.

"Why would he think we were going there?" Puck asked, leaning over Emmi and staring at her phone screen.

Emmi cross-referenced Holyrood with "witch hunts."

"This is why," she said, tilting the screen toward him. The top article was all about a ghost of a witch executed in Edinburgh that haunted the halls of the old palace.

"Ah, so we're going there next?" Puck asked. "I'll need a bit of ash or something to burn..." His voice trailed off as Emmi tapped on her phone again.

"There's a bus that'll take us right there," she said. "You don't need magic for everything."

"Why would you travel by bus when you could travel by sigil?" Puck asked, gaping at her.

Emmi rolled her eyes. She *wanted* to see Scotland, not zip through it in weird ashen portals. And besides, she had some questions for him. Stepping through a portal was too quick—she needed to corner Puck on the bus and get some real answers for once.

NINE OF CUPS

FULFILLMENT, PROSPERITY, AND BEING SMUG

"A bus." Puck's voice was hollow with disbelief.

Emmi didn't look up from her phone. "Actually, full disclosure, the bus schedule confuses me. But the train station is close by, and it looks even better."

"Yay."

Emmi brought up directions on her phone and marched confidently away from the ruins of the old church and the flocks of birdwatchers gathered at the other end of the little peninsula. The little town of North Berwick spread out before them, with darling houses decorated with flower boxes. Some of the area was clearly designed with tourists in mind—a shop had postcards on a rack outside the door, and Emmi was tempted to stop and buy a tiny clay recreation of one of the brown ponies. Seeing the trinket, however, reminded her of the eerie way the ponies had stared at the ruins, as if they could see what she could see. And the way one pony had stared at her and Puck, as if it could see something she couldn't.

Emmi picked up her pace, mind churning. Puck had gotten her to the United Kingdom, and he was seemingly her only shot at figuring any of this out. But she didn't quite trust him, and that scared her. Scotland wasn't exactly alien territory—despite the accents, at least everyone all spoke the same language as she did—but it *was* a foreign country. One where she knew no one.

Not even the boy walking beside her.

Emmi's phone buzzed in her hand, and she glanced at the screen, grateful she had on step-by-step directions. She'd missed her turn. Pausing, she scanned the street signs.

"No one's around," Puck said. "Give me some paper to burn, and I'll make an ash sigil."

He was right that no one was around—the store fronts had quickly turned into what was clearly a residential area. North Berwick was possibly smaller even than Nick Bottom, and that was saying something.

"There." Emmi pointed at the rectangular street sign built into the wall of one of the houses at the corner. She laughed. "Abbey Road."

Puck looked at her curiously.

"The street is called 'Abbey Road,'" Emmi said. "You know. Like the Beatles?" It was old music, but it was impossible for Emmi not to be aware of a band and album as big as the Beatles's "Abbey Road," even if her grandfather didn't love the classics.

"Beetles?" Puck asked, shaking his head in confusion. "An abbey is a type of religious building."

"No, I mean—the music." Emmi narrowed her eyes, watching him carefully. Puck looked like a regular teenager with the grey sweater he'd lifted from the brochure, but he wasn't. She shouldn't let herself forget that.

"Aren't you hot?" Emmi asked. It was chillier in Scotland than in Massachusetts, but it was still summer.

"Should I be?" Puck asked.

Emmi shrugged, but couldn't hide the her expression.

"Well, then." In a blink, the gray sweater was gone, leaving only the black t-shirt over Puck's narrow shoulders.

Emmi swallowed hard. Magic was just so *disconcerting*. She strode past him, leading the way, setting a pace that kept her a little alone with her thoughts.

The train station was tiny—little more than a glass-fronted building sitting behind a car parking lot. Emmi shoved her phone in her pocket and entered the building, waving to the attendant but moving immediately to the kiosk to buy a ticket with her grandfather's credit card. Winding up in Scotland with a fae in tow counted for an emergency, she figured. She tapped out the purchase—a train would arrive soon, taking about an hour to get to Edinburgh, and Emmi hoped they had food available. She'd still not eaten her supper back home, but it was nearing lunch time here in Scotland. She was *starving*.

The tickets spat out of the tray at the bottom of the kiosk. Emmi grabbed them and turned in time to catch Puck's curious, confused gaze. Through the window, the train pulled into the station, sleek and gray. Puck flinched at it.

"Let's go," Emmi said.

Puck looked as if he was going to question her, but he bit his tongue and followed Emmi. A handful of people waited on the walkway outside the building, milling about. The train's doors opened, letting out a few families, children jumping out of the carriage and leaving their parents to wrestle with strollers and luggage.

Emmi boarded as soon as the doors were clear. Despite it being summer, there were plenty of empty seats and enough room for Emmi to feel confident their conversation would be at least semi-private. In moments, the train pulled away, picking up speed as it headed west. Every once in awhile, Emmi caught a glimpse of the blue sea beyond the houses and farms, but for the most part, the train seemed to display no more of the Scottish countryside than pastures and fields.

"Right," Emmi said, turning away from the window and toward Puck. "We need to talk."

"We need to eat."

There was no real arguing with that, especially considering the way Emmi's stomach growled at the thought. Puck started to get up, but Emmi grabbed his arm, pulling him down. "First," she insisted, "answers."

Puck raised his eyebrows, waiting for her to ask a question. A million things flew threw Emmi's mind, but she grabbed onto the most obvious one. "Is Puck even your real name?"

"Nope," Puck said easily.

"Then what's your real—"

"Oh, I'm never going to tell you that," Puck said, his tone light. "I'd kill you first. Come on, let's get lunch." He got up and looked around, as if expecting a food cart to pop up in the aisle beside him.

Emmi's head swam—Puck had spoken with such cheery friendliness that the threat seemed like a joke, even though she was fairly sure it wasn't. She scrambled out of the train's window seat and stood in the aisle, looking for the dining car sign. "This way," she said.

The selection was minimal; mostly sandwiches and chips, which the attendant called "crisps." Puck tried to order three of everything, but when Emmi refused to pay for that much, settled on cookies and seltzer water, a combination that made Emmi's stomach turn.

The whole time they ordered, waited for their food, and then walked back to their seats, Emmi was quiet. Puck kept up a steady chatter of observations, mostly in delight of the food, but now that she had a moment to think, Emmi found herself growing more and more reserved.

And she hadn't forgotten about the Hunter she'd seen in the crowd after she'd used her magic.

"Why won't you tell me your real name?" Emmi asked once they were back in their seats.

Puck crammed a cookie in his mouth. *Delaying tactic*, Emmi thought, narrowing her eyes. After swallowing, he gave her a side-eyed glance. "Look, I don't like wha— who I was before," Puck said. "I don't like that name. I don't like that...person. So I picked a different name."

"From Shakespeare." Emmi forgot about the other half of her sandwich. "Kind of coincidental that he keeps popping up, no? I mean first *MacBeth*, now both you and that pony share names from *A Midsummer Night's Dream*."

Puck shrugged. "Coincidence," he said, although Emmi didn't believe it for a minute. "Besides, I had it first."

"Had what?"

"The name."

Emmi blinked several times. "Are you telling me that you were named Puck before Shakespeare named his fae character 'Puck?'"

"Yeah." Puck eyed Emmi's sandwich, and she shifted it closer to her.

"How old are you?" Emmi gaped at him. Sure, he was clearly fae and had some sort of power that she didn't understand but—

"No idea," Puck said. "Time's...weird. I mean, I *was* ancient, but then I got young again. Then things sort of...stopped for awhile? And now here we are."

Emmi stared. This was the first time Puck actually seemed serious, but.... "It sounds like you...are you constantly being reborn or something? Like..." She struggled to figure out an analysis, but comparing Puck to Doctor Who didn't seem like a likely thing he'd understand if he also wasn't too up-to-date on self-pay kiosks.

"No, no, not reborn. I just...change. Become different." He grinned at her as if all of this made perfect sense. "Sometimes."

"You molt?" Emmi asked doubtfully. "Like a butterfly?"

"Yes, exactly," Puck said, smiling. "Also, not at all. Not like that all. Terrible analogy, really."

Emmi crammed her sandwich into her mouth and chewed on the dry bread.

"Butterfly." Puck chuckled to himself, shaking his head in amusement. "Although..."

Out the window, the fields were slowly giving way to larger and larger towns. They were approaching Edinburgh, and Emmi felt like they were also approaching a deadline of how much she could ask.

I should tell him I saw a Hunter. The thought came unbidden, and Emmi shoved it from her mind. He couldn't give her a straight answer about his *name*. Even if he did answer her, could she trust what he said?

Instead, Emmi took a different tactic. "So," she said, leaning back in her chair and brushing the crumbs from her lap. "Hunters."

That sobered Puck up. Interesting.

"Where do they come from?" Emmi asked.

"Historically?" Puck's brow furrowed in concentration. "There have always been people who hate what they don't have. But they got organized around the time of the Civil War."

Emmi immediately thought of Abraham Lincoln, the Emancipation Proclamation, and antebellum dresses. But a quick glance out the window and the rising cityscape of Edinburgh reminded her she wasn't home any more. Puck meant the English Civil War, fought after King James died and his son, Charles, took the throne. Emmi was grateful for her grandfather's historical background, for once happy about the way they talked more about long-dead kings than pop culture.

There had been a lot of factors contributing to the English Civil War, but religion and fear had definitely played a part in it. At the end of the war, Charles got his head chopped off, and England got a commonwealth government in place of a strict monarchy. That had all happened after Elspeth had immigrated to America, so Emmi wasn't as familiar with that part of history.

"Matthew Hopkins," Puck said.

Emmi dragged her mind back into the present. "Who?"

"The first Witchfinder General," Puck said. All the levity was gone from his voice; he had never looked more serious.

"What is that title?" Emmi asked gently. The train shifted, slowing down.

"The leader of the Hunters." Puck looked down at his lap.

"He decides who lives and who dies." He finally looked up at Emmi, just as the train pulled into the station, the roof blotting out the sun and casting them in shadow. "And the first one decided that *all* witches must die. The Hunters knew about your power as soon as the bottle broke. It doesn't matter to them whether or not you understand your power, or what you intend to do with it. They are not going to stop until they kill you."

Emmi felt her heart thudding in her chest. She doubted most of what Puck said at any given moment, but she didn't doubt this. He spoke with a strange sort of calm that reached deep inside her, confirming fears she had never known she had.

Unsure of what to say, Emmi turned to look out the window as the train slowed to a stop. The station at North Berwick had been nothing more than a shed barely capable of holding a dozen people and a plain platform under the sunny sky. The Edinburgh train station was a huge building, designed to hold hundreds, if not thousands, with multiple train lines coming and leaving.

Outside was a cacophony of people and luggage, schedules flashing by as trains opened and closed doors. Overwhelmed by everything, Emmi stared at the numerous people milling about, all of them with such clear direction that envy washed over her.

They all knew what to do, where to go. Only she was in the dark, paralyzed by fears she couldn't name.

But...

Her eyes fell on someone standing at the top of the stairs, looking down at the various trains pulling into the station. He stood perfectly still, letting the rushing travelers flow past him like water cascading around a rock in the river.

Emmi was still sitting on the train at the window, looking up. The man couldn't possibly see her.

She hoped.

Because he was a Hunter.

His robe hung on his shoulders like a cape, the hood tossed back to expose his long hair and his cold eyes. He almost seemed like any other man, if a bit oddly dressed, but it was Scotland. Oddly dressed men weren't that unusual.

No, it was the beard Emmi recognized. Steel grey, despite the man's relative youth. He was maybe in his late thirties, early forties; the hard lines of his face made him seem older.

"Greybeard," Emmi whispered.

He had followed them from her house all the way here, to Edinburgh.

He was waiting for her.

The Hermit, Transposed

BEING WITHDRAWN, TIMID, OR FEARFUL

"Puck." Emmi reached blindly for Puck's hand, gripping his fingers hard.

The fae leaned down, clearly sensing the fear and urgency pouring out of Emmi. When he peeked through the window, he cursed.

"Maybe he won't attack us," Emmi said in a low whisper. A conductor was clearing the carriage, so they got up, moving to the door. "It's a crowded station," Emmi told Puck. "Maybe he wouldn't risk being seen—"

"We can't be sure of that." Puck's voice was darkly serious, and he wore the most concentrated look that Emmi had ever seen on his face.

The train car's door opened up on the opposite side of where the stairs were, and Emmi was glad to at least have the train between them and the Hunter. She bounded down the steps. "What do we do?" she asked when Puck joined her on the platform.

They could—with enough confidence and luck—steal someone's unattended luggage and cobble together a disguise from the contents, but even that seemed like a stretch.

"You've got to try your magic," Puck said, his eyes serious.

"My magic?" Emmi's heart rate ratcheted up. "How can 'seeing the mystical' help now?!" She hooked her fingers in mock quote marks.

Puck shook his head. "Your magic is about sight, but that includes how other people see you."

"What?" Emmi's brow furrowed, and she tried to think through the possibilities of what he was saying. "I don't—"

"Call it a glamour, call it a shadow, call it whatever you want, but you *do* have the ability to change a person's perception of you. And, hopefully, me." Puck's eyes grew distant.

"How does it work?"

Puck shrugged. "I don't know. I'm not a witch."

Emmi growled in frustration. "Then how—?!"

"Try!" Puck grabbed her shoulders, his face inches from her. "Just—*try.*"

Emmi's eyes grew round—this was fear, real fear radiating off of Puck. She nodded. Seeing the old church had been a matter of forgetting her consciousness, slipping into a different realm. It was like those old visual puzzles that tricked her eyes into seeing something in 3-D out of a chaotic mess of colors.

But how could she turn that inward in a way that would change her outward appearance? She focused on her hands, holding them in front of her face. *I need to hide,* she thought. *I need Greybeard not to see me. I need to...*

Words left her mind as her hands started to fade. With a yelp, she leapt back, but Puck grabbed her arm. "Keep it up!" he said. "You almost had it!"

I need to hide, I need to be safe, I need to be unseen, Emmi chanted to herself, focusing on her hands again. On the way Puck had slipped his fingers through hers, holding her hand tightly, squeezing with reassuring pressure. Anyone who saw them would think they were romantically involved, the way he was staring at her and clutching her hand...

But no one would see them. Because they were invisible now.

"Are you there?" Emmi whispered.

Puck rubbed the pad of his thumb over her knuckles but didn't let go. "I'm here."

"And we're—"

"Invisible. You're not so bad at this, Castor."

Emmi took a shaking breath and stepped forward. If she looked straight ahead, it wasn't so bad, but if she glanced at her feet, her concentration wobbled and a hazy image of her body reappeared. She had to stay focused.

But not too focused. She slammed her shoulder into a pole before turning the corner around the station and heading to the stairs, and her image reappeared so fully and suddenly that a man who'd been hurrying in the opposite direction startled and dropped his full cup of tea, milky brown liquid splashing everywhere.

Puck gripped Emmi's hand even harder, yanking her around. "You have to concentrate!" he said, eyes darting to the wide central staircase. They were still hidden from view of Greybeard, but barely.

"I know, I know," Emmi said. It wasn't just that the magic required her single-minded focus; bumping into the pole had made the illusion jerk back into reality before she dropped her concentration.

The train station was crowded. If anyone bumped into her, it would blow her cover, force her magic to fade.

And Greybeard would see her.

"You've got this," Puck whispered. He hadn't let go of her hand, and his breath was warm. How could she be so *aware* of him when he was invisible?

She gripped his fingers. "Let's go."

Emmi took the lead—invisible, they navigated the outer edges of the crowd, going wide to avoid both Greybeard and the chance of bumping into someone else. Emmi wanted to grab the hand railing, but she worried that would break the illusion, too. They took the steps carefully, both of them deeply aware that slipping now would blow their cover.

Emmi stopped when she was halfway up the stairs. Greybeard turned his neck slowly, looking left and right.

He paused, his gaze resting exactly at where Emmi and Puck were. Her breath caught; she could feel Puck's heartbeat in her palm.

Greybeard looked straight through them, then turned the other way.

Once past the stairs, Emmi risked going faster, racing toward the big exit sign. The station opened up to the street, a blast of warm air ruffling her hair. She pulled Puck to a little alcove around the corner of the station and let the glamour fade.

"Holyrood is that way," Puck said, pointing past the station.

Emmi had looked it up on her phone, and so she knew they would only need to go about a half mile to reach it. On the train, that had seemed easy. Now, with Greybeard hunting them, Emmi wasn't so sure.

"Do you see?" Puck asked.

"See? Like with my power?"

Puck nodded, but he was distracted, looking not down the street but back toward the station entrance. "It's all connected."

"Connected?" Emmi's heart thudded as she followed his gaze. "Can Greybeard trace us?"

"Greybeard?"

"It's what I'm calling that Hunter," Emmi said.

"He likely doesn't have a way to track us," Puck said. He grabbed Emmi's hand and pulled her down the street. "But it won't take long for him to realize he missed us in the crowd, and he's likely going to follow us out here. Do you see anything?" His question was a little more urgent, his grip on her hand tightening.

Emmi trusted Puck to guide her down the narrow sidewalk as she squinted in the direction of the palace. She shook her head.

"It's probably safe," Puck muttered, picking up his pace. They were almost running now, and the crowd from the train station was thinning out as people went their separate ways.

"What do you mean about safe and connected?" Emmi asked. She shot a look behind her, but couldn't see anyone following us.

"Before Elspeth left for America, she set up a series of protections in key places around the UK," Puck said. "Witch bottles are designed for protection. The one in your house was like the central hub for the network."

Emmi's mind raced. If the witch bottle in her home acted as a sort of battery supply for all the other witch bottles her ancestor had scattered throughout the UK, then...

"Elspeth thought it would be safer if the main bottle was in an entirely different country," Puck continued. "She thought her protections would hold. And they did. For centuries."

"Until you broke the bottle."

"Not on purpose."

"So Holyrood Palace has one of Elspeth's bottles?"

Puck nodded. He pulled Emmi closer to the buildings as they walked. The streets were broad, but there were lots of little side alleys and corners to hide behind. For both them and any Hunter tracking them.

"Why would Elspeth make a protection spell for the king who started the witch persecutions?" Emmi asked.

"Wasn't for him."

Emmi looked behind her again. She could see a dark swath of cloth half a block behind them. It could be Greybeard, but it could be someone's fancy rain coat. It was impossible to tell between the long shadows of the buildings and the curve of the street. But—

Puck pulled Emmi into a little alcove. "Hide us," he hissed.

Emmi nodded, throat tight. She concentrated, clutching Puck's hand. She didn't feel anything, but when she looked down, her body was invisible again.

She looked up.

And saw Greybeard.

The black cloth she'd seen *had* been his cloak. Emmi barely breathed. If she reached out, she could touch the Hunter. Puck's grip on her hand was so hard it made her fingertips tingle, but Emmi kept her concentration on staying invisible.

Greybeard sniffed the air, like a hound on the scent. He lingered in front of the little alcove for several long moments, but he never looked at them, and if he did, he would have seen nothing. He strode forward, determined.

Puck and Emmi waited a beat before Puck jumped up. Emmi's spell broke, and they were both visible again. He held his hand out to her to help her wobbly legs stand straight.

"Should we make a detour?" Emmi asked. Even though Greybeard was at least a full block ahead of them, she spoke in whispers.

Puck shook his head. "He's definitely going to Holyrood. Our best bet is to get there as fast as possible."

They started off again, eyes peeled. But Emmi couldn't help but ask, "What were Elspeth's bottles for?" Emmi asked. "Why put one in Holyrood if not to protect the king that lived there?"

"There are places where the veil between mystical and mundane are thinner," Puck said. "Places where other creatures—"

"Fae creatures, you mean," Emmi interjected. *Like you,* she thought but did not say.

Puck nodded tightly. "They come through. It's dangerous for us all."

"Like when a deer crosses a street," she said. "If it's hit, everyone's hurt."

"Exactly."

Emmi looked up, and in that exact moment saw Greybeard cutting through the thin crowd, heading straight toward them. Emmi gasped, yanking Puck back and throwing up her protective magic in seconds. She and Puck pressed into the wall, invisible, as Greybeard strode by.

"Where are they?" the Hunter growled to himself, the words

barely audible. Emmi smiled smugly, but Puck squeezed her hand, as if to say, *Don't get cocky, kid.*

As soon as Greybeard was safely at the corner on the opposite direction of where they wanted to go, Emmi and Puck started racing toward Holyrood. The street was growing wider now, and a traffic circle—and the gates to the palace—were in sight.

"Why didn't you tell me about Elspeth's bottle at Holyrood sooner?" Emmi asked. They were so close now she could see the stone walls rising beyond the gate.

"She made dozens of witch bottles and hid them really well. There are some I don't even know about. Since Holyrood is located over a fae circle, yeah, it's one of the ones Elspeth protected. Your unnamed witch may be there. But...she may not."

"Yes, but—" Emmi started, but then an iron knife slammed into Puck's back.

Emmi screamed, whirling around as Puck staggered and fell to his knees. Greybeard stood there, his hand still poised from having released the dagger he'd thrown at them. A smirk smeared across his face.

Emmi tried to flicker her power back on—he couldn't hit what he couldn't see—but she was too distracted to concentrate on her magic. Puck stood up, ripping the knife out of his shoulder and dropping it as if it disgusted him. "Come on," he said, already loping toward the traffic circle, ignoring the cars that came to a screeching, honking halt in front of him.

Emmi could see it now—a faint bubble of light encircling the palace grounds. "Greybeard can't get through it?" she asked. There were screams and shouts behind her—no doubt the general public didn't take kindly to cloaked men throwing knives, even if it wasn't at them.

"He shouldn't be able to," Puck said. "The only way past it would be if you, as Elspeth's ancestor, allowed him in. But the main bottle broke. All the protections are weaker now."

Greybeard had caused a commotion. People were rushing, panicked—some away from him, some toward him. Meanwhile, they were nearly at the gates—and the guarded ticket booth. Emmi squeezed Puck's hand, forcing her magic to work. Mid-stride, they went invisible, and thanks to Greybeard's chaos, no one noticed as they dashed through the palace gates and past the bubble of protective magic.

Panting, Emmi turned, dropping her concentration and the magic. Safe behind her ancestor's barrier, Emmi could see Greybeard knocking aside people trying to restrain him. Shouting, he reached inside his cloak and withdrew a small leather satchel and something else, something narrow and rectangular that he held like a knife, despite there being no blade.

As Emmi and Puck watched, the Hunter jabbed the square thing toward the little bag. The contents exploded in a burst of shining powder that Greybeard waved over himself, showering his body with the dust. Emmi caught a glance of the rectangular object—it now had the tip of a blade exposed, similar to a prop knife with a retractable blade.

"What's everyone doing?" Emmi asked in horror as she watched the people nearby shrug and start to walk away. They no longer seemed to care about the Hunter who'd been throwing knives and knocking people aside in the streets. It wasn't that they couldn't see him—they clearly did by the way they side-stepped him—it was that they seemed to suddenly be completely disinterested in him.

"He has magic?" Emmi asked, looking up at Puck.

The fae boy glowered. His clothing was spotted with green blood, but not much, thankfully. "He and his kind steal magic," Puck snarled. "It's not as strong, and it only works for a little while and only that against mundane people with no mystical power. But it's enough sometimes."

Greybeard grinned ghoulishly as he strode past the guards and the ticket booth, straight to the gate. He stopped short of the almost invisible bubble that protected Holyrood. Without breaking eye contact with Emmi, Greybeard raised the retractable blade and pressed its tip into the almost invisible light that surrounded the palace grounds.

A ripple of lightning crackled over the surface of the protective bubble.

Greybeard couldn't cross the barrier, but he could break it.

Four of Wands

ACHIEVEMENT, ROMANCE, AND PLANNING
NEXT STEPS

Emmi watched with horror as lightning splintered over the surface of the magical protective barrier that encased the Holyrood Palace and its grounds. Greybeard unflinchingly pressed the tip of his weapon against the edge, but, despite way the bubble's surface crackled, it held.

"We have to hurry," Emmi told Puck, grabbing his hand. She started toward the palace doors, but Puck stayed rooted to the ground. "Come on!"

Puck shook his head. "We don't have much time."

"I *know*, let's go!"

"We need to start with the outside," Puck argued in a low voice. "Work our way in. We don't know *where* your ghost witch is, just that she's somewhere within Elspeth's protective barrier."

"But—" Emmi started.

Puck shook his head, hair flopping in his eyes. "When that barrier comes down, he's heading straight to us. We'll have to leave, regardless of whether or not we've found your witch. We have to be methodical here. If we start outside, we can cover a lot of ground, then head into the palace, where he'll have a harder time finding us. We don't have time to debate this."

Emmi swallowed, her eyes flicking once more to the Hunter trying to break through the barrier. "Okay."

Puck took off with determination, setting a pace so fast that Emmi could barely keep up. She looked left and right as they raced over the flat, grassy lawn of the palace with manicured trees and carefully designed paths. Above , seen only by the two of them and none of the other tourists milling around, the magical bubble of protection was streaked with glowing cracks fizzling up to the apex.

But despite her anxiety and broken focus, Emmi yanked Puck's arm as they rounded the corner of the palace. "There's a guard."

The rope barrier blocking back the path had a clear sign written in English: "No Guests Beyond This Point." Emmi would have simply ignored it, but the guard standing idly near the feeble blockade and the shadow of another around the bend made her pause.

With no other tourists around, Emmi used the guard's bored distraction to hastily pull a glamour over her. She kept her hand around Puck's wrist so the magic would extend to him, making them both invisible. Puck twisted his wrist, threading his fingers through hers, gripping her hand in a way that made her stomach flutter.

Emmi took the lead, pulling Puck off the path and past the rope. Soon, they were near the back of the palace.

Grassy mounds with stone peeking through the dirt dotted the lawn. There were architectural ruins here, just as there had been in North Berwick. Beyond the uneven landscape, the broken remains of what was clearly once a religious building rose in stark contrast to the sturdy palace walls. The desolate abbey—according to a sign affixed on the wall nearby—indicated that the building was centuries old.

But why was it roped off? Nothing looked hazardous, and the signs scattered around the abbey showed that it was usually open to the public. Even though most of the roof was gone, the floor below was made of stone, solid and even. Broken pillars were affixed to the ground, not in danger of toppling over. There was no reason for this area to be blocked off, except—

"Feel that?" Puck asked.

There were no more guards around, so Emmi let the glamour drop. "Feel what?"

Puck's eyes grew distant, his head cocked to the side as he attempted to listen to something Emmi couldn't hear. She strained, trying to use those untapped powers she wasn't sure of, hoping to sense whatever he did.

A cold chill washed over her—not a breeze on this warm, sunny summer day, but a bone deep feeling of ice crawling up her spine.

"What is it?" Emmi asked.

"A Cat Sìth." Puck pronounced the word like "cat-shee," but Emmi distantly recalled hearing about them from her grandfather's books.

Now that it was named and Emmi had felt at least a shiver of its presence, she honed in on the eerie feeling. The shadows flickered not with light, but darkness, a roughly cat-shaped black hole that seemed to be the antithesis to light.

The broken abbey was mostly open to the sunny sky, but the palace against which it was built and a long alcove made one wall dark. Flitting between the shadows of the lichen-covered arched walls, the big cat stalked, barely visible, a trick of the eye made real.

"Cat Sìth usually linger in the Highlands," Puck said. His eyes were trained on the shadowy corners of the ruins of the abbey; he clearly saw more than she did.

"They're supposed to suck out the souls of the dead," Emmi said, unconsciously touching her neck.

Puck laughed, but there was no amusement in his tone. "No. That's just what mortals say. Cat Sìth just happen to be closer to the veil between life and death. Like you're closer to the veil between the mystic and the mundane."

Emmi's eyes adjusted to the dark, and she thought for a moment that she truly could see the Cat Sìth. It was as large as a cougar, silently threading through the shadows. It flicked its tail as Puck spoke, impatient, perhaps, or angry at being disturbed.

There were graves here, Emmi realized. The big table near the center of the abbey was a tomb. Some of the stones in the ruins of the abbey weren't just weather-worn rocks—they were grave markers.

"A Cat Sìth shouldn't be this far south," Puck said softly. "It must have gotten trapped here when Elspeth put the bubble of protection up, and then it wasn't able to escape."

"That was hundreds of years ago," Emmi said.

Puck shrugged as if that information was unimportant. Disturbed, Emmi recalled the way Puck had spoken of himself— old enough to have inspired Shakespeare to name a character after him, young enough to blend in like the teenage boy he appeared to be.

Her eyes drifted back to the Cat Sìth. Rather than fur, black swirls curled over its body, whispy and dark, like smoke fading into a shadow.

Hundreds of years ago...

"Puck," Emmi said, grabbing his hand to pull his attention from the Cat Sìth to her. "Is this fae creature linked to the ghost witch?"

Puck shook his head. "Definitely not," he said.

"But you said that Cat Sìth are close to the veil between life and death. If this one knows the ghost witch, maybe it can lead us..." Her voice trailed off at the way Puck shrugged.

"You can try," he said.

Carefully, Emmi stepped forward. The Cat Sìth stopped its pacing, eyes like black fire turning to watch her. She stopped dead in her tracks. "Er," she said.

"Good start," Puck said. "Eloquence is sure to win the fae over to your side."

Emmi shot him a glare. "Can you tell us about a witch who

haunts this palace?" Emmi asked, returning her attention to the Cat Sìth.

It blinked at her. Black whisps of smoky darkness curled around its eyes, streaming over its lithe body.

"Please?" Emmi asked.

The Cat Sìth stalked away, tail twitching.

"I don't think you're going to get anything from it," Puck said. He had that too-casual tone to his voice that made it sound as if he took nothing seriously, and even if Emmi could tell from the tight way he held his shoulders that he was on edge, his easy voice infuriated her.

"You pushed to explore the grounds rather than go inside the palace," she said, jamming her finger into his chest so forcefully that he took a step back. "You took us straight here. You knew the Cat Sìth was here, didn't you?"

Puck's eyes slide away, toward the shadows where the fae creature had disappeared. "I knew something was here."

"Did you think it was the ghost witch we're looking for?"

"No." There was no guile or guilt in his voice.

Growling in frustration, Emmi stormed outside.

Puck chased after her. "It's not all about you and your witches, you know," he said. He grabbed her wrist, trying to hold her back, but Emmi yanked away. "Elspeth's protective magic affected fae creatures. The Hunters hunt fae, too. I could sense that there was one of my kind here, trapped. Of course I wanted to know if it needed help."

One of my kind. The words clawed at Emmi's ears, distracting her from everything else.

When Emmi had to throw a glamour over them both, she had to hold his hand. She had gotten used to the feeling of his palm against hers, his fingers intwined with hers.

But he was closer to the Cat Sìth than to her. That was his *kind*—dark, feral, mystical.

Not a human like her, not even one who could see through the veil into the magical realms.

Puck looked like a teenaged human boy. He looked like he could go to her school. He looked like he could ask her out.

But he wasn't human.

And he wasn't on her side.

He was on *his* side. The fae side.

And she could not allow herself to forget that again.

As if he could hear her thoughts, Puck said, "I need you to see that your powers aren't just for humans, Emmi." His tone was pleading, but she wouldn't meet his eyes.

Above them, the sky split apart. The bubble of protection that had kept Holyrood Palace—and the abbey ruins—safe for centuries was breaking from the top down. The top of the barrier splintered, evaporating into nothing, and the edge burned down slowly, a bright-yet-dark light eating at the open area in a way that reminded Emmi of the Cat Sìth eyes.

The protection faded slowly, but still, Emmi could tell—they had only ten or fifteen minutes more before the Hunter could break through it.

Two of Pentacles
MAKING CHOICES, STRUGGLING TO FIND
BALANCE AND STAMINA

E mmi rushed inside the courtyard of Holyrood Palace, her eyes darting around, taking everything in. The building was built with giant towers in the front, a main entrance, and a fully protected and enclosed courtyard. A tour group clustered by a stone wall.

"We're going to start with the gallery—keep your eyes out for the portrait of James the Sixth!" the guide said, waving around the little red flag that was the signal for the group to follow her. "And don't worry! We will be ending in Mary's Tower, the oldest part of the building open to the public and site of the infamous murder! It's been kept almost exactly as it looked in that time period, one of the few rooms in the palace to have been preserved to its original appearance."

"Murder?" Puck asked Emmi as the guide led her group away.

Emmi was already turning in the opposite direction, heading toward the exit. Above them, the protective magical bubble burned. *Less than ten minutes,* she thought.

Puck raced to keep up with her. "Do you think this is where your witch was killed? That she haunts this tower?"

Emmi ignored him, trying to process her thoughts. Besides, she was still angry about the stunt he'd pulled to get her to go to the Abbey first, which had wasted precious time. But she knew there could be only one Mary that the tour guide had referred to —Mary Queen of Scots, the mother of James.

Which meant the murder the guide had talked about had nothing to do with Emmi's unknown witch.

Mary Queen of Scots had been something of a fascination for Emmi, a royal story that had all the best bits—intrigue, murder, and even explosions. Mary had a lover who her husband became jealous of. That was who was murdered in her tower, and Emmi could almost recall some legends about the lover's ghost haunting the tower. To be fair, Mary did get her revenge by murdering her husband later—supposedly. Emmi always thought that Mary must have been upset when the building Mary's husband ought to have been in exploded and he hadn't been there, but fortunately he tripped in a nearby orchard and somehow strangled himself. To death. With no witnesses. Despite the aforementioned exploding building drawing a big crowd.

It was such a mystery of the ages.

Emmi pushed past a little sign that said "Exit," indicating that the tower was at the end of the tour. Just in case anyone else was leaving when they were trying to enter, Emmi grabbed Puck's hand, quickly casting her glamour over the both of them.

"You think the ghost is here?" Puck asked.

Emmi ignored him and charged up the steep spiral stone staircase. It was narrow and tight, and her arm twisted around uncomfortably so she could keep hold of Puck. If they ran into a big group, it would be impossible to go around them without being caught.

A sign by the first door they came to labelled it as "Lord Darnley's bedroom." Emmi went past it—that was the murdered husband, not Mary's room. They had to go up another level.

"Emmi!" Puck yanked his hand free, breaking Emmi's concentration.

She spun around, glaring at him. "We don't have time for this!"

"Let me help!" Puck said, exasperated. "Don't just run around medieval towers. I do have some insight; I can help you."

Emmi's eyes narrowed. "Maybe you can," she snapped. "If it suited you."

Puck raked his fingers through his hair. "Will you just tell me where we're going?"

"Mary's bedroom."

"Mary? I thought we were looking for James. Or a witch. Is Mary the witch?"

Emmi rolled her eyes. "No, but—"

"Has it occurred to you that if that Hunter comes up the stairs, we're trapped? This is a narrow, tight spot. We're putting ourselves into a corner."

Emmi swallowed hard. That hadn't occurred to her. But it was too late to change her mind now. They were running out of time. She turned and started up the steep steps again. But with each step, she explained herself.

"Mary is James's mother." Stomp. "And this is the oldest part of the castle, the guide said." Stomp. "This is the best bet of being a place where James would go. He was king after his mother died. He definitely used this tower. And it's been kept in preservation from *that* time period." Emmi paused. Now that she said it out loud, it didn't sound like a good enough reason. Maybe she should have followed the tour group and started at the portrait of James—that at least was directly linked to the old king.

But they were here now. Emmi saw the sign by the door. *Mary, Queen of the Scots. Bedchamber.*

She stepped inside.

True to the tour guide's word, the bedroom looked as if it belonged in the late Middle Ages or early Renaissance. The room was beautifully appointed with a high wooden ceiling decorated with wood railings forming diamond shapes, each one painted with a crest or elaborate pattern. The bed had heavy, embroidered brocade on the canopy, a gold and blue floral lined in red. It stood across from a big open window with a table in front of it.

And to the side, near the door, was a chest. The cabinet was almost as tall as she was, and about the same width as her arms spread wide. It was made of shining black wood, with spiral-carved legs, but the front was decorated in gleaming red hearts surrounded by gold and ivory trim. Two enormous hearts stood at the center of each of the big doors to the cabinet, with smaller hearts on each corner.

"What are you staring at?" Puck asked.

Emmi ignored him. Something was drawing her to the cabinet, something that felt like a physical tug leading her forward.

"I'll, uh," Puck said. "I'll guard the door, I suppose."

Emmi didn't even look at him. No doubt it was a violation of every historical law—and perhaps the literal law of Great Britain —to touch this cabinet, but she couldn't help herself. She knocked aside the little rope that was supposed to prevent tourists from getting too close, went straight to the cabinet, and yanked the doors open.

The inside of the cabinet was just as elaborately decorated as the outside, with two more small doors and a plethora of tiny drawers, all inlaid with the same red material. But that wasn't what caught Emmi's eye.

No—it was the book made of glowing light that enraptured her.

It was propped up on the inside of the cabinet. Emmi reached for it, intending to pick up the book, but her hands went right through it. It truly was made of light, no substance at all.

"What do you see?" Puck called from the door.

Emmi finally spared a glance at him. "Can't you see this?" she asked, gesturing to the glowing book.

Puck shrugged. Nothing there—not that he could see.

Emmi's heartbeat spiked up. This was her magic—to *see*. And she did see. A book—surely that meant something. Desperately, she turned around, but there was nothing else unusual in the room, glowing or not. Nothing else called to her.

The paper! Emmi dug her hand into her pocket, pulling out

the torn and burnt piece of paper that she had discovered in the remains of the broken witch bottle. It had come from a book.

Daemonologie, Emmi thought.

The letters *DAEMONOLOGIE* glowed in gold across the ghostly book in the cabinet.

Her hand shaking, Emmi pressed the paper from the bottle into the glowing book. It burst out in blinding beams of brilliant, shimmering light, and Emmi flinched away. When she was able to look at it again, the book was—

Real.

Breathless, Emmi picked it up. Her fingers didn't go through the book. It was solid.

"Oh," Puck said. "Now I see it. Also, you should know that the bubble broke."

It took Emmi a minute to realize what Puck meant. Her eyes darted to the window across from the bed. Sure enough, there was no longer a protective spell around the palace.

Greybeard was able to come inside.

He has to find us first, Emmi thought, hoping against hope that he'd gone the wrong direction in the vast palace grounds.

She had the book in her hands, but there was still no ghost witch, much less a name to call her by. Emmi ran to the table, slamming the book down. Much like her torn piece of paper, this book seemed to be written by hand.

James wrote this, she thought. She looked around the room. *He wrote it here.* That's why the book was here, why she was called to this spot.

But where was the witch that begged for her to name her?

"I hear footsteps," Puck said urgently. He'd closed the heavy wooden door that led to Mary's bedroom, but that would not be enough to keep the Hunter away.

Emmi opened the book, rifling through the pages. Her heart-beat thundered in her ears, the same heavy thudding of boots on the stone spiral steps. Greybeard was heading right to them—but the steps were long, and maybe he'd be distracted by Lord Darnley's bedroom first—

Emmi sucked in her breath.

At the end of the book, in the section called "Newes From Scotland," King James wrote about the trials he'd personally witnessed. Each witch was listed by name. Emmi skimmed over them, reading through the Scottish-influenced writing that was both old, riddled with non-standard spellings, and scribbled in nearly indecipherable handwriting.

"Help," Emmi muttered, her eyes blurring. The thundering in her ears was definitely not just her heartbeat—Greybeard would be at the door any second. Emmi looked up to see Puck bracing himself against the heavy wooden door, pressing it closed with his weight.

Emmi looked back to the book, her only clue.

"'The elder witch,'" she muttered aloud, her eyes bouncing over the words. "'...stood stiffly in denial of all that was laid to her charge.'" A poor, old widow woman, one who helped birth the babies in the village, known for being a healer. She had little money and little support, and when she'd been accused, she'd tried her best to prove her innocence.

Emmi's heart clenched as she read the torture put to the poor woman's body. Imprisoned, beaten, pricked with needles, "examined." Emmi shuddered. The poor grandmother denied being a witch through it all.

But then they stripped her bare and shaved her head, all to find a so-called devil's mark. *Probably an innocent birthmark or freckle,* Emmi thought. *It didn't matter what it was—they just needed an excuse to say that the woman was claimed by the devil and therefore a witch.*

She sucked in a breath. Stripped and shaved.

The ghost she'd seen in the scrying mirror—she had been wearing nothing but her undergarments, and she'd been roughly shorn of all her hair.

Emmi's eyes flew over the passage, looking for a name—

BOOM.

The blow to the door was enough to make Emmi scream in surprise. She glanced at Puck, his face pale, his mouth narrowed in a grim line.

Greybeard had arrived.

"Hurry!" Puck said.

Emmi nodded, her eyes back on the page. She read the name out loud, her voice strong and clear:

"Agnes Sampson."

Greybeard pushed against the door, and Puck struggled to drop the heavy wooden latch to secure it into place. It wouldn't hold for long—if nothing else, all the noise they were making was sure to draw guards.

But they didn't need more time.

The ghost of Agnes Sampson appeared before them.

She looked just as she had in the mirror, except instead of screaming in furious desperation, silent silver tears tracked down her face. *She wasn't old enough to be a grandmother*, Emmi thought, but then again she had likely been a mother by the time she was Emmi's age. Women who were thirty were often enough grandmothers in the seventeenth century.

"You are Agnes Sampson," Emmi said, and the woman nodded, tears still flowing.

It wasn't fair. Emmi knew this on a bone-deep level. Some rich, powerful men got scared—of the *weather* of all things—and blamed witches on it. But Agnes Sampson was just a woman who'd birthed a lot of babies—her own and others'. She knew herbs. She would have been revered as a Cunning Woman, save for a frightened king with a grudge.

"You are not a witch," Emmi said, looking right into the ghost's silver eyes.

Because that, Emmi knew from the bottom of her heart, was true. Agnes Sampson had been poor. A widow with no husband to protect her. An easy target. A woman in a world where women were not valued.

But not a witch.

Glimmering light flared around the ghost of Agnes, each pulse bursting bright, then fading, fading, fading, until she was gone.

Puck raced to the table. Emmi wasn't sure how much he'd seen, but he saw the book in front of her. "We have to go," he said, snapping his fingers. Licks of yellow-red flames burst over his palms, and Puck slammed them onto the open pages of the book.

"Hey!" Emmi shouted, grabbing the page with Agnes's name on it. She shook cinders off the edge.

Puck yanked the burning book up and waved it in the pattern of a sigil. There must have been enough powdery ash from the quickly-incinerating pages for the magic to work—Emmi's hearth back at the museum glimmered.

"We have to go," Puck said just as the door banged open.

But Greybeard was too late.

Emmi and Puck were gone, nothing but smoke and ash as evidence they had ever been there at all.

THE CHARIOT

IMMINENT SUCCESS, A FOCUS ON THE PATH
AHEAD, AND PURSUING AN OLD AMBITION
WITH NEW INTENSITY

E mmi stepped from the portal in Queen Mary's
bedchamber back into her home. Her foot caught on one
of the hearthstones as she stumbled through, and she fell,
her left palm and right elbow smashing into the sooty ash, her
knees painfully crashing onto the stones.

Puck stepped over her, brushing an invisible speck from his
shoulder.

"Thanks for the help," Emmi muttered as she pulled herself
up, glaring at him.

Although she ached thanks to both her new bruises and the
strenuous flight from and race against the Hunter she called Greybeard, Emmi still held the paper she'd ripped from the book
before Puck had burned it. She'd snatched it up almost without
thinking. Her only intent had been to preserve Agnes Sampson's
name. The poor woman had gone through such torture and had
been all but forgotten in history. Her ghost had wanted nothing
more than to be named.

A thought occurred to Emmi. "Was Agnes a ghost? She
looked like a ghost. There were rumors of the tower being
haunted. But..." That label didn't seem to fit.

Puck blinked at her blearily. They were both exhausted, Emmi realized. Puck may have blithely ignored her when she fell in the hearth, but Emmi suspected that he was far more injured than he was willing to show, plagued by pains from the repeated attacks from Greybeard, which always seemed to draw his blood, green though it was. "I'm not sure, to be honest," he said. "The mystic doesn't like labels."

Emmi's mind tried to figure out what that meant, but she was so tired, she was finding it hard to concentrate. "What do you mean—labels?"

Puck hauled himself up, his eyes resting on the scrying mirror where Emmi had first seen the specter of Agnes. "Just because you see something doesn't mean it has a name, Emmi Castor," he said finally. "It's you humans who use words all the time. Some of the fae love that, but..."

Emmi had heard stories about the way the fae targeted artists and poets and storytellers. She had always assumed that was because the dreamers were the ones who made up the legends about the fae, but now she wondered if it was through a different connection.

A little mewing noise at her feet made Emmi pause. Sabrina wove herself around Emmi's ankles. Emmi bent to pet her cat, but Sabrina's soft steps reminded her of the Cat Sìth they had seen in the Abbey, fur like smoke and eyes like ember.

The fae, Emmi supposed, were a bit like cats. Independent and unconcerned. Emmi seriously doubted her cat would speak even if she could. She didn't need words. Things just were. Sabrina had no idea what catnip was called; she just liked it.

Maybe Agnes had been a ghost, and saying her name had freed her. Maybe Agnes had been an afterimage, like the church in North Berwick, the lingering remains of a traumatic experience. Did it matter what she was called?

She was free now.

That would have to be enough.

Emmi looked down at the paper in her hands, her thumb

moving over the rough scratches made by the pen as it scrawled Agnes's name. The history-loving part of Emmi knew this should be analyzed. If it was, somehow, actually King James's handwriting, it wasn't just financially valuable but also an artifact to be studied. But the growing magical side of her knew what this piece of paper really was:

An ingredient.

"The first item for our new witch bottle to protect everyone," Emmi said. It wasn't lost on her that it was torn and burnt on the edges just like the original. She hadn't meant to purposefully pluck out a near-exact replica of her ancestor's page, but she had.

Emmi shifted her gaze to Puck, who was watching her quietly in the mirror, his reflected eyes scrutinizing her in a serious way.

"What do I do with this?" she asked, feeling suddenly helpless.

When Puck turned, that intense gaze was gone. His real eyes held that same indifferent-yet-mischievous spark Emmi had come to expect. "What do you think we should do with it?"

Emmi's heart skipped a beat. *We.* He said it casually, as if it were assumed, but she still wasn't sure how much she could trust him.

Even so, it wasn't as if the Castor house had a safe, and if Puck truly wanted to do harm to the paper, he could. Emmi only needed a place to store it in the house where Sabrina couldn't get to it. A drawer or—

Her eyes rested on the cauldron across from the hearth, hung up on iron rails. That certainly seemed fitting. "'Double, double, toil and trouble,'" Emmi muttered as she passed Puck on her way to the other side of the room. "'Fire burn and cauldron bubble.'"

Emmi dropped the paper into the dark, shadowy depths of the black iron cauldron. For a moment, she thought she saw the golden glowing light that she had seen when she had found the book in the cabinet. When she looked again, it was just a piece of paper, resting on the black iron.

With the paper safely stowed away, Emmi turned back to Puck, catching him mid-yawn. "We need sleep," she said.

"This body is so annoying," Puck muttered.

Emmi paused. Puck said that as if he wasn't used to a human form, and Emmi was absolutely unprepared to think about what that meant.

"We can do nothing without sleep," Emmi said. "You can stay in my grandfather's room. In the morning, we need to discuss what to do next."

They had one item, but they needed more. The Hunters were hot on their trail, and while Emmi felt mostly safe in the Castor house, she didn't like the way the Hunters always seemed to show up when she wasn't ready for them. Greybeard had been waiting for them at the train station. The Hunters were always a step ahead.

After Emmi got Puck to her grandfather's room, she went inside her own room, shutting—and locking—the door.

Her phone was very nearly dead, so Emmi plugged it in to charge and scrolled through her apps—email, social media, text messages—to see if Grandfather had responded to her.

She took a deep breath. After her parents had died and Emmi lived fully with Grandfather, the two of them had worked out a code for emergencies. It started when Emmi had been old enough to go out on her own. If Grandfather texted Emmi the word "baclava," then she was to call or come home immediately. Emmi didn't always pay attention to the time, but as soon Grandfather sent the secret word, she knew it was time to go or face dire consequences. "I made fresh baclava for when you come home," meant *Come home* NOW, *young lady, or else.*

The same went with her. She had once gone to a party with her friends, and without her knowledge, a boy she had thought she might like had spiked her drink. As soon as she realized the loose feeling in her body was due to alcohol and not having fun—about the same time the boy she'd thought she'd liked had started trying to talk her into going out in the woods with him alone—Emmi had texted Grandfather the word, and he'd come so fast to pick her up that she knew he had to have broken the speed limit and ran every stop sign.

"Baclava" was as powerful as a magical spell in the Castor family. It meant "emergency," and it meant that no matter what, the recipient responded.

Emmi typed the letters carefully in her phone, first as a text message, then as a direct message in Grandfather's social media, then to his email.

But just as she had suspected, there was no response.

———

When Emmi woke the next morning, her eyes still itchy and red from crying, Puck was not in the attic apartment at all. There was evidence he'd been there—a messed-up bed with pillows and the comforter strewn about as if he was a little kid, a ripped-up box of cereal that Emmi suspected he'd eaten from without the aid of a bowl, and the swinging door leading downstairs wide open.

She found him in the hearth room, curled up on the floor around Sabrina, chatting away. Emmi looked down at him, temporarily forgetting her troubled thoughts about Grandfather. He seemed to be having a conversation with the cat, pausing as if listening for answers. But then Emmi realized that she didn't understand any of his words.

"What are you saying?" she asked. She couldn't even place what the language was, other than not-English and not-Spanish, which she took in high school. Puck's language was at times soft and lyrical, but there were trills and guttural noises that didn't seem to make a word at all, just a sound.

"Told you so," Puck said to Sabrina, and he stood up.

"What did you tell my cat?" Emmi asked.

Puck blinked at her as if affronted. "It was a *private* conversation."

"Well, excuse the heck out of me."

Puck straightened his clothes—now without the stains of

battle. Puck looked fresh as a daisy, and despite having showered and changed, Emmi felt as if she were slumming it beside him.

"We have to figure out the next item needed for your witch bottle," Puck said.

He had lined up the things she'd collected from the fireplace along the stony edge of the hearth. A stained pottery shard, a pale gray stone, a coin, a clod of dirt. One of them would take her on their next adventure.

But Emmi didn't move. She felt weighed down by sorrow and worry. "Will this save my grandfather?" she asked in a small voice. She wasn't sure she could trust Puck in any capacity. Whatever he said could be a lie. He obviously had an agenda of his own.

But he bent down, forcing Emmi to meet his eyes. "I promise it will," he stated, and even if it was a lie, Emmi wanted to believe it.

She picked up the earthen clod, carefully holding it in the palm of her hand so it wouldn't crumble. Somehow, she hoped, this palm-sized clump of dirt would bring her only remaining family back to her.

Nine of Swords, Transposed

Acceptance, Facing Fears, and Looking Forward After Leaving Grief Behind

E mmi looked down at the lump of earth in her hands. She could almost feel her hopes draining from her like water through a sieve. "It's just dirt," she said.

Puck crossed over to her, folding her fingers over the clod. "To everyone else, it's just dirt," he said. "But you're a Castor witch. You can see it for what it really is."

"It really is dirt."

Puck rolled his eyes. "Don't give up on me yet, witch." He said that last bit—*witch*—like it was a compliment, a royal title. Like it meant she shouldn't deign to relinquish even an ounce of hope.

Something about his belief in her reminded Emmi to believe in herself. She took a deep breath and let it out slowly. She willed her eyes to unfocus, to see beyond what was there, to know that the hard-packed clay was more than just soil.

To find the truth behind it. The power.

For a moment—the space between blinks, really—Emmi actually did see something. A faint glimmering, warm and glowing. Not like the way the cauldron had seemed to shine, but something dimmer. It reminded her of fireflies, the magic twinkling on warm summer afternoons, the there-and-gone-again dance of chasing them with Grandfather laughing behind her.

Grandfather. The memory jarred her, and with it, whatever magic that may have clung to the clod evaporated.

"I see nothing," she said heavily. Part of her wanted to throw the dirt on the ground, but she didn't dare risk it.

Sabrina wove between Emmi's legs, mewling for attention. When Emmi ignored the cat, Sabrina jumped up on the little table beside the cauldron.

"Shoo!" Emmi said, lunging for her. Sabrina had fallen inside the cauldron once, and not only could the cat not get out on her own—which meant she screamed until someone came to help, and then she clawed her way up her rescuer's arms—but Emmi also didn't want to risk her cat destroying the magical piece of torn paper that already rested in the bottom of the iron vessel.

Sniffing indignantly, Sabrina twitched her tail at Emmi and then leapt off the table, a flash of ginger fur reflecting in the old scrying mirror.

Emmi's eyes lingered on the mirror. It had shown her Agnes's ghost form. Maybe she needed to hold the dirt up to its reflective surface. Maybe that would be enough of a clue.

Emmi could feel Puck watching her as she stepped around him, holding the dirt to the mirror. She caught a glimpse of his worried face behind her, but she refocused on the clod of earth. It rested in her palm, and she was deeply aware of how she could just squeeze and break it apart.

Focus, she reminded herself.

She looked not at it, not at her own reflection, but at the lump of clay reflected in the spotted mirror's surface. She willed her mind to see a ghostly reflection of an ancient witch, but...

Nothing.

Except—

"What is it?" Puck asked sharply, noting the way Emmi's face changed.

She shook her head. "I thought I heard..." But mirrors were for seeing, not hearing.

"What was it?" Puck insisted. "We can use any clue you have."

"A name," Emmi confessed. "I was absolutely certain that I heard a female voice say a name. Joan."

"Joan?" Puck asked.

"Joan," Emmi confirmed.

"That is...not helpful," Puck said. "Are you aware that there are a *lot* of Joans in the world?"

"Even more when you consider that we're talking about history, too."

"This might prove a little difficult, Castor. Anything else?"

Emmi shook her head. One word, one name—she'd heard it clear as a bell, but nothing else.

Puck heaved a sigh. "Okay, that didn't really work as well as I'd hoped."

"I guess we got lucky with the paper and the mirror." Emmi tried not to let her self doubt leak into her voice, but it was hard not to feel as if she'd failed. She carefully wrapped the dirt clod in a dusting cloth and tucked it in her pocket, hoping it wouldn't crumble.

"So, you got a map around here?" Puck asked.

"A map?"

"We need a map," Puck said, speaking slowly as if unsure of why Emmi couldn't keep up with the situation.

"Yeah, um—this way." She led Puck out of the hearth room, down the hall, and into the botanical room. Elspeth Castor had been called a witch in part because of her knowledge of botany. Her herbs were potent medicines, many of them the basis for modern medications today. Hanging on the wall beside the shelf that displayed her many bottles of dried herbs, the labels written in her gothic script, was a map of England. Across from it was another map of America. Both were hand drawn and labelled with a mix of town names and notes about what plants flourished in each area.

Puck grabbed the English map off the wall, slamming the frame on the table as if it weren't a centuries-old work of practical art.

"Hey!" Emmi protested.

Puck ignored her. "Now we need..." He looked around the room, his eyes falling on a crystal hanging from a cord by the window. It wasn't a relic, but a modern bit of cut glass. Emmi had placed it there so it would catch the rainbows from the sunlight.

Puck yanked the cord off the hook and thrust it into Emmi's hands. "There," he said, satisfied.

Emmi looked from the crystal to the map and then back to the infuriating boy.

"Go on," Puck said, actually shooing her with his hands the same way she'd shooed Sabrina.

"And do what?" Emmi said, her voice rising. "What am I supposed to do with glass and a map?"

"Pendulum dousing." Puck stated it as if it were the most obvious solution in the world.

Emmi had, of course, heard of the practice. One couldn't work at the Museum of Magic without being aware of various types of mysticism. She cast Puck a doubtful look. Pendulum dousing meant that she would hold the cord with the crystal hanging down, swinging over the map. The crystal would—supposedly—point to the location she was seeking.

Emmi had always assumed pendulum dousing was a trick, much like pushing the planchette on a Ouija board and pretending that a ghost moved it. But with no real other option, she took a breath, held the cord between her fingers, and moved the crystal over the map.

The glass swung wildly; she hadn't been gentle with her motions. But even though the pointed end of the crystal skittered in a wide circle that encompassed most of England, Puck stared down at the map intently, fingers on his chin, eyes laser-focused. Emmi couldn't look at him; it made her feel both silly for doing the dousing and also nervous that she'd fail at this, too.

She closed her eyes. Emmi was deeply aware of the string between her fingers, of the fear gripping her heart, of the sense of ridiculousness she felt at just standing there, hoping a piece of glass would hit the map correctly.

But then Puck sucked his breath in through his teeth. "Hey, Castor," he said softly.

She opened her eyes.

The crystal circled slowly over the southwestern tip of England. Emmi pulled her hand away, dragging the string east, but the crystal pulled toward Cornwall as if it were magnetic, straining against the force she exerted to move it. Even though she'd seen the ghostly elements of the past, even though the North Berwick ponies had come to her as if summoned, even though she'd witnessed her ancestor's protective bubble around Holyrood, the pendulum was the first time she *felt* the magic like this, from her own fingers.

"Cornwall," Puck said, nodding as if none of this was wildly weird. "Maybe Tintagel?"

Emmi glanced at him, and her concentration was broken— the pendulum swept back over the map as if an invisible thread tying it to Cornwall had been severed. It was so odd, the way Puck seemed to know some things but not others. Then again, perhaps Tintagel was famous enough for Puck to know of it, the location of the legendary castle where King Arthur supposedly built Camelot.

She shook her head, though. "I've read Elspeth's journals. She wrote about how Tintagel was 'devoid and contaminated.'" The words stuck in her memory; her ancestor had described Tintagel with such dismissive terms that Grandfather had written a journal article on it for his history department at the university. Whatever magic that may have been at the old ruins before was, according to Elspeth, long gone.

Puck cast her a look that made Emmi question all she knew, all Elspeth had known. But rather than protest, he turned to the map. "Where then?" Puck drew a circle around Cornwall with his finger.

Emmi, meanwhile, took out her phone. While Puck squinted at the obscure script writing on the map, Emmi tapped out "witches in southwestern England."

"Oh," she said.

Puck looked up. "Yeah?"

"The last trial of an English witch during that time happened in a place called Bideford." Emmi peered down at the map. "There."

Puck frowned. "That's in Devon, not Cornwall."

"It's close, though," Emmi said. "Really close. Almost on the border."

Puck still didn't look convinced. Emmi brought up a Wikipedia article on Bideford and sucked in a breath. "Also, there's a Joan."

"There are a *lot* of Joans."

"But there was a Joan associated with the trial in Bideford!"

"Was she the witch they hung?"

Emmi scanned the page. "No. She was one of the accusers..." That seemed less promising.

"I don't know." Puck's voice was doubtful.

Emmi glanced back at the map. All the cluttered names handwritten on the parchment seemed to blur together, but she saw one more she recognized—Boscastle. That had been one of the towns Grandfather had planned to go to; it also held a museum of magic, one dedicated to witchcraft throughout the United Kingdom and beyond.

Which meant that Grandfather may have been in the area. It couldn't be a coincidence that a witch trial was held so close to a place where Grandfather had planned to go. He may still be there...she could try Bideford, and if it led to no results, she'd find a way to Boscastle and the other museum. Emmi was determined to either find the ghosts of some witches or find her grandfather.

"We need to go," Emmi said, certainty ringing in her voice.

"This is the right place, Bideford. We just got back from the first witch trial—this is the last one. It's symmetry!"

"Magic doesn't care about symmetry," Puck said, still doubtful.

Emmi shook her head. This was far too logical to be the wrong direction. "What do we have to lose?" she asked.

"Our heads, if we fall right into a den of Hunters."

"You say that like they're animals."

Puck cocked his eyebrow. Okay, fine. Point taken.

Emmi turned her phone around, showing Puck images of Bideford. "They have plaques up where the executions took place. And there's...dirt." Emmi's voice trailed off. Obviously there was dirt in Bideford; there was dirt in all of England.

But they didn't really have any other clues.

Puck shrugged. "Okay, let's go."

He picked up the framed map and twisted his hand.

"Wait!" Emmi screeched. "You are *not* setting the map on fire!"

Puck rolled his eyes. "Fine," he huffed, the sparks fading from his fingertips.

Everything happened quickly after that—Emmi drug Puck back to the hearth, where a pile of ash awaited his sigil. Puck drew the magic symbol into the ash, opening a portal. They stepped through, the early morning light of Nick Bottom, Massachusetts, replaced with the warm afternoon sun of Bideford in the county Devon.

Emmi looked around. When they'd gone to North Berwick, they'd known exactly where to visit. But as she and Puck stepped out onto the street, it became immediately clear that there would be no ruins of an old church or a towering medieval castle to beckon them. Bideford was larger than Emmi had expected. Modern store fronts and cafes lined the street, people shopping and eating late lunches.

She glanced at Puck. He looked around in a bemused sort of way, but he clearly didn't think much of the town.

Emmi's eyes scanned the area desperately. There had to be some sort of clue. Being the location of the last witch trials in England was a big deal, surely.

"There!" she pointed to a sign built into the side of a yellow building.

"A market?" Puck asked.

Emmi headed in that direction. "Markets were the center of any medieval town," she said, her voice ringing with authority, even though Puck was an ancient fae being, not a fourth-grader on a field trip to the Museum of Magic. "They were places where people worked and shopped and also a gathering spot, including for legal proceedings and public punishments."

But if Emmi expected to find a medieval gallows standing in front of the market, she was sorely mistaken. While the outside of the building was pale grey stone and red brick, the inside was sleek and charmingly pretty. Any other time, Emmi would have been wide-eyed with joy, walking over the bricked path inside the building with sunlight streaming through the high windows. But overall, the market was more beachy-Victorian than witchy-medieval. Woodworking shops and stained glass demonstrations in some of the booths lining the center walkway were traditional, but not exactly any indication of what Emmi was looking for.

She rushed past the stalls. Puck lingered long enough by a sweets booth to slip some candy into his pocket before slinking away. Emmi raced back, shoved some dollars at the teenage boy minding the till, shouted an apology when he protested her American money, and chased after Puck.

"You can't just take what you want," she hissed at him, her heart racing.

Puck shrugged. "I don't think the police around here have ash sigil portals with which to chase me."

"Can you be serious?" Emmi said. Her hands bunched into fists, and she refrained herself from stomping her foot.

"I am serious. This place is a bust. There's nothing here, Castor."

A different sort of emotion rose in Emmi's throat. He was wrong. There *was* something here. There had to be. A clue to her Grandfather's whereabouts, a hint, something—

"The plaque!" Emmi said. She had only seen an image of the metal square set into stone, with words commemorating the Devon witches that had died in the last major trial. They were at the end of the market now, but there was stall nearby displaying Celtic jewelry. Emmi leaned over the pendants.

"Excuse me," she said to the shopkeeper. "Is there a museum or a tourism place or something where I can learn more about the history of this town?"

"Oh, sure," the woman said. "You want Burton."

Emmi blinked, unsure if this was a place or a person.

"Big white building on the edge of Victoria Park," the shopkeeper elaborated. "Go down the river; you can't miss it. Less than half a mile."

"Thanks!" Emmi said, already dragging Puck in that direction. Cars parked along the edges of the road, but there was a wide walkway along the river. Emmi walked so quickly that even Puck, with his long legs, had to jog a bit to catch up.

"What's the rush?" Puck asked.

Emmi shook her head and picked up her pace even more. "You wouldn't understand," she muttered.

But she couldn't shake the feeling: This was all wrong. Nothing about this town seemed to even remotely remember that there had been deadly witch trials here. Cheery fish and chip stalls competed with ice cream carts. Emmi had lived at the Museum of Magic long enough to know that appearances were deceptive— her home was centuries old, and the Exxon station at the corner didn't detract from that. But...

It was all wrong.

The *feel* of it. She had stepped into North Berwick and had been able to blink and see the history she needed. But here? Nothing.

"There," Emmi said, spotting the wide swaths of green that

meant the park was nearby. Puck tried to speak, but Emmi ignored him, crossing the street. She almost missed the white building that housed the art gallery and museum of Bideford, a triangular-shaped front with red signs obscured by bright green trees.

"Emmi," Puck said, and even though she noticed that, for once, he actually used her first name, Emmi ignored him as she strode into the building.

An older woman with salt-and-pepper hair glanced up. Emmi went right to her, though Puck lingered at the door. Before the museum docent could even speak, Emmi said, "I need to know everything about the witches that were tried here."

The woman blinked. "We have some art exhibits housed in the gallery," she said, "including traditional folklore relics."

Emmi had traditional relics back home. What she needed was a clue.

"What about the trials?" she asked. She pulled her phone out, bringing up a picture of the plaque she'd found that listed the names of the witches who'd been tried and executed in the last major hunts.

The old woman squinted at the screen as Emmi held it out for her. Emmi's eyes flicked to Puck. He stared at her with an inscrutable look. The jovial smirk was gone from his face; his dark eyes were honed in on her in an intense way that put her on edge.

"Oh, that," the woman said, straightening. "That'll be in Exeter."

"Exeter," Emmi said flatly.

"About an hour's drive east," the old woman said. "The Bideford witches were taken there for their execution."

They were in the wrong place. No wonder it hadn't felt right. Agnes Sampson had started in North Berwick and then been taken to Holyrood for her execution, but while the Bideford witches had started in this town, there was no trace of them left here. Not even a plaque with their names.

"Would you like to come inside for the art exhibits?" the

docent said, gesturing. "We also have some books on the Exeter trials, I believe."

"No. Thanks." Numbly, Emmi stepped back outside.

Puck peeled off from the door and followed her. Emmi circled around the Burton art museum, onto the vast green lawn of the big park. All around her, flowers bloomed, birds chirped, and the sun cast cheery rays on them.

Emmi plopped down in the grass.

"Hey." Puck sat down beside her, his voice soft.

"My grandfather is missing." Emmi stated it hollowly. "Maybe the Hunters have him, or maybe something else, something mystic. But he's gone. And he's all I have left."

She stared down at her open hands in her lap.

And then Puck reached over, weaving his fingers through hers. It wasn't the first time he'd held her hand—she had used her powers to cast a glamour over him as well—but it was the first time he'd been so gentle. His thumb brushed over her knuckles until she looked up into his eyes.

"You're not alone," he said, not breaking her gaze. "You have me."

But can I trust you? Emmi wanted to say. She bit her doubts down. She wasn't sure she could trust him—not ever—but he was here.

And right now, that felt like enough.

"You can't go chasing every witch killed in England," Puck continued. "There were a lot. Most of them lost to history."

That just made Emmi sadder. All Agnes Sampson had wanted was someone to remember her name. Someone to remember that she was more than just a witch, tortured and hung and cast aside into an unmarked grave. That she had been a real person.

The impossibility of it all washed over Emmi. So much had happened in the past that was *wrong*, but also so much was happening *now* that was wrong. And she was helpless to do anything about any of it.

Puck pulled his hand from her loose grip. Emmi sat with her

legs straight in front of her, her back hunched over, but Puck shifted so that he straddled her, a knee on either side of hers. He bent down so his face was forced in front of hers; there was nowhere she could look to avoid his gaze.

"You can't save everyone," he said gently.

"I just want to save my grandfather," Emmi whispered. But it was more than that. The witches, innocent and forgotten. Even the Cat Sìth, trapped where it didn't belong.

The only thing Emmi knew for certain was that she wasn't capable of helping them all.

"That's why you went tearing off through the sigil to come here," Puck said, still uncomfortably close. "You thought he was here?"

"Or nearby." Emmi could feel the tears in the backs of her eyes, threatening to spill out. She shifted and felt the dirt clod wrapped in cloth, tucked into her pocket. Dirt. She had chased her grandfather halfway across the world with nothing more than a hunch based off a lump of *dirt*.

Puck ducked his head again, drawing her focus. "I'm going to kiss you, Castor," he said in the most calm, even voice Emmi had ever heard him use.

"What?"

"I am going to kiss you, Emmi."

She blinked. And then he leaned up, his face centimeters from hers, his warm breath on her lips. But he didn't kiss her. Not yet. Instead, he said, "You can say no. You can pull away."

She did neither.

And so his lips pressed into hers. His eyes were closed, but hers were open, burning from unshed tears that were forgotten in the shock of his action. He was crouched over her, but he raised one hand, running his fingers from her back, up her neck, and into her hair, clutching her as the kiss deepened. She slid back, giving in to the moment, closing her eyes. Puck's hand supported her body as she lay down in the park's grass without once breaking the kiss. He was fully on top of her now, knees on either side of her hip, his chest against hers, his hands framing her face as her hair splayed out on the grass.

When he leaned up, she let out sigh. Her eyelids fluttered open.

Puck smirked down at her, that gleam of mischief sparkling in his gaze. "Noted," he said.

"What?" Emmi's mind still swirled.

"One good kiss drives every bad thought from your head."

That snapped her fully into consciousness. Emmi shoved Puck off her. "Who said it was good?"

"Your lips."

Emmi ripped some of the grass up and threw it at him, but he laughed, and that made her laugh, and for that one moment, Emmi allowed herself to hope.

Ten of Pentacles, Transposed

Quarrels, Family Troubles, Loss of Community, Materialism

"So, what next?" Emmi asked, leaning back and looking up at the bright blue sky. *Afternoons in Devon aren't so bad,* she thought. *Maybe, when this is all over...*

She nipped that thought in the bud. When this was all over, there was no chance of Puck casually opening up ash sigil portals for lunch in the English countryside. No, when this was all over, either she would have her grandfather back as well as some semblance of her normal life or...or she wouldn't. And either way, it wasn't like Puck was going to stick around and be there for her.

"We could kiss again," Puck offered. "The option is there."

"No, it's not," Emmi said firmly.

Puck raised his eyebrow, but Emmi ignored him. She needed to focus. They had scant clues—the name "Joan" and a big chunk of Cornwall—but she knew that playing whatever dangerous game Puck wanted to play was just as wrong as trying to find her grandfather in this town.

"The reason I wanted to come here was for Boscastle," she confessed. "Grandfather intended to go there."

"If you wanted to go to Boscastle, why didn't we go to Boscastle?" Puck asked.

"Yeah, I'm starting to wonder that as well."

"Right, so..." Puck made a motion with his hand.

"It's probably not the right place," Emmi said.

"If you had a pull to one specific area, it's at least worth exploring," Puck offered. "Better than running around in places you know are wrong. Your instincts are stronger than you believe."

"Fine." Emmi nodded her head, mind made up. "Let's go there."

Puck gathered together the bits of grass Emmi had thrown at him, some dead leaves, and other detritus. Emmi knelt in the grass, blocking Puck from the view of any stray passersby as he igniting the plant matter, incinerating it into ash. "Boscastle," Puck muttered as the sparks cooled from red to black. "What else is there?"

Emmi had her phone out. She'd known about the Museum of Witchcraft and Magic there, but hadn't done much research into it. She showed Puck a picture, then turned to look at the article about the museum. "Oh," she breathed as Puck piled the ash into a little mound. "There was a witch named Joan. Her skeleton was on display at the museum." Her eyes widened slightly at the thought. She was used to relics on display, but a real human skeleton?

"You know," Puck said, "I have a theory about that name, Joan—"

Emmi was willing to kiss Puck but definitely not trust him. She shook her head. "Focus, fae." She tried to use the same playful tone as Puck used when he called her "witch," but it came out harsher than she intended. Puck's eyes flicked to hers, inscrutable, but Emmi didn't retract what she'd said.

Puck has his own agenda, she reminded herself. He's concerned about the fae creatures caught in the middle of the witches of the past and the Hunters of the present. But if Emmi had to choose, she would choose her grandfather every time.

Puck drew the sigil in the ash, and the portal opened up. They were in a park; anyone could see them. But just as the Hunter had used magic to make people's eyes slide past him at Holyrood, no one seemed to notice or care about the portal hanging in the air in the middle of the park.

"Coming?" Puck asked. He was still grumpy, but he held his hand out to help Emmi stand. Together, they stepped through the portal.

———

Boscastle wasn't that far away from Bideford, but it seemed a little chillier—certainly more windy. Emmi pulled her loose hair into a ponytail as she and Puck stood outside a big white building. The letters "MWM" were plastered on one wall—the Museum of Witchcraft and Magic. On the other wall, a big painted sign showed an older woman selling a knotted rope to men in front of a harbor. Emmi squinted up at the illustration.

"An old belief," Puck explained, noting her attention. "A witch would tie up the wind into knots and sell it to sailors before they left on their journeys. If the sailor didn't have good winds at sea, he could untie the knot and a wind would fill the sails."

"Did that ever work?" Emmi asked.

Puck shrugged. "Not like a sailor could demand his money back when he was in the middle of the ocean."

His eyes slid past her, and alarm bells rang in Emmi's mind. There was more to this than he was saying. Before she could quiz him further, Puck strode toward the entrance of the museum.

Emmi raced to keep up. A little bell at the door tinkled—this one was silver, not iron—but it was enough to remind Emmi of her own Museum of Magic. She took a deep breath. There was something different about air wrapped around relics, a musty smell like old books and older smoke.

It was home.

"Hi," an aggrieved voice said from near the entrance. Emmi turned to see a teenager, probably a year or two older than her. He looked incredibly bored. Emmi could understand; manning the front desk at her museum wasn't always the most entertaining thing to do, but it was also her home, so perhaps her level of pride in it wasn't possible to emulate in a kid with a summer job.

Emmi paid for her own and Puck's admission into the museum. "Have you seen anyone like this?" she asked the boy, holding her phone out to show him a picture of her grandfather.

He shrugged, barely glancing at the image.

"His name is Landon Castor," she pressed. "He owns a museum like this one, in Massachusetts. America."

"I know where Massachusetts is," the boy grumbled.

"He was going to come here," Emmi continued. "Have you seen him? Is there anyone else who works here that may know him?" She felt odd, basically asking for a manager, but this was important.

The boy turned to a computer near the desk by the door. "I'm the only one scheduled for today," he said. "There are some volunteers I guess. But..." He tapped at the keyboard. "Looks like the owner emailed with a man named Landon Castor, but that was weeks ago."

"Is the owner around?" Emmi asked.

The boy shrugged, his default mode of communication, but he grabbed a pamphlet and scribbled an email address on the back. "You can try to message them."

"Thanks," Emmi muttered. She used her phone to send an e-mail to the museum's owner without really looking at the displays around her as she followed Puck deeper into the museum. By the time she hit "send" and looked up, she realized she'd lost track of Puck, chasing shadows rather than him.

The museum back home, made from Elspeth's old house, was packed full of seventeenth century items, most of which could be directly traced back to Elspeth Castor. There were some bad reviews on the internet from people disappointed in the narrow focus of the museum, actually, but looking around this Museum of Witchcraft and Magic left Emmi's head spinning. Rather than focus on one witch, this museum had bits of pieces of witchcraft throughout history, throughout England, and even displays from other parts of the world. While Emmi's home was a microcosm of one witch's life, this museum was a broad view of witchcraft as a whole throughout all time.

Various displays fought for her attention; the labyrinthine dark rooms were filled from floor to ceiling with artifacts, display cases, art work, photographs, and charts documenting various magical practices.

She focused on a black lump under a glass case. The card beside it called it a "Black Lemon: Cursing Charm." Emmi peered closer, a tingle going up her spine.

Apparently, if someone took a fresh lemon, pierced it with pins, wove a string around the pins, and then hid the lemon in someone's house, the person would be cursed, their life fading as the fruit rotted. Whoever had been cursed by this particular lemon must have died horribly, if the curse had worked—the lemon was nothing more than a black lump, more similar to coal than citrus.

"Interesting, no?" an older woman said, stepping closer. She wore a badge on her button-up shirt that said, "Volunteer."

Emmi's heart surged. Was this someone who may have seen her grandfather? Before she could ask, the woman said, "Curses like this are surprisingly common. I know some people who still use it, or knots."

Emmi already had her mouth open to ask about grandfather, but the word "knots" reminded her of Puck looking at the sign outside. "What about knots?"

The old woman reached into her pocket and pulled out a black ribbon. "You tie knots in it to use against an enemy," she said, tucking the ribbon in Emmi's palm. "You can bind up their ill will, or tether them to a curse. It's like the lemon curse, but a little more portable." The old woman's eyes flicked to Emmi's jeans.

Hesitatingly, Emmi moved to put the ribbon in her pocket. The woman nodded in approval.

Puck rounded the corner. He raised his eyebrows, a question in his look, but Emmi shrugged. The ribbon in her pocket felt like a secret.

"Were you looking for anything specific, dear?" the old woman asked her.

"My grandfather." Emmi held her phone out, showing her a picture. The woman shook her head, not recognizing him.

"Or Joan," Puck said. He casually draped his arm over Emmi's shoulders in a move that felt almost possessive. Emmi shrugged, knocking him away.

"Joan?" The old woman laughed. "Well, she's not here any more, but..." She gestured toward a little set of stairs tucked into a corner. Even from here, Emmi could see a large sign and the words *Joan Wytte* etched on it in Celtic font. "Our fighting fairy, our white witch," the old woman said with a smile.

"White witch?" Emmi asked.

"Because of her name. Wytte. White." The old woman's face turned grave. "I was here when they decided to take her down."

Emmi remembered reading the article on the museum, how Joan Wytte's skeleton had been on display for the public.

"The children made a bit of a mockery of it," the old woman continued. "I mean, children will do that with anything, but it was disrespectful, wasn't it? She was a witch, yes, but she was human."

Beside her, Puck stiffened. "All life deserves respect. All death does, too."

Emmi looked at him in surprise. Puck was so rarely serious, but his countenance now was grave.

"Aye, I suppose Joan would agree with that," the volunteer said. "Well, she's at peace now, bless her."

"Where?" Emmi asked. "Can we visit the grave?" It could not

be a coincidence that she heard the name Joan when holding the dirt clod; she felt pulled now to explore that path more.

"What you're going to want to do is go to Minster Church, just that way." The woman pointed despite the fact that the walls blocked a clear perception of where to go. "Joan's buried outside the churchyard, of course, but you'll find her tombstone just off the path behind the gate."

Something about the wording snagged in Emmi's mind. "And that's where she's buried? Just past the church gate?"

The old woman laughed. "Oh, you're a clever one!"

"She is," Puck said in a low voice no one heard but Emmi.

"Joan's not actually buried right at the tombstone. Too tempting for vandals. But if you find the tombstone, Joan's nearby."

"Can you tell me where?" Emmi asked. This felt *right* in the same way that going to Bideford had felt *wrong*.

But the volunteer shook her head. "I'm not sure," she said. "I only know the grave is near the stone. Unmarked. Joan deserved some peace."

The woman left them at that, and Emmi reflected on her words as she followed Puck to the display of Joan Wytte's information. Joan had been respected as a healer and well known for helping people with her skills, but an abscess tooth had caused her to go a bit mad with pain—impatient, more like, and unable to bite her tongue or play nice. She was jailed for witchcraft after that, died in prison, and her bones were put on display after being passed around. She'd only been in her late thirties.

The display had a recreation of the tombstone Emmi hoped to find at the church. The bottom had the words "No Longer Abused" etched into them.

"It may not even be real," Puck muttered in a low voice.

"What do you mean?"

Puck shrugged. "During that time, bones of a witch would have been...a novelty. This is the stuff of local legends. The prison she went to—Bodmin Jail—it's huge. Lots of nameless people, vagrants, beggars and the like, stuffed inside. A jailer wants to make some money, all he had to do was sell a body. Happened all the time."

"Who would want a body?" Emmi gasped.

"Doctors, mostly. They were still learning how to do surgeries. Better to practice of the dead than the living. Grave robbing could make a man rich."

"That's *horrible*," Emmi said.

Puck shrugged. "That's human. Anyway, not the first time some poor woman had her body used for science and display even after she died. Add a local spin, put her in a museum, then you've got a prize attraction."

Emmi felt sick at the idea. The information on the wall in front of her claimed Joan Wytte was well-known as a witch, but Puck was right. Could that sort of thing be verified? She'd died in 1813 and wasn't buried for nearly two centuries. The Museum of Witchcraft and Magic hadn't opened until the 1950s. What had happened in the time between Joan's death and the museum opening? How could anyone even verify that it *was* Joan in that grave, after being hung on the wall?

Another thought hit her then—if the woman in the grave wasn't Joan, then her clue was not a clue at all. No matter how right it felt to be in Boscastle and on this trail, it could be another misdirection, more time lost with her grandfather still missing.

Turning from the display, Emmi was prepared to leave. Grandfather wasn't here, that much was certain, and perhaps Joan wasn't either. They needed to find out and move on, even though Emmi had no idea where the next step of their journey may take them.

Puck let out a little snort as they passed another display case. "Look at that," he said, pulling her closer.

A long pin was on display, along with a little card detailing how that pin was used to pierce a supposed witch's skin. If the wound did not bleed, it was considered proof of her being evil.

More lies, more ways to abuse women. It was an easy parlor

trick to not fully pierce the skin or to fake jabbing a person and "prove" they did not bleed when they should.

But Puck didn't move, even as Emmi tugged at his arm. "It's brass," he said in a low voice. "That's not right."

Emmi's impatience turned to confusion. "What do you mean?"

"The Hunters use iron," Puck said. "It *has* to be iron."

Emmi recalled the black metal device Greybeard had used to destroy Elspeth Castor's protective bubble around Holyrood. Iron. Like the bell on Emmi's front door, the one Elspeth herself had placed.

There was more here than Puck was saying. Emmi stuck her hand in her pocket, feeling the black ribbon. He wasn't the only one with secrets.

Five of Pentacles

HARDSHIP, ABANDONMENT, AND DELAY

A blast of wind from the sea hit Emmi and Puck as they stepped out of Boscastle's Museum of Witchcraft and Magic. Emmi's thoughts were a tangled mess—how could no one there have known her grandfather? Was Joan Wytte the witch they were supposed to find for this element of the witch bottle? And that black ribbon—

That silenced Emmi's mind. Because the black ribbon...it had the same resonance as the page from *Daemonologie* that she recovered for her witch bottle. It felt like it had more potential for magic than even the dirt clod she still carried in her pocket. She had no idea who the volunteer at the museum truly was, but getting that ribbon didn't feel like a coincidence or a random encounter. It felt fated.

It felt powerful.

"What are you thinking about?" Puck asked, and Emmi realized that her face showed how lost in thought she was.

Fortunately, she didn't have to come up with a quick lie to distract him. Emmi sucked in her breath, pointing. "Do you see that?"

Puck turned around, looking over the street up to the puffy white clouds dotting the sky above them. "See what?"

"That's why there are no Hunters here," Emmi said. "There's a bubble of protection around this area, just like there had been over Holyrood Palace."

"Hey, Castor," Puck said, sounding impressed. "Look at you with your seer powers growing. You didn't even have to work to see that."

Emmi tried not to let Puck's compliment go to her head as she squinted, following the golden light that encircled Boscastle with her eyes. "I can't tell where the protection ends," she said. "This is big."

"Interesting." Puck drew out the word, thinking. Then he shrugged as if none of it matter. "Well, I guess not really."

Emmi whipped her head around to Puck, off-put by his change in attitude. "Not interesting?"

Puck shrugged. "You think this museum is important because it reminds you of the museum you live in. But it wasn't here when Elspeth was alive. So she must have been protecting something else."

Emmi thought back to the bones of Joan Wytte, which had been on display at the museum. But Joan had been born in 1775, well after Elspeth had sailed to America, lived a long life, and died.

"We're on the wrong path, aren't we?" Emmi asked. The dirt clod in her pocket felt as if it weighed a million pounds, mocking her for chasing yet another false lead.

"Oh, I don't know about that." Puck said in his trademark chipper voice. "May as well track down the witch's grave, see where that takes us." He headed down the street toward the direction the volunteer had told them Minster Church was located.

"But Joan was buried centuries after Elspeth died," Emmi protested, jogging to keep up. "It's impossible..."

"Impossible?" Puck laughed, as if the words were meaningless.

They crossed a short bridge that traversed the river spilling into the ocean, the crisp air seeming to push at their backs, propelling them forward. Maybe it wasn't impossible that Elspeth

Castor had foreseen her several-greats granddaughter being put in a position to find the grave of a witch who died almost a century after she did.

Stranger things had happened in the past three days alone.

Puck strode with confidence along the narrow street beside the river, but when it intersected with a larger road, he paused.

"I have no idea where I'm going," he told Emmi pleasantly.

Rolling her eyes, Emmi brought up directions to the church on her phone. It was only a little under a mile and a half away—still within the protective bubble Elspeth had cast. They trekked up the hill toward New Road, which did not in the least look new. Emmi's legs burned as the incline steepened. The narrow street was designed for two lanes of traffic, but houses were built right next to one side, and the sheer face of the hill, often lined with stones, was built on the other. There was no dividing line in the center, and Emmi was only grateful that the road was, at least, mostly straight so she could see the cars coming in time to move out of the way. She even saw a caution sign on the side of one of the houses, warning buses not to hit the roof, which hung over part of the main road.

"This is ridiculous," Emmi muttered, ashamed that the walk was making her breathless. Puck trotted merrily up the road, easily lopping along in a way that made Emmi want to push him off the steep side. Emmi's phone buzzed, leading her from New Road to Old Road, which had the advantage of being downhill for a bit before veering up again, and, despite its name, held houses that looked a little newer and a small cafe with sandwiches. It was heading toward dinnertime here in England, but lunch for Emmi. Puck had not complained of hunger, but he ate everything Emmi gave him.

By the time they reached Minster Church, Emmi was sweaty, breathless, and tired. The only thing working in her favor was the way the trees spilled out around them, casting gentle shadows through the afternoon sun.

They were alone now, and it had been some time since they'd

even passed a car on this road which was, somehow, even narrower than any of the other ones they'd passed before. They could see the church through the trees, as well as stone tombstones rising amidst the vines and greenery. Birds chirped overhead, and the wind rattled through the leaves.

I'm glad, Emmi thought. After the life—and death—Joan Wytte had, it felt right that she had a peaceful final resting place.

They came to a spot where the trees thinned, casting a long view of the countryside beyond. Emmi strained her eyes to see. Elspeth's bubble of protection seemed to flicker—less a perfect bubble, and more...

"It's like she's only protecting the forest," Emmi muttered.

Puck looked at her harshly, his eyes intent. "What?" he demanded, more serious now than he had been all day.

"Her protection—it's a big bubble all over this area, but see those fields out in the distance? The towns? They seem...paler. But all the forested areas are cast in a strong golden light." Emmi turned her attention from the protection spell to Puck. "Why?"

"Just...odd. That's all." Puck spoke quickly without looking at her. *He's still not telling me everything,* Emmi thought bitterly, her hand slipping into her pocket to finger the black ribbon.

To the left, a green wooden picket gate was labelled with a white sign, careful black letters spelling out *Minster Church*.

"We're here," Emmi said. She didn't add the word "finally," but she might as well have. She led the way down the steps toward the gate, pushing it open. A paved footpath meandered through the churchyard.

It didn't take them long to find Joan Wytte's grave marker, a replica of the one on display in the museum in town. But while the stone was there, Emmi knew that the grave was somewhere else, unmarked and hidden. Still, it was nice to see a little collection of red flowers tied together with twine, a rolled scroll, and a few other trinkets under Joan's name. She was respected now in a way she hadn't been in death. Or even life.

To think—a well respected woman of her time ends up in jail

for brawling because she was in pain from a toothache—a *toothache!*—and even her corpse ends up abused. All it took for centuries of disrespect after a lifetime of good deeds was poor dentistry.

No, that wasn't entirely true. She remembered what Puck had told her about the grave robbers of the time, how it was possible the bones belonged to more than one woman, or an entirely different woman.

Focus, Emmi reminded herself. She could mourn the woman after she found her true grave. Emmi tried to tap into her powers, but beyond the bubble of protection arcing overhead, she couldn't see anything magic.

Instead, she saw Puck.

He had been cheery enough on the hike up the hilly landscape, but ever since entering the churchyard—no, before that, when she'd mentioned the forests being protected—he'd grown more and more silent. Emmi had assumed it was being in a cemetery, but Puck wasn't the type to respect tombstones or the dead.

Instead, he was looking at the trees.

It was growing late enough for the shadows to be deep and long, the air chilly despite the warm day. A few fireflies even illuminated the deepest shadows. Puck watched them as if mesmerized.

Emmi was on her own.

She reached into her pocket and pulled out the dirt clod. It felt a little ridiculous to have carried this lump of earth through multiple magical portals, but almost as soon as she had the thought, a zap of energy zipped through her fingers. With a yelp, she dropped the dirt on the ground.

"What's wrong?" Puck asked, coming closer.

Noted. The magic didn't like doubt.

Emmi picked up the dirt again, more gingerly this time, but it was apparently done zapping her. Instead, she saw faint glimmers flickering over the clod, glowing and fading softly.

Like the fireflies in the trees.

Emmi looked around, and several meters away, deeper into the trees that surrounded the area, she saw a similar golden glow. "This way," she said breathlessly, rushing toward the spot, Puck at her heels.

Emmi dropped to her knees in front of a small mound of dirt, the light rippling around her feet like disturbed water after stepping into a puddle. Flowers, vines, and grass curled over the soft bump, poking through the golden light. Emmi held out her hand, the dirt clod resting in her palm.

It was grave dirt.

And this was the grave.

How her ancestor had plucked a bit of earth from the exact spot a woman accused of witchcraft after her death had been buried centuries after Elspeth left England, Emmi would never know. But her whole body sang with the rightness of it. As she tipped her hand over, the clod of earth fell as if pulled by a magnetic connection to the exact divot in the ground that fit it perfectly, as if it had always been there.

The golden, flickering lights shined brightly. Emmi watched with wonder as the sparks rose up, like dust disturbed in an abandoned house. The glowing specks gleamed brighter.

Emmi felt Puck behind her, solemn. She should say *something*. "Buried here is a woman whose name I don't know."

The bones may be Joan's, or it may be part of Joan or none of Joan.

"They called her a fighting fairy woman and a witch."

And the term "witch" may have only been tacked on as a play on Joan's last name.

"All I know is that it wasn't fair."

Emmi bowed her head. It didn't feel like enough, even though she could think of nothing more to say. She had known all her life the story of Elspeth and Salem and the witch trials in America. She had not really related those legends to the way they were connected to other legends, other women, across the ocean and across the world. And she had never really been able to distill the factual knowledge of the injustices of the past to the empathetic emotions of real people facing such horrible twists of fate.

If she had been a child in the seventies, if she had visited the museum in Boscastle rather than being raised in the one of her ancestor, would she have giggled at the bones hanging there and never really thought of how they were human?

"Whoever is buried here," Emmi whispered, "whatever actually happened to that person, whatever she may have done, I know she wasn't a witch. She was a person. A human deserving of more than what life offered her."

The glowing lights seemed to hum and vibrate with the flow of Emmi's words. As sound died from her lips, the lights burst forth, scattering.

Emmi felt certain that this was the same type of release as before, when Agnes escaped Holyrood.

The bone witch of Boscastle was free.

Darkness fell. Both the magical lights hovering over the ground and the real light of the fading day evaporated into a mild twilight.

Emmi stared at the ground.

"There's nothing there," she said.

Puck shifted, stepping beside her. It was so strange that he'd been so silent. "What do you mean?"

Before, with Agnes at Holyrood, Emmi traded the paper from Elspeth's bottle for the magic book, and she took a page from that book of light for the witch bottle she would make once she was ready. But now? She'd returned the dirt clod onto the grave, but nothing was given back to her. The light was gone. There was nothing magic that remained.

"There's no magic," Emmi told Puck. She dropped to her knees, running her hands over the ground. "Do I just get some more dirt?" That didn't seem right. She had just said that the bones in the ground here did not belong to a witch; how did stealing dirt from this grave make sense to create a new witch bottle?

"Maybe it's not the grave," Puck said. He was still standing, and he pointed into the dark forest.

The lights. They had seemed to gather on the grave and then disperse, but they had not evaporated into nothing. They had retreated to the forest.

She'd been thinking of them as fireflies, but...they weren't. They pulsed with light, golden like fireflies, but even as she watched, the lights formed an obvious path. And the lights were bigger than the bugs she'd chase on summer afternoons with Grandfather. These lights seemed...

Magical.

And they were obviously creating a path for her to follow into the dark.

The Knight of Cups

INVITATION, LOVE, AND EMOTION

Emmi and Puck stood side-by-side at the edge of the grave, staring into the flickering lights blossoming over the forest. Each light was roughly fist-sized, glowing golden with shimmers of iridescent green.

And they created an unmistakable path deep into the forest surrounding the cemetery.

"Wills-o'-the-wisp," Puck said almost reverently.

Emmi had, of course, heard of such things before. Lights that flickered and illuminated paths, leading people from a common road into the unknown. Some stories said wills-o'-the-wisp led people to their fates, sending them off on an adventure that ended with fortune, love, and happily ever after.

Most stories said the wills-o'-the-wisp pulled people into danger where they usually died.

Emmi had always assumed that the tales happened because the wills-o'-the-wisp were actually the result of swamp gas, a perfectly natural explanation that also meant it was logical for so many people to die if they chased them—bogs and swamps weren't that hospitable for midnight strolls. But this wasn't marshland, and those carefully positioned lights were not natural.

This was the fae at work.

Emmi took one moment to glance at Puck, who was enraptured by the light like a moth to the flame. She recalled the way he'd been watching the woods ever since they'd reached the graveyard. He was fae; they were fae.

You can't trust him, and you can't trust them, Emmi reminded herself.

But if there was a path that would bring her closer to her grandfather, she'd follow it.

Taking a deep breath, Emmi plunged into the dark, Puck on her heels.

As soon as she started, the lights closest to her faded into the dark, and more lights appeared further out, creating an obvious trail for her to follow. But no matter how quickly she and Puck crashed through the forest, the lights seemed spaced further and further apart, always out of reach, always taking the most difficult possible path. Vines snaked around the forest floor, grabbing at their ankles. Roots bulged up, making Emmi stumble.

The shadows grew long and longer still. Emmi squinted in the darkness, tripping over a tree stump.

"Come on," Puck said, grabbing her elbow and helping her up. "If we lose them, we'll never get another chance like this."

Part of Emmi worried at this—it was all too sudden, too chaotic. It felt rash and unwise to so blindly follow the fae. Grandfather used to tell her that if someone was trying to push her to make a decision immediately, it was usually best to tell that person no and walk away. But at the same time, the urgency of the situation snagged at her breath. This *was* magic, and magic did not wait for anyone.

And if Grandfather were here to give his advice now, she wouldn't be so desperate to find him.

With renewed effort, Emmi pushed against the soft earth of the forest, sprinting toward the closest will-o'-the-wisp. She tried using her powers to truly see what the light was, but as she peered into the dark, focused on the flickering glow, a sickening feeling wrenched at her gut, her stomach swooping and her mind going hazy. Gasping, she looked around.

It was darker now, pitch black on a moonless night. Puck's pale face was barely visible.

"A portal," he said, as shaken as she was, if not more so. "The wisps led us through a portal."

"Like your ash sigil?"

"Not really, but yes." His voice was strained. Not from exertion. Fear.

It was too dark for the time of night; either the portal had sent them somewhere in a different time zone, or it had cost them at least a few hours. Far in the distance, almost out of sight, one single will-o'-the-wisp beckoned them forward.

"We have to go!" Puck shouted, racing to it. Emmi could hear the sound of crashing waves and taste salt in the air. It was a shock to have been on a cold hilltop forest by a grave and then emerge somewhere near a craggy shore. She hadn't seen a portal, yet she had stepped through one.

It occurred to Emmi that if she died out here, if she got lost in the light's labyrinth—no one back home would ever know what had happened to her. She was halfway across the world meddling with the fae; if she disappeared now, she would be gone forever.

"Emmi!" Puck shouted, and there was a desperate edge to his voice, as if he, too, realized that the only person on Earth who knew what they were going through was the other.

Emmi bounded toward Puck's voice, barely able to see him. She got fleeting images of winding paths over craggy cliffs, but there was no sign of humanity.

What would happen if I just stopped here? The thought filled her veins with ice; Emmi didn't want to know.

Instead, she grabbed Puck's waiting hand and together they charged toward the last remaining light. It was a pale ghost of a glow, but they reached it before it faded to nothing.

That same rushing feeling, the jolt in her gut, the lurch in her stomach. Emmi blinked. It was, somehow, even darker now. The salty air was replaced with the scent of petrichor; the crashing waves sounded more like a bubbling brook streaming over rocks. The other place had been rocky; this place felt softer. Damp earth under her feet. Moss covering the roots.

"Where are we?" Emmi asked in a shaky breath.

"We went through at least two portals," Puck said. "We could be anywhere."

"What time is it?"

"What day is it?" Puck asked. "Or, rather, what night?"

Emmi turned in a slow circle. Her eyes were adjusting to this darkness, but all that meant was there was no sign at all of the wills-o'-the-wisp.

"Do you see anything?" Puck asked, his voice an urgent whisper.

He meant with her magic. "No," Emmi said.

She was scared, even if her voice didn't shake. She wanted to grab Puck's hand, to assure herself that this crazy dash chasing after the fae lights had not been as foolish as she was starting to fear it was. But as she reached for him, Puck stepped forward.

"There's a building over there," he said.

Emmi's breath came out shaky, but Puck didn't seem to notice. She squared her shoulders and followed him.

It wasn't just one building, but several, all of them crumbling and falling apart. Most of the roofs were gone, the windows nothing but black squares cut in the stone walls covered in moss and ivy.

"Whatever used to be here has been abandoned for a long time," she said.

Puck made a grunt in agreement, the sound almost lost to the loud brook winding over the stones below. These houses were built right on the side of the brook—or perhaps it was a small river? Emmi headed in that direction and found a clear footpath, well worn. "I think I see a bridge," she called back, but Puck was too far away to hear her.

The brook created an open spot in the sky that cast a little starlight over the area. Emmi could see the outline of the land. It looked as if a giant had bent down, raking his fingers through the rocks and mud to create the craggy hills. Trees twisted up, full of leaves that clattered in the wind. It was colder now, not bitterly so, but enough for Emmi to wish she had a jacket.

Emmi turned, heading back to the broken-down buildings, and hit a trail marker that had been hammered next to the foot-path. Her thigh ached from banging into the wooden post, but her heart soared—they were at least close enough to civilization that the hiking trail could guide them back. Somewhere.

She looked around the buildings, occasionally catching glimpses of Puck, who was doing the same. Emmi wasn't really sure what she was looking for, but the fae had led her here. There must be something, surely?

She spotted a large stone sunk into the earth near one of the hollow houses, pale white and round like the moon, with cut marks all along the side. She'd seen this sort of thing before—a mill stone.

"Puck?" Emmi called in the dark. "I think we're near a mill." It made sense—the water nearby would have been used to operate the mill, but with technological advancements, such mills had been abandoned over time.

"Puck?" Emmi shouted again when he didn't answer. Her heart thudded; had the wills-o'-the-wisp returned? Had he followed them without her? "Puck!" she screamed.

"Here!" His voice was only a little distant, muffled by the stream and the trees and the broken walls. Emmi let out a sob; the night was playing tricks on her, and she didn't like how much this all unnerved her.

Before she could wind her way through the broken buildings, Puck popped out from behind a wall. "Emmi? You okay?"

Her hands were shaking. "I'm fine," she ground out through clenched teeth.

Puck rounded the moss-covered wall and stood in front of her. "You're trembling," he said.

"It's cold."

"Not that cold."

Why wouldn't he drop it? But instead of just shrugging and joking as Emmi had come to expect from the fae boy, Puck ducked his head, forcing her to meet his eyes. Her gaze slid away from his, but before she could step back, he grabbed her shoulders, grounding her, his thumbs running over her skin.

"Yeah," he said softly, "it's cold."

And he pulled her against him, wrapping his arms around her shaking frame, holding her until the only thing that still trembled was her heart.

After several long moments, he stepped back, searching her face. "Better?" he asked gently.

Emmi nodded mutely.

"Okay, then, come with me!" Puck flashed her a brilliant smile, turned on his heel, and darted away.

A laugh burst from Emmi's lips as she chased after him. Puck leapt over a rock, around a crumbling wall, and behind the mill buildings, stopping in front of a boulder. "See?" he asked, pointing.

Emmi stepped forward tentatively.

Etched into the rock face was a circular design that wove around itself. Emmi traced her finger over the carving. "It's like a maze," she said, wonderingly.

Puck nodded eagerly. "And there's another one, here." He pointed to a second labyrinth.

"Is this what the wills-o'-the-wisp wanted us to see?" Emmi asked, her eyes still tracing over the design. It was impossible to tell how old the petroglyphs were, but the edges were worn by both weather and time. They date back to the mill, perhaps the seventeenth or eighteenth century, or they could be remnants from an ancient tribe, millennia old. The petroglyphs *seemed* archaic; it was the same sort of weaving-lines design Emmi had seen on Celtic art.

Puck shrugged. "It could be this, I guess. Can you sense anything with your magic?"

Emmi took a deep breath, trying to center herself. Between falling through portals and falling into Puck's arms, it was hard to focus. But as she stared at the lines carved into the rocks, a flickering, trembling glow rose through the stone, highlighting the circuitous path of the petroglyph maze. Emmi gasped, stepping back, and Puck grabbed her hand, squeezing her fingers, reminding her that he was there.

The light in the carving on the rock grew and grew, burning as bright as a bonfire. Emmi staggered back, eyes widening despite the pain the bright light caused. Even Puck could see the magic now, the fire-like luminescence growing, forming a shape. The light burned into solid curves—shoulders, arms, a torso, legs.

From the center of the maze emerged a woman with fire for hair and flames for eyes.

And she was staring right at Emmi.

The Knight of Cups, Again

Invitation, Love, and Emotion

The woman standing before Emmi seemed to be made of fire. Flames licked her head like hair, and her skin was deep black, as if made of charcoal. Occasionally, Emmi got a glance of bright, orange-red beneath the black, glowing embers in place of muscle, lava in place of blood. The woman wore no clothing but had no shame nor even seemed aware of her nudity. She was smaller than Emmi had first perceived, short and slight, but the woman stood with her shoulders thrown back, her chin tilted up as if everyone else was beneath her.

The woman's eyes, flickering with firelight, turned from Emmi to Puck. She opened her mouth, but rather than any words coming from her lips, she spoke in a language that sounded like fire popping and crackling. There was rhythm and cadence to the sound, and Emmi was fairly sure the woman spoke a language, just none that any human had ever voiced.

Puck got on one knee, bowing his head to the woman. "This is one of the ancient beings," he said, flicking his gaze to Emmi. "Joan the Wad."

Emmi stood awkwardly. She wondered if she, too, should bow or curtsy or something, but the fae woman completely ignored her. She seemed entranced by Puck, running her hands over the back of his head, flames falling like raindrops from her fingers and sizzling in his hair.

"I don't know what's happening," Emmi muttered. The fae —Joan the Wad, apparently—completely ignored her.

Puck spoke out of the corner of his mouth. "Queen of the Cornish Piskies. 'Wad' means torch. You've not heard the rhyme?"

A torch brought light. Fire light. That explained the woman's appearance and also her connection to the wills-o'-the-wisp that had led them here.

"'Jack-the-lantern, Joan-the-wad,'" Puck said, his voice lilting into a sing-song tone, "'that tickled the maid and made her mad. Light me home, the weather's bad.'"

Jack-the-lantern...as in a jack o'lantern. The tradition was reserved for Halloween in America, carving pumpkins into ghoulish faces and lighting them with candles, and Emmi had always heard the legend started in Ireland. But Cornwall was on the western side of England, not that far from the Emerald Isle, and if the story could cross the Atlantic, surely it could cross the Irish Sea as well.

Joan fawned over Puck as he stood up, making fond noises that sounded like a crackling campfire. For his part, at least, it didn't seem as if the little licks of flame falling from Joan's fingers burned him.

"She seems to like you," Emmi muttered.

Puck didn't act as casually unconcerned as he usually pretended to be; this was someone important, that was clear. But he said, "It's not so much that she likes me. She just likes my elements."

"Your elements?" Emmi asked.

"She's fire and water. So am I."

Emmi frowned at that, unsure of what it meant. Puck didn't seem to manipulate fire. But...he did make portals with ash. He'd attacked the first hunter with wind, but...

Before she could ponder on this, Joan shifted her attention to Emmi. She opened her mouth, smoke mingling with her popping, crackling style of talk. Emmi wasn't sure what the Queen of the Piskies was saying, but she certainly seemed angrier than when she'd been petting Puck's hair.

"Why is she mad?" Emmi asked, daring to steal a glance at Puck.

"She says she's seen you." Puck frowned, clearly struggling to translate the strange language into something Emmi could understand. "When you look through the veil to see beings on the other side, sometimes the beings on the other side look back at you."

Emmi shuddered and wrapped her arms around herself. She'd been watched? Her powers were in her ability to see, but she'd never noticed anything seeing *her*. "How does she watch me without my knowledge?"

Joan closed her lips. Her eyes seemed to flare brighter as she stared at Emmi.

Beyond her, deep in the forest, lights flickered, golden glows extending into the trees. Emmi turned as more and more lights popped up—over the river, up the craggy hills, scattered over the horizon. For one moment, the entire night was illuminated by the wills-o'-the-wisp.

Wills-o'-the-wisp, piskies, pixies, whatever they were called, they were hers. Joan's. The queen. The ancient one. They were her eyes in the dark, and there were hundreds, thousands of them.

In a blink, every light went out. Darkness flooded the forest. Only Joan still burned.

The queen opened her mouth again, the sound of a roaring fire emerging.

"What did she say?" Emmi asked Puck urgently.

"She says, 'What do you intend to do, witch?'" Puck translated.

Emmi's heart thrummed in her chest. She had always known the fae were dangerous, but it was easy to forget that danger around Puck. But Joan? Joan was wild magic, as vicious as a forest fire.

"Tell her," Emmi started, but Joan opened her mouth, a sizzling scream bursting out. The queen, it seemed, was tired of speaking through Puck. Joan opened her arms wide, fingers splayed, and fire erupted around them. Although she was several feet away from Emmi, the fire created a barrier encircling the two of them, leaving Puck and the forest on the other side. It was hot, bright, and painfully frightening.

The queen demanded an answer. From Emmi's lips.

"I just—I'm trying to save my grandfather," Emmi stuttered, aware of the pleading tone in her voice. "And, I think I can help. To protect. Like—"

But Joan did not want Emmi's words. The fire raged higher, hotter. Emmi stumbled backward, her hair singing. The cage of flame tightened around the two of them. Sweat streamed down Emmi's skin, stinging her eyes. Raw panic ripped through her, and she wanted to make a run for it, dash through the wall of fire and throw herself in the cool river. But instinct kept her rooted to the ground. This was not a simple fire; this was fae magic. Stop, drop, and roll would do nothing.

Emmi was trapped.

So she faced Joan, Queen of the Piskies, and looked into her too-bright eyes of flame without flinching, even though it hurt.

The walls of fire, ever so slightly, seemed to burn a little less hot.

Joan had called Emmi a witch, and she knew she could see magic. If Emmi could not use her voice, she needed to use her powers. She let out a shaky breath and forced her eyes to focus on the flames, to see beyond the pain. Light flickered with shadows. It was mesmerizing, watching the flames leap and pop, bounce and...melt. Shift. Change into shapes.

Within the fire, there was the form of a human girl. Of Emmi. The flames rose and grew and—there. Beside the fire-Emmi was a tiny form of Joan, shrinking and cringing in front of Emmi.

Emmi shook her head; that was all wrong. She was not some powerful being forcing the fire queen to kneel. Before she could blink, Emmi watched as the little fire figures shifted, the looming shape that looked like her growing smaller and smaller as the fiery Joan rose, turning into an inferno that forced the avatar of Emmi to submit.

"Not that, either," Emmi muttered, watching. She may not be an ancient fae who ruled the pixies of Cornwall, but she also wasn't going to cower.

The shapes shifted again, the large, flaming Joan shrinking down as the meek Emmi grew. When they were equal in stature, neither of them towering over the other, Emmi turned to the real Joan. "That," she said. Unwittingly, she raised her hand to point.

Those flames did not burn her.

Joan—the real Joan—nodded. The two avatars disappeared into smoke.

The queen accepted Emmi's promise that they would speak to each other as equals.

All around Emmi, throughout the circle of flames, more figures popped up, dancing around them. Emmi struggled to focus on the different scenarios playing out—she could recognize some of the shapes in the flame. There were several images of her, all doing different things, often with others. Some people she knew, some she did not.

And there—her grandfather!

Emmi made a little startled cry and started to reach for the image of her grandfather, but the flames sputtered and sparked, and this time, they burned her. Emmi snatched back her hand, forcing her powers to focus.

There were three images circling around that area of the fiery barrier. One showed Emmi as a queen, a crown like sun rays bursting over her head. At her feet, all manner of beings, human and fae, knelt. Emmi could not tell if the beings were worshipful or fearful of her as a queen, but she didn't like that image. Her gaze slid to the next one. Emmi stood with a complete witch bottle, casting her arm out, sending protective bubbles over the land like her ancestor had done.

Unbidden, Emmi's hand started to raise. Wasn't that what she wanted—to make a witch bottle and protect the world as Elspeth had? But the bubbles...they protected, but they also caused harm. Emmi thought of the Cat Sìth, trapped at Holyrood. And Agnes, an echo of her former self, unable to leave the bubble.

The image melted into her grandfather, and a tiny flame-made image of herself standing beside him. Without a single doubt, Emmi touched that image.

New scenarios melted into the fiery wall. This circle of images seemed focused on Hunters. The first showed Emmi hunting the Hunters. She rode an enormous wild stag, and she brandished a spear. Behind her was an army of fae, eagerly declaring war against the Hunters.

Emmi glanced at Joan, the real one. Was it her imagination, or did Joan seem to smile at the idea of Emmi leading an army of fae to get bloodthirsty revenge?

Emmi clutched her hands together and shook her head. Even if the Queen of the Piskies wanted her to choose that fate, it was not what she wanted.

With a crackling huff from Joan, the image melted into a different one. Now the avatar of Emmi wore a black cloak. She held a sword that seemed oddly shaped—and she pressed it against a fae boy's throat.

"No, not that either," Emmi said aloud, shaking her head.

Another image bloomed in the blaze. Emmi stood before a Hunter, but she held a shield. Was it literal or symbolic? Emmi wasn't sure, but that was an idea she could get behind. She didn't want to kill the Hunters, but she did want to protect herself and others against them. She touched that image.

Joan seemed a little less pleased, but she waved her hands. The flaming wall was smaller now, the heat still uncomfortable but far more bearable. Through the flickering light, Emmi could see the real Puck.

He watched worriedly from the side, unable to help. Emmi wasn't even sure he could see her. But she could see him.

And then she saw another version of him, one made of flame. This one crawled on his knees toward Emmi, his hands raised and pleading. Emmi shook her head.

She did not trust Puck, but she didn't want him to beg. It felt wrong. He should—

Before she could complete the thought, the image shifted. Emmi squinted, unable to discern what was being shown to her. It looked like Puck, but...monstrous? Flames dripped down his body like mud, clinging to his skin. His face was melted and grotesque. The little fiery image was still recognizable as Puck, but...not.

Emmi frowned. What did Joan mean by showing her that?

The image shifted, and a little version of Emmi flared beside a more normal-looking Puck. The two figures walked through the flames like a dance, weaving in and out of the blaze, their hands meeting before they spun out together. Emmi couldn't help herself; she was charmed by the image, and she reached out for the fiery version of this dancing Puck at the same time that her flaming avatar did.

The wall of fire died.

Emmi was blinded by the sudden absence of light, and her skin prickled in goosebumps to go from blazing heat to cold night air.

"Emmi!" Puck cried, leaping forward. He grabbed her and pulled her close. While he'd been in awe of Joan before, now he glared at her.

"What was that?" Emmi muttered, grateful to have Puck's protective arms around her.

"A test," Puck growled. "And, apparently, you passed."

A sound like a crackling fire poured from Joan's lips. It almost —but not quite—sounded like a laugh. It sent chills down Emmi's spine.

"The Queen says that you have pleased her," Puck translated. "And she will allow you one question."

A question of an ancient queen of the fae? Emmi looked into the darkness, and for a moment, she thought of all the thousands of piskies who worked as Joan's eyes. What knowledge did she have, with so many spies?

"But," Puck said, his voice low and close to her ear, "be careful. The fae are tricky. She'll twist your words if she doesn't like your question. Remember the poem."

Joan-the-wad, that tickled the maid and made her mad...

Just as much as Joan could answer her question and give her the truth, she could obscure it and lead her down the wrong path. The fae notoriously delighted in chaos, and even if Emmi had pleased the queen, it would make Joan just as delighted to torture her.

One question.

One chance.

And a million ways it could go wrong.

Six of Pentacles

GENEROSITY, REWARDS, AND ABUNDANCE

Emmi closed her eyes, trying to think of the right thing to ask—and, just as important, the right *way* to ask it. Puck kept his arms around her, as if he could shield her from the potential wrath of the queen of the piskies.

I could ask about Puck, Emmi thought. She still did not trust anything he said. Puck was too chaotic, too blithe, too clearly focused on some inscrutable goal of his own. He was with her now because their paths aligned, but Emmi had no illusions about how little of his loyalty she actually held.

It was hard to think that now, though, with his arms around her, his head ducked low, his breath on her cheek. Emmi kept her eyes squeezed shut, trying feebly to pretend that this moment could last, that she was not facing down the fae after tripping through portals. What would it have been like if she'd met Puck on her own, without the threat of her grandfather's disappearance and the Hunters at her door? If Puck had just been a new student at her school, someone she could go with to grab a coffee and browse the bookstore? How different everything would have been, if he was truly hers, if she even believed such an idyllic fate was possible.

She took a deep breath, and all she could smell was him—earthy and sunshiny, like gardening on a spring day.

She couldn't waste her one precious question on Puck. Besides, Joan was fae, too. A fae who clearly favored Puck from the way she'd been treating him before. Emmi couldn't trust her, either, at least not with a question about Puck.

Although...perhaps Joan had been trying to get Emmi to ask about him. She *had* shown her visions of Puck—were those visions possibilities? A warning? And why had so many been focused on Puck?

No—*no*. Emmi needed to focus. She needed to find out about her grandfather, her ancestor Elspeth, magic itself. She needed to focus on her own role in this magical mystery.

She pulled away from Puck. He let go of her reluctantly, sorrow in his eyes, as if he wished he could spirit her away somewhere safe and private. A lock of dark hair fell over his brow, and Emmi's fingers twitched with the urge to brush it away.

Emmi took another step back. She needed distance. She needed to think.

Joan burned brightly, fire licking over her body. For the first time, Emmi realized that the small woman didn't stand on the ground; she floated, hovering a few inches above the dirt, one leg bent, the toe pointing down as if Joan was a ballerina caught mid-twirl. Flames trickled down her hair, over her skin, evaporating into smoke at her feet. She was so bright that watching her hurt.

This question offered of her, Emmi knew, was like that fire. It illuminated the dark, but it also burned.

Joan opened her mouth, and a sound of crackling sparks fell from her lips.

"She grows impatient," Puck warned Emmi.

One question. Emmi wanted to know where her grandfather was above all else, but she couldn't think of how to phrase it in a foolproof way that wouldn't lead her astray. It would be too easy for Joan to trick her with something like a location—"in England" would be too vague, but if Emmi asked for specifics,

Joan could say "by the sea" or "on a rock," none of which would help her. Even asking for coordinates wouldn't work; Joan wasn't a GPS. She merely had lots of eyes. Asking for a specific town may lead Joan to give her an older name for the town, or a fae name, or lead her down a circuitous path that would take too much time. No—it would do no good to waste her question on a location, even if that was what Emmi wanted more than anything else.

Part of Emmi wanted to ask what she should do, but she certainly didn't trust Joan on that. Joan would tell Emmi to do what Joan wanted her to do. Emmi didn't want to harm the fae, but she also didn't want to serve them.

Puck made a motion with his hands, widening his eyes at Emmi. She had to hurry. An impatient queen was not a good thing.

The Hunters, then—if Emmi asked about the Hunters' motivation for tracking and attacking her, that question would tie into everything else. It would tell her what power of hers the Hunters feared, or what they hoped to prevent by killing her. *That* may guide Emmi to know what she needed to do, or perhaps give her a hint as to where her grandfather had been taken, since the Hunters arrived at the Museum of Magic right after Grandfather went missing. And Emmi was reasonably sure Joan had no love for the Hunters; she would likely tell the truth in order to give Emmi the best chance at defeating them at their own game.

Squaring her shoulders, Emmi turned to face Joan. "I have my question for you, er, your highness."

Joan made a crackling, chortling sound. Emmi hoped it was amusement.

"Why are the Hunters after me?" Emmi said.

"She means the Witch Hunters!" Puck interjected quickly.

Emmi whipped her head around, surprised at Puck's interruption but more confused as to why he had to clarify the question. *What other Hunters were there?*

Before Emmi had a chance to really muddle through Puck's words, Joan started speaking. Her eyes blazed in blue-yellow fire, and her answer was shorter than Emmi would have thought. She waited a beat, hoping for more. When Joan said nothing further, Emmi turned to Puck.

"She said that she offered you a question, but not an answer," Puck said, opening his palms up as if to show there was nothing he could do.

Emmi's mouth dropped open. She had wracked her brains for a good question to ask; it hadn't occurred to her that Joan wouldn't simply give her the answer!

The crackling sound like laughter echoed over the woods, weaving in and out of the abandoned mill buildings, the sound bouncing all around in a way that told Emmi that the hidden piskies were sharing in the joke, laughing and mocking Emmi's lack of wit. Emmi cut her glance at Joan, and even if the fae queen's eyes burned like embers, Emmi could tell that she was testing her.

"Puck," Emmi said, her voice a command, "ask Joan what the price of the answer is."

Puck sucked his breath in through his teeth. "That's a dangerous game," he said in a low voice, intended only for Emmi.

Emmi didn't look at him. She held Joan's gaze.

"I did not say I would *pay* the price," Emmi said cooly. "I only asked what the price was."

Behind her, Puck spoke to Joan in her strange, burning language. The echoing laughter of the piskies around them faded as the queen cocked her head, watching Emmi closely.

Joan spoke, and Puck translated. "She says the value of her answer will match the value of what you give her." Puck paused. "You have to give her something now, though, Emmi. She won't wait. Do you have anything?"

A human would find the most value in her wallet, but Emmi doubted the fae elder cared about American money or a credit card. Emmi's phone was expensive, but that didn't make it valuable, not to a fae queen.

Emmi had some jewelry. Cheap earrings made of brass. Her

necklace was gold, a simple chain with a locket, but it wasn't a price she was willing to pay—the locket had been her grandmother's, and it contained photographs of her parents. It was too precious to barter away.

Emmi slipped her hands into her pockets, wishing that gold or gems would magically appear inside of them. Instead, she felt the length of black ribbon the woman at the museum in Boscastle had given her.

Emmi pulled it out of her pocket. The thin black ribbon dangled from her fingers.

"Where did you get that?" Puck asked, and from the wariness in his voice, Emmi knew that he did not see it merely as a simple ribbon. He had been in the museum as well, and even if he hadn't seen the woman give her the ribbon, there seemed to be some truth in her advice that it could cast a curse on someone.

Emmi ignored Puck as she held the ribbon up to Joan. "I will give you this for the answer," Emmi said. "It is more than a ribbon, I think we all know that. You also get the knowledge that I will not do the thing I intended to do with the ribbon, which adds value to the bargain."

There was no knot in the black ribbon, but that didn't mean Emmi hadn't thought about it. She resolutely didn't look at Puck as Joan floated closer to her, close enough that smoke stung Emmi's eyes. The heat grew, and Joan reached for the ribbon, her burning palm touching Emmi's pale skin. Blisters singed Emmi's fingertips, but she forced herself to show no pain.

Joan curled the black ribbon into her palm and watched as it burned to ash.

Then she turned to Emmi. She opened her mouth, and she answered the question: *Why are the Hunters after me?*

Puck did not translate the answer. Emmi craned her neck around, staring at him. He had a hard look in his eyes, his jaw set as he shook his head slowly, bitterly. Emmi couldn't tell if he was upset at her for giving away the ribbon or upset at Joan for her answer.

"What did she say?" Emmi demanded.

Puck flicked his eyes to her, an angry glare in his gaze. "She said, 'Silly human, the Hunters are not after you at all.'"

Emmi's brow creased. Of course the Hunters had been after her. They had shown up on her doorstop and nearly killed her!

Emmi craned her head around to Joan, unsure of how to get the truth. She couldn't speak Joan's strange fire language, and there was no one to translate other than Puck. How foolish she had been—not only could she not trust Joan's answer, she also couldn't trust Puck's translation.

As her eyes settled on Joan's face, though, Emmi caught an unmistakable smirk. Joan waved her hand, and little flame avatars burned through the night between them. One was a miniature Emmi; the other a Hunter that looked remarkably like Greybeard. The Hunter strode past Emmi, completely ignoring her.

Joan was confirming Puck's translation. The Hunters did not want Emmi.

Then...what did they want?

"Are they trying to get my grandfather?" Emmi asked desperately. "Why are they attacking if they don't—"

A roar of flames erupted around Joan, bright and hotter than any bonfire. Puck leapt forward, grabbing Emmi by the elbow and yanking her back.

"You only got one question," Puck said breathlessly, stumbling back into the mill ruins. Emmi tried to see through the fire to Joan, but there were only flames, no womanly shape.

And then—

Darkness.

As suddenly as Joan burned, she disappeared, and with her, all the firelight. Emmi broke free from Puck's grasp and raced to the stone. For one second the petroglyph carved on the big rock seemed to glow brightly, the labyrinthine maze illuminated.

And then it, too, faded into the night.

Emmi whirled around, confused by the sudden disappearance of the fae queen. She had gotten no real answer at all, and she was no closer to knowing where her grandfather was or how she could use her powers—much less how she could protect herself and those she loved from the Hunters. The futility of it washed over her. Emmi blinked back tears of frustration and rage.

Through her blurred vision, she saw one glimmering will-o'-the-wisp, flickering in the window of the furtherest abandoned mill building, the faint glow casting eerie light over the broken bricks.

"Emmi!" Puck shouted as Emmi raced toward the light. She ignored him. This was her last chance, and she wasn't going to give it up.

Two of Swords

FINDING COMPROMISE OR REACHING A STALEMATE

I t was no easy thing to chase a flickering light through the broken remains of old mill buildings, dodging exposed roots, crumbling bricks, and tripping vines. Emmi didn't hesitate as she raced after the light, though. Joan had not given her an adequate enough answer, and as much as Emmi had tried to think of a clever question, she was left with very little to go on. The frustrations of the last few days no longer felt like a weight but rather the igniting spark to make her go even further, faster. She ignored the pain that lanced up her elbow when she accidentally skirted too close to a crumbling wall. Even when she stumbled, she didn't let that slow her pace.

Emmi skidded to a stop right in front of a square carved into the brick of a single wall; all the other parts of the building had long since fallen. Sitting on the brick of the glassless window opening was a tiny creature holding a lantern. It looked at Emmi with wide eyes, but she wasn't sure if it was scared or simply curious. Shadows flickered across its face as it swung its legs over the side of the brick, like a child sitting on a stoop.

Puck stopped short behind her. "A piskey," he said.

"I thought it was a will-o'-the-wisp," Emmi said.

Puck shrugged. "It's holding a lantern, so, sure, you can call it that. Doesn't matter."

Emmi shot him a confused look, but didn't linger on the distinction. It seemed to her that a creature should have a set name; was Puck implying that if the piskey let go of the lantern, it would no longer be a will-o'-the-wisp?

Confused, Emmi looked closer at the lantern. It seemed to be made of an actual tiny pumpkin, like the little squat things people bought for decorations in pottery bowls on their table in the fall. Pale orange, the pumpkin had a quarter-sized circle cut out of the front, with a candle smaller than a tea light flickering inside.

It suited the poem Puck had told her earlier—"Jack o' the Lantern, Joan of the Wad."

"Is this one of the piskey king's followers?" Emmi asked Puck quietly. Maybe that was why it had lingered behind; it followed King Jack instead of Queen Joan.

Puck shot her a dubious look. "You're taking things too literally," he said after a moment. "The fae are basically the opposite of literal."

"Well, I don't know!" Emmi said. She turned instead to the lone piskey, the only bright spot in the dark forest. It was watching them both, eyes wide in a way that Emmi definitely thought now showed fear. "Hi, little guy," Emmi said gently, not daring to take another step closer. "What's your name?"

The piskey opened its mouth, and sound like crackling fires and whistling winds emerged. Emmi glanced at Puck for a translation.

His eyes shifted away, and he tried to bite down a smile. "It called you a not exactly flattering name, indicating that your intelligence level would, um, how should I put this, be adequate for tending a fart on a windy day."

"He said all that with a few snaps and pops?" Emmi gaped Puck. "I just asked his name!"

"Emmi, most of the fae don't have names. Names are a human thing, not a fae thing."

"You have a name."

Those four words seemed to have hit a sore spot for Puck. His jaw clenched, and he physically flinched as if Emmi had struck him.

"Yeah," he ground out. "I do."

Emmi's mind reeled, unsure of what she'd said to cause Puck such a deep insult. The piskey had called her something rude, how could it be worse that she pointed out that Puck had a name? Still, this one single piskey had been left behind of all of Joan's subjects; surely that meant something.

Emmi turned back to the piskey in the window just as it started to fade from vision. It wasn't just that the lantern was losing its light; the entire creature was nothing more than a foggy outline, a ghost-like image rapidly disappearing.

"No!" Emmi cried, but that didn't stop the piskey from fading away. She had no control over it.

But she did have control over her powers.

Without thinking too much about it, Emmi blinked and focused her sight, calling up her magical powers immediately. Briefly, she thought: *I'm getting better at this.* There was no struggle here, no fear—her powers came when she called them now.

With her magic, she saw—more than she ever thought she could.

It was as if there were two worlds. She could still, vaguely, sense the remains of the human world. The broken buildings, the dark night, the whisper of the river nearby. But brighter than that was the fae world. It glittered, sparkling in a strange twilight that belied the actual time.

The mill building was there but...different. The piskey sat in the window of a quaint, square building that had a thatched roof and white plaster instead of bare stone. Flowers bloomed, pink and purple and yellow blossoms trailing up vines at the corners of the building. Those same colors reflected in the sky, a brilliant horizon that was vividly bright, but as Emmi cast her gaze up, the sky turned darker and darker until, directly above her head, she could see stars twinkling and a pale white moon that seemed two or three times larger than the moon she was used to seeing.

Emmi dropped her eyes back to the piskey, who watched her intently. She didn't bother trying to speak—it would not answer in a language she knew. She took one step closer, but that seemed to make the piskey's fear rise again, like a rabbit that had decided to run

The tiny creature dropped its lantern, which crashed on the hard earth below the window. Emmi hadn't realized the piskey had wings before, but now they fluttered out, iridescent and impossibly thin. The piskey whizzed straight past Emmi, flying off into the nearby trees and disappearing.

Emmi crouched down to look at the pumpkin lantern smashed at her feet. When she let her magical sight fade, she could still see the pumpkin, small and broken. But when she shifted her vision to the fae world, she didn't see an organic pumpkin, but instead something that seemed to have been made of pure light, seeping into the dirt, like water soaking a sponge.

"Puck?" Emmi asked. "Do you see this?"

She glanced over her shoulder. Puck was still there, but...

Different.

Using her magical sight made Puck appear fuzzy and dark, as if he weren't quite with her. *That's impossible—he's fae. Of course he can see and be in the fae world.*

But he stared blindly about, his eyes unfocused. He seemed to see Emmi, but not the glowing dirt she pointed at. His outline was different, too, as if he wasn't fully in the human nor fully in the fae world, but lingering on some liminal border between the two.

Emmi scooped the glowing dirt up with her fingers. The light remained, a golden shine illuminating what should just be plain earth. She turned to Puck, blinking away her magical sight until she saw nothing but the dark.

With the dirt in her hand, Puck was able to focus on what she held. "That's it, Castor," he said, then looked up at her. "This is the dirt you were supposed to find to replace the dirt you put on Joan Wytte's grave."

Emmi sucked in a breath and stared back at it. She had grabbed it without thinking about it, but now as she looked at the solid dirt clod, she realized it was the exact same size and shape as the other dirt clod, the one that had melted into the grave. And it lingered with the same golden glow of the page from *Deamonologie.*

This was the next element to add to her new witch bottle. They were one step closer to recreating the protection spell her ancestor had cast so many centuries ago, but the success rang hollow. Would every interaction with the fae be this off-putting and confusing? All Emmi wanted to do was help, but the way the fae treated her made her wonder how worthwhile such efforts could be. Joan spoke in riddles, the piskey fled when she got too close, and Puck...

Puck had more secrets than ever. And it was about time she got some answers.

King of Wands, Transposed

Active and Mature, but Possibly Proud and Arrogant

Puck created another portal using an ash sigil. As they stumbled from the forest in Cornwall back to the old Castor home in Massachusetts, Emmi had only one thought in her mind: *I will get some answers from him this time.*

Her shoulders were tight, and every nerve in her body seemed to vibrate with purpose. A quick glance out the window told her that it was either dawn or twilight; the sky was pale pink streaked with orange.

"That's two down," Puck said, brushing ash and dirt from his pants. He shot Emmi a huge grin, something that would have, perhaps, disarmed her had he been a normal boy in a normal situation. "So, what's next for your witch bottle?"

Emmi didn't answer other than to narrow her eyes slightly. Puck's usual unflappable grin faltered. This false cheeriness was forced, so Emmi simply ignored it.

He hadn't seen the fae world, not as she had. But he *was* fae. He should have been able to see what the piskey showed her. And yet, Emmi was absolutely certain he had not.

The witch bottle came first. Emmi deposited the bit of dirt from the fae land into the cauldron, next to the piece of paper from the *Daemonologie*. There were now only three items left from the hearth—a coin, a heart-shaped stone, and a piece of pottery shard stained with either blood or wine. Rather than leave it to chance, Emmi tested her powers again.

Vaguely, she was aware of Sabrina, her cat, mewing as she stepped gingerly into the room. Puck crouched on the floor, petting Sabrina's soft fur, as Emmi shifted her sight, focusing not on the items in front of her but on the magic that clung to them.

Of the three remaining items from Elspeth Castor's witch bottle, the coin seemed to glow, radiating a warm light. It was dusted in ash, but as Emmi picked it up and rubbed it with her thumbs, the gold shined through, both magical and real.

She squinted, holding the coin up to the light so she could read it. She saw the word "Rex" easily—king—but the name wasn't James, as she expected. "Carolus," she read aloud.

"Who's that?" Puck asked. Sabrina was on her back, all four legs in the air, as Puck scratched her belly. Despite definitely being a cat, Sabrina kicked her back leg like a dog when Puck hit the right spot.

"Rex Carolus—the Latin form for King Charles. The first, I think." Emmi frowned at the coin. There were two "X" marks printed beside the portrait of the king on the front. She knew that was the Roman numeral for twenty, but that certainly didn't apply to the king—there was no king who was the twentieth of his name; as far as Emmi knew, there had only been two King Charleses.

While she didn't know what the coin meant, Emmi did at least have an idea of how to find out more. Not in her books—no, Emmi crossed the room and held the coin in the flat of her palm in front of the scrying mirror.

The image in the mirror was not her reflection. It was instead as if the mirror a window. From a distance, a man strode forward, his expression thunderous. He drug a girl behind him, her face hidden by a kerchief and her own long, dark hair. The girl stumbled behind him, unable to keep up with the man's long strides. The two walked straight forward, growing larger as they came near Emmi.

Emmi's breath caught in her throat. It looked as if the man and woman would walk right to the glass and then step through the mirror as if it were a window. When the man finally stopped, his eyes locked onto Emmi's. She couldn't read his expression, and she couldn't see the girl's eyes at all—she was ducking away as if she was ashamed of being seen.

The man, though, did not look away from Emmi. His jaw was hard, his gaze unblinking. He raised his free hand, and he hurtled something toward the scrying glass.

Out of instinct, Emmi threw her own hand up to catch whatever the man had thrown. She flinched, and when she refocused her gaze on the scrying mirror, the man and woman were both gone. Nothing had been thrown out the mirror, but in Emmi's hand was the gold coin, as if she had just caught it.

"So, we're looking for a coin next?" Puck ask, still petting Sabrina.

Emmi stared at it, still unsure of what it meant. "Yeah," she said hollowly.

"That should be easy," Puck said, "finding one random coin that magically fits our requirements out of the eighty billion or so coins in existence."

Emmi was no mathematician, but she knew there had to be more coins than that in this world. But she was starting to suspect that *this* coin was something special in the worst possible way. She pocketed it for now.

"You didn't see any of that, did you?" Emmi ask, jerking her head to the now normal-looking scrying mirror on the wall.

"I was petting the cat," Puck said, as if that were an excuse.

"Even if you had been standing beside me, you wouldn't have seen anything."

"I don't have your magic. I'm not a seer."

"But you are fae." Emmi said the words as if they were an accusation.

Puck looked as if he wanted to say more, but he turned his attention back to Sabrina.

Emmi wouldn't let up, though. "You *are* fae. And you couldn't see the fae lands."

When he didn't answer, she took another step closer to him.

"No," Puck said softly, without looking up. "No, I didn't see them."

Although he kept his back to her, Emmi could see that Puck's shoulders were tense. Sabrina batted at his hand, asking for more pets, but Puck seemed lost in thought.

"I've lost my connection," he said.

"You see some," Emmi protested. "You saw the Cat Sìth."

Puck nodded tightly. "Because she let me see her. I saw the piskies, too. I can see the creatures, if they don't mind being seen, but...I've lost my connection to the world."

Emmi wanted to comfort him. She had never seen Puck seem so upset—truly upset, on a deep, personal level. But she also wanted answers, and she was too angry at being kept in the dark for so long to bend and offer him an olive branch.

She ran over the bits and pieces of information she'd been collecting. "Does this have something to do with your name?" she asked, her voice quiet.

"A name is a cage," Puck answered.

Emmi squated down on the other side of Sabrina. The cat held every belief that they were both there to lavish her with love, and so Sabrina stretched out, tail flicking in anticipation. Emmi scratched the cat's belly, but kept her eyes on Puck.

"The fae don't have names," Puck said. "That's a human thing. Humans go around naming everything. You even named your cat!"

Emmi wanted to press him for more, but she bit her tongue, waiting.

"The fae never should have messed with humans. We were *fine*, just existing. Being. We didn't *need* to name everything. But you don't just *name* things, do you? You tell *stories.*"

"What's wrong with stories?" Emmi asked gently.

"We don't have stories, not the fae. You make them up. And then suddenly a piskey isn't just a little piskey. She's Joan of the Wad. She's a queen. Your stories gave her a name, a title, they made her. She was just a piskey, like all the others."

Emmi's brow furrowed as she muddled through what Puck was saying. "You have a name," she said.

Puck made a disgusted noise in the back of his throat.

"Does that mean you're a king?" Emmi asked.

"No," Puck laughed bitterly. "It means I'm a tool."

"What does that even mean?" Emmi asked, her voice rising. "That doesn't make sense."

"It doesn't have to make sense to be true!" Puck snapped back.

"If you would just *explain* it, I could help."

"Oh, yeah," Puck said sarcastically. "That's all humans want to do. *Help.*"

"I *am* trying to help!" Emmi threw her hands up, and Sabrina mewed in protest at no longer being petted. "I've been doing all this—hopping through portals, finding ghosts, facing down Hunters—just to help!"

"To help yourself," Puck muttered.

"I want to find my grandfather, yes, but I would also like to help the fae," Emmi snapped. "My ancestor made a protection spell..." Thoughts started to unravel in Emmi's mind. Elspeth *had* made a protection spell...but who was she protecting?

Joan had told Emmi that the Hunters were not after her. In fact, the Hunters had never come to her house until after Puck arrived.

Every time a Hunter had attacked, the only one injured had been Puck.

She had thought the Hunters were after *her*. But it had only seemed that way because she had been standing next to *him*.

"They're after you," Emmi said, realization dawning. "The Hunters. They're not *witch* hunters. They're hunting...you."

SIX OF CUPS, TRANSPOSED

DISAPPOINTMENT, DENIAL, LIVING IN THE PAST, AND REFUSING TO GROW

Emmi knew the truth even before Puck confirmed it. His shoulders slouched in defeat. A resigned sigh that escaped his lips, remorse filling his eyes. He leaned back, sprawling on the floor, and Sabrina hopped in his lap and purred. Puck stroked the cat absent-mindedly as Emmi sat down on the carpet across from him.

"The Hunters only care about witches because they're the link—witches like you can see fae," Puck said. "If they track *you*, they find *us*."

Well, that thought was terrifying. Emmi certainly didn't want to be stalked for any reason, but it was worse knowing that she wasn't the end game. She didn't like the idea of being the reasons an innocent was found by a predator.

"It's always been that way," Puck continued. "There are people who seek the magical, even if they don't have the sight as you do. But after the witch trials really got going, some of them realized that among the innocents killed were people who truly did have the power to see realms beyond their own. They got organized." Puck spits the word out as if it were bitter.

Emmi watched Puck. He was careful with the cat in his lap, attentive as Sabrina pushed her head into his palm to guide his petting. But his eyes were unfocused, hollow and even, she thought, a little frightened.

"Are they trying to kill you?" she asked gently. "Is that what the Hunters are doing—hunting the fae?"

Puck made a noise of derision in the back of his throat. "Oh, if it were only that easy," he muttered, then looked up at Emmi. "They don't want me dead. They want to steal my magic."

Emmi hadn't expected that. "How can they steal magic?"

"Iron," Puck said, as if that were the obvious answer.

Emmi knew, of course, that iron had long been considered a bane to fairy creatures. She'd written her AP European history exam on how the evolution of iron as a stronger metal than brass led to a rise in both warfare and a nostalgia for days gone by, giving credence to the superstition that iron made fae creatures— the mythological stuff of legends—weak. Iron marked a new age for mankind, an age where people no longer believed in fairies, and the stories that got passed down shifted the narrative to make iron into the literal, rather than symbolic, killer.

Emmi glanced up and saw that Puck was watching her, a bemused look on his face. "What?" she asked, feeling a blush creep over her cheeks.

"I like to watch you think." His voice was serious, but after a beat, Puck pulled an exaggerated face, scowling, brows down. The corners of his lips still twitched up in a laugh even as he tried to mock her gravity.

"Sabrina," Emmi told her cat, "eat his face."

The cat purred.

"Useless," Emmi muttered, but she reached over and gave the ginger cat a belly rub. Sabrina curled more tightly into Puck's lap, twitching her tail out of Emmi's reach. "Useless and a traitor."

Emmi flicked her gaze back up to Puck. "I did notice the Hunters used iron in their weapons." It was hard to miss the black metal. "But iron is in a lot of things." She gestured to the cauldron that was storing her items for a witch bottle, to the poker by the fireplace.

"Any iron isn't *great*," Puck conceded. "I'm not going to strip down naked and jump in that cauldron."

"I appreciate that," Emmi said sardonically.

"The Hunters use iron purposefully to hurt us and slow us down, like with the knives. But the real danger is in that device the Witch Hunters developed."

The one Greybeard had used to break the bubble of protection around Holyrood.

Puck traced an outline of the device in the air with his finger, and for a moment, a glimmering line of light hung between them in the shape of the weapon. Sabrina jumped up, batting at the magical image until it faded away.

The device had a blocky handle and a sharp tip, almost like a cross between a letter opener and a needle.

"I've seen that design before," Emmi said. "It's a pricker. Like the pins inquisitors poked women with," Emmi said, recalling the display at the museum in Boscastle.

"Same concept," Puck allowed. "But when a Hunter jabs a fae creature with that iron device, it leeches our power."

"What happens?" Emmi's voice was low. There had been much Puck had lied to her about, but this, she felt, was true. The terror, the disgust—that couldn't be faked.

"It kills us eventually." His tone is hollow. "Our magic is our life force. They drain it away and store it, and it enables them to do some magic of their own."

"But it kills you in the process."

Puck nodded. Emmi watched him as he stroked Sabrina. She felt as if she were truly seeing a real fear, and that, perhaps, it took that specific trait to understand what a person was like. Puck could have shared a favorite book, or a happy memory, or a million other things, and Emmi doubted she would have accepted it as entirely sincere.

But fear, she realized, was true in a way not even Puck could manufacture.

She felt the coin in her hand, the metal warm and familiar even if she didn't understand it fully. Emmi rubbed her finger over the embossed image, lingering on the XX mark near the center. This coin, she knew, would take her one step closer to making the witch bottle she'd need to protect Puck—the fae, to protect the fae, and her grandfather, and... She just had to figure it out.

Sabrina mewed and hopped up, dashing for the door in the way cats do, as if she'd suddenly realized she wanted to be anywhere except the place she was. When Emmi turned back, Puck was staring at her.

"What?" she asked, unnerved by his focused gaze.

"You're doing it right now, aren't you?" he asked, his voice soft.

"Doing what?"

"Making up a story so this all fits."

"I wasn't making up a—"

Puck shook his head. "You were. It's what humans do. You tell yourselves little stories, and then they become real. That's your magic, I suppose."

Emmi wasn't sure what to do with the intensity in Puck's eyes. She wanted to pull away, but it would be too obvious if she got up from the carpet, and she was too proud to let him know that he could unnerve her in this way. "You're not making any sense," she said instead. "I can't tell myself stories and change reality."

Puck ran his tongue over his teeth as he contemplated her. "How sure are you of that?"

"Pretty sure!"

He leaned closer, sitting on his knees, inches from her. She could smell mint on his breath; she could see the sparkle in his eyes. "In that library you have, with all those books...there are history books in there, yeah?"

"Yeah." The word came out as a whisper. Emmi cleared her throat and said louder, "Yes."

"Who wrote those histories?"

Emmi rolled her eyes. "I know what you're going to say."

"Oh?"

Emmi wished Puck wouldn't speak in such a low voice. She wished he'd look away. She couldn't think straight with him sitting so close to her. "You're going to say that victor writes the history books, and so they shape the way we think about the past."

Puck smirked. "No, I wasn't going to say that."

"Then what?" Emmi demanded.

"I was going to say that in the end, we all become stories, or we become nothing. There are a lot more people who never got into the history books than those that did. But you only know the stories, don't you, Emmi Castor? You know the stories of the past, and you interpret the world through the stories you know. Stories shape your reality."

"If you want to be pedantic about it—" Emmi started.

"And the story you're telling yourself right now is shaping the reality you currently are in," Puck continued. He drew even closer, and it definitely set Emmi on edge, but she refused to give up any ground.

"I do not."

"You are currently in the process of constructing a narrative where you're the hero, and that gives you the belief that you will triumph in your quest. You'll save your grandfather, you'll save magic, you'll save..." He paused, not finishing the thought. "And because you believe that story you've told yourself, it'll come true."

"You can't know that." Emmi voice was a whisper as she realized Puck was right. She *had* been telling herself a story, thinking of the coin, how it could help, how it would bring her closer to what she strove for. "It might not come true."

"Doesn't the hero always win?" Puck asked. "I wouldn't

know—I'm not a hero. But you've read the stories, haven't you? They've been fed to you like mother's milk. The hero always wins."

"What's true in the stories isn't always true in real life," Emmi said.

"Depends on what type of story you're telling."

Emmi's heart thudded in her chest as she met Puck's eyes. "I don't know what type of story this is going to be."

Puck grinned impishly. "Just look at the way you've told your story to yourself so far. A master Hunter broke into your house and violently attacked, and an entire team of them have hunted you since—you could have turned your story into a horror. Instead, you made it into..."

His voice trailed off, and Emmi caught her breath, held it, waiting. He was so near to her now. Her eyes searched his, wondering if this story was a romance.

"An adventure," Puck concluded.

Emmi's breath released. Puck smirked and sat back on his heels. "So, what's the next step on this *adventure* of yours?"

Emmi stood up, moving away from Puck, trying to make her body listen to her head. "The coin," she said firmly, gripping it.

Across from her, the scrying mirror gleamed. Although Emmi held the coin up to the glass again, she didn't have a repeat of the vision she'd seen before.

Still, those images haunted her. "I think this was a coin used to pay a witch hunter," she said, remembering.

"Makes sense," Puck responded. He held his hand out, and Emmi flicked it with her thumb, sending it flying to his palm. He peered at the face of the coin. "Twenty shillings—that's what people paid them."

Twenty— Emmi groaned. The two X-marks on the face of the coin. XX was the Roman numeral for twenty. It hadn't been anything deeply significant, just the value of the coin.

"So," Puck asked, tossing the coin back to Emmi. "What witch was bought with this coin?"

Emmi snatched the glittering gold from the air. She shook her head. "I don't think this one is about the witch," she said. In the vision, she had never even seen the woman's face.

"Is it about a specific Hunter?" Puck asked. "Matthew Hopkins was the first to really organize it, to bring in iron. Do you think we need to find something linked to him?"

Emmi shook her head. In the vision, the coin hadn't been paid to another man. The person who'd dragged the woman along and flicked the coin had tossed it toward the mirror.

Toward Emmi.

"In the vision I saw," Emmi said slowly, turning to Puck, "*I was the Hunter.*"

EIGHT OF SWORDS

CRISIS, STRUGGLE, AND FEELING STUCK

"**Y**ou were the Hunter?" Puck asked, eyes widening and then narrowing in suspicion.

"I can't help what I saw in the vision," Emmi snapped.

Puck looked as if he wanted to say something else, but instead, he shut his mouth with an audible clack of his teeth. The little muscle in his jaw worked.

"Well," Emmi said, a bit unnerved by his reaction, "I'm not going to do anything until I have a plan. I need to go the library."

Emmi walked past Puck, who scrambled to follow her as she headed straight to the library her ancestor had started so many centuries ago. It wasn't just Elspeth's books along the shelves—in fact, most of them were more modern additions as books had become cheaper and more available in following generations—but Emmi was certain she would find an answer inside her favorite room of the entire house.

Except...she didn't know where to start.

As she stepped inside, Emmi paused. Her eyes flicked over to where she knew the copy of *MacBeth* was, which had led her to the first item for the witch bottle. She had been so sure of herself then, that the right book and the right clue would help her solve every issue.

Now, though...

"Bibliosmia," Puck said, standing behind her in the doorway.

Emmi stepped to the side, letting him in. "What?" she asked, eyes wide. Had that been some sort of spell?

Puck took a deep, loud breath in. "The smell of a good book. Bibliosmia." He leaned down to whisper to Emmi conspiratorially, despite the fact that they were the only people in the room. "The smell is actually the chemical breakdown in the compounds of paper, but that doesn't sound as pretty. Unless, I suppose, you say that the intoxicating smell comes from the death of the book; that's got a little poetry in it."

"I don't care what books smell like, I just need to find the right one," Emmi grumbled.

"And which one is the right one?"

"If I knew that, it would be a lot simpler." She didn't bother hiding her frustration. The library was a place where time was supposed to stop, where she should have the chance to *breathe.* Instead, panic welled inside her.

"Did you know there's a library in the cathedral at Hereford where the books are all chained to the shelves so no one can steal them?" Puck asked idly. "You have to stand by the shelf and read the book with the chain attached."

Emmi gaped. "How is that helpful information?"

"Oh, it's not," Puck said. "Just thought you could use a distraction."

Emmi rolled her eyes but, despite herself, smiled. "Right, well, I suppose we'd better see if there's anything helpful here on Hunters."

She knew which section to go to; this was *her* library, after all. Not even Grandfather cared about the books the way Emmi did. Grandfather had only ever dropped in to see if there was some hidden detail in the archives to put on display or turn into a special event to draw in more tourists. The Museum of Magic was

Grandfather's, a mix of both a popular spectacle and a celebration of history, but Emmi's heart was in the books, the facts, the knowledge bound neatly into the leather-bound spines.

"Let's see..." Emmi said, her voice trailing off as she perused the shelves. Puck had mentioned Matthew Hopkins, and Emmi knew there had been at least one book on him. The man had notoriously commercialized witch hunts, offering to test "witches" with his device, a device that helped him condemn eighteen different innocent people to be killed in one of the largest witch trials not just in Suffolk but all of England, with nearly twice that number sent to jail before the trial, some dying while imprisoned. Emmi took the book and sat on the floor by the shelf with it, reading each name of the victims, lingering over them.

Puck had been right. There was a type of immortality in becoming a story. She would never have known, for example, the name of Anne West, who was killed after her own daughter, Rebecca, testified against her. But so much of that story wasn't told. Rebecca had been fourteen, and accused of witchcraft herself. Had her mother pleaded with her daughter to save herself? Had the girl been swept up by lies and regrets and hysteria? There was more to this story, Emmi knew, but there was nothing else written.

She closed the book and looked up. Puck was watching her in that curiously intense way he had, as if he saw more than she did, even with her magic.

"It's not fair," she said softly. "None of it." One man turned persecuting women into a business, and eighteen people died.

More than eighteen. Because, Emmi knew, his methods had spread. Across England and across the Atlantic. He'd killed eighteen, but the Salem witch trials killed nineteen more, and there was every chance that if he hadn't whipped Suffolk into a frenzy, Salem would not have followed.

"Have you looked at the map yet?" Puck asked.

Emmi shook her head. "Map of what?"

"England. Look at where Hopkins operated."

Emmi pulled out her phone, bringing up a map of Suffolk. She let out a little huff of surprise. "Look, there's an Ipswich here." Many towns in Massachusetts shared the same names as towns in England, but Ipswitch, Massachusetts, was close to Nick Bottom. She could take a bus there. It seemed a little serendipitous that the first town she saw on the Suffolk map was Ipswich, too.

"You're looking too closely." Puck said. He made a movement with his fingers, and Emmi realized he was copying the way she'd zoom out of pictures on her phone. She touched the screen, bringing up the entire lower portion of England on the display. "Compare it to Cornwall."

"Cornwall's in the west. Suffolk is in the east," Emmi said, a question in her voice.

Puck nodded. "And the legends—in the west, there was Tintagel, Joan, the wills-o'-the-wisp. There's magic still, after all this time, in the west."

"Not in the east?" Emmi guessed.

"That's where the Hunters are."

Are. Not were. Despite witch trials being a thing of the past, the Hunters still hunted.

Emmi let out a shaking breath. Did her vision with the coin mean that she would need to infiltrate the Hunters herself? It sounded like even if the Hunters didn't want Emmi directly, they would try to use her to find more fae to leech magic from. It was too risky to confront them, despite the vision.

Reaching up without really looking, Emmi grabbed another book from the shelf, pulling it down.

A shower of white crystal power cascaded down on top of her, followed by a small metal dish that clunked on her head.

"Ow!" Emmi cried, picking the container up. "What is this?"

"Sugar?" Puck asked.

Emmi licked her lips, accidentally tasting some of the power. "Salt!"

"Salt?"

Emmi examined the metal dish, which she now realized was a small salt cellar. It could have even been one from the kitchen, but neither she nor Grandfather were that great at cooking. "What's this doing here?"

"I think it was crammed in with the book," Puck said, leaning over her and looking at the shelf. He ran his finger through a line of salt, sending another sprinkle of white showering over her.

Emmi brushed the salt aside and glanced at the book she'd grabbed. It was slender and not too tall, a black hardback volume with no title on the cover. She flipped open the book and immediately recognized her grandfather's writing.

"These are notes," Emmi said in an awed voice. "His notes!"

The journal fell open naturally to a page near the first quarter of the book, and no wonder—salt was stuck between the pages, little crystals along the inside edge where the book was bound. Scrawled in big, bold letters on that page were three words: *salt destroys iron!* Grandfather had underlined the words, circled them, and—judging from the ink smeared on the opposite page— he had then slammed the book shut.

Emmi turned the page. Blank. She thumbed through the rest of the book. Every page after those words was similarly empty. Before that, there were scatterings of notes, mostly book titles, a few questions, some obscure things that Emmi didn't have enough insider knowledge to decipher, but they all seemed linked with Hunters. She caught Matthew Hopkins's name, a few doodles of the skin pricker or thumbscrews and various other torture devices, and even the words "twenty shillings" and "thirty silver coins."

"Grandfather was researching the Hunters," Emmi said, looking up at Puck. "But...I don't understand..." Her fingers flipped back to the page where Grandfather had marked that salt destroys iron. "I guess saltwater makes iron rust, but...?"

Puck's brow furrowed gravely. "Remember what I said about the weapons the Hunters use?"

"They have to be made of iron."

Puck nodded, excited. "The weapons are limited. They only hold a magical charge for so long. While I can generate as much magic as I need, once they use up the magic they store in their devices, they have to refill it."

By stealing it from another fae creature, Emmi thought darkly.

"But salt..." Puck shook his head. "I don't know, but..."

"But what?" Emmi asked, frustrated.

"Aren't there legends, even now, about salt?"

It took Emmi several moments to remove the idea of salt as a kitchen staple to what she knew of it in folklore and mythology. "A witch can use a salt circle to stay safe when summoning dark powers," she thought aloud, recalling various books and images of women drawing out a white circle with salt—none of it real, as far as she knew, but Puck was right that the legends were there. "It can repel vampires and ghosts—"

"Every story has a seed of truth, Castor," Puck said, excited. "These legends all point back to one thing."

"Protection," Emmi said. Salt was a barrier evil could not cross. "So, what, we throw some salt on a Hunter?"

Puck grabbed the book from Emmi and pointed to the words Grandfather had written. "No—salt doesn't stop a Hunter. It stops *iron.* I think...I think maybe your grandfather figured out a way to ensure that the Hunters' weapons couldn't be used against the fae."

Emmi took the book back from Puck, perhaps a little more forcefully than she'd intended. This was, perhaps, one of the last things Grandfather had written before he disappeared. She couldn't be sure, but she felt certain he would have told her about this. It looked new, the pages white, the ink not dulled.

"You realize what this means?" Puck said. "If the fae didn't have to fear Hunters..." His eyes grew wide at the possibility.

"We need to get our hands on one of those weapons, test this theory somehow," Emmi said, her mind half-elsewhere.

"Yes," Puck said emphatically.

Emmi flipped through the last three-quarters of the book, all blank. She ran her fingers over the smooth, empty pages. "What if the Hunters found out Grandfather knew something. What if they took him or...or hurt him...because of what he'd discovered?"

"They might have," Puck said darkly.

Emmi expected panic to flood her senses, or grief, or anxiety. Instead, she felt eerily calm.

"Then we get him back," she said firmly.

THE EMPEROR, TRANSPOSED

TYRANNY, DOMINANCE, AND MISUSED POWER

Several days later, Emmi was exhausted, tired, and utterly at her wit's end. They were no closer to finding Grandfather or a Hunter that could lead them to him. They'd spent ages researching, testing, *trying*...and yet.

Nothing.

Emmi slung the front door of the Museum of Magic open, blinking in the midday light. "I need time to think," she told Puck, glaring at him, "and you are not helping."

"So, what, you're just going to throw me out?" Puck had been leaning against the front desk, but he pushed off it, striding toward her, hands balled in fists, eyes flashing as his temper flared.

"I just need some space!" Emmi threw her arms up. "Go for a walk, something! Five minutes alone, that's all I'm asking for, jeez!"

"What are you talking about?" Puck's voice rose as he strode near the door. He gestured to the lawn outside, to the sidewalk. Not many people were out, but a couple of kids licked melting ice cream cones on the bench across the street. An older woman walked her dog, turning the corner. A man crossed the street, carrying a box, heading toward the post office. "I can't go out there!" Puck's tone dripped with derision, as if Emmi had asked him to thrown himself into a volcano.

"Why not?" Emmi's voice rung out loudly.

Puck, however, lowered his. "Hunters could be out there."

Emmi rolled her eyes so hard it hurt. "Do you *see* any Hunters?"

"I don't know, do you?" Puck shot her a pointed glare.

Emmi felt her muscles tense as she turned and scanned the area, calling her sight forward, but she was so distracted by the pretentious way Puck had thrown her words back at her that she wasn't sure that the fact everything appeared normal was reality or if she'd just not been able to harness her powers better.

"There's no one out there," Emmi said, unable to keep the doubt from her voice.

"How sure of that are you?" Puck snarled. "I've never see anyone not be able to actually use the powers they were gifted with. Are you really Elspeth Castor's descendent? She would *know.*"

Emmi sucked in a harsh breath through her nose. "That's not fair," she said in a low voice.

"Whatever, Castor." Puck shrugged, but his shoulders were still tight.

"You think there's Hunters out there?" Emmi snarled. "Fine." She turned to the street. The kids were now openly staring at their argument, ice cream dripping down their arms. "Hey, Hunters!" Emmi shouted at the top of her lungs. "You want him? Come get him!"

She whirled around and grabbed Puck's arm, yanking him toward the front stoop. Puck dug his heels down, leveraging more strength than Emmi had expected from his slender arms, keeping himself from moving through the door.

"I'll take him."

The voice was cool and calm, but it was the assurance in the man's tone that set Emmi's spine tingling. She turned slowly, letting Puck go, and saw that the man who'd been carrying the box was not a neighbor or anyone she recognized. The box was gone. The man looked at her with pale eyes, a little smirk on his lips.

She had tried to use her vision and failed. The man was a Hunter.

"Take him then," Emmi said. Her heart rate ratcheted up. How had he moved so quickly and silently?

His eyes roved from her to Puck, still inside, standing behind her. "You have to let me in," he said. "Or force him out. If you can."

Emmi stared at him, hard. That was the line Greybeard had drawn, too, when he'd first knocked on her door. She shifted her powers, focusing on him, and realized that this man *was* Greybeard, the original attacker, wearing a deep glamor of some sort. As she watched, he shivered, letting the illusions fade.

"How much fae magic did you burn up just to merit that disguise?" Puck snarled at the man.

Greybeard licked his lips as his eyes flicked from Puck's shoes all the way up to his unruly hair. "I'll have more soon." He turned to Emmi. "Let me in, girl. It's your house."

Like a vampire, he needs an invitation, Emmi thought. The parallels were creepy, and Emmi remembered the way her grandfather had found out that salt created a weakness for the Hunters, or at least for their weapons. She looked back at Greybeard. Despite it being summer, he wore a long coat, his fists bunched up and hidden by the sleeves.

He's got his weapon ready.

"Let me in," Greybeard said again, his voice stronger, more demanding. He did not take his eyes off Puck.

"Emmi, Emmi, please," Puck said, his voice hitching to a high note of panic. "I know we fought, I know I'm annoying, but—"

"Get out of the way," Emmi said, using both her hands to shove Puck down and across the foyer. She took several steps in, and when she turned, there was nothing between her and Greybeard but the doorway and the thin carpet in front of it. He looked poised for action, his body tightly wound, his eyes glittering.

"How can I be sure you won't hurt me?" she asked him.

"I don't care about you," Greybeard said. "Besides, even if you let me in, the house will still protect you. Castor built it...intentionally."

Doubt seized Emmi's heart, although she was curious about Greybeard's choice of words.

"Emmi," Puck pleaded from the floor.

"Come in," Emmi said to Greybeard.

Grinning triumphantly, Greybeard stepped inside, taking a long stride to the left, completely by-passing the carpet Emmi and Puck had put down on the floor in front of the door.

The carpet that had a ring of salt hidden under it, the white powder caked thick and purposefully intended to trap the Hunter they'd lured inside with their fake, loud argument.

"Well, that didn't work out," Puck said, getting up from the floor, his eyes on the Hunter.

"The salt?" Greybeard smirked. "No. I knew you laid a trap. I'm not a fool, fae."

Inside, Emmi's nerves rioted in sheer panic. They had thought that with a believable enough fight, a Hunter would lower his guard and come inside. They knew they were being watched— they were always watched by the Hunters unless they were in an area that was protected—but they had hoped that bringing one inside would be enough. They'd barely begun the plan, and it was already failing!

But that does prove salt is a weakness, Emmi thought, that one idea giving her hope.

Emmi stepped over the carpet and slammed the door shut, hoping the movement was just enough to distract the Hunter. His eyes followed her, but he didn't move, and he didn't turn his back on Puck.

Puck, who pulled a fistful of ash from his pocket, drew a sigil quickly in his palm, and then flung the grey powder over them all.

Just before Emmi's senses succumbed to the ash sigil portal, she heard Puck cry out in pain—Greybeard had gotten in a blow of some sort, quicker than lighting, but not quicker than Puck's portal.

Warm air assaulted Emmi, and she felt her stomach plunging to her feet as her whole body swooped down in a freefall. Her hair blew in her face, and she scrambled to hold on to something, anything, but there was nothing there, just the salty breeze, the sound of waves, the scream of the Hunter—

A splash below her and a gurgling noise as Greybeard hit the water and sank, sank. Emmi felt cold waves licking at her feet as a hand wrapped around her wrist and swung her up. With his other hand, Puck pushed air straight down, creating a jetpack-like effect to keep him buoyed above the waves of the ocean below. As soon as Emmi was pulled up to his level, the little platform of air extended to her feet.

Her heart raced. "You almost let me fall!"

She got a good look at Puck as she wiped her hair out of her face. His shoulder was stained green with his blood, and his jaw was set in a grim line. Puck hadn't just been hurt, the injury had been bad. "Let's keep this quick, Castor," Puck said.

Nodding, Emmi looked down. Puck kept one hand pointed down, creating the air barrier that kept them afloat, and the other gripping Emmi's wrist, enveloping her in the magic. The air barrier was a meter or more above the ocean, dark blue-green with gently rolling waves, but even as she looked, the barrier slipped down an inch or two. Puck couldn't keep the magic going for long.

With a gasp and a splutter, the Hunter's head burst out of the ocean, a spray of salt water scattering like glittering gems. "What happened?" he shouted. He thrashed in the sea, looking around before he looked up. His eyes narrowed in rage. "What are you doing?" he screamed.

"Right, I'll get to the point." Emmi leaned down. "You can't use your weapon when there's salt, and there's salt in the ocean, so...this should work."

"You think so?" The Hunter grappled with his long cloak, and then Greybeard pulled out the same device that he'd used to attack Holyrood's protective bubble. It looked like an enclosed dagger, the tip pointing out of a metal hexagonal tube that almost hid the whole blade.

Puck's grip tightened around Emmi's hand—fear.

But, even as the Hunter pointed it at Puck, nothing happened. The saltwater worked.

Cursing, Greybeard slammed his arm in the water. But his other hand lifted, an iron knife gleaming. His device wouldn't work due to the salt, which would take magic from Puck. But a regular blade could take Puck's life.

"Throw it, and we go!" Puck shouted, his voice cracking. "Figure your own way home then."

That caused the Hunter to pause. "What do you want?"

"First of all, we want that." Emmi pointed to the device that would suck away magic. Getting that would not only disarm Greybeard just in case, but it would give them something they could examine, perhaps finding a better way to thwart.

"No," Greybeard sad flatly.

Emmi shrugged. "Look around."

They were in the middle of the Atlantic, somewhere between England and America. There was no land in sight, just the curvature of the Earth and water, water, everywhere.

No ships.

No hope.

"You'll kill me?" Greybeard asked in a low voice. It would take time for him to drown, true, but it would be inevitable.

"I don't want to," Emmi started, unsure of how far she could push this.

"I do," Puck growled, the strain of his magic making his voice sound harsher.

Greybeard seemed to weigh his options, then tossed his weapon up into the air, and Emmi scrambled, pulling against Puck's grip as she snatched it by the handle. It dripped with saltwater.

"Now let me out," Greybeard snarled. "Send me back to land."

"Oh, I have a few questions first," Emmi said sweetly.

Puck's hand twitched. "Hurry it up," he said in a low voice. His face was pale, his eyes strained. "I can't hold on much longer."

Emmi focused in on the Hunter, using both her magical vision and her other senses, hoping she could see if he lied to her. "Where is my Grandfather?"

The Hunter's eyes went wide, his body slack as he sank a few inches in the water before he started treading again. "You don't know," he said, marveling.

Puck grunted, and the air platform stuttered—not long enough for them to plunge into the ocean, but definitely long enough for her to feel it. He pulled her closer, and Emmi slipped her hand up to his forearm, careful not to let go of him as he reached into his pocket and pulled out another fistful of cold ash.

"Know what?" Emmi called back to the Hunter. She was distracted by Puck's faltering magic, but not enough to ignore the important question at hand.

"I don't have your grandfather, girl!" Greybeard shouted up at her. "None of the Hunters do. The fae have him!" He threw an accusing finger up at Puck. "The ones like him!"

At that, Puck's magic shattered. The air platform turned to nothing, and Emmi plunged down to the ocean. At the same time, Puck quickly swiped his finger through the already scattering ash. The portal glittered and fell on them—Puck, Emmi, and the Hunter—like snow.

THE CHARIOT

DIRECTION, DETERMINATION, TRAVEL, AND
BALANCE

Emmi smashed to the foyer with a teeth-clacking crash.
Saltwater fell down on her like rain, droplets from the
ocean that had gotten caught up in the portal spell.

Emmi was dazed but only for a moment. Puck was the first to
move, leaping up, fire sputtering on his wet hands.

"Get out," he snarled at Greybeard, who moaned on the floor
at his feet, a dark stain of water spreading out from his sodden
clothes.

The Hunter turned to Emmi. "You cannot trust his kind."

"I can't trust you, either," Emmi quipped.

"Then trust none of us," Greybeard pleaded even as Puck
advanced on him, flames growing. "But don't trust *them.*"

"I said get out!" Puck shouted at the Hunter.

The man struggled to his feet, moving slowly, as if hurt. There
was a chance, Emmi thought, that salt did more than cancel out
the Hunters' weapons; it may cancel out their strength, their
spells, anything about them that had been stolen from the fae.

Greybeard turned to the door, but he cast another look at
Emmi. "I mean it, girl. Humans have to protect each other, witch
or not. To the fae, we are disposable. Gnats compared to their
long lives, worthless. We are fodder for their entertainment."

As the Hunter spoke, the fire in Puck's palms dimmed, worry creasing his brow as he looked to Emmi. But Emmi strode forward, not taking her eyes from the Hunter.

"You need to leave this house and never come back." She spoke firmly with no hesitation or doubt, and at that, the Hunter finally left.

Emmi slammed the door behind him.

"Emmi, I swear to you by any god or king, I do not know what he was talking about," Puck said urgently, his eyes searching hers. "Maybe the fae do have your grandfather, but I don't know—"

In two long strides, Emmi crossed the room, placed her palms on either side of Puck's face, and drew him into a long kiss, silencing his words and his worries. Once the shock wore off, his hands slid up her back, pulling her in tighter. She could still feel the warmth from the flames he'd summoned, the heat radiating through her shirt, and she had a fleeting thought of how easily he could burn her, how little she cared.

Puck started to pull away, but she could still feel the tension in his back, the worry threaded through his breath, so she held on. She kissed him until his breaths grew ragged from it; she kissed him until he could think of nothing but the kiss.

And then she stepped back. A soft sigh filled the space between them, and she wasn't sure if it had fallen from his lips or hers.

"If I didn't trust you by now, Puck, what am I even doing?" Emmi said, looking at him earnestly. "I am not stupid; I can see that you have your own motivations and that you have not told me the whole truth in this situation. But I do not believe you intend to hurt me or Grandfather, and I know you would have told me if you knew where he was."

"I would," Puck managed.

"I know."

He let out a shaking breath.

"And now," Emmi said, smoothing down her hair and

straightening her shirt. "Let's figure out where Grandfather actually *is*." Just because she didn't think Puck specifically had anything to do with his disappearance, it didn't mean the fae weren't involved. She wasn't entirely sure about Greybeard's word, but it was enough for her to consider it.

Puck smirked, his eyebrow cocked.

"What?" Emmi asked.

"I like the way you get down to business." His voice was velvet, and Emmi wasn't sure which type of "business" he was referring to. She swatted him on the arm, just in case. "Right, so," Puck said, "the problem is that saying the 'fae' have your grandfather is rather like me saying a human does. There's...a *lot* of fae. This isn't narrowing the field down all that much."

It also didn't narrow down the location—Puck was proof enough of portals that could put Grandfather anywhere on Earth. *Or* in the fae lands, actually, which Emmi wasn't sure was an entirely different location or an overlay on her own reality. She leaned against the front desk, tipping her head back to look at the darkly stained wooden planks on the ceiling, counting them idly as she tried to figure out a lead.

"Is there any fae that is linked to salt?" Emmi asked. Maybe her grandfather's discovery had something to do with which fae was most interested in him.

"Oh, sure—there's saltwater creatures, of course, some grindylows, sprites, selkies, some of the mer-people."

Emmi tried to hide her astonishment at the idea that all those creatures were as real as Puck.

"Some of the sprites and goblins don't particularly *like* salt," Puck continued, "but that's more about taste than magic."

With nothing left to go on, Emmi checked her phone, hoping that perhaps the curator of the Museum of Magic in Bosworth had sent her a message about Grandfather, or...or something. No human had seen him, though. When she'd spoke to Joan of the Wad, the fiery queen had seemed to imply that the Hunters weren't interested in her or Grandfather, which did lend credence to what Greybeard had told her. If only she had asked about the fae instead of the Hunters.

"Wait a minute!" Emmi shouted so loudly that Puck jumped.

"What?" he asked.

She thrust a finger at him. "When I asked Joan about the Hunters, you made a point to say 'Witch Hunters.' I'd forgotten about that, but you...you knew there was a distinction to be made then."

Puck shrugged. "Joan's crafty. I didn't want her to deflect us with the Wild Hunt."

Emmi's mind surged. The concept of a Wild Hunt existed throughout Europe, although she wasn't as familiar with the British version. Wild Hunts were bloodthirsty, rampaging gods or fae creatures that usually presaged—or feasted upon—war.

"Who leads the Wild Hunt in England?"

Puck bristled. "'England' is too limiting, Castor."

"In Great Britain, I mean. The whole island."

Puck shook his head. "The Wild Hunt comes from the fae lands, and crosses into the mortal realms."

"Fine, but who leads it?"

"Gwyn ap Nudd," Puck said as if the answer were obvious.

That was a Welsh name, and she had to get Puck to spell it for her before she could find it on her phone's search engine. "Associated with Glastonbury Tor," she read, scanning the pages that came up. "Part of Arthurian legends. King of the Fair Folk." Emmi looked up from her phone at Puck. "I get that Joan was queen of the piskies in Cornwall," she said. "What's Gwyn's role? What does it mean to be king of the fair folk?"

"King of all," Puck said. "He mostly stays in the Otherworld, except when he's leading the Hunt. But he's *the* king. Others, like Joan, lead a specific group, but everyone serves the king."

Otherworld—that was the more proper name for fae lands. And Gwyn ap Nudd ruled it all.

"We need to see him," Emmi mused aloud.

Puck reared back, eyes wide. "We do *not!*"

"Why not?"

"Emmi!" Puck crossed over to her and gripped her arms. "You don't just go to the Otherworld and chat with the king!"

"Why not?" Emmi asked again.

Puck shook his head slowly. "Who do you think he's hunting?" he asked quietly.

Emmi had assumed that there was a sort of battle going on—the Witch Hunters versus the Wild Hunt.

"People?" Emmi asked, her voice a whisper.

"Humans," Puck confirmed.

Emmi felt hope drain from her. "If this king hunted Grandfather—"

"He wouldn't kill him," Puck said immediately. He flinched. "Probably."

"My phone said Gwyn was associated with Glastonbury," Emmi started.

"You can't go there!" Puck said. "You do realize you are also human, even if you're a witch? If the Wild Hunt put *you* in their sights...Emmi, I could not protect you."

It cost him something to say that, Emmi could tell. He *wanted* to protect her, but he simply wouldn't be able to.

Emmi reached in her pocket and pulled out the golden-colored coin, the twenty shilling piece. "Everything's been reversed," she said after staring at it for a long time. "Everything I've tried to replicate from the witch bottle has been the opposite of what I ultimately got. I found a piece of paper calling someone a witch, and turns out she wasn't one at all. I found a bit dirt from a grave, and replaced it with dirt from the Otherworld." She caught herself just in time from calling it "fae lands" again. She flipped the coin over in her palm. "This coin was used to pay the Witch Hunters." Emmi looked up at Puck. "What happens if we give to the Wild Hunt instead?"

"It's too risky for you to go," Puck said, already shaking his head vehemently.

Emmi tossed the coin to him. "Then you go."

He caught it mid-air.

"I *can't*," he said with the same anguish he'd spoken with before. Puck did not like limitations. "You saw the way I can't connect to the Otherworld. I can't...I can't even see it."

"I can see it," Emmi shrugged. "I can guide you." She frowned. "But I suppose that defeats the purpose of me staying here, safe..." She sighed. "I have to go, but I can't go. If there was just a way for me to give you my powers..."

Silence wrapped them around.

Emmi looked up. Puck stared at her with a curious intensity. "Would you?" he asked softly. Although he hadn't moved, he seemed closer now that he had been a moment ago. He reached up and almost touched her face, then pulled back. "Would you give me your powers if you could?"

Emmi's heart hammered in her chest. She'd kissed Puck; she said she trusted him. But why did this feel different? Why did this feel...dangerous?

THREE OF CUPS, TRANSPOSED

MISFORTUNE, UNTRUSTWORTHINESS, AND LOSS OF FRIENDS

Would she trust Puck enough to grant him her own powers, lend him her magic—perhaps even her life? *Should* she?

"How would that even work?" Emmi asked, aware that this was a delaying tactic and not a true answer.

Puck didn't seem to mind. "You still have the Hunter's weapon?"

Emmi passed it over to him. Puck weighed it in his hands, contemplating it with an unreadable expression.

"This is a tool," he said. "It takes out magic and can transfer it to someone else. Too much, and it can kill. But it doesn't *have* to drain the person entirely. It could take a small portion of magic without causing lasting damage."

"And that's what you want me to do?" Emmi asked. "Take out my magical vision and transfer it to you?"

"A small portion, temporarily."

Still, it would require a level of trust, trust that she was surprised to find she had. Emmi truly did not believe Puck would do something to cause her harm.

Puck started heading deeper into the house, toward the room with the hearth and cauldron. "The concept of transferring magic—it's such a *human* thing. In the fae lands, you just are what you are, and that's enough. But humans...they always want to change things."

They stepped into the room, and a stray sunbeam caught the scrying mirror, flashing in Emmi's eyes.

"So, what I would have to do," Puck said, turning around to face Emmi, "is carefully pull a portion of your magic out and transfer it to me. That would give me the power to see in the Otherworld and gain access. Really, all I have to do is get in. The doorways are slippery, and even if you know where they are, you have to see where you're going to get through them."

"Can I do it?" Emmi asked. "I mean, can I be the one to initiate the transfer? Does it have to be you who uses the...tool?" It was hard to think of it as anything less than a weapon.

Puck considered for a moment. "You could. But it's dangerous."

"Sounds like it's dangerous either way."

Puck met her eyes unflinchingly. "Yes. It is."

But there was no part of this plan that wasn't dangerous. Going into the Otherworld using borrowed magic, especially considering the way Puck seemed to have been severed from his home lands...

"I'm going with you," Emmi announced.

"Wait, what?" Puck gaped at her.

"I'll just turn myself invisible like before, in Scotland."

"That won't work." Puck was already shaking his head. "That sort of trick can deceive a human, but not a fae, especially not in the Otherworld."

"Can't you give me some sort of magical disguise then?" Emmi pressed. "A glamour or something?"

"Nothing strong enough to get by the king of the fair folk." Puck sighed. "To do that and not be seen as a mortal, you'd need..." He stopped short.

Emmi narrowed her eyes. "Need what?"

"You'd need magic of your own. You could cast a glamour on *yourself*—the fae would see that you were wearing a disguise, but they'd still believe you were fae, if the source of magic came from your own hand. *That* might be enough."

"So..." Emmi mused aloud, not breaking eye contact. "I'll give you some of my magic; you give me some of yours. Then you can enter the Otherworld and see the fae lands, and I can go with you in disguise."

Puck raised his eyebrow. "That would work, except for one problem."

"What?"

"You're not coming with me."

Emmi bristled. "I am, too!"

"No," Puck said flatly.

"Why?"

"It's too—"

"Don't say it's too dangerous!" Emmi snapped. "This is about *my* grandfather."

"And my people."

Emmi refused to budge. "That's the deal. You take some of my magic, I take some of your magic, we go together."

"Emmi Castor, you are infuriating," Puck said, but there was an appreciative glint in his eye.

"Infuriating gets the job done."

Puck raised an eyebrow, and Emmi could almost see the protests about to fall from his lips.

"Trust goes both ways, Puck," she said softly.

His jaw clenched, and he tested his grip on the Hunter's weapon. "You first," he said finally.

She nodded, agreeing.

Puck grabbed two chairs from against the wall and positioned them in the center of the carpet in front of the hearth. When they sat across from each other, their knees bumped together. Puck leaned over, twirling the weapon in his hand so that the pointed end faced Emmi's temple.

"It's going to hurt," he said gently.

"How do you know?" Emmi asked.

Puck's eyes widened, then narrowed.

"Have you felt this before?" Emmi pressed. "Has someone taken your magic before?"

He was close enough that she could see the thrum of his heartbeat in the vein on his neck. "Yes," he whispered, the word coming out like growl.

"Did a Hunter catch you?" Emmi asked.

Puck shook his head silently.

If not a Hunter...who? Before Emmi could ask, Puck pressed the edge of the cool iron against her forehead. "I'll be quick," he promised. "Try not to fight it. It makes it worse."

Emmi felt her body winding with tension. She wished he'd just get it done with; his dark tone and the fear in his eyes made it all the worse. When nothing happened, she refocused on Puck's gaze, and she realized he'd been waiting for her to meet his eyes. "Trust me," he said.

She nodded.

And a needle pierced her brain.

At least, it *felt* like a needle, driving into her thoughts, splintering her emotions, draining—draining *something* from her. Something intangible and yet still an essence of her very being. She gasped, a raspy, violent intake of air that sounded like a death rattle, and then Puck broke away, snapping the device to the side. Emmi clutched her head, pulling her hands away, expecting blood, but there was nothing.

Just a hollowness in her brain.

Puck tapped the device right in the center of his forehead. Emmi stared at him with eyes watery from pain, and for a brief instant, she saw his usually pale eyes glow golden.

He blinked and let out a sigh, his shoulders unconsciously rolling back as the magic washed over him.

"Done," he said. He leaned over, cupping Emmi's face. "Are you okay?"

She tried to nod, but the movement made her stomach lurch.

"Give it a second," Puck said. He stood up to give her space.

After a few moments, Emmi straightened, although she didn't feel strong enough to stand. Puck was pacing, head down, lost in thought. Emmi watched him, then her eyes settled on the scrying mirror behind him. Her eyes ached, but somehow watching Puck in the mirror helped her.

Puck turned to her. "Feeling better?"

"It's weird," she said uneasily. "It's not like anything's missing, and it doesn't really hurt any more, but..."

"But you have a sense of loss?" Puck guessed.

Emmi nodded.

"It'll fade." Puck took the chair opposite Emmi again. "Can you still see? Magically, I mean."

Emmi took a shaky breath and tried to summon her power. It was like reaching into a well that was almost empty, but as she cast her gaze around the room, she settled on the cauldron and saw the familiar golden glow from the objects she was collecting for her own witch bottle.

"I can," she told Puck. A relief; giving him some of her powers had not entirely depleted her own.

"Okay," Puck said, nodding, his eyes unfocused. "My turn. I guess."

He passed the weapon to her. The iron, despite having been in his hand, still felt cold. "What do I do?" she asked in a small voice.

"It's about intent. Hold it here," he said, pulling the iron point to his forehead, "and think about what power you want to draw from me."

"A disguise," Emmi said. "To help me blend in with the other fae."

"The power to make a disguise of your own," Puck countered. "Fortunately for you, that's a magic I can do pretty well. It's basically a trick, and tricks are my speciality."

"I thought fire balls and blasts of winds were your speciality."

Puck shrugged, a satisfied smirk smeared on his lips. "Those too."

"Ready?" Emmi asked. The device was still pressed against his forehead, still cold to the touch.

Puck tightened his lips and gave a curt nod.

Emmi focused. *Power to make a disguise,* she thought. There was tug, not in her hand but at her navel. Puck flinched, but the weapon didn't slip.

The smell of petrichor. A cold breeze, damp and heavy, the chill dragging at her instead of being brisk. Something...oozing, thick and heavy, pulling her down, the sensation of sinking, sinking—

With a gasp, Emmi jerked back, flinging the weapon away. It thudded on the floor, the sound dampened by the heavy carpet. Emmi focused on Puck, who seemed pale, green-tinged lines snaking across his skin. She had taken too much. The pull of his power had been intoxicating.

"Are you okay?" she asked.

Puck's eyes focused on her. "Heh," he huffed. "It worked."

Emmi stared at him, confused for a moment, but then looked down at her hands. Her skin was gnarled, bumpy and brown, like tree bark. She jumped up, rushing to the scrying mirror. She could see a hint of gold around her—the traces of magic heralding the use of a glamour—but her whole appearance looked different. Her eyes were the color of mud; her hair was replaced with a brownish moss; her fingernails looked to be made of tiger's eye stone.

"What am I?" she gasped.

"A brownie," Puck said, chuckling. "And a cute one at that."

Cute? Emmi had imagined that she would turn into a fairy or elf, something that would blend in on the set of *Lord of the Rings*. Instead, she looked like something that was born of the earth, quite literally.

"Brownies are usually tied to a specific piece of land. They're home creatures—the most important thing to a brownie is their home, the place they belong. If a human comes to their land and is nice and builds a house, a brownie will try to help the human's home, make it better, keep it safe, keep it clean. Not because they're a servant," Puck added, a harsh note to those last words, "but because they care. They just...they just want a home."

Emmi wrapped her arms around herself, feeling the differences in her body. This was a good disguise; she almost believed herself to have truly changed forms.

"A creature that wants a home," Emmi said to herself. "I can understand that."

Puck looked as if he wanted to say more. Emmi waited. He stared at her but seemed lost in thought. Finally, he shook himself.

"Okay, so—the fastest way to the Otherworld and to Gwyn ap Nudd is through Glastonbury Tor. Ready?"

Emmi nodded. Puck crossed over to the hearth, drawing the sigil with his finger. It was evening in Glastonbury now, the twilight sky casting a golden glow over the high hill through the portal. Emmi took Puck's hand and together they stepped through.

"Do I need to cover up?" Emmi asked Puck as they stepped out onto a paved path.

"Are you cold?" Puck asked. The sun was setting, but it was still summer.

"No, I mean—what if someone sees me?"

Emmi knew from looking at the map on her phone earlier that Glastonbury was a decently sized town, but from their position at the base of the hill, they may as well be in the remote countryside. There was a wooden fence behind them, trees along the side, and the lone path heading up the enormous hill, cement steps cut into the incline. They didn't see anyone else, but the sound of voices carried; hikers ahead of them on the trail.

Puck shrugged. "If it's a human, they'll see you. The glamour you made is for fae eyes only."

"Oh." Emmi didn't *feel* like herself wearing this disguise; it was strange to think that any human would see her as such. "Well, how do we get to the Otherworld from here?"

Puck heaved a sigh. "That'll be at the top of the tor," he said. "We do like our dramatic entrances."

Emmi wasn't sure what he meant by that, but she followed up the steps heading higher. As the path curved, Emmi realized that at the top of the hill was a structure of some sort, almost like a gate or the remains of a grand doorway. If she shifted to her Sight, she could see a hint of a golden glow in the carved stone entrance. On the other side, she assumed, was the Otherworld.

They passed a few people who were heading down from the path, but no one else seemed to be making their way up. It was a surprise, therefore, when they rounded a curve and saw an old woman sitting in the grass, a cloak pulled over her head.

Puck stopped in his tracks, his muscles tense, which put Emmi on edge. Puck grabbed her elbow, steering her to the side of the path away from the old woman, striding up. Emmi's legs burned from the hike up so far, and her thighs screamed in protest at the quick pace Puck set.

"A coin, a coin," the old lady crooned from her spot on the path.

Emmi's steps faltered.

"A golden coin for a poor beggar woman?" The cloaked woman held her hands out, palms up. It was strange enough to see someone begging on what was a nearly deserted path up a hill, but what made Emmi stop in her tracks was the specificity of her beseeching words.

A golden coin.

Like the one in her pocket, the one from the witch bottle.

THE MAGICIAN

INTENTION, FOCUSING, CREATIVITY, AND
TRICKERY

"P lease," the beggar woman said in a piteous voice. "Have
mercy. A coin, please. A golden coin." Her tone turned
wistful. "Sing a song of sixpence."

"Come on." Puck's hand on Emmi's arm was tight; he was
nervous. His jaw was clenched, and he seemed intent on
completely ignoring the woman at their feet as he steered Emmi
up the path.

She allowed herself to be pulled along a few steps, then dug
her heels in. "This cannot be a coincidence," Emmi told Puck in a
low voice. "A woman asking for a golden coin when I just happen
to have one in my pocket?"

"Of course it's not a coincidence!" Puck shot back. "She's
obviously fae. And you cannot trust a fae disguised as a beggar."

"Why not?" That seemed awfully prejudiced.

"Have you not ever heard a fairy tale in your life?" Puck
growled.

Emmi had grown up with a plethora of fairy tales, but she was
starting to see from Puck's reaction that they weren't simply children's bedtime stories but carefully constructed warnings. She
looked back at the woman, and caught a glimpse of her warm,
brown eyes before she pulled her hood closer over her face.

"She could be a good fairy who will grant you a boon for your generosity. She could be an evil fairy hoping to trick you into eating a poisoned apple."

"Well, how can I tell the difference?" Emmi looked behind her. The beggar woman sat motionless, softly singing a nursery rhyme that Emmi almost recognized but couldn't quite catch the tune of in the woman's flat voice.

"You *can't!*" Puck said. "So, we ignore her. Move on."

"Please!" the woman cried out piteously. She stirred, shifting her body to reach her cupped hands out toward Emmi. "Just a golden coin!"

Emmi shot Puck a pleading look and pulled the coin from her pocket, showing him the gold in her palm. He huffed a breath, defeated. "Deals with the fae are difficult to make." His voice was low, and his eyes were on the woman. Emmi knew Puck was right; she could still remember the pressure of dealing with Joan of the Wad.

"I'm not making a deal."

"If you give her a coin, it's a transaction." Puck's eyes bore into hers. "And that makes it a deal. At least know what you're going to get out of it if you do it."

Emmi swallowed and nodded, then turned to the woman, dropping to a squat in front of her so they were on eye level. Her fingers held the coin in a tight fist.

"Sing a song of sixpence," the beggar woman muttered. She tilted her head up, and Emmi saw that she was young, not old, despite her soft voice. Why had she assumed the woman was old? "Or, in this case," she continued in the same sing-song voice, "sing a song of twenty pence..."

"Why do you need this coin?" Emmi asked, hoping the answer wasn't part of any bargain.

"Why are you so far from home?" the woman said, a sharp edge to her tone now.

Emmi felt as if a bucket of ice water had been dropped on her head, but she kept her face placid. "Why do you think I'm far from home?"

"Little brownie girl, this land is no fae's home. Do you not know the portals are dangerous?"

Emmi almost smacked herself; she'd temporarily forgotten about her fae disguise. Brownies, Puck had told her, rarely if ever left the land they considered their home.

The beggar woman let her hood tip back, exposing silver hair. Not gray—silver, shining like metal, each strand glinting in the dying light of the rapidly setting sun. "How far away from your home are you?" she asked.

"Very far," Emmi allowed. She felt Puck move closer behind her, his legs almost touching her back, but he didn't speak and the beggar woman didn't look up at him at all.

"Why are you so far from your home, little brownie girl?" the woman asked, almost a whisper.

Despite herself, Emmi leaned a little closer. "A home is not a home if it's missing the people you love," she said after carefully considering her answer.

"You seek the one you love?" At this, the woman looked at Puck, smirking. Emmi didn't bother answering. There were many types of love, and if this beggar woman suspected she was seeking a romantic love instead of the grandfather she held dear, it wasn't worth Emmi's time to disavow her of such an idea. Eventually the fae woman in disguise turned back to Emmi, eyes glittering. "Ah, well, many homes of the fae have been disrupted for quite some time, no?"

Emmi nodded silently, agreeing without committing to any idea. *Does she mean when my ancestor erected protective bubbles?* she thought. The Cat Sìth had been isolated at Holyrood—how many other creatures had their homes blocked by invisible fences of power? Surely that wasn't what happened, though; surely Elspeth had not had the power to so violently disrupt the fae...

"A golden coin for me, please?" the woman asked again, drawing Emmi's attention back to her.

Emmi's fist tightened around the coin. "Why do you want it so much?" she demanded, aware the other woman had redirected her the first time she asked.

"It's more than just a coin, and you know it," the woman growled. Her voice was lower now, deeper, a strange dissonance that didn't match her almost-childlike face. The woman shuddered, her entire body rippling, as if she had to settle back into the skin she wore. Emmi felt unnerved in a way she couldn't describe, and Puck took another step closer, supporting her with his presence.

The woman stretched her jaw, twisting her tongue, and when she spoke, she spoke with the same voice as before, a young, soft, feminine voice. "I know where that coin came from, what it was used for. I'm a...collector."

"Collector of what?" Emmi asked, unable to keep the tremble from her voice.

The woman touched Emmi's fist, then tapped her thumb, peeling back Emmi's fingers as if they were petals of a stubborn, unblooming flower. Her eyes were on the coin, wide, greedy. "I am a collector of lives." Her breath cast a fog over the shiny coin. Emmi started to pull back, but the woman grabbed her wrist, keeping her still, her grip so tight it made Emmi's fingers tingle.

"You cannot take that which is not freely given," Puck said from behind her. His voice was steel, barely contained rage.

"I know, I know," the beggar said without looking up. "But I do not have to pay to see."

She cocked her head, then let go of Emmi's wrist, pushing a bit, as if suddenly disinterested. "Oh, it's straight. How disappointing."

"Well, if you don't want it." Emmi stood and started to slip the coin back in her pocket.

The beggar woman scrambled up, proving herself at least a head shorter than Emmi. "I didn't say that!" she cried. She tried to grab Emmi again, but Emmi slipped beside Puck, who threw a protective arm over her shoulders and glared at the beggar.

The woman turned to Emmi, eyes pleading. Emmi realized that the woman's cover seemed to be slipping, her glamour fading. Her eyes were no longer brown; now they were shiny silver like her hair, her pupils tiny mirrors. Emmi thought immediately of the scrying mirror in her ancestor's home, and found herself enraptured, staring at her own reflection in the other woman's eyes.

Puck's arm slid off her shoulder, down her arm, to her free hand. He wove his fingers through hers and squeezed. Emmi took a shaky breath and refocused.

The beggar woman smiled. Even her teeth gleamed, flashing a reflection of the last rays of the setting sun.

"You could bend it for me?" the woman said, a lilt in her voice as if it was a question.

"Bend what?" Emmi asked, unable to follow her train of thought.

"The coin, girl, the coin! A bent coin is lucky. If you give it to me unbent...do you wish me ill luck?" The woman widened her eyes, her silvery pupils dilating.

Emmi glanced at Puck, in part to pull her gaze away from the woman's strange eyes. He shrugged—it wouldn't hurt to bend the coin. Emmi pinched the gold between the thumb and forefinger of each of her hands and tried to force it into a curve. It should be easy; the ancient coin was thin. But it flicked out of her grip, twirling in the air. Emmi was too surprised to move, but the woman lunged, reaching for it. Puck snatched the flipping coin out of the air and slipped it back to Emmi, glaring at the beggar woman.

The coin was still unbent. "Unlucky," the woman muttered. She raised her eyes to Emmi. "Still want it, though."

Emmi held her palm closer to her body. "What do I get in return *if* I give this to you?"

The woman paused, considering. "A little brownie girl like you, what could you want more than your home? And it is not in my ability to give you back your home if it is sealed beyond your reach..."

Emmi waited. The beggar woman smirked, an idea dawning on her. "How about a blessing?" she asked.

"No!" Puck roared before Emmi could even process the offer.

The woman's smile twisted at the corners, positively feral. "The girl has to answer."

"No," Emmi said, trusting Puck. "No blessings in the deal."

The woman sighed, somehow expressing that she was both disappointed but pleased in Emmi's denial. "I have little to offer, a poor, innocent, beggar such as I am," she said finally. "If not a blessing, then a song?"

Emmi had no use for a song, but she looked up at Puck, questioning him with her eyes. He shrugged—if Emmi was determined to trade the coin, a song was as good a price as any.

"Deal," Emmi said, putting the golden coin she's plucked from the ash after the witch bottle broke into the woman's outstretched palm.

The woman's smile stretched wide, wider, wider still, beyond the limits of what a human mouth could do. Her gleaming teeth shone brightly, unnaturally so, perfect white squares vivid in the dim light. Her fingers plucked up the coin, and Emmi noticed that the woman's nails were silver now, too, tiny mirrors on each tip. The old scrying mirror had black spots on it from age; this woman now had similar spots in place of freckles, scattered over her skin.

Silently, the woman turned, heading down the path, entranced by the coin as she twirled it over her fingers, the flickering gold like a flame in her hands.

"Our song!" Puck demanded at the retreating woman.

"It's okay," Emmi started to say. She was already starting to wonder if she had been foolish in this trade, and no song could account for the loss of the coin.

Puck shook his head, glaring at the woman's retreating back.

Slowly, the woman turned. She looked even more feral now than before, her mouth elongated, her eyes too-large, unblinking.

"A song for you." The woman whispered, but they heard her clearly. She took one step forward, and that seemed enough to bring her right in Puck's face, close enough that not even starlight slipped between their bodies. "There was a crooked man," the woman crooned, her voice soft, eerie, "and he walked a crooked mile."

The woman stretched, curving around Puck like a snake before straightening and looking down at her hands. "He found a crooked sixpence upon a crooked stile."

Emmi knew this nursery rhyme, but she had never heard it whisper-sung like this before, the tune flat, the words enunciated so carefully, as if they did not fit correctly in the woman's mouth, as if her teeth were the cage holding the words inside and each breath set another free.

The woman turned to Emmi, holding one mirror-tipped finger against Emmi's temple and drawing it down to her chin, the touch feather-light. "He bought a crooked cat, which caught a crooked mouse..."

Which am I, the cat or the mouse?

The thought came unbidden to Emmi's mind, but the voice that spoke inside her head whispered, just as the woman did.

"And they all lived together in a little crooked house," the woman said. Her nail was pressed painfully at the point of Emmi's chin, and slowly, slowly, she curled her finger back into her palm. "Now, little girl who seeks her home, our deal is complete."

The woman turned on her heel and walked down the path, away from Puck and Emmi, away from the gate at the top of the hill, into the dark.

THE LOVERS, TRANSPOSED

DISHARMOY, STRUGGLE, LONELINESS, AND INDECISION

"You'll see fae like that a lot," Puck said as he and Emmi continued up the hill. Sunset had drifted into dusk, the sky more dark blue than orange. They moved slowly, not because of the climb, but because Puck was on edge, looking out for more such encounters. "The barriers cutting off portals to the Otherworld have created...problems."

Emmi kept quiet at that. Her ancestor had erected the barriers for a reason—the walls were protection, and they kept the Hunters out. But they also were still walls, and every wall could turn into a prison.

"Before..." Puck's voice trailed off, and he actually stopped on the path, a rueful twist to his lips that seemed to leave a bitter taste in his mouth. "*Before*, it was easier to slip between the worlds."

"That's where the legends and fairy tales come from, I suppose," Emmi commented. She had studied manuscripts alongside Grandfather, stories of how a poet fell asleep and woke up in the fae lands, of goblin markets hidden inside regular ones, of changelings living as humans. Shakespeare's own *Midsummer Night's Dream* had a version of Puck that moved freely between the worlds, a fairy queen falling for a human, and both humans and fae shifting from one world to another as easy as crossing a stage.

"Over time," Puck said as he started back up the path, "the doors closed. Sometimes the fae did it, to protect themselves. Sometimes the humans did it, to protect themselves. And other times…"

"People like Elspeth did it," Emmi said.

"The witches have the sight," Puck said. "They can see the weak spots between the worlds, the hidden barriers that keep them closed. No one can lock a door as well as a witch."

Emmi frowned as she trudged up the hill a pace behind Puck. She wondered if a witch could open a door as well as close one.

"Can other creatures make barriers?" Emmi asked.

"Some," Puck allowed. "But a witch wall is strong, in part because it's so well hidden. If a witch makes a wall, no one but another witch can break it."

"Not even—?" Emmi started.

Puck cut her off. "Not even a queen like Joan or a king like Gwyn."

It was strange for Emmi to think she had any power at all, much less a power so strong.

"So, that's why you'll see fae like that woman," Puck said. The path was steeper now, heading straight up to the summit. "There are many that are displaced, no way to go home."

"Can't they go to Cornwall?" Emmi asked. "We saw the fae lands there—"

"Because Joan let us. She controls that gate. And she does not often share. *All* the spaces between fae and humanity are guarded by someone, somehow. And especially the weaker fae cannot traverse the realms."

Puck's tone brooked no argument. Something about this night had soured his mood, and Emmi couldn't really blame him, especially when they crested the top of Glastonbury Tor and Emmi realized that there was, indeed a barrier around the door.

Even here, Elspeth had cast her "protection."

Emmi shivered as she looked up at the wide, pale bubble. It seemed to swirl in silvery light rather than shimmer in gold, like the other protective barriers she'd seen. The hairs on the back of her neck prickled. Emmi looked around. It felt as if she were being watched, but she could see no one other than Puck.

Emmi stepped closer to Puck. He scowled at the barrier.

"I can see why Elspeth made the barriers," Emmi started.

"Can you?" Puck's words were so low that she almost didn't hear them, more growl than anything else.

Emmi slipped her hand in Puck's, squeezing his fingers. "Walls protect, but they also imprison."

Puck turned to her, eyes wide.

"There has to be some other way to keep fae and witches and humans all safe from the people like Hunters."

Emmi stared up at Puck, trying to read his expression. He didn't speak, but he seemed...hopeful.

"And anyway," Emmi continued, "if we want to get to this king of the fair folk and see if he knows what happened to Grand-father, we're going to have to take *this* wall down."

The wind whipped up around them, and it seemed to carry whispers, sounds Emmi could almost piece into the words *witch walls*. Emmi rubbed the bumps on her arms, wondering who —*what*—was out there in the dark. Watching her. Listening. Answering.

With a confidence she didn't really feel, Emmi withdrew from Puck's comforting grasp and stepped forward, touching the moonlit barrier surrounding the arched doorway at the top of the tor. She knew that *she* could go through it as easily as walking. No human without her gift could see, much less feel, this barrier made of magic. It only kept fae magic out.

It was stronger, she thought, than the one that had surrounded Holyrood. When Emmi touched it, she had a distinct sense of *old*. Nothing clear, but—the scent of very, very old books, the pages crumbling, that dusty-bookiness combined with a faint warmth, flickering like a candle flame, and the distant sound of a clear bell, overwhelmed her senses. Some other witch than Elspeth —some ancient witch, millenia ago, perhaps—had made *this* barrier.

She turned to Puck. Beyond every other feeling, she still felt as if she were being watched, and not by human eyes. "If I break this barrier," she said in a low voice, "my disguise is pointless. You said it yourself—only a witch can break a witch wall. It won't matter that I look like a brownie if I take down this wall."

Emmi had gotten so used to her disguise that it felt natural now, but with the creepy feeling of being watched combined with the even creepier woman with silver eyes, Emmi was on edge and deeply aware that she was getting close to the fae, and with that came the primal fear of the unknown. Children knew to be scared of the dark; Emmi was learning that there was a reason for such fear.

"You're right," Puck said. He scowled. "Maybe this was a bad idea."

They could go now, and they would be safe. They could find another way to investigate Gwyn ap Nudd, the king of the fair folk. Another access point, one that wasn't so obvious.

Emmi tilted her head, glancing at the first early stars scattered around the moon. She didn't want to completely blow her disguise, the one thing working in her favor as she entered the Otherworld, but keeping this barrier up felt *wrong* in a way she couldn't fully describe.

I need a sign, she thought.

At that instant, movement caught her eye.

If it hadn't been for the soft, moonlit shine on the protective bubble around the gate, Emmi probably wouldn't have noticed the blackbirds circling overhead.

Her eyes shifted, and she sucked in a breath. It wasn't that the magical sheen that reflected on their pitch-black feathers that made the birds visible. It was that they also had some trace elements of fae. They were blackbirds, but they were also...not.

Shapeshifters, perhaps? Or maybe just blackbirds that were meant to be in the Otherworld, not this one.

They swooped in a low circle, their talons centimeters from the protective bubble around the gate. The birds were silent, barely visible, but tirelessly going round and round the impenetrable barrier, a perfect rhythm to their flight, the same repeated swoop of their wings, tilt of their bodies, flash of their beaks.

Emmi started counting them. Puck, noticing her gaze and her whispered numbers, followed her lead. "Twenty-four," Emmi said finally at the same time Puck said, "Four and twenty."

Emmi looked at him. "Sing a song of sixpence," she said.

"A pocketful of rye," Puck answered, a lilt to his voice as he repeated the words of the nursery rhyme.

"Four and twenty blackbirds," Emmi whispered. "Baked in a pie."

She shook her head. It couldn't be a coincidence that the silver-eyed woman had repeated snippets of those lines to her when she was begging for Emmi's golden coin. But at the same time, while Emmi had asked for a sign, she really wasn't sure what this one meant.

Her instinct was to lower the barrier, even if that meant exposing her true form as a witch and losing her only protection —her disguise as a brownie. On the other hand, what if "baked in a pie" was a warning for her to *not* open the barrier...if she recalled correctly, the maid in the nursery rhyme had her nose snipped off. Emmi's hand went unconsciously to her own nose.

She was sure it wasn't a literal warning, but she didn't really want to risk it. Her gaze went to Puck.

"So," he said, watching her, "what do we do?"

NINE OF PENTACLES, TRANSPOSED

INTRIGUE, DECEIT, AND BEING TAKEN ADVANTAGE OF

"We can't just turn back now," Emmi said, staring up at the protection bubble around the gate and the birds circling high overhead. She wasn't even sure if *any* barrier should remain, but she was certain this one should be broken.

She was certain...wasn't she? A pang of doubt twisted inside her. Was this just selfishness, because this gate would take her closer to the Wild Hunt, which may have her grandfather?

Above her, the birds cawed, a cry that sounded almost human.

"For what it's worth, Castor," Puck said, "if you can, I think it may be best to take this one down."

"What do you mean, *if*?" Emmi shot him a sardonic look before turning back around to the bubble. She held her hands out, and even if the bubble wasn't a physical thing, she felt a connection to it. A shiver ran up her spine. Her magic somehow seemed indescribably warm, but this magic seemed ice cold. Puck's "if" felt a little more real.

Focusing her energy, Emmi reminded herself that she *was* a witch, and she could not only see and make barriers, she could bring them down. And while that may not be the same as Puck's magical connection to the elements, being able to open a door seemed like a special kind of magic.

In front of her, the silvery glow of the bubble concentrated to glittering stars, light flashing in a million different sparkles that drifted down. Emmi acted on instinct, turning her palms up, collecting a hundred million stars in her open hands. The magic called to her, tentative but trusting at the same time, like a skittish kitten stepping toward an outstretched hand. The light cascaded over her fingers, strands of delicate gossamer.

Emmi squeezed her fingers closed. If she shut her eyes, it felt like nothing but a cold breeze slipping through her grip, but when she looked, she could *see* the magic, light vividly powerful, as real as she was.

Emmi held tight and *pulled*.

The bubble shattered in a dazzling display of sparkling stars bursting all at once before fading to the dark.

Emmi's body was awash with the power, stars zinging over her skin, lighting through her blood. She spun around to Puck, and in his eyes she saw every bit of magic shining back at her.

She stepped closer to him and realized he was focused not on the spot where the barrier had been but on her. "That was, uh..." Puck breathed, unable to think of the right word. "Impressive."

"See if you doubt me again." Honestly, *if*.

"Yeah." Puck huffed a short laugh. "Lesson learned. Don't mess with a Castor." He closed the short distance between them, reaching up and touching a lock of her hair that had come loose. "Your disguise is gone now."

They hadn't brought the Hunter's device; Emmi could not replace the magical disguise she'd had. Above them, the birds swooped through the portal, back into the fae lands. Emmi could see shadows moving closer, and she suspected that there were more fae creatures who'd been hiding near Glastonbury Tor, now rushing to the gate to get back home. Her cover had been blown the second she tore down the barrier; there was no use pretending she wasn't a witch if only a witch could take down that magical wall.

"You made a cute brownie," Puck said in a soft voice, dragging her attention back to him. His fingers shifted from her hair to her neck, and he pulled her closer. "But I like this version of you better." His words were a whispered promise on her lips.

Emmi's heart thundered in her chest as she looked up into Puck's eyes. They had kissed before, but when his lips pressed against hers this time, it felt different.

It felt *real*.

A breath escaped her, something between a sigh and a gasp, as their lips parted.

"Emmi," Puck whispered.

"Mm?" She wanted to stay here, in the dark and magic, with him forever.

His voice held an unbroken laugh. "Open your eyes."

Emmi opened her eyes. And she realized they were *surrounded*.

Fae creatures of every size and shape swarmed toward the now open portal back to the Otherworld. Sprites, their forms impossibly small and surrounded in an ethereal glow, zoomed through the night. A swarm of them encircled Emmi and Puck, swirling around their heads, humming something that Emmi could almost hear.

"What are they saying?" she asked.

Puck smiled at her. "They're thanking you."

Relief flooded Emmi—she'd done the right thing in calling down the barrier.

The sprites circled tighter, humming something that made Puck turn a furious shade of red.

"Now what are they saying?" Emmi asked.

"Nothing," Puck growled. "Buzz off." He swiped his hand through the air, and when the sprites continued toward the gate, Emmi distinctly felt like they were laughing.

Emmi's eyes followed the sprites to the portal as they flew through. Although it was fully dark now, the sky a deep navy blue and sprinkled with early stars, through the stone gate at the top of Glastonbury Tor, Emmi could see the fae lands, lit in a twilight orange. *It's magical*, Emmi thought, to see two different times of night at the same time. She almost snorted—of course it was magic.

"Let's slip in now, with the crowd," Puck said. Emmi noticed more creatures making their way to the doors. In the distance, something that distinctly looked like a tree with legs trudged up the hill. Cloaked figures with their faces hidden slipped through, all the other fae keeping distant from them. Puck reached down, grabbing Emmi's hand, his grip tight enough that Emmi knew it was a warning.

Sprites were one thing, but some fae were dangerous.

"Where did they all come from?" Emmi asked as Puck pulled her away from the cloaked figures. There was a bit of a jam at the gate—not even the tiny sprites wanted to draw too near the shadowy people, slowing the mad rush to the Otherworld. "We didn't see anything like this in Cornwall."

"Cornwall is quieter," Puck told her, keeping his own voice low. "Joan rules there, and she...curates which fae she allows in her realm. Those fae like to be hidden among people, like the wisps. She has made a haven for a specific type of fae."

They shuffled closer to the door. There was a little brownie Emmi thought may be a male, if the fae had genders. But when he turned to look at her, he grinned, his teeth in sharped points, his lips curving too wide. Emmi gripped Puck's hand, and Puck threw a protective arm over her shoulder, snarling at the brownie, who just laughed, waggling clawed fingers at Emmi before darting through the portal.

"This portal is linked to the Wild Hunt," Puck reminded

Emmi. "The creatures here are not looking for a home or a haven. They're looking for action."

Emmi could guess just what type of action creatures who wanted to hunt would be looking for. Especially since what they hunted was human.

They stepped through the gate, into the Otherworld. The creatures streamed out in every direction, each intent on going somewhere, but Emmi and Puck paused. Puck drew her away from the gate, near a moss-covered tree.

Emmi was about to ask where they should go next, what they should do, when Puck spun around, pinning her against the trunk of the tree, his arms on either side of her, his face close to hers. Emmi's eyes widened, unsure of what was happening, but then she saw a glimpse of the creatures that had just entered the portal behind them.

They each wore red caps, the pointed tips darker than the brim, the hats strangely stiff and conical. They would look like comical garden gnomes, but there was a viciousness to them that was inescapable. They spoke in a language Emmi didn't know, something that sounded almost Germanic or Celtic, a hard language that somehow was still lyrical. There were at least six of them, gleefully talking among each other, their voices rising above all other noise.

"Don't move," Puck whispered, his voice tight, and Emmi realized that Puck had positioned his body to cover hers, to hide her. Protect her. She shrank against the tree, the scent of the moss creeping over her.

Red caps—these creatures had to be red caps. Violent fae who followed war, dipping their hats in the blood of battle. Emmi peeked out over Puck's shoulder and saw the nearest one reach up like lightning, his arm elongating in a way that was creepily unnatural. The red cap snatched a zooming sprite right out of the sky, cutting its life off with a little squeak and popping the creature into his mouth before its light had fully faded.

Emmi curled against Puck, but she could still hear the tiny bones crunching.

She closed her eyes, pressing her face into Puck's shoulder. He wrapped his arms around her, the hard muscles of his chest a contrast to the soft moss tickling her neck.

After a few moments, Puck released her. They weren't alone, but the mad rush of fae entering the Otherworld from the newly opened portal had slowed.

Emmi let out a shaky breath. "Where do we go from here?" She wasn't sure what she had expected, but a part of her had hoped they'd step through and simply see a sign of her grandfather.

Puck shrugged, shooting her a rueful smile. "Just because this portal is closest to the king doesn't mean he's sitting around waiting for us to show up."

"Fair," Emmi allowed. She looked around. While they had entered from the top of a high hill, this realm showed a rolling landscape that seemed gentler, older. Trees dotted the area, and the sky seemed softer, somehow, warmer. From this side, the portal looked like a golden gate with twisting, branch-like spires, and through it, she caught a glimpse of the night sky and stars. Past the portal, though, more trees, each as indistinct as the other. Emmi had no sense of north or south, could see no path to follow, and there were no truly discernible landmarks beyond the gate.

It would be incredibly easy to get lost forever in these woods.

As the thought struck her, Emmi heard a horn blowing in the distance.

"A hunting horn," Emmi said, looking to Puck, who was clearly thinking the same thing. *The Wild Hunt.*

Despite her fear of getting lost, Emmi was about to risk it all and sprint toward the sound. The horn blew again, close enough for Emmi to hear the sound of baying dogs, too. At least it sounded like dogs. Or wolves.

She took one step in that direction, but then a a burst of black shot up through the trees. She yelped, falling into Puck, a blur of feathers obscuring her vision.

The blackbirds—apparently all twenty-four of them—flew up from the underbrush, soaring over the trees.

Heading in the exact opposite direction of the hunting horn.

Eight of Swords, Transposed

Moving forward, breaking free, and mental clarity

Emmi knew without a single doubt in her mind that she needed to follow the blackbirds as they flew off. "Come on!" she shouted at Puck as she sprinted through the clearing after the birds.

"Wait—Emmi!" Puck raced after her, easily catching up to her head start. The birds flew straight through the sky, clearly intent on heading in a specific direction, but Emmi and Puck had to dodge trees, jump over roots, and go up and down hills. Already, the birds were outdistancing them.

Emmi's legs pumped, her heart racing. "The song, remember? The nursery rhyme," she told Puck between breaths. "'Now wasn't that a dainty dish to set before the king.'"

"You think these birds are going to take you to Gwyn ap Nudd?" Puck sounded doubtful, but Emmi knew her hunch was right. She had given the silver-eyed woman a coin, and the woman had given her a clue.

And hadn't part of it come true already? The nursery rhyme started with the words, "Four and twenty blackbirds baked in a pie." These birds had been trapped by the witch's barrier if not piecrust. Emmi opened the barrier, and the birds flew off—surely they were going to take her to the king of the fair folk, matching the next line of the poem.

She only wished it wasn't so hard to chase birds in flight while she was on land.

In order not to lose them, she leapt over a bubbling brook, her ankle sticking in the muddy bank, making her slip, brown streaking up her pants leg. Emmi dug her fingers into the soft earth, leveraging her way up the bank. Puck was a little faster than her; he grabbed her elbow and hauled her up the steep side. He still didn't seem convinced that Emmi was doing the right thing, chasing after the birds, but he wasn't about to leave her behind.

"Thorns," Emmi groaned as the two of them grappled through a bramble bush, tiny thorns clawing at their clothes and bare skin. Above them, one of the blackbirds cawed, the sound already more distant than before. Emmi charged forward, ignoring the pricks of pain erupting over her skin as nettles scraped her arms. Her t-shirt snagged, the material ripping.

Fortunately, the delays didn't make Emmi and Puck lose sight of the birds. They circled overhead—all twenty-four, Emmi counted. She and Puck slowed down a little as they approached the clearing in the forest where the birds swooped.

Emmi noticed the flowers first, yellow and bright as gleaming gold. She didn't know what kind they were, just simple, delicate flowers, enough to make the air scented with sweetness. "Flowers have meaning," Puck muttered.

"What do these mean?" Emmi asked. She'd heard of things like that before, the symbolism of certain blooms. Roses meant love; forget-me-nots meant...remembrance, probably. She wasn't that adept in flower lore.

Puck shrugged. "What kind of flowers are these?"

Emmi wasn't that adept at botany, either.

Besides, the more important thing was the man standing in the center of the clearing. He was silent, looking out at the petals, his gaze unfocused, his mouth moving. Was he...counting the flowers? There were hundreds, maybe thousands, each one blooming, vying for attention in the gentle breeze. The twenty-four blackbirds did one final circle around the man, swooping down, and as they passed in front of him, they disappeared.

The man looked up. He met Emmi's eyes across the clearing.

"Is that the king?" Emmi muttered to Puck.

"I don't know," Puck said. "I never met the man."

Fair, she supposed. She'd never met the president, and only knew what he looked like from the news. Fae didn't seem to have access to televisions.

The man stared at them, his eyes narrowing. A chill ran down Emmi's spine.

"Use your magic," Puck whispered.

Emmi slipped into her magic as easily as breathing. The flowers seemed to glitter, radiating a glow. But what really drew Emmi's attention was the crown floating like a ghost over the man's head. She couldn't see it without her magical sight; she was certain Puck could not see it at all. But this man had a gleaming gold crown with arching spires, impossibly large, extending out like tree branches, the roots casting down and almost—but not quite—touching the man's dark hair.

He was the king.

Before she could say anything, even to Puck, the king launched himself at her, racing through the flowers, casting yellow petals all around. He had both hands out, and with her Sight, Emmi could see dark power pooling in his palms, his fingers turning into something like claws.

"No witches in my realm!" the king screamed.

On instinct, Emmi threw her hands up, a shield of light bursting out, protecting both her and Puck. The king drew himself up short, stopping just before he hit the barrier. He glared at Emmi, pure hate in his look.

"How did you get here?" he growled. "The witch may have put up the wall around my realm, but at least she kept herself on the other side of it."

"I tore down that wall," Emmi said. "And I only want to talk."

The power faded from the king's palms. "You...you took down the wall?" He cocked his head, as if listening to something.

In the distance, so faint that it was almost inaudible, they could hear the hunting horn.

The king straightened, turning back to Emmi. His entire demeanor changed. His eyes crinkled at the corners as he smiled. "Take away your shield; I will not hurt you."

Emmi wasn't so sure of that, but she didn't want to bring the king's wrath on her any more, and keeping the barrier up would be disrespectful. She twirled her hands, and the protection faded. Puck took a step closer to her, touching her elbow, reminding her that he had her back.

"I have hated that wall for centuries," the king said. "Walls are not good for hunts. We could still find ways to track our prey, of course, but the wall made things...difficult." His eyes raked over Emmi. "You do not look like a witch."

"My name is Emmi."

Puck sucked in a breath through his teeth, and Emmi was reminded too late that names were important to the fae. She may not know her flower lore, but she knew the legends. *Never give your name to the fae,* she reminded herself. Had she or Puck mentioned her name in front of Joan? She didn't think so. But she recalled the way Puck had talked about names limiting people, trapping them. Even queens and kings.

"I am called Gwyn ap Nudd," the king said. "Or, I used to be called such."

Emmi felt tension coiling inside her. It felt...treacherous to just be talking with this man. This king. Joan had been very clear about how dangerous it was to speak with her. But this king seemed more ominous now that he wasn't attacking. She wished she could put the shield back up.

"You are a witch who takes down walls instead of erecting them. And you took down a wall I personally hated." The king smiled, and Emmi felt her knees go weak with fear. "I will grant you a favor."

Emmi didn't need to be told twice. "I want my grandfather back," she said.

Puck's hand snaked down her arm, and he slipped his fingers through hers, squeezing them. A warning. She shook his hand away and took a step closer to the king, not backing down.

Gwyn shook his head. "You ask too much."

"You didn't set limits to your favor. You asked what I wanted. I want my grandfather."

"A trade must be fair," the king said, and there was a dangerous edge to his voice now. "A wall for a person? It is not equal."

Emmi let out a frustrated breath. "Then tell me where he is," she said.

"See, now, that's fair. You gave me information by telling me of the freedom of my realm. I shall give you information in return." Gwyn smiled, all teeth bared. "Your grandfather is with my hunters."

Emmi's hand shot out, grabbing Puck's, gripping his fingers. She could barely process the information. They had been right! Grandfather was *here*, somewhere. The horn sounded again, even fainter, and Emmi tilted her head to the sound.

When she focused on the king again, she saw that his eyes were on the way she held Puck's hand. His gaze drifted up, a different sort of smile twisting his lips as he met Puck's eyes. Something seemed to be communicated between them, but Emmi wasn't sure what.

She only knew that Puck's hand was shaking, trembling.

In terror.

She set her jaw and drew the king's attention back to her. "What will it take for you to give me my grandfather back?" she demanded.

"What will you give me?" the king asked.

Emmi opened her mouth. *Anything*, she was about to say, but

Puck acted quick as lightning, yanking her to him and throwing his hand over her mouth, silencing the word.

Promising *anything* to the fae was a dangerous bargain indeed.

The king chuckled.

Puck's grip on Emmi was viselike, and she could tell that he pressed his hand over her mouth so hard because he was afraid. She wiggled against his arms, letting him know she would be more careful with her words. When he let her go, she didn't say anything at all, lips pressed tight together as she glared at Gwyn.

The king seemed more amused than anything else, and when he presented his offer, he spoke casually, as if he didn't really care about the outcome. "A person for a person. *That* would be a fair trade."

"What person do you want?" Emmi asked, bile rising in her throat. Could she really trade one life for another? What if he wanted her? What if he wanted some innocent person?

"Another witch. One named Orddu. Give me her, and I'll give you your grandfather." The king paused. "Do we have a deal?"

Emmi glanced up at Puck. His brow was furrowed, deep in thought, trying to figure out the loophole or catch. He gave Emmi a little shrug.

"Deal," Emmi told the king. She would find Orddu, somehow, and at least see if the witch would come willingly with her. If not—she would figure out another way to save her grandfather. She didn't *need* the king. She didn't *have* to fulfill the bargain. She could save Grandfather some other way.

Emmi blinked, and King Gwyn was gone. She jumped back in surprise, Puck catching her.

"That was terrifying," Puck said, his shoulders sagging.

Emmi bit her lip. It was clear that King Gwyn was powerful, perhaps even more powerful than Joan, but while the conversation had been fraught, it hadn't felt as frightening as Puck seemed to think it had been. She wondered what he saw when he looked at the king, or what he had seen in the past to make him so afraid.

"Is he really gone?" Emmi asked. She used her magic, but still could not see any trace of where the man had been.

"I think so." Puck let out a haggard breath. He seemed exhausted. "Do you know this Orddu witch?"

Emmi shook her head. The name seemed faintly familiar, but she couldn't place it.

"I think...that may have gone as well as we could have hoped."

"At least we know where Grandfather is," Emmi pointed out.

"And he'll likely be kept alive," Puck added. "If the king wants to trade him."

Emmi felt as if she'd been punched in the gut. She hadn't considered that the fae may kill her grandfather, but of course...it was the Wild Hunt. Its whole purpose was to hunt and kill.

"Let's go home," Puck said. He slipped his hand in his pocket, pulling out ash that he must have picked up from the hearth before they'd gone through the portal.

"Wait," Emmi said. She used her magical sight on the clearing one more time, focusing on the flowers. "Remember the song? 'The king was in his counting house, counting out his money...'" She looked up at Puck. "These flower petals aren't what they seem to be."

She bent down, plucking a single petal of a single flower. The yellow petal glimmered, shining, and even as she pinched it between her fingers, she felt it harden and thicken, shifting into a gold coin.

Puck's eyes widened. "No," he said immediately.

"What do you mean, 'no?'" Emmi said. "We *need* protection, that's clear. If both the Witch Hunters and the fae Wild Hunt is after my family, I *need* to make that witch bottle as soon as possible. I gave the woman on the tor Elspeth's gold coin. Don't you think *this* is the gold coin I need for the next ingredient in the bottle?"

"*No,*" Puck said again, emphatically.

"It's a sign!" Emmi said. "The silver-eyed woman told us about the blackbirds. They brought us to the king, the person we needed to see. And they brought us to the object we need, a gold coin!"

Puck shook his head. "This is a bad idea, Emmi. No. You shouldn't steal from the fae. It cannot go well."

Emmi flipped the coin with her thumb, the golden disk catching the twilight sun's lights, flickering as it fell back into her palm. "I need protection," she said, sure of herself. "I need a gold coin for the witch bottle. *This* gold coin."

It felt right. It felt like fate. But Puck was shaking his head, fear in his eyes. "You can't steal from the king of the fae and expect things to go well, Emmi," he said.

"Next time I see that king," Emmi said, "I'm going to have a completed witch bottle with me. I'm going to have *real* protection. And I'm going to get my grandfather back."

The Hierophant, Transposed

Rebellion, Unconventional Actions, and Questioning Authority

"**A**re you sure?" Puck asked, staring at the coin in Emmi's hand as if it were a venomous snake.

Emmi crammed it into her pocket. "Sure," she said, her voice exuding confidence.

Puck made the ash sigil portal, and they both stepped through. Emmi blinked, momentarily blinded by the difference in light. It had been nighttime in Glastonbury, a weird in-between twilight in the Otherworld, and now dim and dark in Elspeth's hearth room.

Puck flicked his fingers toward some of the candles scattered over the mantle. They ignited in soft flame.

"No!" Emmi said, striding over the carpet and blowing the candles out. "Those are a hundred percent beeswax."

"Aren't most candles?" Puck asked. Even in the semi-darkness, Emmi could see his confusion.

"They're just very expensive," Emmi said, deciding not to explain soy candles to the fae. Grandfather had the same beeswax candles on sale in the gift shop out front, and Emmi knew exactly how expensive the handcrafted items were. "Besides," Emmi added, flicking the light switch and filling the room with bright white light, "this is better."

Puck squinted. "Is it?"

There was still a tiny glowing ember at the tip of one of the wicks, and long wisps of smoke curled around Puck. His jaw was tight, his shoulders bunched up. Emmi could tell that he was still on edge, and his nerves put *her* on edge. She reached into her pocket, pulling the coin out.

The coin was thin—she needed to be careful, because it could have easily bent in her pocket. The metal was warm from her body temperature, shiny and gold. On one side was writing she couldn't read, the clear swirl of markings that looked something between a letter a rune, but she had no idea what it meant.

On the reverse, the coin was etched with a flower, the same delicate simple flower that she had seen in the field. Now that she didn't have the king of the fair folk looking down at her, Emmi allowed herself to look a little closer at the flower's shape. Elspeth's speciality had been in botany, and Emmi had picked up some from what she'd studied.

"It's a primrose, I think," she said slowly. Puck glanced at the engraving and shrugged, unsure. "Well, it's still a coin," Emmi said. "And that's what we needed." She flicked the golden coin into the black cauldron across from the hearth.

As before, the cauldron temporarily emanated with a yellow glow, sparkles of magic bubbling up.

But this time, there were silver, reflective streaks through the yellow. Emmi blinked, and the silvery light seemed to fade to nothing. But she was still certain she had seen it, certain it had been real.

"Everything okay?" Puck asked, watching her.

"Yes," Emmi said firmly. Then her eyes adjusted on what Puck held. He'd picked up the weapon of the Witch Hunter, the cold iron with the hidden needle. "What are you doing with that?"

Puck put it on the mantle next to the now-dead candles. "Just putting it away."

"So, we have the heart-shaped stone and the pottery piece with a stain of...something," she said. Two more items for the witch bottle, and then she would have all she needed to protect herself, her grandfather, and the fae. They were *so* close—more than halfway there—but Grandfather was trapped in the Other-world, and Emmi certainly didn't feel closer to saving him.

Who is Orddu? Emmi thought. How was she supposed to find a complete stranger...and even if she did, how could she turn this person over to Gwyn ap Nudd, even in exchange for her grandfather?

The thing was, though, that name sounded familiar. Like...*really* familiar. But Emmi couldn't place it...

She let out a long breath. Well, she didn't really know what direction to take either of the objects she had remaining to make her own witch bottle, just as she didn't know who Orddu was or what to do with the new task Gwyn ap Nudd had given her. The only real clue she had right now was the flower. Puck had mentioned that flowers had meanings, and she knew Elspeth had devoted her life to the magic of flowers.

"Where are you going?" Puck asked as Emmi headed out of the room.

"Elspeth's botany room," she said. They'd been there once before, when Puck had asked for a map, but they hadn't examined any of the countless little vials and bottles Elspeth had gathered over her lifetime of study.

Walking through the halls of the home-turned-museum gave Emmi a little familiarity that she'd been missing. There was so much out of her control, but at least she knew where her roots were. That was more important to her than she'd ever realized before.

It reminded her of brownies, the type of fae she'd been disguised as earlier. She used to think of fae as otherworldly, important creatures with grand destinies. The only fae in the stories she'd read as a child cast the elves as mighty hunters, the trolls as powerful brutes, the fae as guardians of the mystical with vast power that could bend the forests to their will.

But there were a lot of creatures Emmi hadn't really considered before. Little wisps that just wanted to float and glimmer in the dark shadows of the trees, brownies that wanted to care for their homes, sprites that buzzed around like hummingbirds, with no grander purpose than to take joy in their own flight.

Emmi didn't think she was the type of girl who would have wanted to fight alongside hobbits or go through the wardrobe and be crowned a queen. But she did think that, maybe, doing something to help the brownies and the wisps and the sprites might be within her reach.

It was definitely worth trying.

"At the very least, anyway," Emmi continued, pushing open the door to the botany room, "I want to find out what primroses symbolize. *If* the flower the coin came from actually was a primrose." It wasn't much of a lead to follow, but it was the only direction she had.

Morning light poured through the windows as the sun started to rise. Because this room faced the back yard, Emmi rarely bothered with the curtains, so the sun was unfiltered as it painted the room in yellow and orange.

Puck wandered over to the maps as Emmi headed to the books. Emmi knew that it had been the Victorians, long after Elspeth's time, who had done most of the "language of flowers" and symbolism behind blooms, but Emmi had also spent her summers categorizing and reading Elspeth's books, the real ones, written in her own hand accompanied by tiny, faded illustrations.

Elspeth's private journal listed flowers in roughly alphabetical order, although Elspeth had made various out-of-placement additions and revisions throughout the book as she came across new flowers and herbs to record. Still, it was fairly easy for Emmi to find to the page on primroses.

The watercolors Elspeth had used were faded, but there was still a hint of pale yellow clinging to the blossom she'd illustrated. Emmi had no doubt left in her mind; the flowers Gwyn ap Nudd had been standing in, counting as if they were gold, had been primroses.

"Primroses are symbolic of protection," Emmi said to Puck, reading Elspeth's scrawling handwriting. "I definitely think taking the gold coin from Gwyn's field was the right thing to do."

Puck cringed more than smiled, which was not very reassuring.

Emmi looked back at the book, ready to close it and carefully return it to the shelf, but then her eyes fell on the opposite page. A delicate purple-pink flower that looked like a crocus was illustrated along the spine. Elspeth had written out the word *Colchium* across the top of the page, the name of the species of flower. The symbolic meaning of the flower was scribbled underneath it.

My best days are behind me.

It seemed ominous at best, especially the way the ink was so thick, as if Elspeth had written over the words two or three times, truly believing in them.

But what drew Emmi's eye was the list of sub-species under the Colchium. There were several different types of this flower. Meadow saffron, which Elspeth noted created a deadly poison. An autumnal variant nicknamed "naked lady."

And, at the bottom of the list, a variant of the flower called "ordu."

Emmi brushed her finger across the word. While Emmi was fairly certain that Elspeth had been the one to add the name to the list, she thought there was a good chance that it had been added later. Not only was the ink a different color—blue instead of black—the handwriting was a little shakier and thinner.

"Ordu," Emmi read aloud, looking up to Puck.

He turned to her. "What?"

"There's a flower called 'colchium ordu,'" Emmi said.

"A flower?" Puck's eyebrow rose. "You think when Gwyn ap Nudd said 'Orddu,' he meant a flower?"

"No, but this can't be a coincidence." Emmi had thought from the start that "Orddu" sounded familiar. Perhaps she had read it in this book. That didn't feel right, though. She didn't remember this exact book among the many in the room.

She shoved the thought aside. There was one more thing she could check.

Emmi headed deeper into the room, closer to the windows. She could hear Puck following at her heels. "Elspeth took detailed notes, but she also gathered samples," Emmi said. "She was really scientific about her studies."

The science part of Elspeth's history—making medications from herbs, studying the properties of plants, and even creating her own hybrids—had been the source of Emmi's fascination with her ancestor. She had always assumed that Elspeth's contemporaries called her a witch because they didn't understand how a woman could be a scientist.

Now she was realizing that Elspeth had been a witch, a scientist, and a woman—a dangerous combination indeed.

Emmi stopped in front of the shallow shelves that lined the back wall, tiny glass bottles with wax or cork stoppers standing in neat, carefully organized rows. This part of the room was carefully organized. Emmi should know; she was the one who most often took the bottles down and cleaned them. She ran her finger along the shelf, pausing at the row of colchium flowers that had been preserved. Elspeth had used salt to preserve the flowers, and while many had crumbled to dust at the bottom of their jars over the centuries, some still remained, the petals crisp but beautifully curled. Each bottle had a tiny label written in Elspeth's own hand.

"This one," Emmi breathed, plucking a finger-sized vial off the shelf. The label affixed around it with a bit of twine labeled the flower *Colchium ordu*.

"What's wrong with it?" Puck asked, looking over her shoulder.

Emmi tilted the bottle, and the gray-beige flower rattled against the glass. Emmi was meticulously careful in how she handled the delicate flowers when she cleaned this room, and she had always moved the bottles with such care that the contents didn't shift in their glass chambers. This one, though, clinked as if the flower inside was stone. Now that she had the illustration from the book fresh in her mind, Emmi realized that this flower should be purplish, not pale and sandy colored.

"There's something on the back," Puck said, pointing to the label.

Emmi turned the card over. "It's the location of where she got the sample," Emmi said, reading the text. "Knaresborough."

Excited, Puck raced back over to the maps on the wall. "There's a town in Yorkshire with that name," he said, pointing.

Emmi looked at the map. It wasn't much to go on—a stone flower and a town name.

But it was something.

FIVE OF SWORDS, TRANSPOSED

EMOTIONAL TURMOIL, REJECTION, MISFORTUNE, AND REGRET

Emmi stared at the map, then looked down at the vial with the stone flower in her hand. She felt like she was heading in the right direction, but it also seemed painfully clear that she was missing *something*. It frustrated her, like trying to remember something that was on the tip of her tongue or forgetting the answer to a question the moment the teacher called on her.

"I just *know* I've heard the name 'Orddu' before," Emmi muttered. And it didn't have anything to do with a flower, one made of stone or not.

"Oh, yeah," Puck said casually, shrugging. "I know Orddu."

Emmi's head snapped up. "What?" She realized that while Gwyn ap Nudd had asked her to find Orddu and she had no idea who that was, she hadn't actually told Puck that she was uncertain. She's just been musing on it silently. "You know this witch?"

Puck leaned against the wall, his shoulder on the map, tilting the frame until Emmi pushed him off it. "Orddu's not *a* witch," Puck said, readjusting his position as if he'd meant to be there all along. "Orddu's a title."

Emmi shot him a look which Puck accurately interpreted as, *Get to the point before I hit you.*

"In the early times, witches were more..." He bit his lip, thinking of the right word. "They were closer to magic. It's not that they were more powerful, exactly, but they were more in tune with magic. And, okay, look." Puck pushed off the wall, spreading his hands out, leaning in as he got more impassioned in his speech. "So magic is kind of like on a spectrum. And the spectrum lines up with the different elements and types of magic. And also life and death."

Emmi knew her face was twisted in confusion. Puck glanced at her, screwing up his lips as he tried to think of a better way to explain.

"On one side," he continued, shaking his left hand toward Emmi. "There's black magic."

"Black magic?" Emmi said. "Like...evil?"

Puck shook his head. "No, no, black magic is night magic. The spells that work better in the dark, or under a certain moon. The creatures that are nocturnal. And spells involving death."

"Death? Death sounds evil." Emmi was envisioning the red caps again, as well as every superstition she'd seen cycled through media.

But Puck was even more emphatic in his answer. "No, death isn't evil. It's just a thing. A part of the spectrum." His arms were still spread apart, and he shook his right hand. "On the other side of the spectrum is white magic. Daytime stuff. Sun spells. Diurnal animals."

"And life."

"Well, healing spells are white magic. But it's not like black is evil and white is good. It's just day and night."

Emmi frowned, still unsure about this description. "Well, where is Orddu in all that?"

Puck spread his fingers out, as if he were gripping the air. "Witches and fae—any creature that taps into the magic—they're *also* on the spectrum. And it *is* a spectrum. Some creatures are strictly on one side." Puck shook his left hand again. "And some are on the other." Puck shook his right. "But there are a lot of creatures that are sort of in the middle."

Emmi's brow furrowed. "Like how Joan came to us in the night," she started.

Puck nodded. "Wills-o'-the-wisp and Joan are black magic, nocturnal."

And they're known for killing, Emmi reminded herself. Wills-o'-the-wisp weren't just pretty lights that only appeared in the dark; they were mischief makers who'd guide nighttime voyagers astray, leading them to their deaths.

"Meanwhile," Emmi said slowly, "in the Otherworld, through the portal...it was like it was twilight there."

"Crepuscular."

"What?"

"Crepuscular—creatures that aren't akin to the night or the day, but instead prefer twilight and dawn hours." Puck spread his arms even wider. "It's a *spectrum*."

"Okay, fine, it's a spectrum, but where is Orddu?" Emmi said, losing her patience.

"Most witches fall in the middle—they're not necessarily linked to black or white magic. They're neutral. They see things, but they're not inclined toward one action or another. But," Puck said, continuing when it looked like Emmi would interrupt him, "some powerful witches *are* on the edges of the spectrum. A black witch is known as an orddu."

"So... an orddu is basically the manager of the night shift of magic?" Emmi asked.

Puck smirked. "That'll work. And a white witch is known as an orwen."

That name again...Emmi knew she had heard both "orddu" and "orwen" before, and not like how Puck was describing them. She pushed the thought from her mind, focusing on Puck's information. She supposed she herself was somewhere in the middle ground, a person who could see magic but didn't really have an affinity toward any specific type of spell. She was a neutral observer, in the middle of Puck's spectrum.

But that meant some witches weren't. Some were powerful enough to do more than see. Emmi's eye roved around the botany room. The samples of flowers and handwritten books had always felt...comforting to her. But Elspeth seemed to be more powerful than Emmi had realized before. Was she a white witch or a black witch? Even if "black magic" was more about a specific affinity than anything monstrous, it was hard for Emmi to shift the years of subtle messaging in everything from *The Wizard of Oz* to medieval texts that "black magic" meant an evil witch.

Puck finally dropped his hands, satisfied that Emmi understood him. "Honestly, though, I'm surprised this information got lost in time. Powerful enough witches to be called an Orddu or an Orwen are rare, true, but I would have thought there would at least be stories..."

"Stories!" Emmi shouted, snapping her fingers. "That's it!"

Puck's eye grew wide at her outburst.

"I've been trying to think of where I heard those names before—they're from a *book* I read!" Emmi turned and headed to the door, Puck at her heels. "I used to love those books as a kid. And they made a movie! A cartoon—no one's ever heard of it, but I was obsessed as a kid."

"A movie?" Puck mused. "I've always wanted to see one of those."

Emmi stopped in her tracks, and Puck crashed into her. "You've never seen a movie?"

Puck shrugged. "Why would I have?"

Fair enough, Emmi supposed. Puck was so modern compared to the other fae she'd met. He almost seemed like a regular teenage boy.

But he's not, she reminded herself, the words twisting inside her. She swallowed them down, the taste bitter.

"I forget you're fae sometimes," Emmi admitted.

Puck raised his eyebrows.

"It's just...you at least *know* about movies, right?" Emmi asked. Puck nodded, and she continued. "I don't think Joan or Gwyn ap Nudd or the sprites are aware of anything so...human."

"No." Puck's voice was low. Sad. "I don't think they are. They spend more time in the Otherworld."

"And you've been blocked from it."

Puck's jaw was tight. Emmi wanted to ask more, to press him for information, but she waited, silent. They were in a dim corridor, partway between the botany room and the library, probably the area of the house furtherest from a window and any natural light.

Weariness settled over Emmi like a blanket. She needed sleep, food. Rest. A moment to think and reassess. But she reached toward Puck, grabbing his hand, her thumb running over his knuckles. "Where have you been?" she asked. He hadn't been in the fae lands, but he hadn't really been here, in the regular world.

Puck cringed. "A sort of...in-between place," he said. "Not in the Otherworld, not in this world. But I was more in this world than the fae world, and I got impressions as time passed."

So he picked up on the idea of movies, without ever seeing one before.

Emmi's heart thudded. "How...how much time passed?" she asked.

Puck pulled his hand out of hers. "A lot." He looked over her shoulder, as if he wanted to push past her, but he wasn't sure what direction to take. Elspeth's house could be labyrinthine, especially this corridor that wasn't a part of the regular tour of the Museum of Magic and therefore had no helpful signs pointing out where to go.

"What was it like?" Emmi asked.

Puck didn't meet her eyes. "A dream. A nightmare." His mouth moved, as if he wanted to speak more, but the words were gumming up his teeth. "I'd go in and out of awareness. I picked up some things, but time was...different."

Asleep for centuries, drowsy and just on the edge of

consciousness. Emmi couldn't imagine it. But looking at Puck's face now, she thought it must have been horrible, wherever he was. *Under a spell, I suppose,* she thought. She wanted to ask him how he broke free, how he winded up, of all places, in *her* house. But Puck looked as if he were going to be physically ill as he spoke of it.

Emmi rearranged her face into a sunny smile. "Well, I'm pretty sure the king of the fair folk wasn't talking about a cartoon from the eighties. When all this is done, you and me are going to watch that movie together, okay? Popcorn's on me."

One corner of Puck's lips twitched up as he focused on her. "Deal," he said.

"It's a date," Emmi said, tentatively, watching Puck's face for a flicker of recognition at what her words may connote.

Puck, however, seemed oblivious. "So...the library?"

"Yup!" Emmi said with forced cheeriness. "This way."

She pushed open the door and looked at the shelves of books. It wasn't always great, living in a museum, but having access to her own library whenever she wanted it was probably the best perk there was.

She crossed over to the shelves against the north wall, where fiction was kept. It took her only seconds to find a copy of the Prydain Chronicles by Lloyd Alexander, a large book that collected the first three volumes of the series into one binding. "Here," she said, tossing the book to Puck. "This is the story I was thinking of. The movie is called *The Black Cauldron*, and it's about a boy who's an assistant pig keeper, and he becomes a hero by the end. It's really good." Emmi's voice trailed off as Puck turned the book over in his hands, his fingers running across the cracked and worn spine.

This wasn't just any copy of the book; this was *her* copy. The pages were soft, some of them bent, some of them smudged from her finger running over the ink.

These were the books Emmi had read after she lost her parents. Grandfather had given them to her on the first night *he* had tucked her into bed, not her mother or father. He told her how he first read the books to her mother when she was a little girl, how they'd stayed up late at night together, sneaking past Emmi's grandmother in order to read just one more chapter together.

Emmi hadn't let Grandfather read them aloud to her. "I know how to read!" she'd shouted at him. As a child, she had been ignorant of anyone's grief but her own, cognizant only that her father and mother were gone, one after the other, without realizing that meant Grandfather had lost a daughter and son-in-law of his own.

Grandfather had left the book on the nightstand for her.

And Emmi had started to explore Prydain. She'd gotten lost in the pages of that book. *That* book, the one in Puck's hands now. It wasn't just the story, it was that specific book, the one her grandfather had read to her mother as a child, the one she had plunged into in order to escape her life, and instead found a new one.

Part of her wanted to snatch the book back. It was too precious. It held not only the story, but also a part of her heart.

But Puck held the book gently in his hands, like a woodland animal that needed help. He tucked it into his pocket carefully, patting the material of his pants. He must have used a form of magic as the book was too large to fit in a normal pocket, and this one seemed to disappear inside.

When he looked up, Puck's eyes were sincere. "I promise to take care of this book and to read every word inside it," he said reverently. For all that Puck joked and for all Emmi knew of how fae twisted words, this was a vow she knew without a doubt Puck would keep.

Her story was safe with him.

Three of Cups, Transposed

Misfortune, Stagnation, and Untrustworthiness

The system to organize books in Elspeth's library was odd, to say the least, but Emmi knew it like the back of her hand. It was a system she had made, after all.

"Huh," Puck said, looking at an old leather bound book curiously. *The Banishing and Summoning of Powerful Fae* was scratched on the cover, almost invisible due to age and wear.

Emmi plucked the tome out of his hands and slid it home on the shelf. "We need *this* section," she said authoritatively, leading him to the far side of the wall. She didn't recall Knaresborough specifically, but there were books on York here, and that was close enough. She pulled down a few appendices and catalogues, including a handwritten pamphlet of herbs that Elspeth had made, the pages crisp with age, prone to crumbling.

Emmi carefully opened it up, peering at the index her ancestor had carefully printed in the front. She saw nothing in there about colchicum flowers, in real life or made of stone.

"This is probably what we're looking for," Puck said, reaching over Emmi's shoulder and pulling a thin book down. Emmi was about to snap at him—*she* knew this library better than anyone—but then she saw the title on the spine: *The Witch of York.*

"Ah. Yeah. I suppose that might be it." Emmi took the book from Puck, and they sat down next to each other on the floor, the book open between them.

Emmi read as quickly as possible. The book was a biography of a woman named Ursula Sontheil who had been born to a young fifteen-year-old girl who never revealed the father. Orphaned, destitute, and with no one to aid her, Ursula's mother lived in a cave and gave birth alone.

"It's so sad," Emmi said, touching an engraved illustration in the book of a young woman holding a bundled baby at the mouth of a cave. Ursula's mother had been at least two years younger than Emmi was now, and, according to the book, died not long after her baby was born. The townspeople called the mother a witch and the daughter the spawn of Satan. *Meanwhile,* Emmi couldn't help but think, *whoever had sexually abused Ursula's mother got away with it. Or at least never faced the same punishment they did.*

Mother and newborn daughter spent two years living in the forest, scavenging, barely surviving, before an abbot intervened, separating them. The mother was sent to a convent where she soon died; Ursula was given to a foster family and never saw her birth mother again.

Emmi turned the page of the book, where a crude illustration of a woman peered back at her. With a large nose covered in pock marks, dull eyes, scraggly hair, and even a pointed hat, this portrait of Ursula seemed to illustrate every cliché of a witch there was.

"Do you think she really looked like this?" Emmi asked Puck, unable to take her eyes off the illustration.

"Who knows?"

The text described Ursula as having crooked legs and a hunched back. That could have been the result of her birth or malnutrition or injuries she had as a young child, barely surviving in the woods. Or it could be exaggerations, the smallest flaw blown up to hyperbolic proportions to excuse the cruel behavior of the townspeople who never accepted her. Emmi was struck by the futility of it all; Ursula had been doomed before she'd been born.

"Descriptions like this could be a response to her power," Puck said. "I've seen that sort of thing happen before. She was called the Witch of York for a reason—her power was renowned. And if a woman has one type of power..."

"People try to take away her other type." Loathe as Emmi was to admit it, there was power in beauty. Superficial, yes, but a beautiful woman could leverage her looks in astounding ways. Anne Boleyn was proof enough of that, as was Helen of Troy and Marilyn Monroe. So if this Ursula Sontheil had respect for her witchcraft, it was shockingly unsurprising that the locals would try to tear her down in other ways, mocking her appearance and exaggerating her every flaw.

Emmi's stomach soured. Here, once more, was a woman who was treated cruelly, all because she was different. Just like Joan Wytte, whose toothache sent her to jail, or Agnes Sampson, an easy target after being widowed, Ursula Sontheil had been cursed by her gender, her status in society, and misfortune.

Even when Ursula married, she was dogged by loss. Her identity was changed, and she became known as Mother Shipton. When her husband died soon after, the townspeople blamed her for the death, driving her out of town and back to the very cave she'd been born in.

The next page showed a twist to the story. Mother Shipton, as she'd become well-known as, carved a spot for herself in the society that had rejected her. She took the claims of being a witch and wore the label with pride, turning simple charms into a business, making herbal potions, telling prophecies, and becoming so well known that records of her witchcraft reached the king of England. When she died, she died of old age in her early seventies —not on a stake or in a prison cell.

She survived, Emmi thought, smiling. She had been given the worst possible cards in life, and she had survived it all.

"Do you think she had real magic?" Emmi asked, staring at another picture of Mother Shipton, this one a kinder portrayal.

"Maybe." Puck sounded noncommittal. His eyes were not focused on the illustration, but Emmi couldn't tell what he was looking at.

Emmi stared at the portrait in the book, shifting her eyesight. It was almost like those Magic Eye renderings Grandfather liked, where Emmi could see a leaping dolphin or a floating heart amidst a chaotic mess of patterned colors if she just let her eyes unfocus. Mother Shipton's face blurred in her vision, and she almost...she *almost*...maybe she did see something there? A bit of a sparkling sheen, a golden halo clinging to the image...

"Maybe she really did have magic," Emmi said softly. "Or maybe she got it."

"Got it?" Puck asked. "Magic cannot be transferred without a tool like what the Hunters use. Do you think she—"

"No, not like that," Emmi interrupted. "I mean, the fact that she wasn't killed for being a witch came in part because she claimed the title. People were going to be afraid of her, so she just made them afraid in a way that kept them from killing her." Emmi nodded to herself. "Their fear gave her power, and she used it."

"Are you saying because they called her a witch, she became one?" Puck asked in a flat tone.

"At least enough of one to ensure that she was strong enough to survive."

Puck scowled at the book. "It doesn't work like that," he said. His tone was carefully measured, but Emmi could see emotion welling inside him, strangling his throat. "Naming something— forcing a label on someone, one they don't want—it only ever hurts."

Emmi chewed on her bottom lip. This wasn't the first time he'd said something like that before, but she didn't fully agree with him. Sometimes, there *was* power in claiming a label thrust upon you. Emmi had been called weird in elementary school—something she could almost understand, since she grew up in a witch's house—and it wasn't until she'd started self-identifying as strange that the other kids realized they couldn't hurt her with the name calling.

But Puck seemed to mean something more than school ground taunting, and until she fully understood his story, she resolved not to press the issue.

"I don't see how this is linked, though," Emmi said, pulling out the vial with the stone flower in it. "I'm going to try to...you know. See." It felt awkward to state flatly she intended to use her magic.

Puck leaned back, watching her. Emmi tried to ignore him as she focused. Her vision shifted, the magic coming more readily than it had when she'd tried to get a read on Mother Shipton's illustration. That had been a faint, ghostly overlay that could have been nothing more than her imagination. But this?

This was magic.

While previously all of Emmi's magical sight had been linked to her vision, her other senses came into play as she stared at the beige stone flower. The air felt chilly, enough to make the hairs on her arm stand up. A shiver tickled her spine. Emmi could smell the distinct scent of water, the air moist, not in a humid way, but a damp way. Distantly, she heard the steady pulse of a *drip, drip, drip*. It felt like...

"The cave," Emmi breathed, opening her eyes. When had she shut them? It had all felt so *real*. Her gaze met Puck's. "We have to go to the cave," she said. It was where Ursula—Mother Shipton—had been born, and where she had died. It was where she claimed the label witch. A place designed to bring her low, an exile from civilization, a life in the wilderness—it had all become the source of this woman's power. It all centered on the cave.

And it was where, Emmi was certain, there were answers.

Puck went to a small desk under the window, picking up a

crumpled piece of paper and holding it in his cupped palm. The paper burst into flames, then pooled into ash. Puck drew the sigil, and a portal sprang up.

There it was—the scent of damp earth, mossy and green but still fresh. Emmi let out a sigh, relief flooding her system. This was *right* in a way she couldn't describe.

"After you," Puck said, gesturing.

Emmi stepped through the portal into Knaresborough.

———

A cool breeze rushed her as her feet landed on soft earth. Puck followed her, the portal closing.

"No one around," Emmi said, looking around. They stood on a path near a broad river that curved into trees that cast long, dark shadows. Emmi's eyes trailed up, taking in the full breadth of an enormous, towering stone viaduct that traversed the water. While they seemed to be in a park, across from them, the river's edge was dotted with picturesque houses, ivy covered brick home beside quaint cottages of white plaster. Flowers spilled over the sides of window boxes, and a few rowboats meandered lazily over the water.

The calm serenity of the scene was broken by the sound of a loud hammer pounding, punctuated by a little boy's excited voice.

Emmi rushed down the path. Tucked into the glen were a dozen or more tree trunks, branches sawed off, laying on their sides, the wood black with age and damp. Each of the enormous trunks was riddled with round metal disks, so many that it looked like metal dragon scales had replaced the bark of the fallen trees.

"Sorry!" an older man called to them as a young blonde-headed boy whacked at one of the trees with a hammer attached to a chain.

Emmi shot Puck a look, and the two of them climbed up the low hill toward the boy and, presumably, his grandfather. "What are you doing?" Emmi asked. The little boy had not paused in his single-minded focus of hitting the tree trunk with a hammer, driving a coin into the wood.

Emmi could tell now that she was closer that all the disks in the wood were coins jutting out, hundreds of them. Most were British, but she spotted lots of euros and even pennies and dimes from America.

"Do you need the hammer?" the grandfather asked. "Hurry up, Sam."

"No, it's okay—" Emmi started to say.

The little boy, Sam, didn't look up. "I. Am. Getting. My. Wish," he said, slamming the metal hammer against his coin with each word, missing the mark at least half the time.

"Wish trees," Puck said in a low voice, touching Emmi's elbow and leading her away, back to the path. "It's an old tradition, and they've sort of bungled it, as usual."

"Jamming coins into logs is an old tradition?" Emmi asked.

"The fae don't do anything for free," Puck answered. "But in the old days, if you offered them something they wanted, they may help you."

Emmi recalled the stories of leaving out a bowl of cream for brownies or dropping something shiny for the elves of the woods.

"Does it work?" Emmi asked.

"Who can say? Sometimes you leave an offering, and no one takes it. Sometimes they do." A flicker of a scowl crossed Puck's face. "And the fae always pay their debts."

A few yards away, the little boy whooped in joy, having finally hammered the coin into the tree trunk to his satisfaction. Emmi cast her eyes over the logs studded with metal.

Here were hundreds of coins, each an offering to the fae, a request for a wish. What would have happened if Emmi hadn't given her ancestor's coin to the silver-eyed fae woman in Glastonbury? If she had saved it and instead hammered the coin into the wood...would that have meant another coin would have appeared to her here, glowing with the golden light that meant it was perfect for the witch bottle?

Unease twisted inside her. Emmi had felt so confident to take the coin from Gwyn ap Nudd's meadow, but now she realized she may have acted too rashly. Here was an alternate, safer option had she only been willing to wait. To listen to Puck.

Puck looked down at her, expression grave, as if he could read her thoughts.

"I don't know about you," he started, his voice low. Emmi's stomach sank. He was going to blame her, he was going to tell her how wrong she had been, he was going to— "But I'm *starving,*" Puck finished.

"What?" Emmi blinked.

Puck nodded down the wooded path at an enormous teapot next to a truck that had been converted to a food stand, both painted in charming Tiffany blue. "You're paying!" Puck called cheerily as he headed toward the cart, leaving Emmi behind with her dark worries.

THE DEVIL,
TRANSPOSED

FEELING TRAPPED AND FINDING A WAY OUT

W hile there were a few white metal tables and chairs in front of the tea truck, Puck plunked down on a trimmed tree trunk that had clearly been positioned as overflow seating. He balanced a paper plate with an enormous scone on his lap as Emmi paid and picked up her own scone, as well as two cups of tea.

"Do we have to sit on a log?" Emmi asked, but she was already throwing one leg up as she shimmied over the dark, worn surface.

"I like this place." Puck wriggled on the log, getting more comfortable. "And I like this food." He inhaled the still-warm scone, his eyes rolling in the back of his head.

"How do we do this, anyway?" Emmi muttered. The lady in the tea truck had given them small tubs of both jam and something that looked like whipped butter. Emmi dabbed a thin layer of the creamy substance on the corner of her scone and nibbled.

Puck's eyes narrowed at her.

"What?" Emmi asked.

Shooting her an *I-can't-believe-you* look, Puck dumped the entire tub of the buttery stuff on the top of his scone, then scooped out the whole container of raspberry jam on top of it.

With another look, this one plainly saying, *This is the proper way,* Puck shoved the slathered scone into his mouth.

"That was like an inch of butter!" Emmi protested.

"Not butter," Puck said, crumbs flying from his lips. "Clotted cream."

"Clotted" didn't sound that appealing, but Emmi tried the scone Puck's way, piling the stuff on thick.

Heaven.

It was pure heaven.

Unlike scones Emmi had gotten in America, this scone was soft and decadent, somewhere between a cake and a biscuit. The clotted cream cut the sweetness of the jam but made the whole scone taste richer.

"Now tea," Puck said, lifting his paper cup and taking a sip while there was clearly still a bite of scone in his mouth. Emmi copied him, relishing the hot, slightly sweet liquid that made the scone melt. Grandfather would dunk his donuts in his coffee, but this? This was so much better.

For several minutes, neither of them spoke, busy chewing and sipping. When she was done with her scone, Emmi pressed her thumb into the crumbs on the paper plate and then dragged them through the remaining jam before licking the remains off her fingertip.

"Okay, okay, I get it now," Emmi said, sighing blissfully. She put the empty paper plate on the log and leaned back. "The Brits really have something going for them if this is what tea time actually is."

"What did you think it was?" Puck asked.

"I don't know, just drinking a cup of tea?"

"Without a biscuit? Or a pastry? Just nothing?" Puck gaped. "What kind of savage do you think we are? We need both caffeine *and* sugar to be civilized."

Emmi snorted; Puck was hardly civilized, just as he wasn't truly British, despite his accent. But it was nice to pause for a moment, to have a tea party even if they ate from paper plates on top of a fallen log.

Emmi's fingers traced a crack in the old wood, slender and jagged. Just thick enough for a coin's edge to be pressed into it.

"Do you think I made the wrong choice?" Emmi asked, her eyes on the dark, crooked line in the log.

"Probably," Puck said. "About what?"

Emmi rolled her eyes. "About the coin. I gave the coin from the witch bottle to the silver-eyed woman, and then I took Gwyn ap Nudd's coin from the meadow. I thought at the time it was obviously the right thing to do, but seeing the wish trees..."

"Oh, yeah," Puck said, nodding enthusiastically as he cut her off. "You absolutely, without a doubt made the wrong choice."

"Thanks for the confidence."

Her sarcasm was lost on him. "No problem. That was a *really* stupid thing to do."

Emmi glared, but Puck just blinked blithely back at her. Emmi sighed, admitting defeat. "Maybe Gwyn won't notice."

Puck snorted. "He's the king of the fair folk. He *will* know you took something from him."

"One coin!" Emmi protested. "Actually, just a flower petal. Not even a whole flower—one petal."

"Doesn't matter. You made a deal, and then you took something more. The deal is now unbalanced. He's going to take something of yours in trade."

"What?" Emmi asked. "A different coin?" She shoved her hand in her pocket, imagining loose change. She had no coins on her, just the heart-shaped rock from the witch bottle and the glass vial with the stone flower, but it wouldn't bother her if Gwyn stole a quarter or a dime from her.

Puck shook his head gravely. "You didn't agree to a bargain with his coin; you stole it. He'll steal something from you. And you didn't give him a choice on what you took, so he won't give you one."

It felt ominous—at some point in time, Emmi would lose

something, and she wouldn't know what and wouldn't be able to stop it. At the same time, though, it *was* just a coin. If it was important for the deal to be balanced, then he wouldn't take anything *too* valuable from her in return. Emmi squared her shoulders. She would deal with it when the time came, but she was pretty certain she'd be able to handle the consequences. Besides, taking that coin had given her an item for her witch bottle. Maybe it wouldn't even matter if she was able to make the protection spell before Gwyn made his attempt at theft.

She hopped off the log. "Let's go," she said. The sooner she made that witch bottle, the better.

Her worries were offset somewhat by the beauty of the walk. She could almost forget that she was on a mission to save her grandfather and protect the fae. In the distance, she could see some kids goofing off at a playground, and occasionally she and Puck strolled past someone else, but the area was pretty deserted. They walked in silence, the birdsong and the sound of running water wrapping around them. Through the trees on the left, Emmi could glimpse the glittering waters of the broad river; to the right, she saw a creek slithering around stones and trees like a shining snake.

It was...nice.

Emmi glanced up at Puck, his face flickering in shadows from the trees swaying the breeze above them. *How does this work?* she wanted to ask. *You and me...is there a chance of...anything?*

She swallowed her worries down. Puck had showed up in the hearth room without much of a warning, and he would no doubt disappear once she'd remade the broken witch bottle.

Questions, both full of hope and full of fear, flickered on the edge of her consciousness. She would ask them later. After the witch bottle was made. After she knew if Puck would stick around long enough to answer them.

The path curved around, and the sound of trickling water grew louder. A map displayed on a wooden sign along the path told them they were nearly at the petrifying well.

"Petrifying well?" Puck asked when Emmi read the sign aloud.

Emmi had seen a petrified forest, on a road trip out west when her grandfather had done a research project in the Navajo Nation. She knew that something petrified was made of stone, but weren't lots of wells made of stone? She vaguely recalled Snow White in the Disney movie, singing about her prince as she pulled water up in a bucket from a stone well with a little roof atop it.

As they rounded the corner, though, she saw this well was nothing like the one in *Snow White*. A large rock jutted over a pool littered with ferns and moss, forming a natural well. Water trickled over the top of the rock, splashing through greenery into the pool below, the sound cacophonous.

The enormous boulder sticking out over the water was slick and shining, but someone had affixed dozens of thin ropes all around the edge. A random assortment of items hung from the ropes, positioned so that water dribbled over them. A top hat, a rubber duck, several strings of small teddy bears, a teapot, and even what looked to be an actual, real lobster—red and cooked— all dangled over the side of the rock.

And they all looked as if they were covered in clay, hardening into stone.

"It's like the flower," Emmi said, pulling the glass vial from her pocket and looking up at the other objects. The flower was the same beige as the objects hanging over the well, with the same rough edges forming stone.

"The water turns things into stone," Puck said, peering up at the rubber duck-shaped rock hanging from the rope.

"That's what they meant by petrifying." A nearby sign explained the process of the mineral-rich water calcifying objects relatively quickly, turning the small teddy bears into stone within three months. Emmi's ancestor Elspeth must have come here with a flower and let it be petrified. It was like magic but merely science. Although, Emmi supposed, the two could co-exist.

Emmi took several steps back, trying to get the full image of the well in her vision. It was larger than she'd expected, and the boulder hanging over the well was oddly shaped. "It almost looks like a skull," she said. The ferns and moss rounded over the top of the head-shaped rock, the water eroding grooves along hollows that could be eyes, trickling down jagged edges that gave the impression of a broken jaw.

Emmi shuddered. She could just imagine what it would be like to live in the 1500s, to walk through the forest along the edge of the river in search of a witch who could tell her future. It was not hard to believe Mother Shipton had been a witch if she had lived here, in the shadows of a well that looked like a skull.

"This way!" Puck said excitedly, racing to her and pulling Emmi's hand, leading her further up the path. "There's a wishing well!"

"Another well?" Emmi asked. Puck dragged her up some stone steps. The temperature dropped as they stepped into the naturally formed cave. Emmi blinked in the darkness. Sound was muffled as they crept deeper into the cave, and if it weren't for the artificial lights, they would be blind.

Emmi started to pull her hand away from Puck so she could rub her chilled arms, but he gripped her tightly, and Emmi realized she didn't really mind.

She moved closer to him when he stopped. In front of them, about waist-height, was another pool of water, the colored lights angled over the surface. This was the wishing well.

In America, Emmi was used to the custom of tossing a coin into the water to make a wish. While she may have had doubts about the coin she'd taken from Gwyn ap Nudd, Emmi had no doubt at all that this well before her needed no money. She reached into her pocket, instinct calling the heart-shaped stone from Elspeth's witch bottle into her hand.

"Emmi?" Puck's voice was a whisper, barely audible.

She shook her head gently and slipped her hand from his. This was right—she knew, deep inside her, her magic resonating within her chest—*this* was right. Putting the heart-shaped stone into the well was the right choice.

She didn't want to splash the water; that felt too disruptive. Emmi let her breath out, then lowered her hand holding the stone into the water.

The cold was sharp enough to bite at her as the water covered her skin. *One step closer to the bottle,* she thought. *I just wish I could find Orddu so I could figure out a way to save Grandfather.*

Emmi opened her fingers up, the heart-shaped stone gliding through the crisp water, disappearing past where the artificial colored light shone.

Water dripped from her hand as she pulled it from the well. "I guess it takes more than a few minutes to turn something into stone," she muttered. Not that she minded. She didn't really want her hand turning to rock.

When Puck didn't answer, she looked over at him. His eyes were wide. "Do you feel it?" he asked, shivering. "The magic."

Emmi called her powers up, shifting her eyes from seeing to *seeing.* She expected a golden glow, like the light that flickered over the items touched by the fae.

She saw no light.

Instead, the shadows moved like liquid. Emmi raised her hand in front of her face. She could *feel* the water dripping over her skin, but she *saw* shadows, not water. Darkness swirled through her fingers, over her palm, dripping down.

"Emmi?" Puck's voice was taut with fear. He could feel the magic, but she didn't think he could see what she saw.

The dark shadows drenched around her hand coalesced, swirling. *Tugging.*

"They're pulling me," she whispered. "They want me to follow them."

"They?" Puck asked. "Emmi, what are you talking about?"

"The shadows," she said, her voice cracking. "They want me to follow them."

EIGHT OF PENTACLES

GAINING KNOWLEDGE, PERFECTING A SKILL, AND SELF-MOTIVATION

The shadows swirling around Emmi's hand tightened, the pressure building on her palm almost as if another hand had slipped into her grip, fingers weaving through her own, gently but determinedly pulling her deeper into the dark.

"Emmi?" Puck's voice sounded far away, muffled but tight with fear. She whirled around, straining to see him, but there was only a faint outline. The light seemed dimmer, flickering like a firefly's glow rather than the bright bulbs of artificiality that had been set into the stone.

"Puck?" She wasn't sure if she said the word aloud or not; she could not seem to hear her own voice.

The blurry shape that seemed to be Puck's shadow lunged for her. "Don't go where I can't follow!" Puck cried. These words cut through the dark, straight to her core. Puck's hand burst into Emmi's vision, grabbing for her, but his fingers drifted through hers as if they were made of smoke.

Emmi staggered forward. She should collide with Puck, or the stone wall of the cave, or—*something*.

The cave was gone.

Puck was gone.

And Emmi was alone.

A cold, stuttering breath escaped her trembling lips as she strained to see through the dimly lit area. She seemed to be in a valley, gray granite bursting out through scraggly, pale grass. The floor in the cave hadn't been even, but now she was on the side of a hill, the steep incline leveling out in some areas. She climbed up, finding something like a trail, the dirt at her feet exposed as if this path was well-worn.

Mists boiled down the sides of the hills that surrounded her, constant waves of visibly moving fog, swirling over mounds of that looked far too much like graves for Emmi's comfort. She turned in a slow circle. There was no indication of a portal, no door, not even a flicker of possibility that she had come from a cave in Knaresborough to...here. Wherever here was.

A flicker of movement disturbed the mists to her right, rippling down closer to her. Emmi's heart thudded, and she took a calming breath, but before she could screw up the courage to run or scream, the fog parted.

A black cat made of shadows stood before her. Larger than a normal cat but just as silent, it flicked its tail, the gray mist swirling away.

"I know you." Emmi's voice was a whisper, but that didn't matter. She *did* know this cat—this Cat Sìth. It was the same one that she had seen in Holyrood, after Puck took her to the ruins behind the castle, where the tombs were. She had only ever seen the one ghostly cat before, and perhaps all Cat Sìth looked alike, but this one dipped its head in greeting, padding closer to her. Approaching her, well, not like *friend*, but at least like an acquaintance. And in this cold, desolate land, that felt positively sunny.

Emmi instinctively reached her hand out to pet it. The Cat Sìth was tall enough that she didn't even have to bend down to touch it, but her palm didn't feel anything more substantial than smoke, softly billowing over her skin. This was a cat made of shadows, not fur.

Puck had told her the Cat Sìth wasn't even really a part of this world or of the fae world. It was a creature that lived close to the veil between life and death.

Is that where I am? Emmi wondered, frowning. Somewhere between life and death?

Emmi pulled her hand away as the Cat Sìth kept moving, lithe and graceful yet somehow determined in its steps, just like her cat, Sabrina. She felt a pang in her chest, a longing for Sabrina, for home. Fear washed over her.

Those mounds under the mist looked *so* much like graves.

"Am I dead?" Emmi asked the dark, her voice cracking.

She did not expect the dark to answer.

But it did.

"No."

The voice was resonant, but the one word was all Emmi was given. Emmi whirled around, but she saw nothing more than fog and rocks—nothing that could have answered her so clearly. She squinted, then shifted to her magical sight, searching for glimmers of golden light that indicated fae magic.

Nothing.

Emmi had nearly convinced herself that there had been no voice, when she felt a tug on her hand, just like when the shadows had pulled before. She jerked her arm back, not liking the sensation of something invisible grabbing her, but the grip on her fingers tightened, her arm lurching forward as the shadows *pulled*.

"Hey!" Emmi protested as she was dragged down the path. She stumbled, trying to pull her hand back, but the dark shadows swirled tighter, pinching off the circulation at her wrist when she tried to break free. Her shoulder ached, her elbow screamed in protest, but Emmi could no sooner fight the force yanking on her arm than she could see it. Even when she fell to one knee, her shin smashing into granite, the shadows didn't relent, pulling harder so that Emmi scrambled to make her feet move quickly enough over the craggy ground before her shoulder dislocated.

As abruptly as it had started, the dark shadows evaporated, the otherworldly grip on Emmi's hand disappearing in the mist.

Emmi fell to her knees, crying out in pain, but as she looked up, the fog cleared a little more.

A black cauldron as tall as her waist and wide enough for three of her to stand in loomed in front of her. There was no fire —not that she could see, and certainly no warmth—but as Emmi pulled herself up and peered inside the black metal pot, the liquid inside bubbled, steam rising up, the dark liquid boiling somehow. A curving line cut through the steam, and Emmi could see with her magical vision the outline of something that looked like a spoon handle or a thin staff, stirring whatever potion brewed in the cauldron.

Emmi followed the outline of the handle up from the slow circle it cut through the steam. She could see the ghostly image of an old woman, sheets of long white hair framing her face, her cheeks baggy and wrinkled.

The spoon stirred.

The woman shifted—shorter now, with wide hips and a round face, curly hair cascading down her back.

The spoon stirred.

Another person—male or female, Emmi could not tell— shrouded in black, a hood pulled over their face.

The spoon stirred.

A teenager with braids, glassy eyes watching her, staring at her through the smoke.

Every turn in the cauldron revealed a different ghostly outline of a different person.

But every person watched Emmi.

"Hello," Emmi whispered, fear and confusion choking her. "My name is Emmi."

"I," the young woman said, the spoon completing its circle, "am Orddu." Before the words faded, the young woman shifted to an old crone, one eye missing, the gaping hole in her face where it should be turned toward Emmi.

"*You* are Orddu?" Emmi asked.

The spoon stirred. Now the person holding it was a middle-aged man, bald on top, with a knotted beard. "I am," he said. The spoon stirred. A girl half Emmi's age blinked at her, the ghostly outline of her hair fading in the mist.

"Which one of you is Orddu?" Emmi asked as the shape shifted again. The spoon faltered; the woman who appeared now had only her left hand, and she had to adjust the spoon's handle.

"Orddu is a title, not a name." This was said by a woman with a hunched back, a tumorous lump protruding out of her neck in a way that looked painful.

"An orddu is a type of witch," said a young boy with clear, pale eyes. "One who can see better in the dark."

Beyond the orddu ghost, which was now a woman with a face painted in black runes and a shaved skull, Emmi saw the Cat Sìth, tail twitching as it watched them. *An orddu can see better in the dark,* Emmi thought to herself. See. Like her powers of vision. She shifted to her magical Sight but didn't See any better.

"Why am I here?" she asked.

"You wished for it," another woman said. She was plump and looked kind, but her teeth were filed into fangs when she flashed Emmi a smile over the steaming cauldron. Another circle complete. She was now about Emmi's age, tattoos all over her bare arms.

Emmi tried to trace the words into her mind, keep the thread of thought focused. She *had* wished to meet Orddu when she stuck her hand into the wishing well. She couldn't recall the exact words, but...

Emmi shook her head. It didn't matter. This ghostly, shape-shifting...thing...wasn't someone she could trick or kidnap and hand over to Gwyn ap Nudd. The orddu was not a trade she could make for her Grandfather to be returned to her. Emmi felt both desperate and relieved—she had not relished the idea of trading one person for another, but she felt even more hopeless at the seemingly impossible task of saving Grandfather from the Wild Hunt.

An idea occurred to her as the spoon stirred and stirred the cauldron's bubbling liquid. "Can you help me?" Emmi asked. "I—"

"No," the orddu said. It was simply stated, no anger or malicious tone, but it was also definitively emphatic.

Emmi's eyes drifted back to the spoon. It was easier to think when she didn't look at the ever-changing image of the orddu and instead focused on the constant, steady stir, stir, stir. A perfect circle cut through the steam, parting so the bubbling liquid beneath was *almost* visible, but never quite entirely...

What's inside? Emmi wondered. She didn't bother asking. Cauldrons were odd things. Places of destruction and creation. Cauldrons were once so common that every household in England had one—a universal pot into which went any root or vegetable or scrap of meat, and out of which came pottage or stew or something edible. Ingredients were destroyed, consumed by the broth and the bone and the burn, and they became food. Just like how, at home, in the Museum, Emmi was tipping magical ingredients into Elspeth's old caudlron, hoping they would become a spell of protection.

Many thing melt into one. That which is destroyed, creates.

Stir. Stir. Stir. Each turn of the spoon was a turn of the cycle, a reminder of how everything was in constant death and life, creation and destruction, an eternal cycle—

"Mrew!"

Emmi startled, shaking herself as she looked down at the Cat Sìth. It had pounced closer, not quite at her feet, but near enough that Emmi felt it land on the ground, heard it snarl at her. The Cat Sìth arched its back, impossible black eyes that seemed to eat the light boring into her.

Pulling her attention away from the hypnotizing spoon in the cauldron.

Emmi shook her head harder, trying to clear her thoughts. She had spun out into a darker place, losing herself. Had any of those thoughts even been hers? She didn't think about cauldrons like that—the one in the hearth room had simply been a convenient storage place for her to put the items needed for the witch bottle.

Emmi looked down at her hands.

The smoked wrapped around them, threading through her fingers, drifting down, swirling into the cauldron.

She held her left hand in front of her face. There was no obvious source of light, but is seemed to Emmi that her skin was paler than normal. Almost translucent.

Almost like fog, swirling down around the spoon.

Emmi looked up. The orddu now was an old woman, pock marks on her face. Her hair was braided and neat, but there were streaks of mud on her clothes, dirt that showed up even in ghostly form.

When the pot stirred again, the woman remained the same. Silent. Watching Emmi.

"Am I an orddu?" Emmi asked.

"It depends on what you see." The spoon circled again, and the woman held her shape, becoming sharper with each turn. She had a hunch in her back and a large nose, but she had a defiant glint to her eyes, as if daring Emmi to judge her appearance.

As the other woman's outline hardened, Emmi seemed to be fading. She could not feel her own skin, only a faint coldness, as gentle as the fog.

"Or," the woman continued, her voice growing louder, "perhaps it depends on what you believe about what you see. You can look at one thing and see something entirely different than someone else. It is not your eyes that mark the change, but your mind."

The steam over the bubbling cauldron coalesced as the orddu stirred faster, cranking her arm with effort, as if the liquid inside was growing thick and unmalleable. The pale steam twirled, funneling and then spreading out, forming a shape.

A shape Emmi knew.

Puck in ghostly mist hung over the boiling potion inside the cauldron. As Emmi watched, his features sharpened, softened, sharpened again, as if he were constantly being reformed out of steam.

"Do you see the truth before you?" the orddu asked, her voice echoing so that the question bounced off the rocks and struck Emmi again and again. "Or do you see what you want to see?"

The flickering cloud in the form of Puck seemed to dance as the orddu's rapid stirring grew even more manic.

Suddenly, she stopped. The spoon melted into the liquid, disappearing. The cloud faded, and through it, Emmi saw the old woman staring at her.

"Or do you see only what *he* wants you to see?"

Emmi wanted to run away. She wanted to run back to Puck, back to the cave, back to Earth.

But she couldn't move.

ACE OF CUPS

INSPIRATION, NEW RELATIONSHIPS, RENEWAL, AND SPIRITUAL INSIGHT

Thoughts—voices—swirled around Emmi's mind like smoke, burning through the panic rising inside of her, obscuring the need to stay in the here and now.

No, she thought, a pinpoint of focus.

Silence cut through the fog.

She would *not* be distracted; she would *not* let the unknown cloud what she did know.

She was in the Shadowlands. She was surrounded by danger.

And she needed to find a way back.

Emmi's gaze zeroed in on the orddu witch stirring the cauldron before her. It was still the same woman, hunched back and pock-marked face watching her with cloudy, cataract-filled eyes over the steaming, bubbling liquid, but Emmi could see the shadows of the other orddu witches. They each took a ghostly turn with the spoon, cranking it round and round the cauldron, their faint outline merging with the more substantial, older woman, but each ghostly witch flickered to other areas of the Shadowlands at the end of the spoon's cycle, a blur of motion that added to the foggy, opaque landscape.

Emmi tried to use her magic to track the various different orddu witches, but it was hard to hone in on just one. Not only was each witch like a pearly ghost, blending into the shadows, but they moved too quickly or too slowly to really track with either her regular vision or her magical sight. Blowing a frustrated sigh through her nose, Emmi forced her eyes to the distinct outline of an orddu witch as she peeled away from the cauldron.

This witch was tall and slim, long white hair braided down her back. She had black paint or perhaps soot on her forehead, streaking down to her cheeks, silver runes scratched over the obsidian color. Her ghostly form slipped away from the cauldron as the spoon stirred, and Emmi squinted, determined to not to lose sight of the woman.

The slender orddu witch zoomed supernaturally fast across the Shadowlands, paused at a ridge crest carved at the top of the craggy valley. The horizon was spotted with the jagged, sharp edges of the stones that jutted up from the earth, but the slender orddu witch stopped and hovered over one of the elongated barrows, dirt rounding softly over what looked like a grave.

As Emmi watched, the dirt spilled over the hill, a few clumps at first, and then the skeletal remains of a hand clawed up through the earth. Emmi had seen movies and video games with zombies before, but nothing could have prepared her for the way brown dirt clung to the grasping knucklebones of the hand pushing up, the remnants of rotting flesh peeling over the wrist, showing the gaping, stringy muscle that clung to the forearm bones.

With the arm out, the mound of dirt shifted more violently, a miniature earthquake as the corpse broke through its grave, the chest burst forward in a spray of dust, the head dragging behind before snapping forward with an audible clack of dry jawbones. Straggly strands of hair clung to the broken skull under a gold band that shone and flashed as if it were on fire.

The slender orddu witch knelt over the mound, and the clattering skull turned toward her. Emmi's heart thudded as the witch lifted a sword in her hand that had not been there before. "Back in with you," she whispered gently, almost lovingly, the sound somehow carrying to Emmi's ears despite the distance.

The corpse retreated back into its grave at swordpoint. The earth over the barrow knit back together, the grave mound looking, once again, old and undisturbed, a soft pillow of dirt.

The sword in the orddu witch's hands melted into smoke. Slowly, purposefully, she turned back to the direction of the cauldron. Her eyes instantly met Emmi's, pale green and sparkling through the black paint over her face.

Her lips curved into a malicious smile.

In a blink, the orddu witch moved from the grave mound to inches from Emmi's face. The air felt ice cold, but the coppery scent of blood drifted to Emmi's nose.

"Little witch, you *see*," the rune-covered orddu whispered, the last word fading into a silent hiss.

Emmi swallowed, her body shaking. She blinked.

The witch was gone.

A tingle went up Emmi's spine. She saw the Cat Sìth watching her, its black body still except for its tail twitching, as if it waited to pounce.

Emmi turned her gaze to the cauldron. The hunchbacked witch stirred and stirred, and with each rotation of the spoon, a different orddu peeled away, ghost-like, into the Shadowlands. Emmi caught glimmers of the other orddus, each one with a different task. One dipped her hand into a dark spot on the earth, her fingers coming away red with blood. She flicked the scarlet drops into the mist, and Emmi saw the pale outlines of red caps staggering through the fog, disappearing. Another orddu witch sat under a black tree, branches twisting impossibly, with a black dog in her lap.

"Warn them," she whispered, and the dog disappeared. A second more, and she did, too.

Emmi couldn't stop trembling. It wasn't the cold, although the air was growing more and more frigid. Seeing the different orddu witches slipping through the shadows, each one with a different task, each one sliding back into rotation to stir and stir the cauldron before her, gave Emmi a greater idea of what it meant to be an orddu. It wasn't just a title; it was a shared position, a membership into a unity, each task performed in perfect rhythm, following the rhythm of the cauldron stirring.

When Emmi looked back to the witch with the spoon, she saw the hunchbacked woman watching her. Her eyes glittered with thought. "You see us," she said, her voice crackling, as if it had been a very, very, *very* long time since she had spoken so much. "You *see* what we do."

Emmi nodded, not trusting her own voice to not betray the horror rising in her throat. She could almost—*almost*—understand the complicated dance. Each ghostly shadow of the witches knew the steps, perfectly in sync as they kept the dead in their graves, wove weapons from the dark, poured potions on the ground, plucked black fruits from burned husks of trees.

"If you see the need, fulfill the need." The witch at the cauldron narrowed her eyes at Emmi.

There was an invitation in her tone. Emmi's gaze shifted to the spoon in the witch's hands. She held the wooden stick gently, and as Emmi watched, her fingers flexed, opening.

Offering to let Emmi stir.

The shadows curled and spun, round and round.

"What happens if you stop stirring?" Emmi asked. Her voice felt far away, distant. A whisper on the wind, already gone before she could reach for it.

"Look," the orddu witch said, releasing the spoon's handle. "*See.*"

The wooden stick stood straight in center of the cauldron, not tipping to one side or another. But even as Emmi's eyes peered into the bubbling liquid, the steam stopped. The *world* stopped. And, Emmi realized with dawning horror, *she* had stopped. There were a million cacophonous sounds thundering inside a living body—a heart beating, two lungs breathing, the rustle of hair, the slip of air between teeth—all of life was noisy, deafening in a way that defied itself—and it was all gone from her.

She could not flick her eyes away. She could not shift her

thoughts. She could only exist in the moment, and the moment was dead.

Only one thing moved, and that was the Cat Sìth, its tail still twitching impatiently, its black form somehow uncaring that everything around it was unnaturally unmoving.

"It's time, girl," the orddu witch said, her voice breaking the spell as her hand grabbed the spoon. She stirred the cauldron.

And time began again.

"This is orddu magic," the witch said. Her body was old, her back hunched, her eyes cloudy, but her voice sounded young and clear. Not innocent, but youthful. There was a difference "We see all. A witness to the world, to every version of the world. But to see all, to be all, means to see nothing. Be nothing."

The orddu spun the spoon faster, cranking it round and round through the bubbly steam, faster and faster.

"We exist outside of time, but we are a part of time."

And Emmi understood—at least as much as she was capable of understanding—that what moved within the cauldron was time itself.

From the steam rose an image. Emmi recognized it immediately: Puck, just as she'd seen him in the steam before. But this time another image rose above him.

"Grandfather!" Emmi gasped, longing rising in her chest. It had been so long since she'd seen him, and this faded image wasn't enough, but it was more real than her memory.

"See everything," the orddu witch whispered.

Emmi forced herself to look at the entire tableau rising through the ghost-like steam over the cauldron. There was Puck and Grandfather, but while Grandfather beamed down at Emmi, a blithe smile on his wrinkled face, Puck stared at Grandfather.

Horror twisted his face, pure revulsion choking his throat as his eyes widened with disgust.

"See nothing," the orddu witch whispered.

The image disappeared.

What did that mean? Puck looking at her grandfather with

such obvious distaste? What had Grandfather ever done to him to make him stare like that?

"I have to go back," Emmi said. She needed answers, not riddles and ghosts.

"If you see the need, fulfill the need," the orddu witch said in the same tone of voice she'd said the same words before, almost as if they were recorded, pitch-perfect matches. But then she added, "If you see the path, take the path."

Emmi spun around, mists swirling. There were grave mounds and ghostly shadows and creatures that lurked in the dark and stark standing stones and the jagged ridge tops on the horizon.

But there was no path.

With an impatient *Mrow!*, the Cat Sìth leapt forward, landing on the rim of the cauldron. Inside the black vessel was time itself, stirred forward with rhythmic precision by all the orddu witches of the Shadowland, but the Cat Sìth swatted at it as if it the burbling surface was a toy.

The Cat Sìth looked at Emmi and sat, perched on the edge of the cauldron. The tip of its tail twitched.

The Cat Sìth was clearly waiting.

Emmi drew closer reluctantly. She didn't like the way that it had felt when the spoon stopped, when time itself had stopped. But as she stood on her tiptoes, staring down into the steam, she saw—

Puck.

In the dark cave.

Searching for her.

She was looking at the present.

And she didn't hesitate to climb into the cauldron, to slide through time, to go back.

To him.

THE MAGICIAN

FOCUSING YOUR WILL, CREATIVITY, SKILL, AND MAGIC

I t felt as if Emmi had been pulled into two different pieces, the different dimensions tugging her soul apart, and, like a snapping rubber band, she slammed back home into her own body, the motion so staggeringly powerful that she bent over, sucking in air with an audible gasp.

"Emmi!" Puck rushed over, wrapping his arms around her so forcefully that she staggered back, her legs hitting the wishing well. Puck clung to her, pulling her tightly against him. She could hear the hammering of his heart, chaotic and loud. His grip loosened as she sagged against him, and he ran his hands up and down her arms, as if she were chilled. Then his fingers seized against her shoulders, pulling her back a little so he could look down at her.

"I was so worried about you," he said, his whispered voice cracking.

She could feel his warm breath cutting through the chilly air in the cave. It was dark, but not so dark that she couldn't see the strain in his eyes, the red-rimmed gaze that told her that even now, he wasn't sure she was really here.

"I went...somewhere else."

Puck nodded tightly. "But you're back now. Safe." He leaned closer. All she had to do was tip up on her toes, and they would kiss. All she had to do was tilt her chin. All she had to do was claim his lips with hers.

But his last word lingered between. *Safe.* Was she safe?

"I was in the Shadowlands," Emmi said, unsure of how she knew, inherently, that was the right word for the place.

"*What?*" The spell was broken. Puck took a step back, his mouth agape as he stared at her. "You went *there* and...just came back?"

"Should I not have come back?" Emmi asked.

"No! No—I'm glad you did!" Puck ran a shaking hand through his tousled hair. "I just didn't think...they don't often let anyone go."

"Who?" Emmi asked, wondering how much Puck knew of the orddu witches, of the Shadowlands.

He didn't answer, though. He kept shaking his head, as if he hadn't heard her question and was still muddling through his shock. Puck leaned against the rough, curving stone wall opposite the wishing well. "That's a dangerous place, Emmi, full of dangerous creatures."

Emmi hadn't felt...well, she hadn't felt safe in the Shadowlands, but she also hadn't necessarily felt in danger, or at least not *immediate* danger. The orddu witches had spoken with her, and while their words had been riddles, they hadn't been threats. And the Cat Sìth had actually helped Emmi, far more than it had when it'd been at Holyrood. "What kinds of creatures?" Emmi asked. She wished she could have seen deeper into the dark.

"Red caps, banshees, trolls and goblins." He paused. "Boggarts. Boggarts are made in the Shadowlands." He shuddered. "If it's a fae that deals with blood or revenge or rage, that's the type that goes there. It's a horrible place."

Emmi watched Puck's face. It had grown distant, almost morose. "You've been there," she said, realizing the truth of it as she spoke the words aloud.

Puck cringed as if she's punched him.

Emmi took a step closer to him. She didn't want to cause him harm, but she couldn't shake the feeling that this was significant in some way. "You've been to the Shadowlands," she pressed. And then another question rose within her. If he had been there, did that mean he was a fae that dealt who blood, revenge, and rage?

He guessed the question she didn't voice. "I have been many things over my life. The reason why fae are not named is because a name makes something permanent. I've been light; I've been dark. But once I was named, I became nothing more than Puck."

Puck spat the words out as if they were bitter on his tongue. But Emmi took another step closer to him. Puck looked away, almost as if he were ashamed of how Emmi didn't flinch at his words, but she put her hand to his cheek and drew his gaze back to her. "To humans," she said gently, making sure he heard her, "it's different. Your name does not define you. You have the freedom to be whoever you want to be."

Puck's face twisted, but he didn't look away. "You're wrong, Emmi Castor," he said finally. "You just don't want to admit it."

She shook her head, unwilling to give up an inch of this argument. "Change is *always* hard, whether it's changing your name or your nature. But it's also *always* possible." She leaned up on her toes and pecked him on the cheek. "I promise," she whispered in his ear.

When she pulled away from him, she could see the hope in his eyes. Still, he added, "Fae are inherently shapeshifters. Whether they appear to be a light in the dark and are actually lures to danger, or whether they appear to be beautiful and are actually monsters, you have to remember that fae—*all* fae—are tricksters and shapeshifters. We can be anything until we are caged in by a name."

"You forget that humans are the same way," Emmi said. "You don't think a monster can't wear a human face? I thought you knew better than that."

Puck let out a breath that broke into a snort of a laugh at Emmi's sardonic words, his shoulders relaxing. "So, what did you see in the Shadowlands?"

"You."

Puck's eyes widened.

"As a vision," Emmi said. "Have you ever met my grandfather before?"

Puck shook his head.

"I saw you and him, and you were mad. At him."

Puck's brows creased in confusion. Emmi knew he wasn't feigning the reaction—this was sincere. He had never met Grandfather before.

But Emmi also knew that the orddu witches had given her a vision of a possible future, and there must be conflict of some sort coming.

"If the orddu witches were showing visions and letting you strut around the Shadowlands—"

"I didn't strut!" Emmi protested.

"—have you considered that maybe...maybe *you* are an orddu witch?"

Emmi bit her lip. That thought had crossed her mind, although she wasn't sure what to think about it. On the one hand, if she were an orddu, she could trade herself for Grandfather's freedom. Maybe that was why Puck was angry at Grandfather—Emmi didn't think Puck would like it if Emmi just swapped places with him.

But it wasn't a possibility she had ruled out. She wanted to find another solution, but if she could free Grandfather from the fae as easily as just changing places, perhaps...

"Well, I'm not there now," she said. "Frankly, I'm half sick of shadows."

She led Puck out of the cave, but not without looking at him for a reaction. Puck had known Shakespeare, but if he recognized the Tennyson quote, he didn't show it.

"We do still need a stone to replace the one you sent to the shadows," Puck said, looking around in the bright sunlight. "Do you see anything in the calcifying well? That would make sense. The well makes thing turn to stone; look for a stone there."

Emmi felt a headache coming on. When had the sun gotten so bright? But even when she shifted to her magical sight, she didn't see anything in the petrifying well.

Puck pointed to another cave. "We could try there."

"What's that?" Emmi lowered her eyelids a little and shaded her face with her hand.

"That's where Mother Shipton lived," Puck said. "Nice little cave system here, a cave to cast spells, a well to turn things into stone, and another cozy little cave to live in. What more could a witch want?"

"Electricity?" Emmi asked, already heading to the other cave. "Air conditioning?" It was getting hotter out here; Emmi had grown used to the coolness in the cave and the shadows. She mounted the steps two at a time to get to the other cave.

It was better lit than the cave with the wishing well, but there were still shadows stretching from the artifical lights. In one corner stood a stone statue of Mother Shipton, the face blurred with age and the body of the statue bent over like an old woman. But even as Emmi tried to focus on the statue, she was distracted by the shadows.

There were more shadows than there should be in the dark.

They swirled and shifted, as if there were creatures in the cave that moved unseen. Emmi watched one shadow leap up and rest on a ledge in the cave. It had a distinct cat-like shape, and it appeared to be watching her.

"Hello," Emmi whispered, smiling at the shadow.

"What?" Puck asked. He was looking at the state of Mother Shipton, peering up at the weatherworn face as if it would answer him.

Emmi ignored Puck's question. "You know," she said, stepping closer to him, "I started this whole thing assuming that every witch that burned at the stake or was hung by the executioner was just an innocent woman who was too vocal or too different or simply too in the way. And maybe that's true, but only because the real witches didn't burn."

As the words left her mouth, Emmi felt saddened by them. Real people had died throughout history, victims of prejudice and hatred and bigotry and fear, and only the powerful lived—whether that power be nobility, wealth, or literal magic. Had Mother Shipton been an actual, real witch? She'd claimed she was, using the label as a source of power. And she had not burned for it, despite the way she accepted the name of "witch."

Perhaps Puck was right. Perhaps there *was* power in a name.

But only in the name *you* accept. It wasn't that other people calling Mother Shipton a witch had given her any type of safety; for most women, that label spelled death. It was only when Mother Shipton took a name for herself that she claimed and reveled in that she'd became a force to be reckoned with.

Emmi's eyes drifted from Mother Shipton's statue down to the long shadow playing at her feet. The shadow was deep and dark and although it was clearly extending from the statue, it did not form the same shape. The shadow's back didn't curve; its head didn't bow. It was the shadow of a proud woman, hands gripped in fists at her side, chin tilted up in defiance.

And in the center of the shadow glowed a golden heart.

Emmi knelt down, ignoring Puck's question as her knees hit the cold floor of the cave. When Emmi scooped her hand toward the heart of the shadow witch, her fingers did not hit stone. They dipped into the dark, slipping inside, the sensation just as it had felt when Emmi had dropped the other stone into the wishing well in the other cave. Her hand felt cold, but not uncomfortably so, as her fingers touched the rough edge of a stone.

When Emmi withdrew her hand from the shadow, a new stone heart rested in her palm, the faint gold glow of magic still clinging to it.

Two of Cups, Transposed

Dissatisfaction, Envy, Miscommunication, and Arguments

Emmi blinked, her eyes refocusing on the familiar hearth room as she stepped out of the ash sigil portal Puck had made. She took a deep breath, relishing the scent of home, so different from the mineral water and damp earth smell at Mother Shipton's cave.

"Here, kitty," Puck said, the portal closing behind him. He squatted down on the carpet, holding his fingers out toward Sabrina.

Sabrina, however, merely twitched her tail. Her green eyes were focused on Emmi.

"Hi, Sabrina," Emmi said. She was grateful that Grandfather had invested in an automatic feeder and litter cleaner, the gadgets she had once thought pointless now giving her a little peace of mind that her cat was safe even when Emmi disappeared into other realms for who knew how long.

Sabrina's tail flicked slowly, left, right, left.

"Your cat's mad at you," Puck said, straightening.

But Emmi wasn't sure of that. Sabrina was pretty independent, and this cold way her cat watched her now didn't seem to be anger.

It was how she treated strangers she didn't trust.

Emmi rubbed her hands over her arms, even though she wasn't cold. The Cat Sìth had not liked her at Holyrood, but had treated her like a friend in the Shadowlands. Had she changed so much as her magic grew that the cats—one mystical, one not— realized she was different now? Emmi wasn't sure she *wanted* to be different, not if it made Sabrina dislike her.

Sighing, Emmi headed to the cauldron, ignoring the way Sabrina darted off, racing out of the room as if her tail were on fire.

Emmi looked down into the dark depths of the iron pot. Inside, nestled in shadows, lay the page from *Daemonologie*, the clod of earth from the Otherworld, the golden coin from Gwyn ap Nudd's field of flowers. An effervescent light emanated from the objects as Emmi lowered the new heart-shaped stone into the cauldron. While each object had once had its own unique glow, now it seemed as if light made them into puzzle pieces, fitting against each other, the spaces between them filling in the gaps with a golden glow that almost...*almost*...looked like a bottle.

"The last piece," Puck said, picking up the pottery shard from the mantle over the fireplace and carefully avoiding touching the iron weapon from the Witch Hunter that had rested beside the broken clay.

Emmi took the shard from him. "It's not the jar that's important, but whatever this stain is. Something liquid was poured into Elspeth's witch bottle when she made it." Emmi glanced at the cauldron that still glowed faintly. She did not think she would need to add a clay bottle; the magic seemed to be forming it into the shape of a vessel. But it wasn't done yet. She needed to add in one last ingredient before the witch bottle would complete itself.

Before she had the protection it would offer.

When she'd started this journey, she had believed that she only needed protection from Hunters, like Greybeard when he'd burst into her house. But now she was worried about the fae—Gwyn ap Nudd may seek revenge for her theft, and the red caps terrified her.

The orddu witches, too…Emmi didn't think they had wanted her to leave the Shadowlands.

"You okay?" Puck asked softly, his eyes on Emmi's face.

She offered him a reassuring look, but she didn't think he bought it. "It's just…" she started, unsure how to phrase her worries. "I need protection from the Witch Hunters. Protection from the fae."

"*Some* of the fae," Puck interjected. She shot him a weak smile.

"Protection from the orddu, maybe. And it's not like any of my…normal friends could help me. I can't call the police. If people saw me now, I'd probably need protection from humans, too."

Puck's lips thinned, and he nodded sympathetically. "Feels like everyone's against you?" He said it as a question, but from his tone, she knew he knew the answer.

Wordlessly, Emmi stepped closer to him, sliding her arms around him and hugging him. He was stiff at first, startled, but then his arms wrapped around her. He rested his chin on the top of her head as she buried her face into his chest. She could hear his heartbeat. Emmi closed her eyes, just listening.

After a moment, she stepped back.

"Better?" Puck asked.

She nodded silently, then looked down at the pottery shard in her hand. The broken edges had made indentations in her palm from where she'd squeezed them. Emmi let her eyes unfocus, slipping into her magical sight.

"It's blood," she said, staring at the brownish-red stain on the shard. "But it's magic blood of some kind." She didn't know enough to tell whether the blood had come from the fae or from a witch, but she was certain it had been the unifying magic that had formed the spell into a bottle shape.

Historically, witch bottles were spells of protection. Someone who felt like they'd attracted the eye of a malicious witch would make a bottle and fill it with things to keep the witch away—bent nails, slivers of glass, things like that. But the idea behind Elspeth's witch bottle was to protect magic from Hunters. She had gathered items linked to magic—symbolizing that which harmed witches—and then hid them away to protect the witches from such evil.

Emmi looked up, past Puck, to the mantle. To the Witch Hunter's weapon they had stolen from Greybeard. It was designed to draw out magic from a fae, but it could likely draw out blood from a witch.

"Protection comes at a price," Puck said, oblivious to Emmi's thoughts. "Magic doesn't happen without a sacrifice. You can *want* to protect others, but it means nothing unless you're willing to make a sacrifice of some sort. Blood is the sacrifice, but for a spell to cover the whole world like Elspeth's did...it would take some sort of magical blood." His voice sounded odd, distant.

Emmi strode to the mantle, snatched the weapon up, and crossed the room to the cauldron. "Do you think *my* blood's enough?" she asked Puck without looking at him. She stared down at the cauldron, the glowing light of the different pieces seeming to call out to her, singing for magic to unify the object.

Emmi pressed the iron tip of the needle-like weapon into her palm. She winced in pain, even though it hadn't yet pierced her skin.

"Wait." Puck's voice was hollow. "We, uh...we need to research this."

Emmi turned, lowering the weapon as she did so. Puck looked pale, his brow creased.

"What aren't you telling me?" Emmi asked.

"Nothing," he said too quickly.

She raised an eyebrow.

"That's dangerous." Puck nodded to the weapon in her hand. "And...this is too important to mess up. Surely Elspeth has something that will help with the final step? This witch bottle, the protection it cast—it seems to have been her legacy. There's got to be something about it in the library, or…"

His voice trailed off when Emmi didn't break eye contact. He ran his fingers through his tousled hair and looked away.

"Okay," Emmi said finally. He was right—they couldn't mess this up. But she didn't like the way he was being so cagey.

"To the library!" he said loudly. Emmi wondered how much of his cheeriness was forced.

By now, Puck knew the Museum of Magic almost as well as Emmi did, and he led the way, turning on his heel and heading to the stairs. Emmi trailed behind him, lost in thought. She wasn't even sure what time of day it was—evening, she guessed, but hopping through portals and timezones messed with her perceptions. The windows were dim, though, sending out just enough light to make the shadows long. Her eyes drifted to Puck's shadow, long and bouncy behind him as he strode down the hallway.

His shadow was dark.

Darker than the other shadows, growing darker the longer she looked.

Emmi paused, watching as Puck's shadow expanded. His shoulders bulged. The shaggy edges of his floppy hair curled and spun, twisting out like snakes. As Emmi stood, transfixed, the shadow seemed to writhe. Arms, wide and muscle-bound, nothing like Puck's real arms, ended in fingers that curled in like claws, black leaking off the pointed tips. Wisps of smoky gray spun off the shadow, poison drifting toward her.

Puck's shadow was *monstrous*. It seemed almost like a separate entity, but she could see it attached to his heels, an irrevocable reminder that, when it came to it, Emmi did not know who or even what Puck truly was.

But what she did know was that Puck was in the list of creatures she might have to protect herself from.

"Emmi?" Puck asked, finally noticed that she had stopped.

Emmi shook herself, swallowing hard and unclenching her jaw. "Yeah?" she said, forcing her voice bright and unconcerned.

Out of the corner of her eye, Emmi saw Puck's shadow shift as he walked the few steps back to her. By the time he was close enough to touch, his shadow was back to being normal, showing only the shape of a boy.

Whatever he used to be, he's not now, she reminded herself firmly. *He told me he had been a dark fae before. He hasn't lied about who or what he is.*

And then another, niggling voice in the back of her mind said, *But he also hasn't told me the whole truth.*

"I'm hungry," Puck said, oblivious to the turmoil in her mind. "You go to the library; I'll go to the kitchen."

"Sure," Emmi forced out.

Puck stepped around her, heading to the kitchen. Emmi wanted to run in the opposite direction, but she forced herself to walk at her normal pace. She breathed in and out deeply until her heartbeat wasn't racing.

Emmi had so few allies left in this or any world. She wasn't going to freak out just because the one person closest to her had a dark past.

Being surrounded by books in the library helped calm her more than anything else. She stared around at the shelves, trying to orient herself. She needed to find something about witch bottles. She needed to find answers.

To stop her hands from shaking, Emmi spread her arms as she stepped into one of the aisles, stretching to touch the shelves on either side. She closed her eyes, walking down the aisle by feel alone, her fingertips bumping over the spines, some leather, some laminate, some nothing more than corded-pages held together by dust more than glue. Down one aisle, another, another. She felt the tension coiling inside her like a spring about to break.

What would Puck say if he saw me now? Emmi wondered. And then: *What would he do if I asked him about his monstrous shadow?*

She stopped.

He had a past, she knew. And he would tell her about it when he was ready.

With that clarity in thought, Emmi heaved a sigh. She looked up—she was near a window, and the sun was just setting, the barest sprinkle of stars visible in the navy-blue and orange-streaked sky.

Her eyes landed on a book resting on the wide windowsill.

The book was bound in forest green leather, with a single word printed in gilded letters on the cover: *Mabinogion*.

The long shadow of the tree outside the window snaked over the book, the branches like fingers beckoning her closer. Emmi shifted to her magical sight, her eyes unfocusing and refocusing through the shadows and the golden glow that streaked out from the pages. Her footsteps echoed over the wide planks of the old hardwood floor as she drew closer.

Emmi slipped her fingers into the pages, opening the book at the exact spot glimmering with magic. "Culhwch and Olwen" was written across the top, the title of the short story in the collection of Welsh fairy tales. But the word that drew Emmi's attention swirled in shadowy black, more than halfway down the page:

Orddu.

Nine of Wands, Transposed

BARRIERS, BEING UNPREPARED, FACING
TROUBLE, RASH BEHAVIOR, AND SETBACKS

Emmi sat cross-legged on the old hardwood floor, the open book in her lap, her body bent over it as she carefully scanned the pages. She heard Puck come into the library, but she didn't say anything until he sat down across from her.

"Good book?" he asked. His tone was cheerful, but there was a wary edge to it as well.

Emmi turned the tome around to show it to him. "The *Mabinogion*," she said. "Welsh fairy tales. I've scanned through the rest of the book and looked online." Her phone lay facedown on the floor beside her. "This is the first and one of the only known instances of 'orddu.'"

Emmi had painstakingly been parsing through the archaic language. This translation was in English, thankfully, but still written in a style more obscure than Shakespeare.

"It's kind of a quest story," Emmi continued, looking down at the pages. "A man wants to marry the daughter of a giant, and before he'll grant permission, the man has to go on a quest for all these weird items. But get this." Emmi turned the book around, offering it to Puck. "One of the items is the *blood* of the orddu."

Puck was watching Emmi; he barely glanced down at the book. She pulled it back into her lap. "You think this has something to do with the stain on the pottery of the old witch bottle?" he asked, his voice low and oddly serious.

"It can't be a coincidence, can it?" Emmi said. Her question was sincere—she was no longer sure if she was just chasing...well, shadows. It was a phrase her grandfather used often, but now it seemed to be far darker in connotation.

"The witch in the story, the orddu, she lives in a cave, just like Mother Shipton did," Emmi said. "It doesn't even read like a fairy tale. It reads like history."

"Most fairy tales are history," Puck said.

"This one includes King Arthur," Emmi said. "He's not *doing* anything, which I thought was kind of weird. The story's about this other man, one of Arthur's knights, and how he's supposed to be getting all these items for the giant. But he doesn't do much either. It ends up being kind of a team effort, which is weird since the prize is a bride."

"What happens to the witch?"

Emmi looked up and saw that Puck was staring right at her, his face grave. "She dies," Emmi said. "It takes multiple attempts from all of Arthur's best men, but they get her blood." Emmi snorts. "By cutting the witch in half."

There was no humor in Puck's face, and that in itself was strange enough. "That's the part that's a fairy tale," he said. "It's not that the witch was literally cut in half. I doubt she even died. It's that when they took her blood, they took her magic. She was half of what she had been before. She'd been a witch and a woman, and when they took her magic blood, the witch part of her died."

Emmi suppressed a shudder. "That...that can happen?"

Puck nodded gravely. "What do you think the Hunters do? They don't want the blood; they want the magic. They just take it from the blood."

Emmi rubbed her hands over her arms, feeling the thin bones

over the blue veins in her wrist. She had not been a witch for very long, at least not to her knowledge, and the idea of someone taking that part of her away...

"Arthur and his men, they were Hunters, of a sort," Puck continued.

That matched with the story. Among the knights who accompanied Arthur on this quest was Gwyn ap Nudd, who became the king of the fair folk and leader of the Wild Hunt. They may not be like Greybeard and the Hunters who persecuted the witches, but they hunted magic nonetheless. Apparently, according to the story, to kill or control it.

"That's why there are no more written records of an orddu, I bet," Puck said. He was still watching Emmi in a way that unnerved her deeply, as if he were not talking about an unknown witch but *her*. "If this orddu witch—a powerful one, I'm guessing —lost her title, her name...no wonder future orddu witches guarded it so closely that the word fell out of use."

Emmi felt her brow crease in a frown. He *kept* mentioning how names mattered, but he also kept dancing around the subject. "I understand," she said finally after carefully thinking through her words. "Names are important to the fae."

"To all magic."

"You said once that you'd kill me before you told me your real name."

Puck laughed.

Emmi did not. "Do you still feel that way?"

Puck's smile faded. "Maybe I don't want you to know what I was before. Maybe I just want you to see who I am now."

Emmi swallowed down the rest of what she had planned to say. Whatever she had seen in his shadow, it was not for her to have seen. Puck deserved the privacy of his past. He could tell her who—what—he was when he was ready to tell her.

"I don't need your name," she said finally. She shifted the book to the side, careful with its peeling leather spine, then she turned toward him, leaning up on her knees so she could look him in the eyes. "I don't need your name to know who you are. You're kind."

Puck laughed at that. "You can never trust the fae; has no one told you that before, Emmi?"

She smirked, but didn't deign to answer him. "You care more than you let on, and you hide behind jokes, but I know."

His eyes were round with an emotion Emmi couldn't read. Anticipation? Fear? "What do you know, Emmi Castor?" Puck asked, his voice barely audible.

She could feel his breath, warm and sweet with the scent of mint. *I know that, as much as you try to deny it, you actually care about me,* Emmi thought.

Puck's eyes, somehow, grew even wider as she gazed at him. Before he could say anything, though, she leaned up and kissed him. Emmi closed her eyes, pressing her lips against his, swallowing the startled noise he made in the back of his throat. She was perched on her knees, wobbly and off-balanced, and Puck reached for her. She could feel his hand trembling when he pressed it against her back, steadying her.

When they broke apart, his gaze was heavy-lidded and out of focus. Emmi smiled, pleased that her kiss could rattle him when nothing else could.

"I know everything I need to know about you," she whispered against his lips.

The Lovers

RELATIONSHIPS, LOVE, DUALITY, COMMUNICATION, AND COOPERATION

Emmi stared into the darkness. She couldn't quite shake the feeling that the darkness stared back at her.

The walls in the attic apartment were just thin enough that Emmi could hear Puck snoring in the other room, the bedroom her grandfather usually occupied. She contemplated waking him, but what good would it do?

He wouldn't be able to see the shadows she could see.

This house has a history. That was the thought that pierced her mind. This house had a history. Generations of Castors. Starting with Elspeth, an actual witch.

How many of her ancestors were also witches, even if they didn't know it? How many had lingering shadows clinging to the walls? She could almost see a flicker of movement in the corner of her eye, but when she turned...

Nothing.

Still, she could feel them, the shadows.

Watching.

Waiting.

Emmi knew she *should* feel afraid, but the shadows didn't seem to be malicious. Instead, they were almost like echoes, ghostly afterimages of past lives. It felt...well, not scary. Not quite comforting. More like an awareness that this place she called home had been home to others. She was more curious than scared, and she got the impression that, just on the other side of the darkness, the shadows felt the same. They existed whether Emmi saw them or not, but now that Emmi was more aware of them, they wanted to know what she would do. How close she would come to them.

But no matter how much Emmi tried, she could just not *quite* see them. It was like watching clouds on a windy day, trying to catch a recognizable shape.

Or perhaps it only felt like that because Emmi was so desperate to see two shadows in particular.

Emmi got out of bed—she hadn't slept a wink anyway, despite the late hour—and went to her closet. She shoved the clothes hanging on the bar to one side and kicked her shoes out of the way. There, in the center of the floor, were the remains of a black candle, the wax so deeply embedded in the carpet fibers that it was impossible to remove.

She knelt down and touched the familiar spot, her fingers tracing the swirls of wax, thinner on the outside where she'd tackled it with everything from bleach to industrial cleaners. Nothing had removed the stain.

Emmi had been in middle school when she'd come up with the idea to hold a séance in her closet. As much as she'd come to love her life with Grandfather, nothing could replace her mother and father, both gone far, far too soon. Emmi had gone through a bit of a witchy phase in middle school, leaning into the names some of her classmates had taunted her with. What was the point of being mocked for living in a witch's house if she didn't at least try a séance?

Wanting to find out more about ghosts had lead Emmi to Elspeth's library. She knew her parents would come to her if she called them, if they could. She gathered herbs and crystals and candles, using some of the precious stores her ancestor had collected. At midnight, when Grandfather was asleep, Emmi had tried to summon her parents, a desperate hope coiling around her that didn't die until the candle did.

But now...

She peered into the dark, and she could *almost* see impressions, afterimages of movement slipping from one dark corner to the next, but she couldn't really see the features, make out who the person was, much less whether or not it was her mother or father.

So close, but unreachable. Still.

Emmi shook herself, standing up and grabbing a robe before leaving her bedroom. She headed downstairs. While her séance had not worked, that experiences had marked a shift in Emmi. An acceptance not only of her parents' deaths but also of her own love of books and the library. From that moment on, Emmi no longer believed magic was possible, but she fell in love with the Museum of Magic.

These thoughts almost drew Emmi to the library now, but she veered down the steps, heading to the hearth room instead.

Everything had started here. The witch bottle had broken, and Puck had appeared, and the shards had fallen into the mounds of unswept, soft gray ash, and the entire adventure had begun.

Emmi's bare feet made no sound as she crossed the worn carpet and stood in the center of the room. A different flash of movement out of the corner of her eye made her jump. The orange streak of her ginger cat blurred as Sabrina, startled by Emmi, leapt from the spot on the floor where she'd been sleeping onto the little table that had once held the witch bottle. When Emmi drew closer, Sabrina jumped down, bounding to the corner.

A piece of Emmi's heart broke. Sabrina was her cat, her constant. Emmi crouched in the center of the room, holding her hand out.

"Pss, pss," she said, then, her voice cracking, "Please, Sabrina."

The cat twitched its tail. Emmi didn't like the way Sabrina no longer seemed comfortable with her. Had going to the Shadow-lands and meeting the orddu witches changed her that much?

Even as her legs cramped, the cat crept forward. Emmi's heart surged as Sabrina dared to butt her head into Emmi's palm, letting her stroke the cat's long back, tail winding around her wrist like a snake. She could cry, it was such a relief. When Emmi finally stood, however, Sabrina fled, but the cat did stop at the door way, looking back.

It was a start.

Emmi's gaze went from the doorway to the cauldron. Now, in the dead of the night, she could see the glow even stronger than before. The items resting in the bottom had arranged themselves, as if drawn together magnetically, so that they created a shape similar to the bottle that had broken. The light formed the curved edges, and even though Emmi knew it wasn't substantive, it still almost appeared that she could pick it up.

Something was missing, though. Something magical.

Much like looking into the shadows, the idea of *almost, but not quite* hung around Emmi like a fog.

Her eyes flicked over to the mirror hanging by the cauldron. She couldn't see herself from this angle, but that same feeling washed over her. She knew her image was *almost, but not quite*. Almost a witch, but not quite enough to finish the bottle. Almost an orddu, but not quite enough to see fully into the shadows.

Sighing, Emmi picked up the broken shard of pottery from the mantle over the hearth. She turned it over in her hand, musing. The stain was definitely blood, but magic blood. Was *she* magical enough for it? She thought of the orddu in the *Mabinogion*; that had been a powerful witch, and the knights had drained *all* her magic away. What if Emmi tried to give her magic to the bottle, and she both lost it all and it wasn't enough?

Another flicker out of the corner of her eye.

Emmi looked up quickly, half expecting to finally see the actual shapes in the darkness that seemed to be calling her, but instead, all she saw was her own image reflecting back to her from the old scrying mirror.

Emmi stared with both her real eyes and her magical sight at the reflection of the pottery shard, trying to glean something more from the bloody stain. She could still see the faint echoes of magic there, and she knew she was right—a magical creature had donated its blood for the bottle. But she got no true sense of *what* magical being.

She shifted her gaze to her own reflection. It was hazy, and not just because the mirror was spotted with age and dulled with time.

She could see more faces than her own.

It wasn't clear enough for her to distinguish individual people, but it was as if she wore multiple veils over her own face, each one a shadowy echo of someone she almost recognized. Emmi peered harder at the glass. Her face could—*almost, but not quite*—fit into the features of these other faces. The button nose. Full cheeks. Dark eyes. Heavy brow. Thin lips and sharp jaw. These were repeated features, over and over again, each of them distinct but similar.

"They're my family," Emmi whispered aloud. She was seeing her family in her own face. Her eyes scanned for her mother, her grandmother, but it was too faint for her to really identify any individual, too many overlaid visages.

She wasn't alone.

Emmi bit her lip, emotion welling inside her.

At the thought, the darkness around her surged. The veil-like images of her family's faces faded in the mirror, leaving only Emmi's own eyes looking back at her.

That was what the shadows had been trying to tell her all along.

Emmi wrapped her arms around herself, the sharp edges of the broken pottery in her hands digging into her skin.

She wasn't alone.

Weariness dragged at her, and Emmi felt that, finally, she could sleep. She started to turn, but—

The mirror had one more thing to show her.

In the reflection, she could see herself from the shoulders up to the crown of her head, taking up most of the glassy surface. But over her left shoulder, she saw the corner of the hearth reflected. It was so common to her that she might not have noticed it at all, except...

In the reflection, the hearth was clean.

Emmi glanced behind her. Sure enough, in reality mounds of old ash piled over the bricks. She looked in the mirror again; the ash was gone, the hearth shining and clean, the bricks themselves scrubbed to perfection.

As she puzzled over that, she saw movement over her mirrored self's shoulder. Emmi froze. She knew that if she were to turn around and check again, nothing would be behind her.

But the mirror showed someone cleaning the hearth.

The person was wearing a brown and green tunic and dark pants. The curved mirror didn't give her a good sense of the size of the person or even the gender, but she could tell that it was someone young—perhaps her own age. The person worked industriously, cleaning the already clean hearth, sweeping vigorously. And...there was something *almost but not quite* human about the creature. Even though they were doing a mundane task, there was a lithe grace to the way the person moved, something almost otherworldly...

"A brownie," Emmi whispered aloud. That's what this had to be—a brownie. Puck had disguised her as one, and she knew some of their lore. Brownies cared for houses, made them homes. This house—*her* house—had once had a brownie.

Emmi turned around. As she'd known, there was no brownie currently sweeping the hearth. In fact, she knew from the way the ash was always piled up that there had been no brownie in the Museum of Magic for at least as long as she had been alive.

What happened?

Emmi put the shard of pottery back up on the mantle, then

knelt down in front of the hearth, something she hadn't done since first picking up the pieces of the broken witch bottle.

Why did they never clean the hearth?

It was ridiculous—there was so much ash and soot piled up on the bricks now that it would be impossible to lay a good fire here. Emmi vaguely recalled Grandfather saying the ash looked good for tours, but...

This was too much. Too dirty. It wasn't aesthetic; it was just gross. Emmi stood up, grabbing the broom propped up against the mantle. Although it was handcrafted and another item Grandfather felt added to the atmosphere in the Museum, it was also still a broom, and at the very least, Emmi could sweep some of the ash away.

Except—

She couldn't. Emmi held the broom out to the ash, and...it *caught*. It felt as if there were a barrier preventing her from touching the broom straw to the ash. She pushed, and it bent but did not give way. Emmi shifted to her magical sight, and she could see a fine overlay of silver webbing over the hearth.

"I've touched the ash before, though," Emmi thought. She'd reached into it to get the broken shards of pottery and items that had fallen from the bottle. Puck scooped up handfuls to make portals. Emmi looked at the broom in her hand. It was normal; there was no hex on it.

The hex was on the hearth. Emmi dropped the broom on the floor and knelt back down.

"I'm going to scoop out the ash and throw it away," she said aloud, focusing her mind on the thought. She held her hands out—

And the hex stopped her.

She strained against the silver webbing that was invisible unless she was looking for it, trying her best to push through, but she wasn't strong enough.

Sweating from exertion, Emmi sat back on her heels.

"I just want to touch the ash," she said, realigning her mind to think of only feeling the ash, not cleaning it. She closed her eyes to concentrate on that image, and she reached forward.

Her fingers sifted through the soft, gray ash.

Now I can clean the hearth, she thought, and her hands flew back so violently that she toppled over, her body splaying on the carpet.

Emmi got back up carefully, leaving gray fingerprints on the floor. This was a hex with intent. If Emmi tried to clean the hearth, it rejected her. If she didn't have that goal in mind, she could do what she wanted.

The hex must have played on her mind, too, and Grandfather's, making them not *want* to clean the hearth. Briefly, Emmi wondered if there were more hexes scattered around the house. There were certainly plenty of dirty spots in a house this old.

Why make a hex that specifies a place cannot be cleaned? Emmi wondered, staring down at the hearth. Her gaze shifted to the hex itself, a fine, carefully woven net over the bricks, almost like a spiderweb. She scooted closer, fully awake again.

It may take her all night, but she was going to figure this out.

Six of Swords, Transposed

BEING IN A DEAD END, FEELING STUCK, AND
UNFORESEEN FORCES AT WORK

Emmi leaned back on her heels, ash coating her hands and the cuffs of her robe. Sabrina, who was now curled up in a spot by the door, yawned at her.

"I'm getting nowhere," Emmi told the cat. Sabrina flicked her tail.

Emmi hadn't brought her phone with her, and clocks, according to Grandfather, were too "modern" for this part of the Museum of Magic, but Emmi guessed it was about halfway between midnight and dawn now. Despite testing the boundaries of the hex and using her magical sight, Emmi still hadn't broken it.

Sighing, she stood up, wiping her ash-covered hands on her robe. It was dirty enough that she'd have to wash it later anyway.

If she couldn't break *this* hex, perhaps it would be better to see if there were other hexes around the house.

Sabrina watched her leave the room, but the cat emphatically didn't care enough to follow her. Emmi went to the library first, going so far as to peer behind the books on the shelves. Then to the botany room, using her magical sight to see through the shadows. Emmi checked out the kitchen, the front hall, even the gift shop.

Nothing.

Then again, the hex in the hearth hadn't appeared to her before she triggered it by trying to clean it. There could be hexes all over the house, invisible until certain things happened.

"I should check..." Emmi paused in the corridor. The Museum of Magic took up the entirety of the old part of Elspeth Castor's house. While Emmi felt that the library was as much her home as her attic bedroom, and the hearth room had become integral to her magic, there were other parts of the house that were equally old and important. Elspeth's old bedroom was a huge draw for the historians; Grandfather had all the original furniture from the seventeenth century on display.

Something tugged in Emmi's belly. No... no, she didn't want to explore all the depths of the old house in the middle of the night. She turned on her heel and went back to the hearth room.

Sabrina was gone again. Emmi knelt down in front of the ash. She'd tried to be clever about breaking the hex, she'd tried to use her magic, and nothing worked.

Maybe brute force would.

Emmi took a deep breath. The hex hung across the opening in the hearth like a massive cobweb blocking the fireplace. Emmi hooked her fingers like claws through the hex's opening and *pushed*.

She strained as hard as she could against the hex, shifting her weight from her knees to her feet, leaning down with her whole body. Sweat beaded on her head. It felt as if the hex was bending, and Emmi's feet slipped on the rug. She grappled with her footing and—

The hex knocked her back, sending her flying halfway across the room.

Emmi was winded as she crouched up. She was nearly at the cauldron on its display hook. She gasped for breath, propping herself up on her elbows.

The door burst open. "What is happening?" Puck shouted, thundering inside.

Emmi cocked her head, looking up at him. While she'd landed on the floor with a thud, there was no way Puck could have heard her from the attic bedroom where she'd left him. She scooted across the floor on her knees and stuck out her hand, wrapping her fingers in the thread of the hex and twisting.

Puck flinched.

"You're connected to this!" Emmi shouted, unable to keep the accusation from her voice.

An unreadable expression crossed his face. He started to back out of the room, but Emmi scrambled up and grabbed his wrist, leaving grime on his skin. "What is the deal with this hex?" she demanded.

"I...can't say."

Emmi narrowed her eyes. "Can't? Or won't?"

Puck shrugged.

"How do I break it?" she demanded.

"Why do you want to break it?"

"Why do you care?" she shot back. "Just tell me how to break the hex!"

"It would...take a lot of skill for someone to break that hex." Puck's tone was reluctant, but his eyes were wide, like he wanted her to question this more.

"How do you know that?" Emmi asked. She narrowed her eyes. "You clearly know what's going on, so just tell me what I need to do."

There it was—a twitch at the corner of his lips. She'd asked the right question. "I know about the hex because I made it," Puck started.

Emmi gaped at him. "You?" She dragged him over to the hearth, then sat on the floor and pulled him after her. "Tell me everything," she demanded, drawing her knees up and staring at him.

Puck shot her a rueful smile. His hair was tousled—messing

with the hex had, apparently, woken him up from a deep slumber, but he didn't look any more disheveled than usual. "I followed Elspeth from England to America," he said.

Emmi's eyes rounded. She hadn't expected him to say *that*. Elspeth had crossed the Atlantic in the early sixteen hundreds. Was Puck nearly four hundred years old? She wrapped her arms around her knees tighter. Puck seemed her age, but, she reminded herself, he emphatically was not.

"I was a young brownie," Puck said, his eyes distant. He snorted bitterly. "Really young."

"You're not young now." Emmi couldn't help but snap.

Puck focused on her, noting the way she'd drawn away from. "It's...complicated. I told you, time works differently for the fae. For me especially."

"Why?"

He took a deep breath in and let it out slowly. "Let me back up to the beginning. I was a brownie."

It clicked in Emmi's head then—the brownie she had seen in the mirror...

It had been Puck.

"Brownies only want a home," Emmi whispered.

Puck nodded. "Elspeth found me. She could tell what I was; she had the sight. Almost as much as you."

That made Emmi's mind reel; Puck spoke as if Emmi was more powerful than her ancestor.

"Elspeth offered me a home if I'd help her relocate. The journey was...difficult. But once we landed, we found a place to build a house. As soon as the hearthstone was laid, I could use my powers to help."

He looked at the ash-covered stone fondly.

"But then why..." Emmi started, hating to interrupt him now. "Why did you hex the hearth? Why make it so that everything's covered in dirt and ash?" That seemed antithetical to what a brownie wanted.

"To protect what's under the ash," Puck said as if this were the most obvious thing in the entire world.

Emmi's brow creased in confusion. "What's under the ash?"

"I made that hex a long time ago." Puck laughed in a self deprecating way. "And I made it pretty good, huh? For it to have lasted...lasted *this* long..."

"What's under the ash, Puck?" Emmi asked again, louder.

His eyes focused on her, but he didn't answer.

"Tell me what's under the ash!" She was practically shouting now.

"My contract," he said. He let out a sigh, his whole body shaking. He seemed almost relieved to finally answer her.

"Your contract?" Emmi asked.

Puck nodded. "Written in stone."

Emmi looked back at the hearth. "I want to see it. Can you take the hex down."

"What? No." There was something in his voice that made Emmi look back at him.

She could tell he wasn't telling her everything.

"Why won't you take it down?" she asked.

"Why do you want it gone?" Puck countered.

"I just do. I want to see it. Take the hex down."

Puck's eyes widened a little, trying to communicate something to Emmi.

"What aren't you telling me?" Emmi asked. This whole conversation had been strange so far. Almost as if...

Puck ducked his head, his eyes meeting hers, wide with urgency. But despite his odd facial expression, all he said was, "You didn't say please."

"Please take the hex down?"

Tension uncoiled around Puck as he leaned back. "Three is the magic number," he whispered, his attention on the hearth. He stuck his hands in the hex and started to unpick the strands of the cobweb-like magic.

Three is the magic number?

Emmi watched him while she thought about what he'd said. Once the hex was pulled away from its anchor points all along the hearth, it disappeared.

And Emmi realized, Puck took it down only when she had ordered him to three times. Just as he had only answered her question about it after she'd asked three times. He hadn't been too distracted to answer her; he needed her to repeat the question before the magic would let him answer.

Emmi was in over her head. There was magic here she didn't understand. Magic he *couldn't* tell her about. He was restrained somehow, and Emmi thought it had something to do with the contract.

With the hex gone, Emmi stood up and grabbed the fireplace tools—an ash bucket and a small metal shovel—and worked so quickly to uncover the stones at the bottom of the hearth that a cloud of fine gray powder rose up, coating everything in grime.

Soon enough, though, she could see it.

Symbols and runes were etched into the stone. Emmi thought one of the symbols was close to the same one Puck used to make portals, and that thought drew her up short. If Puck could make portals that would send him across the world, why hadn't he done that for Elspeth? Why go on a months-long journey across the ocean in treacherous conditions when he could have sent her to America in the blink of an eye?

Because portal magic is beyond a brownie, Emmi thought. *And Puck's* not *a brownie any more.* It wasn't just that his physical appearance was different—although it certainly was; he didn't look like the brownie she'd seen in the mirror. Puck had told her, though, over and over again, that the fae changed. He had changed.

"Can you read it?" Puck asked, his eyes bouncing over the runes carved into the ashy stones.

Emmi shook her head. The sigils were indecipherable to her.

"The fae don't like writing. Writing makes a thing permanent, much like a name. But a contract..." He snorted. "Even the fae will write down a contract."

"What does it say?" Emmi asked quietly.

"This is where she named me," Puck said, his eyes still on the stones. "Elspeth. She named me as a protector of this house and its magic. Puck the protector." He made a derisive noise in the back of his throat. "She bound me—she bound *Puck*—to this house and its magic."

His gaze slid to her. "Do you understand?" he asked, his voice resonant. Urgent. "She bound *Puck*."

Emmi shook her head, lips pressed together. She understood Puck bound himself to the Castors and their house, but she didn't understand why he was emphasizing his words so oddly. She didn't understand what he wasn't saying.

"I was a brownie. All brownies want is a home," Puck said. "So the idea that I would be bound to a home—that made sense to me. I wanted to protect the *home*."

"What changed?" Emmi asked.

Puck's lips tightened.

She had asked the wrong question.

And he *could not* offer her the information he wanted her to understand.

Emmi chewed on her lip, thinking. "You *wanted* to protect the home."

"I wanted to protect the *home*," Puck said, slowly, carefully.

Emmi nodded. "Wanted to. In the past tense. So, you don't want to be bound by this contract any more. Right?"

Puck was motionless.

Maybe she had asked the right question, but he couldn't answer.

"You said the contract named you?" Emmi asked.

"Elspeth named me."

"In the contract."

One tight, quick dip of his head. *Yes.*

"I am the heir to this house," Emmi said. "Do I have the power to break the contract?"

Another nod. Yes.

"Do you want me to break the contract?"

Puck stood motionless, eyes wide, jaw clamped shut. She could see a little muscle working in his throat, as if he wanted to speak, but the words would not rise.

"Okay, different question," she said, and Puck's body eased immediately. "If I break the contract, will you no longer have the name Elspeth gave you?"

"Yes," Puck hissed through clenched teeth.

Emmi could almost see what needed to be done, but she wasn't sure. How many times had Puck told her that he didn't like being named? That a name was a cage, something that limited him? No fae wanted a name.

But here, now, it seemed that if she broke the contract with Puck, if she released him from being bound to the house, then he would shed his name. He would be free.

That seemed to be everything he had ever told Emmi he wanted. But his body was rigid and stiff, his eyes wide and wild.

There was *something* Emmi was missing.

Something important.

"Can you tell me what do?" she asked, the question barely audible.

"No," Puck choked out. And then: "I'm sorry."

Emmi had heard of gag orders in contracts before, but this was a cruel exaggeration of one, forcing Puck to silence on something that affected him on a soul level. Emmi swallowed down the emotion rising in her throat.

She could only act with the knowledge she had now.

Puck had bound himself into a contract with Elspeth, a contract that bound him to the house.

A contract that named him.

Puck hated his name.

If Emmi broke the contract, he would no longer have the name he hated.

It was the freedom he'd insisted he'd wanted before. And, it seemed to Emmi, it was another sort of freedom, too. A brownie may want nothing but a home, but the contract seemed to imply servitude in a deeply uncomfortable way.

"No matter what," Emmi said, "this house can be your home. You can stay here even without a contract."

Puck did not speak, but the tendons in his neck drew tighter, as if he were desperate to speak.

"I free you from the contract and from the name Puck," Emmi said.

The hearth stones started to glow, the runes lighting up as if they were made of fire.

But nothing else happened.

Three is the magic number, Emmi thought.

"I free you from the contract and from the name Puck," she said again. The runes blazed brighter, hairline fractures of light spreading over the stones.

Puck's whole body was still. His fists were bunched, the veins popping out on the backs of his hands, his knuckles white. His chest didn't even rise and fall with breath, although his nostrils flared. His eyes, wide and unblinking, bore into her, trying to communicate...*something.*

Emmi let out a shaking breath. She wanted Puck to tell her this was what he wanted, that this was the right thing to do, but she knew he couldn't answer her.

All she had to do was say the words one more time.

Temperance, Transposed

Imbalance, Shifting Goals, and a Need to Refocus

The third time's always the charm.

As Emmi said the words one more time—*I free you from the contract and from the name Puck*—the very air seemed to sizzle with magic. The hairs on her arms and at the back of her neck stood up, and power crackled around the room, tiny sparkles of miniature lightning bolts sizzling all around. An enormous, teeth-jarring *crack* emanated from the hearth stone.

Emmi whipped around. The sound had been so ear-splitting that she'd assumed the actual stones had broken in half, but instead, she witnessed the way the runic sigils splintered, the stone shifting over the words until they were gone.

The contract was broken, quite literally, but the rock was still intact.

And Puck was free—both from the obligations to the house and from his name.

Emmi turned to him, hope surging inside her.

But rather than Puck, she faced a monster.

A scream ripped from her before her mind could even fully

register the being that stood where Puck had been. Easily eight feet tall, the hulking beast had to hunch to fit in the room, broad shoulders tipped with curving spikes that scraped the ceiling. Black antlers sprouted from a wide forehead, protruding from the misshapen skull made even more ungainly by the roots and vines snarling on the monster's head instead of hair. The creature's entire body was covered in fine green moss like fur. An overwhelming earthy scent filled the room. Claws like black thorns, pointed and sharp, jutted out of the monster's too-long gnarled stick-like fingers, and shiny white tendrils—worms or roots, Emmi wasn't sure—dripped around its knuckles.

The monster's legs were reversed, the knees bending backwards, the way a dog's legs do, and rather than feet, twisted tree knots thudded on the floor.

It opened its mouth as Emmi's scream faded, echoes drifting up the cold chimney. Rather than any language, the beast made gagging, snarling sounds that Emmi couldn't discern. Already, it was twisting, the white tendrils that had only been at its knuckles snaking out of the moss, turning the grass-like skin inside-out, twisting it to show roots and mud instead of flesh and blood.

Emmi was backed against the mantle, her feet slipping in stray ash, the stone digging into her back. There was nowhere to run, no place to hide.

No way to escape.

The monster made a groaning, keening sound. Its back snapped painfully. The spikes on its shoulders gouged into the ceiling above, scarring the wood. It doubled over, its head swinging back close to Emmi.

Her eyes met the monsters.

And she realized then—they were Puck's eyes. Exactly the same.

And full of terror.

Blackness swirled up, like dark embodied, deeper than any shadow, and then—

He was gone.

There was nothing but the smell of ash remaining.

The suddenness of it all startled another scream from Emmi's lips. He had *been right there*, but now?

Gone.

Emmi was sure whatever she had seen, monster or man, had been Puck, only forced into a different form than the one she'd known.

"Puck!" Emmi screamed.

But that wasn't his name anymore.

And he was still gone.

Breaking Puck's name had broken whatever bonds to the human world that had been forced upon him.

Emmi shuddered. She could not forget the fear in Puck's eyes, pure, visceral terror. She had not imagined it, she knew that much was true. She had thought she was doing the right thing, freeing Puck and taking away the name he had so clearly hated. But now...

Something was deeply, terribly *wrong*.

She gazed around the room. All evidence of Puck's monstrousness was gone as well—not even the scratches on the ceiling remained. The blackness had taken it all.

Silver glinted. The scrying mirror. It had helped her before, shown her truths... Emmi bounded across the room in three long steps, her eyes on the reflective surface.

In the mirror, she saw herself. But behind her, there was the hearth.

And there was Puck.

It was like an instant replay of what had just happened—Emmi stood in a way that blocked her past self, but she could see Puck over her shoulder, his body rigid as he could not speak under the spell. The hearth glowed and cracked.

But rather than turn into a monster, Puck's regular body stood there. Black hands, blacker than any shadow, scooped out the air around Puck, grabbing him and pulling him into a void.

"What does that mean?" Emmi cried, her voice cracking. She

had seen a monster made of pure nightmare; the mirror showed a kidnapping.

Either way, Puck was gone. But how could she find him? She didn't even know his name.

"Pendulum dousing," Emmi whispered. She turned on her heel, heading to the botanical room where Puck had shown her how to douse with the crystal over the map. She grabbed an atlas and slammed the book on the table in the center of the room. She reached for the same crystal she'd used to find Bideford.

A sob cracked over her lungs, sharp as glass. That had been such an adventure, she realized.

Not like this.

Not...not like this. Not terrifying.

Not *so* alone.

Emmi squared her shoulders, forcing her mind to concentrate. She closed her eyes and saw it all again—the monster, the black—and then she turned the grief squeezing her heart into a blade of focus. *Find him,* she thought, unable to even give her mind a name to whisper.

Pinched between her fingers, the cord that held the crystal started to swing. Low, swooping circles grew wider and wider.

Emmi opened her eyes.

The crystal spun, circling and circling, faster and faster. Emmi's hands were decidedly not moving, but the crystal at the end of the string shot around the map of the world, the cord tight, the stone glinting as it spun and spun. Friction caused her fingertips to burn, and Emmi let it go.

The crystal did not drop.

It swung around and around the map. The cord was still taut, even if it was being held by nothing, and the crystal zoomed, zigging from the Pacific to the Atlantic, pole to pole, zipping across the entire map without slowing.

Puck was everywhere.

Puck was nowhere.

Even as Emmi took a step back, the crystal continued its erratic roving over the map, back and forth, up and around, faster and faster, a manic, frenetic energy that showed no sign of stopping.

She left the room.

With nowhere else to go, Emmi went to the only place she felt truly safe and at peace. As she stepped inside the library, she thought of the *Mabinogion*, the book Puck had helped her read. They'd sat across from each other, their knees touching. She had kissed him, and he had kissed her, and even if Puck wasn't his name, Emmi knew she had seen the truth of him in that moment.

She looked up.

Shadows enveloped the shelves. This was not the utter void of blackness that had snatched Puck away. No—these were true shadows.

The kind that had become her friends.

Emmi gazed around the room. She was used to spending hours among the books, finding answers. But the darkness seemed to push her back.

No, the shadows said as they wrapped around the books, making their spines too dim to read. *This is not where the answers are.*

Then...where?

Helpless, Emmi staggered back into the corridor.

A flicker of movement. Emmi had shifted into her magical sight without even realizing it. The shadows that she had longed to see before were more visible to her now, forms with almost no shape that seemed to beckon her. The shadows moved like a gentle sea, drawing her steps down the hallway with a tug almost too subtle to feel.

They stopped in front of a room Emmi rarely went into.

Elspeth Castor's bedroom.

The Museum of Magic prided itself on authenticity, and as Emmi pushed open the door, she knew exactly what she would see. The same bed her witch ancestor had slept in nearly four hundred years ago, rope stretching between wooden frames with a lumpy mattress atop. A handwoven black quilt made from wool raised in this area. A nightstand and a candle in an iron holder by the bed, a travelling trunk—which had carried all of Elspeth's belongings from England—at the foot of the bed. A handmade broom in the corner for "character," according to Grandfather.

"Why did you bring me here?" Emmi asked the shadows.

Because as much as she knew every stick of furniture that was in the sparse room, Emmi also knew that Puck was not here.

She stepped inside the room, trying to figure out why the shadows had summoned her. She moved to the nightstand, glancing at the decorations on the table—a candle, a bottle, a book—before turning to gaze around at the rest of the room.

The shadows surged in, filling the bedroom with a heavy blackness. Emmi stumbled, crashing into the table at her knees. She groped for the candle standing in a little iron dish, lighting it with matches she knew where there—she lit the candle before every tour, letting the flickering light cast long shadows, adding a spooky effect to the museum.

Now, that warm glow dispelled the strange shadows.

And cast a light on the objects atop the table, the ones she had ignored. The ones the shadows had wanted her to see.

A book and a bottle.

Emmi looked at the book first. There was no title, but the first pages showed a handwritten language Emmi didn't recognize.

The shadows grumbled.

Emmi peered closer. Oh. She *did* know this language—she couldn't read it, but she could identify it as fae sigils and runes, similar to what had been etched into the hearthstones.

Emmi slammed the book shut. "What good is this?" she said into the empty air. She couldn't read the book; how could it help? She turned on her heel—

And the door slammed shut.

The shadows wanted her to stay.

Growling in frustration, Emmi looked back at the table. A tiny glass bottle flickered, reflecting candlelight.

She picked it up.

Written in careful, even letters across the label were five words: *To sleep, perchance to dream.*

Six of Swords, Transposed

Struggle, feeling stuck, being blocked, and unforeseen Forces at work

E mmi picked up the bottle of potion, weighing it carefully in her hand. The liquid inside was black as ink, but there was a glittering sheen to it, a thread of silver that she couldn't quite focus on.

Emmi looked around at the shadows. They were quiet.

Watching.

Waiting.

"You brought me here for a reason," Emmi whispered, not knowing if they could hear her. "Let's hope it's this."

Before she could talk herself out of it, Emmi pulled the cork from the small bottle and downed the sip of potion.

Too late, she remembered why the quote on the label had seemed familiar. *To sleep, perchance to dream.* That, too, was a Shakespearean reference. Emmi felt her mind fogging, her senses dulling, but a flare of panic burned bright within her—if she was correct, that had been from *Hamlet*. And sleep had meant death.

"No—!" Emmi gasped and collapsed on the bed.

———

Her dreams were nightmares.

In the darkness of her mind, a horse galloped, thundering hooves so violent that Emmi crouched on the ground, hands over her head.

Before the dust settled, something wet touched her arm. She startled, falling backward, but only saw a dog, tail wagging, cold nose sniffing at her fingers. "Hello," Emmi whispered.

Low grunts made her whirl around.

The dog disappeared.

But the grunting, snorting hog did not. Black-and-white, with steely bristles prickling over its skin, the enormous pig scratched at the ground and lowered its head toward Emmi as if it intended to charge her. Emmi's heart rate kicked up, and she scrambled back.

And felt thick fur. Her fingers recoiled from the black, coarse hair, and Emmi looked up to see a towering bear on its hind legs, arms reaching out.

She choked on a scream even as the big hog squealed and ran way.

The bear had no head.

In its place was a fire, flickering in the darkness. The bear stumbled down, embers dropping out of its hollow neck, the thud of its heavy body on the ground jerking Emmi awake.

———

She gasped and sat straight up in bed.

Emmi's body felt as if she'd slept for a decade, slow and heavy, and morning light streamed through the bedroom window. Even as the nightmare faded from her mind, her eyes adjusted, and she saw—

"Puck!"

He sat at the foot of her bed, watching her. Emmi wanted to throw herself at him. She wanted to kiss him. She wanted him to hold her.

Instead, she burst into tears.

"Hey, hey now," Puck said in a placating voice.

"Where have you been?" Emmi gasped through sobs. "I've been so—" She couldn't quite bring herself to say *terrified*, but surely he could see it in the way her body trembled, her voice shook.

"It's going to be okay," Puck said, confident. "But I need you to listen. I don't have much time. I have to tell you what I can, while I can."

Emmi sucked in a breath, held it, let it out slowly. She scrubbed her eyes with the heels of her hands and focused her blurry vision on Puck. "What is it?" she asked, proud that she sounded stronger than she felt.

Puck leaned forward, his eyes searching hers. "You found out one of my names, and you broke it."

"I thought that's what you wanted." It occurred to Emmi that Puck wasn't even Puck any more. She didn't know what to call him.

Puck nodded at her, his mouth a tight line. "I need you to find out my other names," he said, carefully enunciating each word, never breaking eye contact with her.

"How?" Emmi said, the sheer impossibility of the task weighing down her voice.

Puck gave her a sympathetic smile. "I can only tell you that Elspeth named me Puck, and the house knew me as Puck. But the longer I'm away from the house..." His smile turned sorrowful. "And the longer I'm away from *you*, the less Puck I will be."

Emmi recalled the shadowy visions of monsters, and deep in her subconscious, she felt the echoes of her most recent nightmare. She shuddered. "What is going on?" she asked, her voice pleading.

Puck bit his lip, then said, "I *can't* tell you."

"Because of magic."

He nodded tightly. "But I can answer questions."

"If I ask the right ones?"

Another nod.

Emmi heaved a sigh. "Does this—all of this—have something to do with your contract with my ancestor?"

Puck widened his eyes in a telling way. *"Sort of."* His voice was tight, his body language strained.

Close to the right question, but not close enough.

Emmi tried again. "Does it have to do with the witch bottle? The old one, the one Elspeth made, the one that broke?"

"Yes." He spoke the word as if it were a relief.

Okay, she was on the right track. What did she not know about that bottle?

"Whose blood was inside the bottle?" she asked, thinking of the stained shard, the last piece to the puzzle.

"Mine."

Emmi's eyes rounded in surprise. She didn't think Puck was lying, but... "Why?"

"Magic requires a price," Puck said, back to carefully constructing his words. "And magic that big required a big price."

"Your blood was the price?"

"Elspeth didn't want to make a sacrifice," Puck said. The cords on his neck stood out from strain; he was dancing close to the edge of what he couldn't say.

Realization settled on Emmi's shoulders, so heavy her body sagged. "She didn't want to sacrifice her magic," Emmi said, "so she forced you to sacrifice yours."

Puck nodded, jaw clenched.

Emmi wasn't sure of the witchcraft behind it all, but she could make some logical guesses. The Hunters took magic from a fae being's blood; Elspeth must have done the same. To Puck.

But then...how was he here, now? And...

"You have magic now," Emmi said, her voice trailing off. Did he not have it before, after Elspeth drained him? Did it replenish somehow?

"Yes," Puck said, eyes wide. "I have magic *now*. Since the *bottle broke.*" He spoke slowly, emphasizing the last words.

Since the bottle broke...

Emmi's brows furrowed as she watched him closely. "How did the bottle break?" She thought back to that night, so long ago. It felt like ages. She had been worried about Grandfather, lingering in the old part of the house. Just about to leave the front desk when there had been a crash...

The witch bottle had broken, smashed on the floor, and there had been Puck...

"Sabrina knocked the bottle over," Emmi mused aloud. "And it broke, and..."

But Puck was shaking his head.

Emmi stopped, both her body and her brain freezing. "How did the bottle break?"

"I broke it," Puck said.

"But you appeared after it broke," she protested.

Puck shook his head. "I appeared *because* it broke."

"Why did you break the bottle?" Emmi asked.

Puck's body relaxed. She had asked the right questions. "Because," he said, "I was escaping it."

Emmi's mind reeled. "You were *in* the bottle? Like a genie?"

Puck actually laughed at that. "No, not really a genie. More like a battery. It was my magic that powered the protection spells. Elspeth made the spell, but..."

"She trapped you—you and your magic—in the bottle in order to make the spell work." Emmi's voice was hollow.

"Exactly."

Emmi thought of how Puck told her he was old, but time moved differently for him. He had been born a brownie centuries ago, but he stopped truly aging when Elspeth trapped him. Somehow, he had been inside the witch bottle, in a magical stasis, fading in and out of time, trapped behind clay walls.

"How did you break out?" Emmi asked. All those centuries,

he'd been contained, growing more and more impatient, drifting through consciousness and lives.

"I'm not sure," Puck answered. "Something...changed. It rippled everywhere."

"Maybe Grandfather did something," Emmi mused aloud. He had gone missing close to when Puck had arrived. Did he somehow trigger a weakening in the witch bottle's magic that enabled Puck to finally break free?

"Or maybe Gwyn ap Nudd did." Puck looked pointed at the nightstand. Emmi followed his gaze, her eyes settling on the book written in fae sigils.

She could tell that she was missing something. Something important. But she couldn't quite figure out what questions to ask to realize what needed to be revealed.

She took a breath and tried again. "So the bottle broke...*somehow*...why did you stay? You were a prisoner inside the witch bottle for centuries. Why stick around?" *With me*, she didn't say.

Puck snorted. "I could have escaped then, but the house would have brought me back."

"The contract."

"The contract," Puck confirmed.

"But you helped me. Was that because of the contract?"

"No." Puck cringed. "And I didn't help. Not at first."

"I don't understand."

"In the beginning, I thought I could trick you. I was going to manipulate you." Puck's face filled with anguish. "Emmi, I'm so sorry. But you need to know. The witch bottle's protection—that's a powerful spell, but it *only* works if you back it with a magical sacrifice. Elspeth sacrificed me."

"And you wanted to sacrifice me?" Emmi gasped.

"At first," Puck said in a rush. "I was going to trick you into making a bottle that would protect the fae but have you power it with your blood."

Emmi remembered how she'd held the Hunter's weapon over

her hand, wondering aloud if her blood could make the bottle complete.

She remembered Puck yelling at her to not do that.

"My blood would finish the bottle?" she asked.

He nodded. "But it's too great a sacrifice. If you gave your blood to the creation of the bottle, it would *drain* your magic. You would still be alive, I think," he added, "but you'd lose all your power. You would no longer be a witch."

Emmi wrapped her arms around herself. She hadn't known about her powers until recently, had barely even claimed the title of witch. She looked around the room, at the dark shadows she knew were listening. She couldn't fathom their silence.

"I can't use your blood," Emmi said. "I will *not* trap you like my ancestor did. And I can't use my blood. But then, how can I possibly make a witch bottle without..."

"Without a sacrifice?" Puck smiled ruefully. "Ah, there's the rub." His gaze grew darker. "But Emmi, you have to figure something out. You need to make some sort of protection. The fae are restless. Elspeth made her barriers, and she made them strong, but without the witch bottle, they're cracking."

"What am I supposed to do?" she asked desperately.

"The protections are failing. I see now that the world has changed—on both sides. But some fae? They're angry."

Emmi thought of the red caps, of the Wild Hunt.

Of the manic gleam in the fae king's eyes.

"You've got to protect magic," Puck said. "You've got to remake the bottle."

Emmi let out a shaky breath. "Well, at least you're here now," she said. "We can figure this out together."

"But..." Puck frowned. "I'm not."

"You're not what?" Emmi asked.

"I'm not here."

———

Emmi opened her eyes with a start.

It had been a dream.

Puck was still gone.

Grandfather was still missing.

And she was still alone.

Justice, Transposed
Unfairness, Loss, and Being Overwhelmed

Emmi's hands bunched into fists, and she slammed them against the bed, ignoring the way the old, lumpy mattress creaked in protest. It wasn't *fair*. Grandfather had been taken by the fae, and she had no one but Puck—and he was gone. Tears sprang into her eyes, and she swallowed down the shout of frustration and rage building in her throat.

And then she remembered there was no one in the house but shadows and her cat, and she tipped her head back and *screamed*.

The acrid scent of smoke coated her senses, startling her out of her furious, futile self pity. She turned to the scent—the candle on the nightstand by the bed guttered and fizzled out, a soft mound of melted wax spilling from the iron holder onto the table. She should care about the wax, the table.

But all Emmi focused on was the book.

She picked it up, snatching it as if it were a lifeline. It was written in the strange sigils and runes of the fae language, and although Emmi couldn't read it, Puck had cast some curious glances in the book's direction, making her think it was significant.

In the light of morning, Emmi could see that the leather of the book was more red than brown, although there was nothing scratched onto the cover to indicate what the book was. She turned the pages slowly, looking for some sort of clue—a translation in the margins, something underlined in the text, or a clue hidden between the pages.

Nothing.

Why had Puck made it seem as if the book was important? He knew she could not read the fae language.

He wasn't even really here, Emmi reminded herself.

It had been a dream.

He had been a dream.

Her breath came out shaky, and her eyes burned. *No.* She couldn't think like that.

She had only one clue. A book she couldn't read.

And if that wasn't a clue, then she had nothing.

That word echoed around Emmi's mind:

Nothing.

Nothing.

Nothing.

There was enough cash in the house for her to survive for a bit. She could maybe scrounge up about a thousand dollars, if she pillaged the register at the front desk of the Museum and looked in the places she knew Grandfather kept money for emergencies. That would barely cover a ticket to England, if she even knew *where* in England she needed to go. But she had no direction, and even if she followed one clue, how could she chase down the next and the next? Puck had been able to travel across the world with nothing more than ash and a sigil, but Emmi didn't have portals.

She had *nothing.*

"I have this," Emmi muttered, looking down at the book in her lap.

Not that she knew what it meant.

Well, it was a book. And books belonged in the library. And Emmi could not bear not moving, not trying.

So she got up. And she did the only thing that she could think to do.

She returned to the library.

It had always given her answers before. She had found a love for *The Book of Three* in this library. A love for reading. A comfort after her parents had died...

The shelves seemed to mock her now, the words on the spines blurring in her burning eyes, giving her no answers.

Emmi stumbled down one aisle and then another, clutching the fae book in both hands, pressing it against her chest as if she could somehow use it to temper the war between hope and despair battling in her heart.

And then she fell flat on her face.

The fae book went skidding across the hardwood floor, and Emmi crawled over to it before examining her arms for bruises and then turning to look at what tripped her.

The *Mabinogion*, the book she and Puck had read together.

The book she'd pushed aside to kiss him, to confess she trusted him no matter what lay in his past or his shadows.

She swallowed down the bitterness in her throat and reached over for the *Mabinogion*, intending to put it away.

"Huh," she said, weighing the book in her hand.

It was almost the exact same shape and heft of the fae book.

She opened the first page of the fae book.

Her fingers bounced over the symbols. She couldn't read them, but what if...

Emmi shook her head. Languages weren't as simple as that. She'd taken one semester of German at high school so far, but she knew there wasn't a direct letter-for-letter code for languages. There were different vocabularies, different sentence structures. The Germans split up some verbs and gendered their nouns; the fae didn't even use letters Emmi could recognize.

Except...

On the fifth page of the *Mabinogion,* there was a table of contents, showing twelve different stories. And on the fifth page of the fae book, there was also a list with twelve different titles down the side of the page. The seventh tale in the *Mabinogion* was called "Culhwch and Olwen," the story that charged the knights to find the blood of an orddu witch.

And the seventh thing listed in the fae book had two words and a symbol that almost looked like a plus sign in the center of them. It could represent the word "and"...couldn't it? Those words in the fae language could say "Culhwch and Olwen"...right?

Emmi turned the *Mabinogion* to the page with the story of "Culhwch and Olwen," and then she turned the fae book to close to the same page. The mention of the orddu witch was on the last page of the story in the Welsh book. Emmi made a guess at the fae book, scanning it for anything that looked like—

The word "orddu" happened only once in the *Mabingoion*. And there, in the center of the page in the fae book, clear as the morning light streaming through the window, were five letters written not in fae sigils, but in the Roman alphabet:

Orddu.

Emmi sucked in a breath. It could *not* be a coincidence—this fae book was the *Mabinogion*.

And that meant...

The first sentence after the mention of the orddu witch in the *Mabinogion* started with the words "Gwyn ap Nudd," the name of the knight who aided King Arthur in the quest of the story. Only Gwyn ap Nudd was not a man but a fae, king of the fair folk, leader of the Wild Hunt...

The fae who held Grandfather prisoner.

Emmi's finger shook as she traced over the unreadable fae sigils, looking for some sort of punctuation that meant the end of one sentence and the start of another. In theory, maybe, the first words would be Gwyn ap Nudd's true name.

Emmi bent over the book. She had so little to go off of, but...

"I think it's this." She tapped a series of three runic symbols. They repeated throughout the text in the same general areas where Gwyn ap Nudd was named in the *Mabinogion*.

She knew the king of the fair folk's true name, written in the fae language.

"Now what do I do with it?" Emmi wondered aloud.

Puck's true name had been enough to bind him to Elspeth Castor's house for centuries, trapping him in the witch bottle and funneling his energy for barriers throughout the fae world. Emmi had no desire to do the same—she wanted to contact him, not control or enslave him. But she didn't know how to speak the symbols, and it wasn't like the fae king was Beetlejuice—saying his name three times wouldn't summon him.

She had only the runes that she thought may be his true name in the fae language.

Puck used ash to make sigils that turned into portals. Emmi picked up the fae book, walking toward the hearth room while musing about the puzzle. Sabrina was inside, sleeping in the center of the rug. The cat yawned as Emmi crouched in front of the hearth.

Despite sweeping, there was still ash clinging to the now plain bricks and stone at the base of the fireplace. Emmi swiped her finger through the ash, tracing out the sigils she thought meant Gwyn's name.

Nothing happened.

She sat back on her heels, staring at the runes and chewing on her lip, trying to concentrate. Sabrina padded over, walking over the stones and pressing paw prints over the design Emmi had etched. She absent-mindedly scratched the cat's back, her ginger tail winding around Emmi's wrist as she thought about what to do. Sabrina curved around her, and Emmi sat down, her back to the hearth, still petting the purring cat.

Her eyes lifted to the scrying mirror.

Not just a mirror. A *scrying* mirror—a mirror designed to give supernatural information and communication.

Emmi stood up slowly, dipping her finger in ash again. She strode to the mirror, and, holding the book out for reference, she slowly traced the sigil out over the shining, silverly surface. Her breath caught.

Nothing happened.

Emmi's shoulders dropped, and she turned away. Sabrina mewed at her.

What can I do? Emmi thought, lifting her gaze back to the reflection.

Mirrors showed things in reverse.

What if she needed to write the sigils as a mirror reflection?

Before she could talk herself out of it and doubt the possibility, Emmi swiped the mirror clean with the hem of her shirt and then dipped her finger in the ash at the hearth again. She went back to the mirror and carefully, slowly etched the fae runes in reverse on the mirror's surface.

Nothing happened.

And then—

The surface glowed in white light. Emmi blinked away, temporarily blinded, and—

"What by all the hells of all the realms have you done, witch?"

Gwyn ap Nudd, king of the fair folk, glared furiously into the mirror, right at Emmi.

Emmi's eyes widened.

"Well?" Gwyn growled. "You summoned me. With my *name*." His lips twisted in a snarl. "What do you want?"

Emmi dropped the book. "Do you have Puck?" she asked, stepping closer to the mirror. "What happened to him?"

Gwyn snorted, a humorless sound. "Puck? Is that even his name any more?"

Emmi shook her head silently.

"That boy had more than one name. More than one contract. If he broke his ties to your family, then he had others he owed debts to." Gwyn ap Nudd's angry eyes narrowed. "And the fae *always* ensure their debts are paid. One way or another."

Emmi's blood ran cold. She thought of how she'd taken a

flower petal—a single gold coin—from the fae king's treasury. She had believed before that had been the right thing to do, but now...

There seemed to be a look of triumph in the fair folk king's gaze. Emmi met his eyes without flinching, refusing to give him the satisfaction of acknowledging her theft. He couldn't know, not for sure.

"Puck may be out of my reach," she said, "but you still have my grandfather. And I want him back."

Gwyn's lips curved into a smile. He looked to the side, somewhere Emmi couldn't see, and made a motion with his hands.

In moments, an old man with pale hair was pushed into the mirror's frame.

"Grandfather," Emmi whispered, shocked, her eyes drinking in the haggard way Grandfather's cheeks were hollowed out, the haunted look in his gaze, the way his hair was wild, the way his back was hunched, meek and fearful.

He mouthed something, his words so quiet Emmi couldn't hear them, but she knew what he was trying to say: *Help me.*

The old man was shoved by someone out of sight, and he fell to the side. Gwyn ap Nudd resumed his spot in front of the mirror. "Well, witch?" he said. "Are you ready yet to bargain for your grandfather's life?"

The Hermit

CONTEMPLATION, WISDOM, AND SOUL
SEARCHING

"Give him back to me!" Emmi screamed, rushing toward the scrying mirror. She clutched the oval frame, and the only thing restraining her from ripping it off the wall was the knowledge that it would do no good whatsoever.

Gwyn's face filled the glassy surface. He contemplated her, his eyes roving over her rage, and he tilted his chin in a way that almost seemed respectful. "We had a deal," he said. "I will honor it, if you will."

Emmi breathed hard through her nose, trying to regain control of her emotions. "You wanted me to trade Orddu for Grandfather," she said, biting out the words. "But that's impossible, and you know it. 'Orddu' is not a name but a title."

Gwyn shrugged. "You are what you are named. Usually." He glanced to the side, where Emmi could almost see her grandfather. "What is a 'Landon Castor?' Weird, human thing, names. 'Landon' means 'long hill' among your people, no?"

Emmi's jaw clenched. It would do no good for her to explain that while her grandfather's name had been a traditional name in her family, the Old English it had been derived from had long since died out.

"Are you a hill, human?" the king of the fair folk called over to

Grandfather. "You look like a human, not a hill!" Gwyn shook his head. "Strange."

"So," Emmi said, carefully enunciating her words. "You want *any* orddu witch."

Gwyn shrugged as if he did not care, but there was a glint in his eyes. Emmi highly suspected that he had been thinking of a specific witch, perhaps one he hated.

"Why?" Emmi asked bluntly.

"Who are you to demand answers of a king?" Gwyn snarled back.

Emmi met his eyes, the full fury of her desperation behind her gaze. She let out a slow breath through her nose and spoke with a soft, steady voice. "I am someone who knows your true name, king."

Gwyn's jaw tensed, the veins of his neck standing out as he swallowed, hard. "Any witch can cast a barrier," he said finally, "or at least any good one can. But one made with an orddu's blood would be stronger than any barrier formed by spell or potion."

Emmi didn't let her emotions show as she considered this. Glastonbury Tor had been protected by a silvery barrier, one different from the ones she'd encountered that had been made by her ancestor.

"What if I make the barrier you want instead?" Emmi said.

Gwyn shrugged, dismissing her offer. "You make the barrier, you control the barrier. I want control of the walls around the fair folk. Why should a witch have such power?"

Because the fae are cruel, Emmi thought. She couldn't see her grandfather in the mirror any more, but she had books and books of fairy tales in the library that confirmed her thoughts. To the fae, people were cheap toys, easily discarded once broken.

But Puck...

Emmi shook her head, gritting her teeth. She couldn't think about Puck. Not now.

Emmi refocused her attention on Gwyn. In the *Mabinogion*, he quested not for the witch herself, but for her blood. Given the way Elspeth had used Puck's blood to syphon magic into the barriers, it was worth a gamble.

"I can't give you an orddu," Emmi told Gwyn. Before he could answer, she continued, "but I can give you a barrier made by an orddu's blood. Will that suffice?"

The king narrowed his eyes. "Which orddu?"

"Me."

He tried hard not to show Emmi his surprise, but he failed. "You, little witch?"

"Will you accept this alteration to our deal?"

"I want a specific type of barrier," Gwyn said. "I don't want to be caged inside the Otherworld with no access to the mortal realm. I should have free rein to leave whenever I want."

"I don't believe your barrier should be a prison," Emmi conceded, "but I don't want innocents hurt."

Gwyn snorted. "What human is innocent?"

Emmi opened her mouth to make a retort, but no words came.

Gwyn laughed bitterly. "I want to hunt again, girl. And no one wants to hunt behind walls."

Emmi chewed on her lip, thinking. She had to be fast; she didn't know what she would do if Gwyn severed their communication. Using his name had worked once, but it was magic she didn't understand, didn't truly control. Still, she did not need to read the old stories to know the terrible tales of the Wild Hunt, the way monsters rode, ravishing towns and slaughtering any in their way. She didn't need to recall the red caps, the easy way they killed.

"You want to hunt?" she said finally, "Then hunt the Hunters. I will make you a barrier with my blood, but rather than enabling you to make a bloodbath of my world, you can only track and hunt the Hunters who are cruel to your kind."

Gwyn looked skeptical, and Emmi held her breath. The Hunters had played a dark game for centuries, using the witches to guide them to fae to drain of magic, killing innocent women and fae in their wake. Emmi did not particularly like the idea of opening up either the fae or the Hunters into a bloody battle, but if that was what she had to do to ensure innocent lives were protected...the Hunters had chosen their path.

"You seek to limit my hunt?" Gwyn sneered.

Emmi feigned innocence, widening her eyes in mock surprise. "I simply thought you were a skilled enough hunter to want a challenge." She shrugged as if she did not care.

"Witch, I am more hunter than you could imagine." The king's voice was low, threatening.

"Then accept what I offer. You can cross into my world, but only in pursuit of a specific prey. That's what a hunt is. Targeted. Precise. Not some rampaging bloodbath or cutting down anything in your wake. If you have skill, use it."

"*If* I have skill!" Gwyn said, so angry his voice dropped even lower.

Emmi shrugged again, her expression a careful mask.

Gwyn considered her. One side of his mouth titled up in a smile, almost as if he appreciated her bargaining. But the half-grin easily shifted into a snarl of utter distaste, and Emmi had no idea what he was truly thinking.

"I don't even know if you can make such a barrier," Gwyn said finally.

Without breaking her gaze from the mirror, Emmi backed up, pausing when her feet hit the hearthstones. She groped behind her without breaking eye contact with Gwyn, pulling down the metal weapon she and Puck had stolen from the Hunter.

"With this," she said, hoping she sounded more confident than she felt, "I can pull the magic from my blood. I'll make a new witch bottle, one with a new intention."

"And you'll give that bottle to me?" Gwyn asked.

Emmi's insides quaked with fear. What if she was doing the wrong thing? Puck wasn't there to tell her if she was accidentally bargaining too much away...

"Yes," she said.

She had to hope that what she'd made so far would be enough. She still wasn't very clear on how witch bottles worked, but they were forms of protection. Elspeth had made her bottle to build barriers between the Otherworld and this world and thereby protect humans. But her walls were prisons. Emmi had gathered different ingredients, and she had a different intention from the start, albeit by accident.

Elspeth's items in the bottle were proof of the cruelty against witches—a page from the *Daemonologie*, a coin used to pay a Hunter, the grave dirt of an innocent woman accused of witchcraft. But Emmi had replaced each item with her own interpretation. She only took a page from a book accusing a woman of witchcraft after declaring her innocent. She traded grave dirt for fae earth.

Elspeth had wanted to identify and protect the women like her, women on the border between fae and human realms, woman who were hunted on both sides.

Emmi, on the other hand, had wanted to identify innocents, people who did not deserve the cruelty the world tossed at their feet, fae and human alike.

And so, while Elspeth's bottle had created magical barriers to protect the witches from Hunters, to erect walls between the worlds, Emmi's bottle would—she hoped—create barriers that blocked evil but allowed free reign between fae and human with good intentions.

Gwyn's eyes seemed to burn as he stared at her through the mirror. "You know that all magic must be powered," he said. "Do you know the cost of a spell like the one you're considering?"

Elspeth's bottle had leeched Puck's magic, slowly, a constant battery constantly drained for centuries.

Emmi held the Hunter's device up, holding the sharp edge to her finger. Ostensibly, it was a needle, but she knew that rather than draw blood, the clever weapon would pull her magic from her.

Puck warned me not to do this, Emmi thought.

But Puck wasn't here.

And Grandfather needed her.

"I make your bottle. You give me Grandfather. Deal?" Emmi asked, her voice cracking.

"Deal," Gwyn ap Nudd, king of the fair folk, said.

Emmi turned to the cauldron beside the mirror. Gwyn watched from his position, straining against the edges of the frame. Emmi knelt in front of the cauldron, took a deep breath, and drove the needle into her fingertip.

There was no pain.

And then, suddenly, *everything* was pain.

Emmi screamed, silvery light pouring out of the Hunter's device, spraying sparks.

"You have to channel it!" Gwyn shouted from the mirror.

With pain blinding her, Emmi tipped forward, her left arm connecting with the cold iron of the cauldron. Inside, the various items she'd uncovered in her quest with Puck shifted as her body weight leaned on the edge of the vessel. Emmi grabbed her right wrist, magic pouring from her index finger, and forced it inside the cauldron.

Light washed inside the black iron, the items—a stone, a bit of dirt, a coin, a paper—and then the silver light turned rusty. Red.

Red as her blood.

Emmi looked at her fingertip. The silver light was gone, and a bright drop of glistening red blood pooled below her nail. She tipped the blood drop into the cauldron.

The sound of breaking glass crackled across her mind.

But inside the cauldron, stoppered with red wax, was a clay bottle. Shaking, Emmi picked it up. It rattled, and she knew the items she'd collected were inside.

"Mine," Gwyn ap Nudd whispered.

Emmi turned to the mirror. Her eyes were bleary, barely focused, but even as she watched, the image of the king of the fair folk faded from the glass, leaving nothing but the spotted, silvery surface behind.

"No!" Emmi shouted, lunging for the mirror.

Her heart stuttered. She looked down at her hand.

The bottle was gone.

Her fingers flexed over air. The bottle was gone; Gwyn was gone. She spun around. Shadows crept along the walls, but they were nothing but shadows. No images stirred in the dark, no whispers gave her comfort or guidance.

Her magic was gone.

"No," Emmi whispered.

A bell resonated throughout the house.

The doorbell.

Emmi stumbled forward, heart hammering. She opened the front door of the Museum of Magic.

Grandfather stood on the stoop. His hair was messy, his beard prickling through his wrinkled skin, his eye haggard. But it was him.

"Well?" he said gruffly, a smile of relief flickering at Emmi. "Can I come in?"

"Yes!" Emmi gasped in a sob, grabbing his arm and pulling him inside. "It's you!"

He gave her that grin she knew so well. "It's me. As soon as you made the bottle, the barriers shifted. Everything Elspeth did had been breaking; now your protections are up instead of hers. Gwyn snapped his fingers and then..."

"You came home."

His smile softened. "And then I came home."

Emmi's whole body sagged in relief. She had lost her magic, but that was a small price to pay to save her family.

EPILOGUE
THE STACKED DECK

Puck could only visit in the short minutes between twilight and night, between night and dawn. When the sun was gone but not its light.

He stood outside the Museum of Magic, his gaze roving over the cold glass windows, trying to see inside.

She was just there, somewhere, just behind those walls.

But he could not reach her.

The light faded. Already, the first stars glimmered. Soon he would be called away. And he would have to go.

Oberon did not like his servant to stray too far.

But he could not control these moments, the in-between times as the sun gasped for breath, the moon clawed for dominance.

"Emmi," Puck whispered, his voice broken.

Something had changed.

He could no longer reach her in her dreams.

Puck looked down at his hands. He was not sure she would recognize him outside of her dreams, where he could shift shapes into the form she knew. Would she scream when she saw him? Would any part of her realize that he was still Puck, beneath the monstrous form?

There was a movement behind the window. Puck rushed forward, pressing his palm to the cold glass. The curtain shifted.

A flash of orange. It wasn't Emmi. It was Sabrina. The ginger cat pressed the side of her face against the windowpane, mewing so loudly Puck could hear it outside.

The cat, at least, recognized him, despite his new form.

The light was fading fast. Already, he could feel himself slipping away.

"Sabrina," he said, knowing the cat couldn't understand him, couldn't communicate a message to Emmi, "I can't get in. Try to tell her that. Something's blocking me now."

In the darkness, Puck could see the hexes binding the house together even clearer. They stretched over the stone like spiderwebs, silvery and strong.

The cat hopped off the window ledge and bounded away, the curtain swishing closed.

Puck felt the call of his master. He could not stay.

He could not warn Emmi that she'd been trapped and tricked.

That she lived in a house of hex.

Historical Notes

Everything in this book is real, except for the parts that aren't.

Emmi and the Castor family are my own invention. I tried to give a nod to how history deviated around Elspeth Castor in the form of her immigration; the *Speedwell* ship she sailed on was a real ship intended for the voyage from England to America alongside the *Mayflower*, but in reality, the *Speedwell* was deemed unsafe and did not make the famous voyage.

Every witch named in this book is based on historical research and real people, and aside from the mystical adventures Emmi has with the echoes of their past, they are presented as factually accurately as possible.

Agnes Sampson was a victim of the Scottish trials and sentenced at Holyrood. James I and VI witnessed and wrote about the trials and judgment in *Daemonologie*, which he also worked on at Holyrood. The chest in which Emmi discovers the magical copy of the book is an actual item on display.

Joan Wytte lived near Boscastle. After a tooth abscess or similar ailment, she grew short-tempered and aggressive, and was therefore condemned as a witch. She died in the horrific Bodmin Jail, and her bones were much later put on display...although they may not have been her bones at all. Her grave is hidden, just as it is in this story. The Museum of Witchcraft and Magic can be visited in Boscastle.

Ursula Sonthiel, better known as Mother Shipton, is among the most famous witches of England. The book of prophecies she wrote is often cited as proof of her power, although it was published well after her death. Her cave can still be visited today, and it is England's oldest tourist attraction. The well actually does calcify objects, turning them into stone, and the current visitor attraction sells miniature stone teddy bears in her honor.

Witch hunters truly did exist, the most famous of which is probably Matthew Hopkins. Hopkins appointed himself with the title of Witchfinder General and commercialized the idea of hunting witches for profit, capitalizing on the chaos and fear during the English Civil War.

Whenever possible, I've used real legends and mythology to supplement this story. Iron is often associated as a bane to fae, perhaps a commentary on how the evolution of metal and crafts-manship pushed out the old magic stories. Joan the Wad is a Cornish legend, often paired with Jack o' the Lantern. The Wild Hunt is an epic myth told throughout most of Western Europe with many different variations.

Gwyn ap Nudd is considered the king of the fair folk, with access at Glastonbury Tor, and he's mentioned in the *Mabinogion*...alongside the first and one of the only known instances of the word "orddu." Historians have argued about whether or not "orddu" is a name, a title, or something else; the true meaning of the word has been lost over time. The most famous use of the word remains the name of the witch in Lloyd Alexander's wonderful *The Book of Three*.

There is a reason why the first witch of this story—Agnes Sampson—asked Emmi to say her name. Real people died horrific deaths or lived in cruel situations often for a crime no more serious than being female and powerless.

Say their names.

And do not let history repeat itself.

AFTERWORD

Museum of Magic is over, but Emmi and Puck's story continues! *House of Hex* will be published first in serialized form, available at Kindle Vella and Patreon at patreon.com/bethrevis. Once complete, the sequel will be available as an ebook and paperback.

Visit bethrevis.com/serial for more information on this and all Beth's other serial novels.

WITH SPECIAL THANKS

This book was originally written in serialized form, releasing one chapter at a time, with input from readers to determine the outcomes of twists and turns. In particular, thanks goes to my active Patreon community and friends in Discord for supporting, sharing, and shaping this story! Deep gratitude to:

Christina Vourcos
Glauber Ribeiro
Andria Henry
Heidi Wilson
Sarah Haasl
Cassie Gustafson
Jessica Fisher
Elyse LeMieux
Kathlene Brown
Emily Bedwell
Jennifer Rodriguez

Additional thanks to my author group of friends who helped me bring this and my other serialized novels into fruition. Thank you, Megan Shepherd, Christina Farley, Scott Tracey, Brook Hatchett, and Mindy McGinnis! Author and designer Jessica Khoury developed the cover for this book, and it could not possibly be more perfect or more beautiful.

Much as I wish I could travel through ash sigil portals like Puck does, most of my research had to be done online. The Museum of Witchcraft and Magic in Boscastle, the Mother Shipton attraction in York, Google street view, Wikipedia, Gutenberg.org, and various travel vlogs and blogs provided endless inspiration and aid in developing this story. Special thanks to the Facebook group "North Berwick Ponies"—finding a real Exmoor pony named Oberon gave me a great plot twist and a deep desire to head to Scotland and see him in the flesh!

Finally, as always, thanks to you, the reader. Stories are nothing but ink and paper until they come alive in your imagination. Thank you for making mine real.

About the Author

Beth Revis is a *New York Times* and *USA Today* bestselling author with books available in more than twenty languages.

Beth is best known for science fiction and fantasy, but she has published widely in multiple genres and formats. Beth is the co-owner of Wordsmith Workshops and the author of the Paper Hearts series, both of which aid aspiring authors. She is currently working on multiple new novels. She lives in rural North Carolina with her son and husband.

Subscribe to her monthly newsletter at: bethrevis.substack.com or discover her latest serialized novel and weekly writing advice at patreon.com/bethrevis. For more information, visit bethrevis.com.

Also by Beth Revis

Fiction

Across the Universe

A Million Suns

Shades of Earth

The Body Electric

Star Wars: Rebel Rising

A World Without You

Give the Dark My Love

Bid My Soul Farewell

Star Wars: The Princess and the Scoundrel

Blood & Feathers

Museum of Magic

Night of the Witch

Nonfiction

The Paper Hearts Series

A collection of advice &
interactive workbooks
designed for writers.

Printed in Great Britain
by Amazon

16270045R00193